Glory

By: Deborah S. Jones

Concrete Rose Publishing Presents···

Library of Congress Control Number: 2009920992
ISBN-13: 978-0-9823295-0-4
ISBN -10: 0-9823295-0-4
First Edition: January 2009

Cover Design: LaVonda Howard
Author Photo: Corinthia V. McCray

<u>*Dedication*</u>

Here's to the second time around!

This book is dedicated to YOU
This book is inspired by YOU
This book is for YOU

No more morsels….Here is the meal!

Cheers…

Acknowledgments

The encouragement and support that I've received since The Princess of Pride was published has been astounding. There are so many of you I want to thank for standing behind me. You have helped me realize the talent for story telling that I have been blessed with. If it weren't for you, I would probably be content storing countless stories on my computer at home where no one else could read and enjoy them, but me.

The Princess of Pride was my baby, the dabble of a toe into a refreshing pool on a hot summer day. Glory is just as special, but in the same breath VERY different – there was no dabbling this time around. I jumped in - head first! I've poured so much of myself into this book, day in and day out. Now countless reviews later, here is the finished product – an intense story which, in my opinion, epitomizes the meaning of 'the second time around'.

Someone I love completely, in every sense of the word, reminded me each, sometimes stressful, step of the way that a good book is not written – it's RE-written. If that is indeed true, then you're about to begin, what is in my humble opinion, a PHENOMENAL book.

I would like to thank everyone who offered me creative feedback and suggestions. To name only a few: Dionne, Jennifer, Nancy, Carolann, Maria, Shana, Diane, Chaz, Michelle, and finally my beautiful mom. They were there from the beginning, when the sexy, heart-felt compilation of thoughts you hold in your hands, was just a pile of rambling ideas on paper. A huge thank you has to go out to Mishella. She came in and helped me tie together all of the loose ends. Her enthusiasm, thoughtfulness, and insight were welcomed and she was indeed instrumental in the cohesive, well thought-out finished product.

I want to thank the best publicist around, in advance, for all of the hard work I know she'll put into this book, like she did with my first novel, in getting the word out there.

Lovern has been one of my biggest supporters. If she could've walked around with the cover of my book plastered over every inch of her body for advertising, and STILL look cute, she would've done it! Both she and my father are determined to make me a household name. Lovern, I would like to take this opportunity to let you know how much I appreciate what you do.

Again, I can't thank you all enough for your continued support. Book number three is in the works and I will keep you posted on its progress.

I know you are not going to be able to put down GLORY. So I'll apologize in advance for the sleepless night ahead of you and say 'you're welcome' for the special benefits some may reap as a result of reading it.

You've all waited patiently for this (some more patiently than others ;-) ....so without further ado...may I present for your reading pleasure....

GLORY

Deborah S. Jones

PROLOGUE

"*If you don't want them all over you, then you'll have to pick one. Choose a geeky one and stay with him all night. You may have to kiss him, but usually with the shy ones you can work your way around not going any further.*" *Ignoring the look of disbelief played across my face, she continued to pace the room, blurting out her instructions.* "*Be a flirt and touch them a lot. That way they will barely notice that they aren't touching you.*" *I couldn't believe what I was hearing. Did my Aunt really want me to pretend I was a prostitute?*

I massaged my temples. "*I can't do this Miranda.*"

The veins in her neck and forehead were already starting to bulge. "*Yes you can and you will!*"

I groaned in frustration. "*But why?*"

"*Why? I'll tell you why. Because I've taken care of you for the past two years, fed you and gave you a place to stay; it's the least you can do, you ungrateful brat! You showed up on my steps, and I helped you when you had no where else to go. That's why you're going to do this.*"

I scoffed at her use of the word 'care', becoming more agitated by the second. She really had a nerve. "*I work and pay my way. Don't you dare imply that I've been living off of you for free! Before my mother died she asked if I could stay here my last year of high school and you agreed. I'm trying to stay on top of my grades, applying to colleges, and I still manage to work twenty hours a week at the hospital. So don't go there with me.*" *She was rolling her eyes, making it clear she wasn't interested in any of those things.*

"*Glory stop being such a stiff. You're a pretty girl, not that anyone would notice, the way you dress and wear your hair. Kim is sick, probably pregnant,*" *she stated matter-of-factly,* "*and Carlos promised this guy I would show up with twelve girls. I swear you won't have to do anything; you're just the fill in. Listen, if you ask me, this could be the best thing that has ever happened in your boring, uneventful life.*"

"*Uneventful is good. It's safe. I am not like the other girls. These men are going to take one look at me and know I don't belong there.*"

"If you don't talk, all they'll see is a beautiful girl. Just don't open your mouth, is all! Pleeeease... they are paying a pretty penny just to have us show up. I'll give you Kim's share of two hundred dollars on top of ten percent of whatever you make."

I think my jaw was touching my chest as I looked at her in amazement. "Make?!? I don't plan on making anything."

"Fine, then sit in a corner all night for all I care, but I need you to come."

I was silent, mentally checking off all the reasons I shouldn't do this. Except for tonight, she had never asked anything of me, and I knew it was paining her to have to ask at all. So I decided it was the least I could do, since she could've very easily thrown me out a long time ago.

"Alright Miranda, but I swear to God, if it goes too far, I'm out of there! Do you understand me? I'm out of there," I tried to make my voice sound as serious as possible.

"Perfectly. Now get dressed and put on some make up. No one wants a plain Jane."

I replayed that conversation a thousand times in my head, and each time it still sounded like an awful idea, but I went to the party anyway. All this time my mom thought her half-sister ran a night club for high powered execs. Little did she know it was more along the lines of a brothel and catering service for sating any sexual appetite. Both Miranda's career and clientele disgusted me, but she seemed so comfortable with it. I'd made it clear that I resented what she did; but she couldn't care less what my opinion was or what they asked of her as long as she was paid, and paid well.

Miranda did a nice job of keeping the club, her clients, and our home separated – *most of the time.* The exception to the rules came when she met some rich beast of a man who she thought would change her life forever. After a much too brief courting period, those men were allowed to spend the night at the house. I tried to keep to myself and mind my own business, but the first time it happened, I came down to the kitchen wearing just bikini panties and a t-shirt (four sizes too small) that my mom had bought me, to find an ogre of a man leaning against the sink having his morning brew; I almost had a heart attack. Let's just say, things didn't go very well. I bolted back up to my room before he could say anything, since his eyes had already said enough. I could hear them arguing downstairs. He seemed upset, accusing my Aunt of holding out on him; by keeping back some of her girls. She was adamant that I wasn't one of her girls, but he wouldn't listen. Needless to say, I never saw him again.

The relationship between my Aunt and I became even more strained. She felt the same way about me as I did about her. I would've left a long time ago, but the truth was that I had no where else to go; and she knew it.

Between work and school, we never saw each other, which was fine with me. The last thing I wanted to do was argue with her about how I dressed or wore my hair, being too drab or needing a life. I hadn't bought anything new since my mom died, not even underwear. Every penny I made at my part-time job and odd jobs around the neighborhood went into my savings for college, just in case all the scholarships I applied for didn't pan out. My mom had left me some money, but it wasn't much after all the hospital bills were paid, and Miranda was nice enough to take half as her dues for taking me in. The two hundred dollars she gave me tonight would go a long way.

The party was supposed to be at some mansion in Pahrump, a town about sixty-five miles outside of Las Vegas. It was for some Ivy League fraternity on a trip to Sin City before finishing their final year in grad school. Once we got there, I did like Miranda said and looked for a geeky one, but there were none. If anything, they all looked like a bunch of wealthy jocks – very 90210'ish. After the second guy offered me three hundred dollars to join him upstairs, and became belligerent when I said no, I realized the bar may not have been the best place to "lay low". I told him he would have to take a number, since I was about to join someone. I grabbed my soda and went to sit by the pool, scooting behind the shrubs whenever I heard someone coming. It was going to be a long night.

Someone was coming. "What's wrong baby? You've paid all this money and now don't want to play?" It was my Aunt Miranda's voice. I peeped between the leaves and saw her following a man over to the pool. She was practically draped all over him, but he kept taking her hands from around his neck.

"No thanks. There are plenty of guys in there that would kill for you, I'm just not interested." He was right, Miranda was a gorgeous woman; there was something sinful about her. She had the same long, curly dark hair as my mother, and those almond-shaped bedroom eyes. I once heard a grossly obese client of hers say that she represented everything bad in his life that his nutritionist said he couldn't have: sugar, salt, and spice. And that was Miranda to the tee, with her syrupy sweet talk in a skin-tight fitted red dress, she was spicy.

"Okay bebê, but you don't know what you're missing," she drawled in an exaggerated accent turning away to head back inside.

"Yes I do," he mumbled under his breath as he sat in a lounge chair admiring the view of the mountains and the faint Las Vegas city lights. I could tell Miranda was miffed. That was a first for her. Usually, she had men wrapped around her finger within seconds of knowing them, but this one was different. Over the next hour I saw him turn away three more girls. I was afraid to move, not knowing what he would think if he knew I was hiding nearby the entire time.

A blonde haired man came out to the patio and yelled for him, running down to where he sat. "Hayden, what's up with you man?"

His name was *Hayden.*

Nonchalantly he shook the man's hand. "Nothing, I'm just not in the mood."

"Not in the mood? We planned this trip for a year, you twisted your Dad's arm to get this house rented to us; we have a bevy of beauties here to grant our every sexual wish, and you're *not in the mood*? Jesus! What the hell is your problem? I hope you aren't out here thinking about Lisa?"

Hayden started to laugh. "No, I'm not thinking about Lisa. Don't be ridiculous. She's the last thing on my mind. None of those girls are my type."

"Bullshit! I wasn't aware you even had a type."

"Well I do, sort of," he smiled.

"Listen, I just had the time of my life with the one in the red, she's superb. Do you want me to send her out here? Maybe you can take her to the pool house." They were talking about Miranda. If there was one thing I knew she insisted on, was that all her 'girls' wore different colors when they attended these functions. It made it easy when there were compliments or complaints to differentiate between all the blondes and the brunettes. After a while they all started to look alike, so it was easier and probably even more degrading to be called red dress, blue dress, black dress, white dress, etc.

"First of all, I already met the one in the red, and she's definitely *not* my type. Second of all, why the hell would I want to sleep with someone you just had ten minutes before?" He was still laughing. "Or should I say, a minute ago?" His friend didn't think it was funny, but I had to cover my mouth to stop from joining him with laughter.

"How about I get you the one that every body has been talking about; they're all saving their money for a turn with her. She's wearing a painted on navy blue dress, has thick dark hair past her waist, and a body from heaven - very exotic. She gives new meaning to the term hour-glass figure. The boys all had their eyes on her when she walked in, but she went to the bar and now no one can find her. Some lucky bastard got to her before me, and now has that gorgeous specimen on lock down in one of the rooms."

Was he talking about me? People were looking for me? Body from heaven? None of the other girls were wearing blue. This wasn't good. I had to get out of there, since I immediately felt faint at the thought that "they were all waiting for a turn" with me. My imagination started to run wild with what could happen during one of these turns.

"No thanks."

The man threw his arms up in frustration. "Fine, if that's how you want to be! I can't believe you sometimes. What a waste. It just means more for me."

"Good, enjoy yourself. Hey, where are your car keys? You're blocking me in, and I'm going to take a drive down to the strip, then head back to the hotel."

"You're leaving?" Disbelief was plastered across his face. "Sometimes I don't know about you H." Taking his keys out of his pocket, they exchanged their keys. "Take care of her, I just had her detailed." The man went back inside shaking his head in disapproval. Hayden was leaving. This could be my only chance to get out of here. As he headed down the stairs towards the front of the house, I ran after him.

Trying to run in my stilettos wasn't working; I yelled for him. "Excuse me, sir?" He didn't turn around. "Excuse me," I yelled again. He stopped then, as if he'd just realized I was talking to him.

"Me?" He looked at me from head to toe.

"Yes, you. Are you leaving?"

"As a matter of fact, I am." There wasn't the slightest hint of an invitation in his voice as he turned back to the car.

"Would you mind terribly if I got a ride with you back into the city."

"What makes you think I'm going into the city?" I could hear the annoyance in his voice.

"It was just a guess, but if you aren't, I will go as far as you can take me." He was hesitant, looking around as though he expected someone to jump out of the bushes any minute and take his car.

"I don't know if that's such a great id…"

"Hey beautiful, there you are," came a gruff voice from behind me as someone picked me up and twirled me in the air. "I've been looking for you all night. If three hundred was too low, I'll double it. You're by far the prettiest one here." I was squirming against him. His hands were rough as he rubbed them back and forth across my bottom and his face was now planted squarely between my breasts.

I tried to be as firm as I could. "Please put me down," but he didn't move. "Put me down! I'm sorry but I can't," I repeated, proud of myself for not letting my voice waiver as he let me slide back to the ground, but didn't release the hold he had me in. I was trying to pull on the bottom of my dress, since it had slid up my thighs.

"What do you mean you can't?!? It's what you're here for! You drive a hard bargain, a thousand, that's my final offer and I'm cutting the line." He was barking at me and becoming obviously upset. One thousand dollars? This man must be out of his mind. He was still holding me by the wrist and as he tightened his grip I tried not to wince in pain.

"I'm sorry, but I was just about to leave." I looked past him, my eyes pleading with Hayden's.

"Leave?" and turning around he saw his frat brother with the driver's door open. He immediately snatched his hands from around me, like a child who got caught with his hands in the cookie jar. "H, I'm sorry man; I didn't know she was taken."

"Umm, yeah…I guess she is. We were just about to leave." He shrugged his shoulders.

"Jesus, I don't know how you end up with the belle of the ball every time, but good for you man. Enjoy her for me. There are a lot of disappointed men in there — me included," he said, his voice dripping with fake well wishes. He was doing a poor job of hiding his anger.

"That's too bad, ya snooze ya lose." Hayden replied with the smallest of smiles. And without looking back in my direction, the man stormed inside.

"Good riddance asshole!" the man grumbled, under his breath.

"Alright, get in. I guess I'm going to have to take you now."

"I would really appreciate it."

"Fine, fine, get in," he said impatiently. I got into the black BMW, and we sped away. I couldn't believe I had just done that, but the alternative wasn't an option. I had to choose the lesser of two evils, and I chose to leave with a perfect stranger. We were driving a few minutes before he asked why I wanted to leave. I had to think of something smart, something Miranda would say. Be nonchalant and indifferent, don't encourage him.

"It wasn't my type of crowd."

"Really? What *is* your type of crowd?" he still hadn't looked at me, but I had definitely looked at him. He was gorgeous, almost like he'd stepped out of a Ralph Lauren magazine ad, chiseled to perfection.

"It varies, but tonight just wasn't it."

"And here I was thinking we were the pick of the litter." His voice was oozing with sarcasm. "Business must be good if you can turn down work that pays a thousand dollars for a night."

"Actually it would've been for an hour and as I said before, it varies. Thank you for giving me a ride though. I know you didn't have to." It was a desperate attempt to change the subject.

"You're welcome. It's clear to anyone with eyes that you didn't want to be there. Where are you heading?"

"No place in particular. Take me where you're going, and I'll find my way from there. I don't want to inconvenience you any more than I already have." I looked out the window and for a long time we drove in silence.

"Why are you so quiet?"

I was a little surprised that he even wanted to talk. "No reason."

"All the girls at that party tonight were chatter boxes. Looking for business every chance they got. *You*, however, leave the party early, turn down a thousand dollars, and sit quietly in the corner of my car like a lost school girl. You aren't acting like any prostitute I've ever met. Not that I mind," he said glancing over at me. Think, Glory, think. Just go along with this until you get back to the city. Tonight you aren't Glory Strair.

"You don't get very far in this business by being like everyone else. Originality is key, and chatter boxes are annoying. It's pretty obvious you aren't like anyone else. So tell me, why did *you* leave the party?" I was still looking out the window, trying to act as though I was slightly bored.

"I guess it wasn't my type of crowd either."

I turned to look at him. "Don't you like women?"

"Yes I like women; actually I would go as far as to say I love them, but..."

"You have a girlfriend," I interjected.

"No, I *had* a girlfriend; we broke up before I came on this trip."

I was enjoying poking at him. "So what, now you're feeling guilty?"

"Guilty? Oh no. I planned this trip, I guess I should've gone a step further and actually selected the girls as well." There was a hint of disgust in his voice. He found us repulsive and I immediately felt cheap, looking down at the thin piece of blue material barely covering my body, even I was disgusted. I decided I would end the conversation there. As I looked out the window, I began to review my mental flash cards for my Advanced Calculus exam on Monday. Once again, we drove in silence.

Finally he spoke when it became apparent the silence was killing him. "I hope I didn't offend you with my last comment."

"I don't get offended easily. Everyone is entitled to their opinion."

"That's good to know, but if I'm driving you all the way into the city, the least you could do is provide some good conversation." He was smiling at me, and I could've sworn I felt my heart flutter.

"Alright. What would you like to talk about?"

"Umm, I don't know. Anything."

"How about what most men like to talk about?" I couldn't help grinning.

"Oh yeah, and what's that?"

"Themselves." We both started to laugh.

"True, but I would actually prefer to talk about you. I honestly find your ability to do what you do quite fascinating." What did I get myself into? The minute I opened my mouth he's going to know I'm the farthest thing from a prostitute.

"Well it is the oldest profession in the world, so that should speak for itself, but I really don't like to talk about work when I'm working."

"You aren't working though."

"Either way, I don't want to talk about it. It's just a job. I'm sure you don't want to talk about your job." I didn't mean to sound as snitty as I did, but talking about my fake life as a prostitute was not my ideal conversation. I wanted to talk about him.

"I don't have a job, yet, but I guess you're right. If I did, I probably wouldn't want to talk about it either. So what *do* you want to talk about?"

"Umm…How about we go tit for tat about anything, but I won't answer any questions about my work." He agreed, and over the next forty-five minutes he learned how I'd grown up in Brazil, and that my father was a musician from Harlem and met my mom touring with his jazz band in South America. I told him we moved to America when I was fifteen after my father died, and then to Vegas with my aunt, once my mother was diagnosed with breast cancer.

I learned that he was about to graduate from Harvard Business School with an MBA in International Finance. He admitted that because his father knew the right people, he was able to bypass the two-year work experience admission requirement into the program. It was a sore spot among most of his friends. He would likely join the ranks at his father's investment firm at the beginning of the summer. He had a younger sister and was on the national water polo team. I found everything about him fascinating. Talking to him came so easily. His voice was unbelievably sexy and those eyes, as the girls at school would say, he was definitely a hottie. Before I knew it, we were in front of the Bellagio.

"Here we are," he announced sounding surprisingly disappointed.

"Wow that was fast." I mimicked his tone and didn't try to conceal my disappointment. "Well thanks again. I hope my conversation made the ride a little more pleasurable."

"It did." He jumped a little when the valet opened his door. "Would you like to come up for a drink? I could....uh, use the company."

"Umm… I don't think that's a good idea, plus I'm not your type remember?"

"I don't have a type," he pressed. "Please, one drink, I promise nothing will happen. I'll be a complete gentleman. I'm enjoying our talk." He lowered his voice slightly, obviously not wanting the doorman, to hear him.

"Aaah, I don't know," I whined, not trying to hide my discomfort. What did this man want from me? *He* wanted to have a drink with *me*? I must've missed something.

His eyes were pleading with me. "Please, one drink."

Those eyes…I couldn't resist. "All right, one drink."

Maybe Miranda was right and tonight could be the best thing that ever happened to me. Things like this never happened to boring Glory Amelia Strair; I had far too many responsibilities. I didn't have time for boys or parties. Don't get me wrong, the boys at school had approached me plenty of times, but my mom had taught me well, and I saw straight through their compliments and hormone-raging facades. So in that split second, sitting in a BMW with the most gorgeous man I'd ever laid my eyes on, I decided tonight I would lie. I would take whatever he was willing to offer. In a couple of months I would be leaving for college, I would never see him again, and he would never know I wasn't a prostitute or that I was *almost* eighteen years old. Taking his arm, we walked into the enormous lobby of the hotel. I know at first glance I didn't look like a prostitute, but I still felt as though no one could take their eyes off of me. We took the elevator to the 36th floor and he led the way to his Bellagio suite.

It took every ounce of my strength not to act like a first timer, screaming over the magnificent view and the ornate furniture, or the size of the bathroom for that matter. He would never know this was the nicest place I had ever been in. I walked directly out onto the balcony like I'd been there a hundred times before, taking in the view of the city. He made a call and then joined me.

"It's beautiful, isn't it?" he said slipping off his coat and draping it around my shoulders, obviously noticing the shiver that had just crawled up my spine. A shiver, I wasn't entirely sure was caused by the cool night breeze and not his close proximity.

"Yes, thank you. It is beautiful." I pulled the opening of his blazer closed as I curled my shoulders inward. I could smell his scent and feel his warmth.

"Do you mind if I ask your name? We've been together for over an hour and I don't know what to call you."

"Actually I do. I would prefer no names."

"But we need to call each other something," he stated matter-of-factly.

"Call me whatever you want."

"No," he firmly returned.

"Okay then we'll make up names like we're characters," I playfully suggested, since that's exactly how I felt. We couldn't help but laugh.

"That works," he responded.

"All right, you first. What's your name?"

He was hesitant for a moment and then he replied. "My name is Hayden." *Hayden?* Why did he give me his real name? That caught me off guard. Shit!

"That's a nice fake name," I mumbled.

"Yeah, I've always liked it." He was still laughing. "What's yours?" I thought for a second before I responded.

"You can call me Glo."

"Glo?"

"Yes. I've always liked it." For once my nickname would come in handy.

"I like it too." He was staring at me. There was an awkward silence as we continued to look at each other.

Looking for any topic to break the staring contest, I finally said something. "You must be thrilled to be almost finished with school."

"Yeah I'm pretty excited, but I'm sure I'll feel a lot better once I take this literature final on Wednesday. I took this class as an elective. You know a fluff course, and it's turning into my worse nightmare. I couldn't care less about Shakespeare and sonnets. I had to pull a lot of strings to get an extension on this final before graduation, two weeks away."

"My, oh my. You've certainly had to "pull a lot of strings". Is that how you've gotten through school, by pulling strings?" I asked with a laugh.

"No, of course not. I worked my ass off. That's why I'm here," he chuckled. "But this professor can be a real hard ass. The thing with my dad, well I didn't have much of a choice. Plus I would've ended up doing the MBA anyway. So why wait. It only meant two *extra* years of college." His voice was strained as he became serious and I could tell there was some contention there. I decided if I pressed the subject, the night would go downhill relatively quickly, so I changed it.

"What type of poems are you studying? Maybe I could help you, because you're cutting it close taking this trip before a major exam."

"*You* help *me*? I don't think so. Most of these poems *I've* never even heard of."

"Try me," I said in a defiant tone, a little annoyed that he automatically assumed I was stupid. Walking into his bedroom he yelled that he thought his professor was a little crazy.

"I mean we've worked from this one book for the entire semester and for the mid-term all she did was write a hundred excerpts from different poems and then gave us a page with a hundred names on it and then we had to match them. Needless to say, I didn't do very well on that exam. I just don't know how she expects us to memorize all the poems in this book." He returned carrying a thick text book, "I brought this thinking I could get in a little studying, but no luck yet." I was smiling, enjoying his little temper tantrum. "What's so funny?"

I couldn't help laughing. "You are. She doesn't expect you to memorize hundreds of poems silly. She expects you to be able to identify the different writing styles of the poet or author. If you identify their style then you can pick their work out of any line up. When you master that, retaining literary work isn't as difficult." He was looking at me sideways.

"You make it sound easy, but it's not. Believe me."

I squared my shoulders for an obvious challenge. "Try me."

"All right," and opening the text book he began. "Here's a good one: *My mistress' eyes are nothing like the sun; Coral is far more red than her lips' red...*"

"Shakespeare's sonnet 130," I said defiantly.

"Umm, that was an easy one. Shakespeare is always a no-brainer," he said, flipping the pages again as he looked from the book to me. *"Pillow'd upon my fair love's ripening breast, to feel for ever its soft fall and swell..."*

I didn't let him finish as I ended the quote. *"Awake forever in a sweet unrest, still, still to hear her tender-taken breath, and so live ever – or else swoon to death.* John Keats. Bright Star, Would I Were Steadfast as Thou Art." I was showing off and enjoying his reaction.

He flipped several pages and began again, *"If thou must love, let it be for nought, Except for love's sake only..."*

Again I cut him off. *"Do not say 'I love her for her smile – her look- her way, Of speaking gently, - for a trick of thought..."*

"Enough!" I couldn't tell if he was genuinely upset or impressed.

"Elizabeth Barrett Browning's Sonnets from the Portuguese, number 14," I said turning away from him to hide my laugh.

Then he began again, this time each word was deliberate and perfectly annunciated as he came forward slowly and stood behind me. I could feel the heat from his body. *"I gave myself to him, And took himself for pay. The solemn contract of life, Was ratified this way, The value might disappoint, Myself a poorer prove, Than this my purchaser suspect, The daily own of Love.* Should I continue or have I finally stumped you," he whispered, a hint of triumph coating his voice. He was so close my breath caught in my throat. I closed my eyes.

"Emily Dickinson's Poem 22, entitled I Gave Myself to Him," I replied softly. "That's a nice one; it could be my new favorite."

"I hope you realize that right now you're shattering every preconceived notion I had of prostitutes, or should I say women of your profession. How do you know all of that?" he asked in obvious disbelief shutting the book loudly.

"I love to read, plus my Literature teacher in school has – I mean, *had* similar tactics. It also helped that my mother was a romantic." I smiled nervously.

"You're right, that crowd tonight was definitely not your type."

I raised my eyebrows. "Really, why do you say that?" There was a knock on the door as he turned away.

"Because you actually have a brain," he said with a small laugh. I was flattered and proud of myself that I'd impressed him.

It was room service with champagne and a tray of caviar with oysters on the half shell. I tried to pretend like I could truly appreciate the pairings of the expensive snack he'd ordered just for me, but that night I came to the realization that champagne was not for my taste. How people could even drink it was beyond me. Hayden laughed at my wrinkled nose as I slipped the first oyster into my mouth and tried to get use to the slightly gross feeling of it effortlessly sliding down my throat. I wanted so desperately to appear comfortable and accustomed to the attention he was lavishing on me. He casually sat beside me on the sofa, and I listened to him talk about his college experiences and his plans to start at his father's firm immediately after graduation. He learned about life growing up in Brazil, my dad's music, my mom's bakery, and how I felt once they both died, knowing I had no other family. I had never met anyone like him. We talked the night away.

It was a chore, but I finally finished my glass. "More champagne?" He was reaching for the bottle.

Slipping my feet into my pumps I stood up. "No, no, thank you. I've had my one drink and now I have to be on my way. It was nice meeting you. Thanks for such a pleasant evening."

"Wait, wait! Why are you in such a hurry to leave? I thought we were having a nice time."

"I am not in a hurry and we were – I did have a good time, but I said I would stay for one drink and I did." My voice protested and my feet were still inching their way towards the door, but something in me wanted to stay.

"You aren't acting like you're not in a hurry. Is it the money? Because I will pay you for your time if that's what you're worried about." He walked over to the desk and removed his wallet. Once again I felt cheap, painfully reminded of the type of person he thought I was.

"It's not the money. Please put that away. You're insulting me," I said with a deep sigh. "I guess I don't know what you're expecting from me. You asked me to stay for a drink and I did." He walked towards me and placed his hand on my shoulders.

"To be honest, at first I expected nothing, but after talking to you I'm now completely intrigued. I don't think I've ever met anyone like you. I guess…I want the full experience of *Glo*. I've enjoyed your company, your sense of humor, your intellect, and your conversation. Now I want to experience your magnificent body." He was in front of me, towering over my 5' 8" frame. I couldn't breathe:

What had I gotten myself into? He looked at his watch and then back at me.

"I will pay you five thousand dollars to spend the night with me. It only seems fair, since you would've likely made the same if you'd stayed at the house."

I turned away from him, my mind racing as I tried to convince myself good conversation and good sex were two different things. And because I may have faked my way through one didn't mean I would be as successful with the other.

The sad and despicable thing was I *wanted* to stay. I *wanted* to make love to this man I didn't even know. I could feel my hands shaking and hear the deafening creaking of my parents turning over in their graves. *Pull yourself together!* I screamed in my head, as he continued to move his hands over my shoulders, running them gently across my skin and down the full length of my arms to my fingertips.

"What do you say Glo? Will you do me the honor of spending the night with me?" he asked turning me around to face him as he moved the tendrils of my untamed mane away from my face. I quickly blinked my insecurity and fear away. And as I stepped into his arms, I padlocked sweet innocent, college-bound Glory in the attic of my mind, and *Glo* came out to play.

"I don't talk money up front. You can pay me after. You never know, five thousand may not be enough," I said with a coy smile. That's what I always heard Miranda say to her customers over the phone, hopefully he bought it.

"That works for me," he whispered, taking me in his arms to kiss me. I was hesitant and he sensed it. "Kiss me," he said in a soft yet firm tone, and I did as I was told. My heart pounded as I lifted my chin to receive his kiss. His lips and his tongue were so sweet, as I laced my arms around his neck standing on the tips of my toes. He tasted divine – champagne in this form was delicious. I wasn't sure what to do, so I just twirled my tongue around his, darting it in and out of his mouth; periodically letting him suck on mine as I squeezed and massaged his back, warm flushes traveling over my body. It was like paradise. My first real kiss.

He picked me up without much effort and carried me into the bedroom not taking his face away from mine as he bit and nibbled hungrily at my lips. I refused to let myself think or rationalize what was happening, as I relished in his touch and the unfamiliar sensations taking over my flesh. He let out a little laugh once my dress was finally off and I stood before him.

"What's so funny?" I whispered, scared of what the answer would be, wondering if the sight of me half-naked was so hysterical.

He smiled showing me a row of perfect white teeth, his eyes glistening. "You're wearing cotton underwear, not lace or satin, but cotton." Slipping his thumbs into the sides of my hi-cut panties, he pulled me closer.

"You're exactly my type!" he said as he slowly peeled the remainder of my underwear from my body. I stood naked in front of him as he longingly admired my every curve. He made me feel beautiful. I knew I should be uncomfortable or even nervous, but I felt nothing but complete joy.

For the first time in my life I was thankful I'd taken up one habit from Miranda and maintained a neatly trimmed and cropped mound. When I moved in with her she almost had a heart attack the first time she saw me naked, "Now I know why you love bananas so much," she said implying I looked like a monkey. She spent the next hour lecturing me on her only pet peeve, "excessive body hair", and I have to admit, I was guilty to the tenth power. Although I often wondered how that could be a pet peeve in her line of work. Some of the men I saw her with were the spitting image of King Kong. It took a couple months to make shaving and waxing a part of my routine, but I did it and Miranda was proud, paying me the only compliment I would ever get from her. I figured no one would ever see down there anyway, so I got creative with it. The current design was that of a chess board, small perfect squares, separated by equally sized squares of smooth skin. I'd done this design before, but the second time was a charm, even I couldn't help but admire it once I was finished.

Hayden was still looking at me as he sat on the bed and brought me forward planting soft kisses across my smooth abdomen. "You play checkers?" he asked as a sexy laugh rumbled out of him.

"No chess." I smiled shyly.

While gazing at me his voice became more serious. "Interesting. I know you probably hear this all the time, but you are simply flawless," he said tenderly.

My skin was warm where his eyes trailed and soon his mouth and hands were on me. I was almost feverish as he gave each part of my body the utmost attention in ways I'd never imagined, only reading about it or hearing stories from the girls at school. Although their experiences under the bleachers and in parked cars paled in comparison to what was happening to me right now. My body wasn't my own as I relaxed and followed his every lead, having almost an out-of-body experience, reality only coming through the millions of sensations running across my skin. I was thankful he'd taken control. I was of no use to him at this point, becoming a malleable piece of warm flesh in his hands.

He seemed determined to taste every moist inch of me and find each delicately hidden crevice, using his tantalizing tongue to drive me to the brink of insanity. His intermittent humming and childlike suckling, against my quivering lips, seemed to reverberate straight up my spinal column causing rippling waves of fire to wash over me.

Our eyes met.

"Check mate," he whispered with a small laugh, to which I could only smile, closing my eyes. The flashes of red lights behind my lids were mesmerizing. The way he made me feel was just unfathomable. There must be some law against such carnal pleasures. He was tender and loving as he stroked and licked me into oblivion. I was open to everything he did, convincing myself that I was someone else, as I in turn tried to do what he asked of me to the best of my ability.

After what seemed like an eternity of him playing with each toy on the playground of my body; exploring and enjoying it, I did the same to him. Aptly learning the spots that rendered him speechless and the ones that made him growl my name. I loved the feel of his hands caressing my jaw as I moved his enormous thickness in and out of my mouth. The salty sweetness of him made me want to stay there forever – content to live off of the delectable nectar that left me ravenous.

I didn't know the woman in bed with him, she seemed confident and strong, nothing at all like the shy book worm that tried to get as far in the back of the room as possible, so she would never be chosen. I liked this person better.

That night I let him make love to me in ways I had only dreamed about, hoping and praying once he'd finally entered me that he didn't notice my discomfort or feel the wetness of my sudden tears on his shoulder. Hoping when I cried out he took it as a form of erotic expression. The pain sliced through me unexpectedly and if it had lasted a minute more I wasn't sure I would've been able to keep going. Discomfort I was expecting, but this hurt like hell and just when I parted my lips to tell him I couldn't take much more, I felt *something*. He pulled out in long strokes and the friction of his flesh inside of me sent a sensation across my body that was almost blinding. The pain was fleeting, as the pleasure far surpassed it, and soon I was enveloped in such unbridled want for him that wild abandonment over took my body as we rode each other into the night; the velvety walls of my womanhood clasping his shaft in a smooth perfect grip.

The fireworks spreading through me were intense, as I dug my nails into his back pressing my hips into his, swirling them around his hardness in a rolling motion. I was determined to take every hearty, satisfying inch of him, regardless of the paralysis I knew would ensue if he hit that dangerous obscure spot within me one more time, with the same deadly precision he'd been using for the past hour.

The sounds and smells of our love making filled the room, intoxicating me more, propelling me into a drunken stupor. I was in a sinful heaven with my inner thighs and abdominal muscles begging for salvation, quivering uncontrollably at the cataclysmic eruption threatening to happen. My toes curled and my calves stiffened. The sensation was foreign, yet inevitable. Hayden's passion was relentless and my determination to keep up with his pace was fading fast.

Calling his name, in what seemed more like a purr than my normal voice; I brought his lips to mine. The lower part of our bodies continued with its jack hammer rhythm, but our mouths moved to a slower hypnotic beat, gliding across each others. Slipping his bottom lip into my mouth, I gently rolled my tongue across it, nibbling at the sensitive flesh and felt him buckle in my arms.

I'm not sure if it was the kiss or the combination of our sensual acts that finally caused the primitive roar which escaped from him. My arousal was at new heights as I held onto him for dear life, letting the wall of our climax crumble in pure ecstasy, brick by beautiful brick, nerve by firing nerve, my name flowing off his lips: "*Glo, Glo, Glo.*"

I was glad we'd given each other our real names, since I didn't know if I could handle hearing him call me by someone else's name at this crucial point of our love-making. Knowing Hayden was *his* name made what I was experiencing even more intimate and natural. It made it all seem real and not like the fictional play it started out as on my part.

Once we collapsed in each others arms for the last time that night, panting and sweating like the wild animals our actions had just embodied; he pulled me into his arms. I would never have imagined that orgasms could be so *strong*, but after that massive one I just had tempted to cripple me, I knew otherwise.

"That was…unlike…anything I've ever experienced," he said in a deep breathless voice, tenderly running his thumb over my still sensitive nipple and nuzzling against my neck.

"I knew what you needed," I breathed softly, kicking myself for such a stupid response. But since he'd just taken the words right out of my mouth, I didn't know what else to say. *He* was unlike anything *I'd* ever experienced.

"Oh really? And what did I need Glo?" His eyes were questioning as he rose up on his elbow so that he could look at me more intently.

"You needed to make love to someone and not be screwed." Even though I was smiling my voice was steady and sure. He just looked at me as though he was trying to see past my face and into the window of my heart.

"Exactly. I haven't made love in such a long time. Although after experiencing you I have to wonder if I've ever made love at all. You felt so fragile in my arms. It all seemed so…so natural," he whispered closing his eyes. "So many men must be in love with you."

"Dozens." I rolled my eyes at the almost ridiculous thought.

"Well I'm glad you decided to stay with me tonight." Sleep enveloped us.

I was up before the sun had risen. The strange, but distinct soreness between my legs and in my lower abdomen, where he had masterfully pummeled my core, was the pinch I needed to convince myself I hadn't dreamt last night. Looking over at Hayden's muscular torso under the blood smeared sheets, I was overwhelmed with the feelings I had for him, wondering how I could've been so lucky, wondering if it was possible to utterly and completely love someone after only one night.

I contemplated staying until he woke up, but that thought lasted all of two seconds before I reminded myself how crazy it was. I lied to him when I let him believe I was an experienced woman. The sheets would tell him the truth, so there wasn't anything I could do about hiding it now, except leave. Nothing more could come of *this* anyway. I was a poor seventeen-year-old, and what happened last night could easily destroy him and everything he was working so hard to build.

I moved gingerly to the bathroom, since anything faster than a stroll was out of the question, wiped the dried blood, sweat, and semen from my body, dressed, and went over to the night table where he'd left the money. I had to smile inwardly as I counted out seven thousand dollars. Grabbing some paper from the desk, I wrote a note that I would never forget.

I gave myself to him,
And took himself for pay.
The solemn contract of life,
Was ratified this way,
The value might disappoint,
Myself a poorer prove,
Than this my purchaser suspect,
The daily own of Love.

You were worth every penny!
Priceless even...
Love, Glo

~

I didn't take his money and instead left my heart. That night changed my life forever. As I would later find out, he had given me so much more than exquisite physical pleasure.

CHAPTER ONE

" ax darling." I was gently tapping his shoulder as I tried to peel the blanket from around his body.

"Mmmmm," he moaned trying to scoot further under the covers.

"It's time to get up. I'm dropping you off this morning and I don't want to be late getting to the hospital. Rise and shine sleepy head, I'll meet you in the kitchen. Hurry up!"

I ran downstairs and whipped up a quick breakfast of scrambled eggs and toast. I was almost finished when I realized I still hadn't heard any movement upstairs. Yelling for Max again, I went to the foot of the stairs.

"Max, please get up. I have clinic this morning and Jeff is letting me sit in on a big case this afternoon. I don't want to be late. It will throw off my entire day. Get down here now."

I knew he was tired and I felt terrible since I hadn't picked him up from Nancy's house until after eleven last night, but I couldn't be late for clinic, not today. I swore to him I would be home by six yesterday, but just as I was leaving the office a case came into the ER and no one would touch it: The excuses were flying, so I jumped on it. I had to. Being the only female cardiothoracic surgeon on staff at the hospital wasn't easy, so I needed to grasp every opportunity I could to prove my worth. I knew Jeff had come up on a lot of resistance when he offered me the position last year after my residency, and I was intent on making sure he and the other staffed surgeons didn't regret it.

I was drinking my juice and skimming the morning paper when I felt his arms around my waist.

"Happy birthday, Mom," Max said kissing me on my cheek. Oh hell, was it really my birthday? This would be the third year in a row that I'd forgotten about it.

I was hesitant before I responded; checking the calendar mentally to make sure it was indeed my birthday. It was. "Awwwh, thank you sweetie." I reached back to kiss him.

"You forgot again, didn't you?" He was looking at me with an exaggerated frown.

"Noooo, actually I thought *you* may have forgotten."

He laughed at the thought and so did I, since he never forgot anything. "Me forget? Never. We have a date tonight, remember? My treat." I most certainly did not remember, but like the millions of time before I pretended like I did.

"A date with my wonderful son, I could never forget. Your treat? Does that mean you're driving as well?"

"Mom I'm twelve I can't drive." He was laughing as he made a silly face, wolfing down his eggs.

"*Almost* twelve. Chew sweetie, chew," I said rinsing my glass. "Did you finish all your homework last night?"

"Of course."

"Are you ready for your exam today?"

"Of course…not. Ms. Murphy is crazy, I hate her class. Poems and sonnets, thous and my beloveds, it is the biggest pile of rubbish I've ever heard." I unintentionally dropped my glass, but thankfully it didn't break. "Mom, are you alright?" he was standing beside me with his empty plate.

"Umm, yeah I'm fine. When you said that, you reminded me of someone I met once. I know Ms. Murphy can be difficult at times but give it your best, you need that class. Done already?" I asked taking his empty plate.

"I can finish my toast in the car. Let's go Dr. Strair; we wouldn't want to make you late for your clinic."

I started reviewing the afternoon case in my head while Max listened to his music. Dr. Jeffrey Bruckheimer had sought me out several years before and this would hopefully be another opportunity for me to prove my worth. If it hadn't been for him, I wouldn't be on the fast track to success right now. He was the prestigious head of the cardiology and surgical departments at the hospital and had significant pull at our institution and nationwide. He was a cut-throat bureaucrat, knee deep in hospital politics and on the board of trustees, but before all of that he was a superior surgeon. Every doctor wanted to be on his good side, so it helped that he'd taken me under his wing.

Traffic was light since it was Friday. I pulled up in front of St. Bernard's School for Boys just as the first bell rang.

"All right, Nancy will be dropping me off at your office around six. This place doesn't take reservations, but I didn't want to wait. So Uncle Jeff called and they'll hold a seat for us. Please don't be late." He leaned over and kissed me, hurrying out of the car, but I held on to him.

"Darling, I'm sorry about last night. A case came in that I had to take." He just continued to look at me, not indifferent, but like he'd heard it all before and he had. "It won't be like this for much longer, you know that don't you?"

"I know Mom. You work hard and you're the best doctor I know. At some point everyone will start to notice, Uncle Jeff has. I just hope they don't take much longer." His friends were calling him as he looked away. "I love you Mom. Don't forget tonight, okay?"

"I won't," I yelled after him.

"Oooh and Mom, wear something pretty. No scrubs," he shouted back, waving at me over his shoulder.

"I'll try." I had to laugh at the things he said sometimes.

As I watched him walking up the stairs I couldn't believe how fast he'd grown up. As fate would have it, one of my first patients was the President of St. Bernard's School for Boys. After having performed a flawless procedure, and Mr. Nash having an equally flawless recovery, Max's admittance into one of the top high schools in the nation, was a cinch. Max was a great student, and was moved two grades ahead of the students his age; all his teachers loved him. Everything he did made me proud. I couldn't have asked for a better child. He was obedient and always understanding. I'm all he had, and he was my world.

These last four years had been hell for us. With a rigorous and competitive residency, I had to put a lot of things relating to Max on the back burner – frankly, I had put Max on the back burner. Sad, but true. I was fighting to be in an elite group of doctors and surgeons, where women were rare and the well-known and successful ones even more so. I had to give two hundred percent when everyone else gave a hundred.

Things were harder for Max, between school and my absenteeism; he'd learned to be relatively self-sufficient from a young age. I'm not sure if that was something to be proud of or not, but for right now it helped knowing I didn't have to baby him. St. Bernard's was an excellent school, and it also kept Max busy. I guess my hope was that he would barely notice my absence if he was constantly occupied with some sports team or club meeting.

I always tried to be honest with him when it came to my work and school so he knew everything I was doing was for him and making a better life for us, but in the same breath I could see he was becoming tired of the excuses and my lack of participation. Other mothers came to school shows, swim meets, and were part of the PTA. I could barely manage my parent-teachers conferences, but those I tried not to miss even if I did it over the phone and had copies of his work faxed over. I knew first hand how much a good education mattered and I'd be damned if I ruined that aspect of Max's life. My participation could be lacking in any other area except that. He needed a full time mother and I was eagerly looking forward to being one, hopefully it wouldn't be too late when I got the opportunity.

My cell phone started ringing as I drove off. I recognized the Nevada area code immediately.

Miranda.

"Hello?"

"Uh, uh Glo? It's your Aunt Miranda?" Miranda. I hadn't heard from her in months, which usually meant she was either in trouble, needed money or both.

"Hi, how are you?"

"Good, good," she said nervously, "What's that noise?"

"The radio. Max was listening to something before I dropped him off to school." I turned the radio off.

"Oh."

"What's going on, are you ok? We haven't talked since... since....?"

"-since I got out of rehab. Yeah I know. I'm fine, doing a lot better. I'm sorry to ask, but I was wondering if I could borrow some money?" I knew it.

"How much are we talking here?"

"Ten thousand dollars"

"Ten..."

"I'll pay you back, I swear"

"Like how you've paid me back the seven grand you already borrowed over the years? I don't have that type of money to spare Miranda." What I really wanted to say was 'You must have lost your mind, or fried your last brain cell with cocaine, if you think I'd ever give you another penny!'

"We're family. I took you in when you..."

"-had no where else to go. Yes, so you keep telling me."

"You're rich now. A big time doctor, it's not like you're going to miss it!" I couldn't believe she was talking to me as if I still owed her my life.

"I'm not rich and me missing it is not the point. I can't keep giving you money. You'll just end up using it on drugs and I can't have that on my conscience if something happened to you."

The fact was I honestly didn't have it to give. Yes, since being asked to join the Cardiac Surgery practice at the world renowned Biltmore Hospital, I was making more money than I ever had in my life. But because of that increased income, we lost Max's financial aid this year, and I certainly hadn't budgeted for the additional thirty-five hundred dollars a month it was costing me to keep him at St. Bernard's. Between our new house, my eleven year old car on the fritz, and school loans, I had just enough for Max and I. After having two relatively young parents die, I was smart enough to know that I had to be prepared if anything happened. Max had no one else. I'd given Miranda my nest egg once before and lived to regret it. I couldn't do it again.

"IT'S NOT FOR DRUGS! I TOLD YOU I'M CLEAN!" I had to pull the phone away from ears as she screeched at the top of her lungs.

"All right then, fine, what do you need it for?" Why was I even asking?

"I'm trying to move and buy a house, but my plans fell through. I was going to use the money for a deposit. I gotta get out of this neighborhood, you know what I mean? It's just not helping my recovery."

"I can understand that; well are you working?" I could feel the tide of my will, to say no, turning. A new house may be just what she needed to get her life back on track for good.

"I still have the club. Carlos took care of it while I was…away," Ahh, the infamous Carlos. I tried not to cringe at the mention of his name, because I remembered him and his pimp like influence over my aunt far too well. "I don't see the point of your question." I could hear the agitation in her voice. "Can you lend me the money or not? Damn it Glory! You know this place isn't good for me and there's no way in hell your mother would let me stay here if she were alive." I hated it when she used my mother to bait me.

"Miranda, I just need to know if you have a job that can pay the bills and pay me back." I was trying to remain calm and put myself in her shoes, but her 'I'm entitled' attitude was not helping. "Listen, I have a better idea. Do you think you can send me the information on the house you're looking at?"

"Why?"

"Just send it. Do you still have the computer I bought you last year?"

"Nope. It's broken."

"Broken? What happened to it? It was brand new."

"Carlos spilt beer on it by accident and it hasn't worked since."

"Alright fine…are you working with a realtor?"

She interrupted me abruptly, "Listen Glo all I need is the money, either you can give me or you can't."

"I'm not going to just give you ten thousand dollars, especially when it's all I have. I need to know what it's for. So you have two choices: You can get me the information I need so I can help you, or find someone else to lend you the money. It's that simple."

"You know, you've turned into a real bitch."

"So I've been told. Be safe and I'll wait to hear from you with that info." *CLICK*. She hung up on me before I could even finish. That woman had some serious issues.

Miranda kicked me out the moment she found out I was pregnant. I never thought to hide it from her, but then again I never thought she would throw me out on the street either. I couldn't understand why she never asked me who the father was. I guess she just assumed it happened the night of the party.

What wasn't surprising was the fact that she never gave me Kim's share of the money, attributing it to the fact that I'd made her worry when I left the party. I told her that one of the guys was leaving, and I got a ride back into town with him, but nothing happened. Somehow I knew she didn't believe me, but she didn't seem to care that I'd left with a stranger either. Thankfully I found out I was pregnant just before I left for college. So she kicked me out a few days before I was scheduled to move into my dorm on a full scholarship. I spent two days sleeping in a train station bathroom, but no one needed to know that. As the years went by, that two-day homeless experience became the least of my memorable stories.

I asked for her help so many times after Max was born. I even offered to help move her to Connecticut while I was at Yale when I heard about her drug habit. I was on a full scholarship and the off campus apartment was completely paid for. I thought it would've been good for her to get out of that environment, while helping me raise Max, but she refused.

Miranda's run-ins with the law were becoming more frequent. I tried again to get her to quit that lifestyle, but she didn't want to – the money was good she would always say.

Once when I had a weekend cardiology course in Nevada, I became desperate and asked her to watch Max for the weekend; she refused, so I had to bring him with me. I can still remember the looks I got, but once I opened my mouth, people seemed to forget the toddler in the stroller next to me. Dr. Kensington, who ran that course, is still a great colleague of mine. He always talks about my tenacity, taking whatever money I could spare to traipse all over the nation with my son in tow to attend weekend cardiac courses, academic meetings and symposiums. It was a huge financial sacrifice, but the educational and networking rewards were invaluable.

It was the obnoxious car horn behind me that brought me back to reality. Whenever I got a call from Miranda, it dredged up old memories of the house, the club, her clients, the drugs, and that entire atmosphere. Life was hard back then, but all I had to do was look at my baby boy and it made all the stress worth while.

I tried to forget his father. The man I convinced myself never really existed. The man I tried convincing myself I never really loved; but I couldn't. I saw his face everyday when I looked at Max and everyday I relived that night, and for a minute or a split second, my body would come alive.

As I walked into the office, I could already see eight to ten people waiting although I was half-hour early. The difference between me and the other new surgeons on staff was that they waited for patient referrals to fill up their OR time. I couldn't do that. Most surgeons hate clinic time; they just want to be in surgery, but until I'd built a name for myself I knew there would be slim pickings, so I added three cardiology clinics during the week and self referred: Most, if not all, of the patients on my surgical schedule came out of my clinics. It worked out well, because I got to build relationships with the patients outside of their surgical needs.

Then there was the ER where I would hang around constantly hoping that they needed an extra pair of hands. They always did. Yes I had gone as long as three days with no sleep, but it was getting to the point where patients and staff were becoming familiar with me, which is what I wanted. All I needed was to keep my schedule available and when I met a patient for the first time, I treated them the way I would want to be treated. In return they would become as loyal to me as I would be to them.

"Good morning everyone," I announced smiling at Rebecca and Amy, who were both in deep telephone conversations about my schedule. There were smiles and 'good mornings' all around. I waved as I passed the nurses' station and went into my office, slipping on my lab coat. Just as I turned on the computer there was a knock on the door.

"Come in." A couple of nurses and Becca walked in. "What's up ladies?"

"We wanted to give you this before you got bogged down with patients. It's from all of us," announced Joy, one of the senior nurses. "Happy Birthday," they said simultaneously.

"Oh you shouldn't have." I smiled but was a little taken aback and surprised so many people knew about my birthday. I usually tried to sweep it under the rug. "How did you find out?"

"Max told us a while ago. He's such a sweetheart," said Becca, as I gave each of them a hug. Janice put a small gift wrapped box on my desk.

"You can open it later," she said heading for the door.

"All right, back to the grind," Becca announced. "You have twenty-five patients this morning and the case with Dr. Bruckheimer scheduled for this afternoon."

"Thank you." I said to the already closed door as they had quickly dispersed. I pulled my schedule up on the computer, did a quick skim to see who was coming in, and then jumped right into my clinic.

It was a little before two, when I finished up and got a chance to sit down before meeting Jeff for a 2:30 scrub in. Peeling a banana I quickly reviewed my charts. In addition to my regularly scheduled patients, I had three walk-ins, an emergency add on from the hospital and two referrals from outside physicians, for a grand total of thirty-one patients in six hours and four booked procedures.

At this rate my practice would grow more than I could ever hope, with referrals coming in and surgical slots booking up quickly. I know many of the other surgeons at the hospital weren't pleased, but there was nothing they could say. I wasn't doing anything underhanded or sneaky. The only thing I could be faulted for was working my ass off. My work spoke for itself: Forty-two independent successful open-heart surgeries my first year alone. It could've been more, but since I'd added regular clinics I lost some of my OR time. That number didn't take into account the ER cases or when I 'assisted', which really meant I got to do all the work while the tenured surgeon played golf or slept in. They still got credit for those cases, but I was thankful for each opportunity to practice my skill and build relationships with the OR staff. Working with Jeff wasn't like that; you were lucky if he let you tie a suture. With him it was all about answering questions, watching and learning techniques, and I was glad to do it.

When I was finished with my charts from the morning, I continued to study the chart on the patient I'd be assisting Jeff with this afternoon. When he asked me late yesterday if I wanted to join him, I had readily agreed; and after my case in the ER last night, I managed to find and copy the patient chart so that I could study it at home. Yes I was only assisting, but it never hurt to be prepared.

My pager went off, and it was the number from the surgical lounge so I quickly swallowed the last piece of banana and called upstairs to double check the time to make sure I wasn't late. The nurse who picked up firmly told me to come upstairs immediately. That was all I had to hear, and I was in an all out sprint to the OR thinking of the many scenarios that would've precipitated the call; none were right.

I was promptly led to a patient prep area. I thought I was going to meet Dr. Bruckheimer and the patient then, but it was Jeff in the bed. He was deathly pale with a large portion of his right hand wrapped in a blood-soaked bandage. My mind was reeling as the nurses hustled and bustled around him.

"What the hell happened?" I was looking from him to the nurses and back again as I placed my hand on his shoulder.

He cleared his throat, swallowing the pain I could see behind his eyes. "I had an accident…"

"What kind of accident? How bad are we talking?" Although with the amount of blood on the bandage I knew it couldn't be good.

He explained that one of his patients was having problems breathing during a post-surgical exam, so he tried to adjust the bed, in an attempt to make the patient more comfortable but there was a malfunction. It slammed down on his fingers crushing them between the bed and the frame. None of the buttons worked and the bed was locked in place. It didn't help that the patient in the bed was morbidly obese, having a check up after his bypass surgery. Between getting him out of the bed and manually unlocking the frame, it took almost fifteen minutes to get Jeff's hand free. At which point it was fair to say that they thought he'd lost use of his second and middle fingers.

"Jesus, Jeff, tell me what to do. Did someone call Clay?" Clay was Jeff's partner and life-long best friend. He was a good man and devoted partner. Jeff would want him there.

"Yes, he's on the way. About the case you were going to assist me …"

"Don't even worry about it. I'm sure it can go on Dr. Nolte's surgical schedule for tomorrow," I blurted out before he could finish his sentence.

"No, no, no. It has to be done today before the patient's children return on Monday. They don't want them to know…just yet. Today is the only option."

"Dr. Bruckheimer, I can do it," Dr. Everton quickly piped in, pushing me aside to stand next to Jeff. I hadn't even realized he was in the room. He was one year ahead of me and chomping at the bit to be in that elite group of surgeons. He only showed his eagerness when there were other tenured surgeons around to see him, Jeff in particular. Last night in the ER, however, he'd been one of the first ones to turn down the double-bypass on the seventy-three year old man and head in the opposite direction. If the patient had died, it would've been a notch on the wrong side of the belt. I didn't care. He still deserved a chance, which I gave him after a successful procedure.

Jeff was looking at me for a response, but I had none. He winced as the nurse started to prep his hand for surgery.

"All right Everton. Tell me your game plan."

"Uh…well…I'll have to look at the chart and…"

"You haven't looked at the chart yet?" I knew if Jeff hadn't been in pain he would've ripped him to shreds. Actually, it was fair to say that he was going to rip him to shreds anyway. "What the hell were you waiting for? We were supposed to be going into surgery," he paused to look at the clock behind us, "right now and you have no fucking idea what we're doing? How exactly did you plan on assisting me, by standing there and looking pretty? Jesus Christ! Do you even know who we're operating on?" He was yelling, his face beet red, as Dr. Everton continued to take small steps back and the nurse cringed from Jeff's voice. "Dr. Strair I hope you have a better fucking answer for me or else you can both consider this the last case you'll ever assist with in this hospital." Turning to glare at Everton he hissed, "And if you don't know what that means for your career you'd better hope and pray that Strair here tells me what I want to hear." This is it Glory. This is it – deep breath.

My voice had never been steadier. "We have a 65 year old male with a history of angina due to ischemic heart disease and no surgical history. I estimate that he'll need a quadruple bypass, based on the coronary angiogram taken this morning. It looks like we'll be bypassing four vessels: the LAD, RCA, LCX, and the first diagonal artery of the LAD. But we won't know for sure until we get in there and look. I'm interested in what the left-main lesion looks like because if it's as bad as I think, it will place Mr. Weiss at a higher risk." I paused to take my first breath, and then continued reciting the patient history and *my* game plan as Jeff, Everton, and the other staff stared wide-eyed.

When I was finished, Jeff wasn't successful at hiding the smirk on his face. "My sentiments exactly, well done. Let me talk to the patient and his wife and then you can go in and introduce yourself.

Everton get out of my sight and send up Willis to assist Dr. Strair. You don't deserve to be in my OR. There's nothing worse than someone who pretends to be something they aren't." I turned to leave as Everton whisked passed me, embarrassed and probably mad as a hater, but Jeff called me back. He was smiling. "Good job."

"Thanks."

"Listen this patient is…well, he's a close friend. It's fair to say that I consider him a brother. He's done a lot for Clay and I, and this hospital. Glory when I say a lot, I mean *a lot.* The new cardiac care center is named after his mother and father." The name was ringing a bell now as I could feel my panic rising. *The* Edward Weiss. Maybe this wasn't a smart idea after all. "This will be the ultimate test for you at this stage in your career, and I won't lie and tell you it'll be easy. They don't know about my hand and they won't take kindly to you doing this procedure — not because you're a woman — but because you're young in age and experience. I know you can do it, but it's still their choice. Do you understand?"

"Perfectly," with that I left the room promptly to go and throw up. Twenty minutes later I was called into the room with the Weiss' and right away I knew they weren't pleased.

"I'm…," I reached out to shake their hands and accidentally knocked the small pitcher of ice water onto the floor. Not now Glory…not now! Get your shit together. This is not the time for Clumsy Clarisse to make an appearance. I was mumbling my pathetic apologies as the nurse scurried to dry up the water and I bumped into every piece of equipment visible between the door and the bed trying to shake their hands.

"When can we expect the doctor?" a woman I could only assume to be his wife barked, all but ignoring my outstretched hand and stepping around me to look out the door.

"Actually Mrs. Weiss, *I'm* Dr. Glory Strair." She didn't try to conceal her shock and annoyance as both their eyes popped out of their heads.

"You've got to be kidding me. Jesus, Jeff told us you were young, but not this young."

"And not this clumsy," her husband added, turning his attention to his wife. He told her he was having second thoughts and that maybe they should wait and have Nolte do it the day after tomorrow.

"Well Raymond, I mean Dr. Nolte, has been on the staff here for several years and is a very capable doctor."

"Yes, but his bedside-manner leaves a lot to be desired," added his wife bluntly. I smiled since I knew what she was saying was absolutely true. Almost instantly I liked them, even though they didn't like me. "We had a consult with him once when Jeff's slots were filled and let's just say he wasn't our cup of tea." She was right. Nolte was the number two cardiothoracic surgeon after Jeff – in respect to years of service and *not* skill level, but his poor bedside manner left nothing to be desired, and in this day and age patients didn't take too kindly to it, which left him with an open surgery schedule.

"Bedside manner or not, at least *he's* out of diapers," snapped Mr. Weiss. I don't think I'd ever been made to feel so inadequate. "All of that being said Dr. Strair, I've always been a numbers man, and I look at numbers, stats, if you will, and you don't have much. But from what Jeff tells me, you're the next best thing, a steady hand and a good heart." I tried not to blush at the compliment, wondering if Jeff would've told them the same thing about Dr. Everton.

"Mr. Weiss you flatter me, but ultimately all that matters is that you're comfortable with your surgeon. I'll hopefully have ample time to prove that Jeff was right. I do have a good heart and steady hand, but right now you need to decide if you want me to perform your surgery. That should be our most pressing concern. Yes I'm young, but I'm driven. I graduated at the top of my class, was hand-picked by Dr. Bruckheimer after residency to be on staff here, and I've studied your chart front to back since he asked me at six o'clock yesterday evening to assist him. Next to him, no one knows your case better. I can do this, and I know it's too much to ask you to trust me; so I'll ask you to trust Jeff. He's told me how much you mean to him. I know its killing him that he can't do the surgery, but if he feels I can perform it in his place, then you should feel confident in that as well. Give me a chance. "

His wife was crying, placing her hands akimbo, she glared at me. "Give you a chance? This is the *only* chance you'll get. If you mess up I lose my husband forever," her voice was now trembling as tears flowed from her eyes like a river, "You have the rest of your young idealistic life to regret it, realizing you weren't meant to be a surgeon, and picking up a modeling career or something. It's not a risk I'm willing to take!" Her husband reached over to take her hand in an attempt to calm her down, which only made her cry more.

"Dr. Strair I'm sure you're a very promising surgeon, but if anyone is going to cut open my chest and work on my heart, they have to be the best…"

My voice was softer than I intended. "I understand completely. Let me talk to the nurse and see if there is anyway we could get Dr. Nolte here today or first thing tomorrow."

"…and if Jeff thinks you're it, then so be it. Right now I don't care how old you are, just do your best is all I'll ask."

I couldn't believe he was going to let me do it. His wife opened her mouth to protest, but quickly realized his decision was final. This was a huge thing. "Th-thank you. I'll give you a couple more minutes, and then the nurse will be in to prep you." I shook his hand, but Mrs. Weiss refused to take mine. I left before they could see my tears, heading straight to the bathroom to throw-up again.

The procedure took a little over five hours and when I emerged, happy as a clam to tell Mrs. Weiss things went text book perfect; I had never felt better. I held her as she cried and thanked me. It was only after I said my goodbyes and promised to come see them first thing in the morning, that I realized the time. Shit, Max! The OR staff and Dr. Willis were trying to congratulate me as I ran through the corridors, but I couldn't stop. How could I make this up to him?

At ten after nine, I wasn't sure what I expected, but the office was vacant and Max was no where in sight. I quickly dialed Nancy's number. She told me that Clay called to tell them what happened, but Max was already dressed. They were on their way to meet me, so she just brought him upstairs to wait with Clay. Just before she hung up, I asked her if he was mad and she said what I expected her to say; if he was, he didn't show it.

I was already late, but I was still in an all-out sprint, mad at myself for disappointing Max yet again. After finding out which room Jeff was in, I went straight there. Max was in the corner reading, when I barged in the room. Clay was sitting on the bed next to Jeff as they all looked at me like I had eight heads.

"There's the birthday girl," Clay announced trying to sound cheerful.

"Max… I'm…so …so… sorry." I was trying to catch my breath and failing miserably. Max looked up and instantly I knew he wasn't mad as a smile spread across his face.

"How did the case go?"

"Uh…well. I think it went well. Can you forgive me?"

"Well? From what we heard, it went better than well," Jeff chimed in. "Your first solo quadruple bypass in five hours and ten minutes is fantastic, especially when I'm hearing terms like "her fingers were moving like a well choreographed ballet" and "she just entered a zone and was all business". Glory this is great! I hear you were superb in there, a real natural. Jen from the OR called me when it was over and said it was like she was watching the female version of me. This must've been one hell of a birthday present for you." I still hadn't said anything as I continued to look at Max and my reflection in the window dressed head to toe in my surgical attire. He asked me not to wear scrubs.

"Glory say something. Aren't you thrilled?" Clay asked.

"Yes, yes of course I'm happy things turned out well." I quickly turned my attention back to Max. "Max, I'm sorry I made you wait, by the time we got into surgery it was after three, and I lost track of time." I wanted to be more excited, but felt surprising sick as I looked at Max dressed in his suit. When would I stop putting everything before him? I rushed over to take him in my arms. He was almost as shocked as I was at my sudden embrace.

"Mom, it's fine really. Uncle Clay called so I knew what happened."

"I know, but I always break our plans, and I know how frustrating it is for you."

"Glory we moved the reservation to tomorrow…"

"No. You told me this place doesn't take reservations. If you want we can still go out tonight. It's Friday and relatively early, plus I'm starved."

"Glory its fine, really. Jeff knows the cook …umm…chef, and he said it wasn't a problem," Clay tried to reassure me.

Max protested and said he was tired, so we finally agreed to celebrate tomorrow, but I still felt lousy. Once that was settled, I turned my attention to Jeff, and we discussed the Weiss case and his own recovery. They were able to insert five metal pins, two into both the middle and second fingers and one into the tip of the index finger. It was unlikely that he would be able to operate again. He choked up then and Clay slipped his arms around his shoulder as we held him. Just like that, in the blink of an eye, his career had been over.

I went to see my seventy-three year old ER patient and Edward, bright and early Saturday morning while doing my rounds. They were both doing well. Even though Edward was in some pain, things looked extremely promising for him and I was pleased with how things were coming along. Jeff had been down earlier to see them and apparently had nothing but good things to say about me and the procedure. They had warmed up to me slightly, but *slightly* was a far way from completely.

I was home and dressed, patiently waiting for Max when he got in from swim practice. He laughed at the fact that I was an hour early, but I told him I refused to be late again. He was ready in no time and we were walking through Central Park shortly there after.

"Where are we going?"

"Dinner I told you," he replied bluntly. He was so independent.

"Dinner where?" I was excited since I'd heard him on the phone firming up the plans and calling Clay to make sure things were all set. I couldn't wait to see what he had in store for me.

"You'll see when we get there." He was smiling at my questions. Fifteen minutes later we were walking into Viva's Diner, where the most expensive thing on the menu cost around thirty dollars.

"Max, this is very expensive. Are you sure?"

With some degree of pride Max patted my hand and assured me he was all set. "Mom, its fine, all taken care of. Uncle Jeff knows the owner and Becca knows the chef, so everyone's expecting us. I told you this is my treat." I was trying my best to contain my smile as he walked up to the little old lady at the front, whom I recognized immediately from the hospital cafeteria, greeted us.

"Strair, a six o'clock reservation?" The woman winked at me and then looked back at Max, before glancing down at the book.

I couldn't help the grin played across my face looking at the handsome young man on my arm. He wasn't yet twelve and stood just a few inches shorter than me. The thick black curls that covered his head were always too long and wild for my liking, but only added to his striking features. Thanks to my side of the gene pool, he was blessed with a smooth olive complexion. If one had to choose a distinctive feature on Max it would be difficult, from his hair, to his eyes and sickingly-long eyelashes, to his height, and already athletic physique. I constantly had to beat the forced-ripe little girls at his previous school away with a baseball bat, hence my putting him in an all-boys' school. The last thing I needed was him thinking about girls. People were always mistaking him for a fifteen or sixteen year old, which helped a little with his transition into the new school and grade level, but presented more social problems with him hanging out with older kids; although he seemed to be holding his own relatively easily. He had a good head on his shoulders Jeff kept reminding me.

"Ah, yes Strair right this way," leading the way, the woman took us to a beautifully decorated table at the back of the diner that looked out across park. "Can I take your shawl ma'am?" she asked.

"Yes, of course," I responded slipping it off.

"Mom you look beautiful," Max exclaimed, admiring the gold satin dress that hung on my every curve. I rarely got dressed up, but when I did, *I did*. "I can't believe you don't think that men find you pretty. No one can keep their eyes off you," he said raising his voice as he looked around the diner.

"Ssshh, lower your voice," I said with an uncomfortable smile. He was right, people were staring. Once she helped me to my seat and walked away, I turned to Max, "Why would you say something like that?" My voice was stern. "I never said that! You embarrassed me."

"I'm sorry, but I wish you could see what we all see, if you did you wouldn't be lonely."

"What makes you think I'm lonely? I don't have time to be lonely Max."

"Mum, you don't have a husband or a boyfriend and your only friends are your patients or your staff, especially Becca," he said in a matter-of-fact type of voice. He was painfully right. Rebecca and I had worked together a long time. She was a single parent like myself and somehow I related to her struggles and wanted to help her as much as possible. She was going to nursing school at night and was my administrative assistant during the day.

"I don't need a husband or a boyfriend," I said in a low voice, "I have plenty of friends and you, so that's all I need."

"You need to go out more."

"Are you trying to get rid of me?" I asked with a playful laugh, trying to hide my embarrassment at the direction the conversation was taking.

"No, believe me, that is the last thing I want to do. I just think you work too hard and …," his voice trailed off as the waiter stepped up, and we ordered our drinks. "I just worry about you, is all."

"You don't have to worry about me sweetie. I have everything I need," I said tapping the back of his hands with a smile.

"I don't believe you. You try to make busy, but your eyes tell me you're lonely, and maybe if you had a husband you would want to be home with us," and with that he quickly turned his attention to the plastic covered menus that had been placed in front of us. I was glad he dropped it, because I didn't have a single response; for the moment he'd left me speechless.

Dinner was lovely, but I couldn't get what Max had said out of my mind. I had been on several dates; I don't know what he was talking about. Although I guess I would conveniently go out only when someone happened to mention that I never went out. For so long between Max, school, and work, I didn't have time for a relationship; I didn't have time for anything. But now that things were going so well and he was older, I should probably start to make the time, if not for myself then for him. I think Max had learned how to pretend things were okay even when he was bothered, and the last thing I needed was for him to think that the reason I worked so hard was because I didn't want to be with him.

They brought out a cake for dessert and sang me happy birthday, I closed my eyes and made my wish. He was so cute, taking out his wallet and paying once the check came, refusing to let me see it.

"Dinner was wonderful, sweetie. Thank you." I leaned over and kissed his forehead.

"You're welcome. Did you wish for the same thing again this year?" he asked.

"I did."

"You've been wishing for the same thing for as long as I could remember," he said with a chuckle. "I hope you get it soon, whatever it is."

"So do I," I whispered "so do I. Let's head home, it's late."

That night I fell asleep and as usual dreamt of the man I try so hard to forget.

CHAPTER TWO

etween Jeff and Edward's surgeries, Max and I saw them constantly. Jeff had taken leave from the hospital for his recovery, but not before he'd done my annual review. He gave me an extremely generous salary increase and designated me as the covering surgeon in his absence, much to Dr. Everton's dismay. Things were looking up for me. A large part of my day was spent in surgery and the other small part on the phone when I called my patients. My schedule was becoming more regimented, and I was usually too tired to take on any extra work, so Max was pleased. With Edward I had taken a very personal role in his recovery; checking in almost on a daily basis.

Three times a week Max and I would join Jeff and Clay for dinner. It was becoming the norm for the Weiss' to join us on those occasions and on the weekend trips to Jeff's cabin. Over the next couple months they'd warmed up to me considerably, and we became friends. We all seemed to get along well. They had taken to Max almost immediately and for some reason, I really liked them. I guess, except for the extremely wealthy part, they reminded me of my parents.

One afternoon when I came out of the OR, I got a message to give Harriett Weiss a call. I had an initial wave of panic at the thought that something may have happened to Edward since she'd never called me at work before.

"Weiss residence." Came the soft voice on the other end of the phone and I knew it was Lolita, the house keeper. She and I had never met, since I'd never been to the Weiss's home, but we'd briefly spoken a few times when I called.

"Hello Lolita. Is Harriett available? This is Glory returning her call."

"One minute Dr. Strair." Moments later Harriet picked up.

"Glory, how are you darling?" She was barely able to contain her excitement.

"I'm fine, busy. How about you and Edward? Is everything all right?"

"We're great. He's doing well. Listen, the reason for my call is because Edward and I have tickets to the ballet tonight, but we won't be able to go, something came up. Jeff and Clay already have plans. Do you think you can go?"

"Well Max is away. He left this morning for a school camping trip, so it's just me."

"I know, but that will be even better. We have a family friend that has been dying to see this show. If you didn't mind, I could give him the other ticket.

"No I wouldn't mind at all. I'm sure he and his wife would enjoy it more than I would going by myself."

"No, no dear, you don't understand. Eric isn't married. I was suggesting that you two go together," she said enthusiastically.

"Um, no I couldn't."

"Why not? He's completely respectable and one of the top partners at my son's firm. Please say you'll go. He's a really nice man; besides, Max is gone, and you've got a free weekend from the hospital; I'm not taking no for an answer."

"Harriett,"

"Harriett nothing, I'll have your ticket couriered over, and you can meet him there. It's that simple. I'm sure you'll have a great time." I couldn't believe she was playing match maker. But what did I have to lose?

"All right, I'll go."

"Great! That's what I want to hear. I'm sure he'll be thrilled. The courier should be at your office any minute."

"Any minute?"

"Yes, I sent him over about forty-five minutes ago."

"But…but…how did you know I would say yes?"

"I just knew. We'll talk soon. Don't work too hard. And please try to have fun tonight. This is a good thing."

I couldn't help but hang up with a smile. That was one feisty woman. I guess she had to be, being married to that powerhouse of a husband.

I finished up my rounds at about 5:30pm and stopped by the office to pick up my ticket, then headed home to get ready. Too bad Max wasn't here, I would have to save my ticket stub so he could have proof that I really went out on a date.

I arrived at the New York City Ballet fifteen minutes early, then it dawned on me that other than the fact that I knew this man's first name was Eric, I knew nothing else about him. The valet took my keys and handed me a ticket. There were a few people standing outside as I nervously looked around. I was about to walk up the steps when someone called me.

"Glory?" I turned to find an attractive man in a tux looking at me.

"Yes. Eric?" I couldn't help the small smile on my face since I was pleased with what I'd seen so far.

"Yes, I was nervous I wouldn't be able to find you, but Harriett did an excellent job of describing you. Please let's go inside," and without waiting for my response, he gently placed his hand on the small of my back and led me inside. "Would you like me to check your coat?" "Yes, thank you." He was cute, in a Frodo Baggins type of way just taller. Harriett had done well. The night was perfect, and Eric was a complete gentleman. I couldn't find one visible flaw in him, and I was certainly looking. We had excellent seats and great conversation. Once the ballet was over, he suggested we sit in our booth a little while longer until the crowd died down.

"Tell me a little about yourself." He turned to me, his face filled with intrigue. Over the next ten minutes I told him about Max and my work at the hospital. "So you aren't married?"

"I am, I just decided not to bring my husband with me on my date tonight," I replied with a laugh. He couldn't help joining in as well, when he really thought about his question.

"I'm sorry that was a stupid question. I guess what I was trying to ask was if you've ever been married."

"That's fine, I knew what you meant, but I wanted to pull your leg. No, I've never been married."

"What about Max's father?" I didn't mean for my face to change the way it did, but it did and he saw it immediately. "I'm sorry I shouldn't have asked such a personal question." Ah get over it Glory, it's been twelve years. Everyone thinks you're lonely, and after only two months, a woman you barely know saw it fit to set you up on a blind date. Max needs a man in his life, a father, so build a bridge and get over yourself. You're running out of excuses.

"It's okay; you caught me a little off guard, but its fine. I got pregnant with Max the spring before I started Yale. His father and I weren't in a relationship at the time, so that's really all there is to it," I said, shrugging my shoulders. Summing up the night Max was conceived into one mere, insignificant sentence seemed like such a mammoth understatement. Yes what we shared couldn't even be remotely considered a relationship, but it was also so much more than a one night stand. Maybe it was all in my head how special that night was…I mean he probably did stuff like that all the time and here I was twelve years later, still pining like a stupid teenager.

"Okay, I'm sorry I asked," he apologized again.

"Eric it's fine, really. How about you? Were you ever married? Kids?" I needed to change the subject and the direction of my thought process.

"Nope, never married and I don't have any kids. I was in my last relationship for four years, but just couldn't see myself with her for the rest of my life; so I broke it off. She wasn't too happy to say the least."

"Well better now than later, right?"

"Exactly what I thought," he said with a smile. We were just looking at each other when I realized the theater had cleared out.

"We should get going," I said looking around, but before I could get up he took my hand.

"I would really love to see you again."

"I think that could be arranged," I replied with a small smile, slipping my hand from beneath his.

"Great." We got my evening coat and he waited while they brought my car around, but I didn't see him give them a ticket.

"Where did you park?" I asked.

"I didn't drive. I thought it was safer to take a cab," he responded.

"Well let me take you home. It's the least I can do after such a lovely evening."

"That's really not necessary."

"I insist, plus it would give us a couple more minutes to talk." He seemed to perk up at the thought of that. If he cared about the jalopy of a car that pulled up, he didn't let on; getting in without a care in the world. We drove to his house and he offered to have me come up for a nightcap, but I declined. I knew from a previous experience that I was not the best person at walking away.

"Would you like to have dinner or something tomorrow evening?"

"Sure that sounds nice. I really had fun tonight Eric. I'll have to send Harriett a nice bottle of wine."

"Wine? I was thinking more along the lines of the Hope Diamond," he chimed in. We both started to laugh.

"That must've been some ballet."

"It's not the ballet I would be thanking her for." I became uncomfortable then, shifting in my seat as he continued to look at me. I could tell he wanted to kiss me. Did I want to kiss him? "Good night Glory," and leaning forward he kissed me at the corner of my mouth.

"Good night Eric." He reached to open the car door and I stopped him. "Wait; take my number, that way we can make plans for tomorrow."

"That would help, wouldn't it?" He rolled his eyes as he slapped his hand against his forehead. We exchanged numbers and I went home, pleased with myself – but more importantly, pleased with him.

Over the next few months Eric and I went out at least a couple times a week. Initially Max was excited for me, but once he met Eric, he didn't seem to care for him. He came over for dinner once or twice during the week, on the nights we weren't at Jeff's; and we'd gone on a few day trips on the weekends, but still Max wasn't warming up to him. It wasn't obvious to Eric that Max didn't like him, but because I knew him like the back of my hand it was obvious to me. Harriett was proud of herself, checking in regularly to see how things were going. The girls at work seemed more excited than I was at the flowers and little gifts that were delivered every other day from my new suitor. Eric was really sweet, and for the most part seemed perfect, but something was missing. On a physical level we had only kissed, but I could tell the time was fast approaching when he would want to go further.

Today I had gotten home early from the office, I could hear Max upstairs. "Max," I yelled and almost immediately I could hear him running down the stairs.

"Mom, how come you're home so early?" The excitement in his voice was bubbling over as he thundered down the hall.

"Eric wanted to come over for dinner," I responded and he stopped in his tracks. His foot was still in the air for Christ's sake.

"*Eric*," he said in total annoyance, rolling his eyes.

I slammed my keys down on the marble kitchen counter. "That's it! What's going on with you? Four months ago you were telling me how lonely I was, how I needed a husband or boyfriend, and to go out more. So I find a man I like, I've been going out on dates and now you're giving me grief. What is the problem?"

"I don't like him, alright? I just don't like him."

"Why? He's been nothing but nice to you and -"

"And I've been nothing but nice to him!" he shouted over me.

"Yes you have, but I know how you really feel and it doesn't make this easy for me Max, knowing that you don't like him. I thought this is what you wanted."

"I did…I do, just not with him. Forget it, what I think doesn't matter."

"How can you say that to me? It does matter. The only reason I even considered going out with him in the first place when Harriett asked was because I was tired of you constantly saying I was lonely. And now you're telling me he's not the one. If not him, then who, Max?"

"You don't love him!"

"What?"

"You heard me, you don't love him, like how you loved my father," I could tell he was close to tears. I was dumbfounded. Where the hell did that just come from? I could remember the five separate occasions I'd talked to Max about his father and the last time was years ago.

"Of…of course I don't love him," I stumbled across the words as I mentally stumbled across the almost ludicrous thought of me being in love with Eric. "I barely know the man, that's the purpose of dating; it's getting to know each other. I can't believe what you're saying to me."

"You barely knew my father and you didn't date him, or try to get to know him better. I know you love my father; I can see it in your eyes when you talk about him. You will never love Eric the same way!" he shouted. Then throwing his arms up in complete frustration said, "Do what you want! I'm going to Patrick's house," walking away from me.

"What? Going to Patrick's? Don't you dare turn your back on me Maximus; I'm still talking to you! We need to talk about this and get to the bottom of what's really bothering you."

"We don't have to talk about anything! You like him and that's all that matters, right? It's stupid to argue about it, what I think never matters," he snapped. His attitude was beginning to irk me and the patience that I prided myself on was quickly evaporating into thin air. "Now can I go to Patrick's or not?" he yelled. Had he lost his mind? Did he have a fall today at school that the teachers forgot to tell me about? There must have been some type of head trauma that occurred between me dropping him off at school and walking through that door just now, for him to even lose his senses long enough to talk to me this way. I stormed towards him, grabbed his cheeks between my hands and dragged his face a few inches from mine. I could see the fear in his eyes and rightfully so. I had never had to spank him before. He wasn't that type of kid. Discipline never included anything that talking, icy looks, or little taps on the butt couldn't fix. But now he had crossed the line, and I didn't tolerate this type of behavior from *anyone*, especially him.

"Perdeu sua mente?" *Have you lost your mind?* "Now you listen to me because I'm only going to say this once," purposely squeezing his face a little harder. "Don't you ever, *ever* raise your voice to me in anger, do you understand me? Especially over a *man*. I am a grown woman, who makes her own choices. If I want to continue to see Eric I will. Why? Because that's *my* choice. I will *never* put anyone above you, but you have to talk to me. What has gotten into you? If you ever disrespect me again Maximus Strair, you will see a side of me that you never have before." I was silent for effect, wanting to make sure he heard exactly what I'd said. Then I snapped my hand from his face and walked away. "Now pack your things. You want to go to Patrick's? Then go! Então vá!"

I picked up the phone and called Patrick's mom. She was here twenty minutes later. Max didn't even say goodbye and my heart sunk in my chest as I came to the realization that this was our first real fight. Eric called a short while later to say he was on his way over. Making dinner would have to wait. Tonight we would order in. I had a shower and put on some sweats just as Eric was ringing the bell.

CHAPTER THREE

$\mathcal{B}$y the time the movie was over, Eric was nuzzling against my neck and rubbing my thighs. I tried to sit up, but he was practically on top of me, kissing me.

"Glory," he whispered, "let's go to bed. I want you so badly." My body and my mind were both screaming *hell no*, but my mouth said something different.

"Okay, you head up I need a minute."

"Are you alright?"

I reassured him that I was fine but needed to check on Max, at which point he headed upstairs. I called over to Patrick's, but Max was conveniently busy. I hung up and started pacing. Tonight may be just what I needed to put Las Vegas behind me. I needed to come down off my twelve-year high. I walked into the kitchen and put the bottle of dessert wine to my head and drank. I needed to loosen up. When the bottle was finished, I let out the most un-lady like belch I'd produced in my entire life, took a deep breath and went upstairs.

Eric had already taken off his sweater and was pulling the shades of my bedroom window. He held out his hand for me to come to him. Against every fiber in my body telling me to turn around and run - I went to him.

"Do you have protection?" my voice was shaky, "because you know I'm Fertile Mertle." I added a little laugh, desperately trying to ease my nervousness. Why wasn't that damn wine kicking in?

"Yes," he responded as he pulled me into his arms. I wanted this to work. I wanted to *feel* something. I was tired of silently hoping and wishing that I found what I had lost that night twelve-years ago. He was kissing me, his thin lips on mine, as usual I felt nothing. The kiss wasn't unpleasant, but there were no sparks, there never was. I wrapped my arms around his neck and closed my eyes, trying to visualize myself the night I made Maximus. I was a different woman then, or was I? As soon as we lay down on the bed, Eric's clothes were off and he was tugging on my sweatpants, slipping my underwear down my legs. I didn't even get a chance to fling them from around my ankle before he was between my legs and *there*. I opened my mouth to stop him, but then I felt his hand, putting on the condom. *What the hell is he doing? Isn't there more to this, more prep work?* He was spreading my legs as my mind raced to try and process what was happening. It all seemed so out-of-sync and awkward. I tried to slow him down, bringing his face to mine as I kissed and nibbled on his mouth, but that didn't help. He was pressing against me and soon panting as he buried his face in my neck. I could feel his mouth open against my flesh. His teeth and tongue against my shoulder, warm saliva on my skin. *What in God's name is he doing?!?* I screamed in my head. I could feel my anger rising. *We haven't even started yet, have we?* I was at a complete loss and decided I would squeeze my muscles "down there" to feel what was going on. The moment I did that he stiffened.

"Oh baby...oh baby...don't ...don't do that...you feel sooooo good...I'm coming," he moaned against my ear. He was actually in there? Did he just say he was coming? What was wrong with me I couldn't feel anything? For Christ's sake, Max was a big boy, but he wasn't *that* big. I thought maybe I was too low so I raised my hips up to meet his, and immediately felt him stiffen again and shudder. "Uhhh, uhhh, uhhhhhhh," he groaned, dropping all of his weight on me, as he was obviously exhausted, from what, I will never know.

"Ahh Glory… that was everything I thought it would be." I was glad his face was still buried in my neck because the look on my face could've killed somebody. I glanced over at the clock and only four minutes had passed since we had laid down. Is this really what normal sex was like? *Four Minutes?* Now I knew for sure I would never get over Las Vegas. He was kissing my face, and I had the urge to throw up as I felt the sticky warmth of the condom against my thigh. I moved from under him. As I walked to the bathroom, I flicked my foot out of my panties that were still wrapped around my ankle. Washing myself, I promised I would never do anything like that again, not that I did anything just now. If that's what I had to look forward to, then I could definitely go without it. Eric was beckoning me to come back to bed, but I told him I had to write a couple chart notes. I promised I would be up in a little while, forcing myself to kiss him tenderly before heading downstairs. I was gone long enough so he could fall asleep and insure there wouldn't be any chance of a repeat session.

When Eric woke up I was already dressed and making breakfast in the kitchen, so he didn't know that I never came back to bed last night. We ate, and I made up an excuse about not wanting Max to come home and find him there; so he left and I told him I would call him later.

It was early afternoon when Max finally came home. I was in the living room, and he came in and went right upstairs - no hello, no nothing. I waited a few minutes before I called him downstairs, when I didn't hear any movement I called again in a louder voice.

"Max I don't think you want me to come up there and get you. Enough is enough, get down here." Then I heard his bedroom door open. "I'm in the living room."

He walked into the room and stood in front of me.

"Yes?" He was looking at me like he had no idea why I'd called him. I patted the empty cushion beside me, inviting him to sit down. He did, trying to get as close to the opposite arm and not to me as he could.

"I said enough is enough. Talk to me." There was silence. "I intend to sit here as long as it takes for you to tell me what's bothering you."

He finally began, "I feel as though you haven't told me everything about my father, and I've been patient. You just...you just don't seem like the type of girl who would..."

I cut him off, "That's not true and you know it! Whenever you've asked about your father I've answered the questions I could. And what exactly do you mean by 'I don't seem like the type of girl'? The type of girl who would what?" I asked, afraid of what his answer would be.

"My friends at school say that only whores sleep with men they don't know, and I know you aren't like that. Mark's mother says you probably know who my father is, but you two don't get along. So the only other explanation is that you know more about my father than you've let on, and you just don't want to talk about it, but I think I should know. He has a right to know about me. It's not fair." I couldn't speak. The thought that *I* was the topic of discussion at his school and that his friends' parents were talking about me openly, made me angry. I closed my eyes trying to contain my anger. Since this was about my son and our relationship I would deal with the other issues later.

"The first thing I'm going to say is that I don't want you using that word, here or at school. It's very disrespectful and that's not how you were brought up. Secondly, I've *never* lied to you about your father. I've been extremely honest with you, to the point where I've portrayed myself in a less-than-favorable light. Oh, and by the way, I don't want you talking about our family's business at school..."

"I don't, just this one time when they were asking about my father..." he interrupted.

"Either way I don't want you to. Anyone asks you anything, you tell them to ask your mother. Anyone has any theories, you send them to me. Do you understand me?

He was looking down at his hands. "Yes Mom."

"Now, what exactly do you want to know about your father?"

"There's nothing I can think of that I haven't already asked. I guess I want to know if there is anything you haven't told me that maybe I never asked." I smiled inwardly at his approach.

"No, there's nothing else to tell, I've told you everything I think you should know. Now about Eric…"

"I'm sorry about how I behaved yesterday. I just want you to be happy and if he makes you happy then that is all that matters," he paused. "I…," his voice trailing off.

"I what?"

"I just don't think he makes you happy, and I don't want you seeing him just to get everyone off your case." Yeah, he was definitely an observant kid - maybe too observant.

"Can I tell you something?" I scooted closer to him. "*You* make me happy, always have. Eric is a nice man, but you're right, I don't love him, and I probably never will. It's just been a nice change having adult company. Can you understand that?"

"Yeah, Mom, I understand. I'm really sorry. I guess what the kids were saying at school got to me more than I thought."

"It's ok, but you have to talk to me. There's nothing I care about more in this world than you. Don't you know that?"

"I know." I hugged him then like I thought we would never see each other again. I never wanted us to be mad at each other again, not like this.

After that day I didn't pull away from Eric completely, but conveniently became inundated with work and Max. I only managed to see him once a week; although he didn't seem to notice that I began to distance myself. I met him for lunch one afternoon and told him I wasn't ready for a relationship with anyone, and I didn't think things between us were going to work out. He was completely shocked; I don't think he saw it coming. He said I could take as much time as I needed, but he was convinced that we could be so happy together. I'd spoken to him a couple times after that, but stopped seeing him.

The Weiss' had invited Max and I to their annual winter getaway for seventy-five of their closest friends and family, at a private mountain-resort in Colorado. My first inclination was to decline, but at Max's urging, decided to go since his newest hobby was snowboarding with his friends. The trip would fall right around his birthday and February school break. I was sure Harriett had invited Eric since she was still pushing that union, but I was confident I could ignore him and have fun once we were there. I worked the few weekends before we left to accommodate the patients that would've had to be rescheduled; so by the time we did leave, I was mentally and physically exhausted.

It was a little before twelve when we arrived at the resort and checked in. Max wanted to hit the slopes right away before the seven o'clock welcome dinner. Since I'm not a big skier, I hired one of the instructors to be his buddy, which he didn't appreciate. But once we met blonde Lindsay in the lobby, all his complaints ceased. I never thought to request a man, because she seemed very capable. I gave them both walkie-talkies and specific instructions that Max needed to be back by six.

I went up to our room, unpacked and took a nap. It was the phone that woke me.

"Hello?"

"Glory, its Harriett Weiss." I tried to focus as I looked at the clock, 3:45.

"Hi there," I was groggy, still between consciousness and sleep.

"Did I wake you? You sound like you were sleeping."

"I was, but I need to get up. What's going on?"

"Well we wanted to make sure that you got in alright, and we would see you tonight at the welcome dinner. Max just blew past us on the slopes and told us you were in your room."

"Yes. I did some unpacking and fell asleep, but we plan on being there."

"I'm sorry I woke you. I know how tired you must be. I was going to take a walk over to the shops in a little bit, would you like to join me?"

"Sure, that sounds nice, what time?"

"How's 4:30 in the lobby? We could get in an hour of shopping and still have plenty of time to get ready."

"That sounds like a plan."

"Dinner is at seven, and don't forget it's a black and white affair, with all the girls wearing white." How could I forget? I had spent more money on a new wardrobe for this trip than I had in my entire life, but it felt good. If anything...I deserved it.

"Yes, I remembered, so I'll see you in the lobby in forty-five minutes."

"See you then." And with that we hung up.

I stretched and walked over to the window, admiring the view. I was glad Max convinced me to come. My body was tired and needed some well-deserved rest and relaxation. The phone rang again, but this time it was Edward, needing a favor. There was a perfume that Harriett always got from the Flora shop that he wanted me to pick up for her as a surprise, but he couldn't remember the name. So while I was out with her, he wanted me to grab a couple samples so he could pick it up later. I told him it wasn't a problem.

It was quite a task trying to get away from her long enough to get to the perfume shop, and when I finally found a moment, they were out of samples so I had to use the testers. I sprayed the three testers on both arms and just behind my ear, wrote down which one was placed where, and then hurried back before she missed me. We had a fun time and I picked up the cutest scarf for Max. Harriett thanked me for the company and went up to her room to get ready, just as Edward, Jeffery and Clay were exiting the resort lounge. After our hellos and hugs, Jeff and Clay went to get ready, and I gave Edward the piece of paper with the names of the perfumes.

"None of these blasted names look familiar," he said with a frown. "Shopping for her can be so annoying sometimes. This *Demure* could be it," he said with raised eyebrows as he studied the small piece of paper.

"Well here, smell it," and leaning into him I pulled the bulky collar of my turtleneck away as he stepped in to smell just below my ear. Over his shoulder I could see a man standing by the elevator glaring at me. I could almost feel his eyes cutting into me, before snapping his head away, and quickly stepped onto the elevator as Edward was leaning back.

"I think that's the one," he said, taking a second sniff of my neck. "Thanks Glory, I'll stop by and pick it up before I come to dinner." I tried to look past him to the elevator, but the man was already gone. Unfortunately, the dim hallway lighting didn't afford me the opportunity to get a good look at him; but somehow he seemed familiar. "Glory?"

"Uh, sure, sure. It wasn't a problem," I replied turning my face back to Edward.

I returned to my room, showered and began to get ready. I couldn't get that man out of my mind, coming to the conclusion that he may not have even been looking at me, although it certainly felt that way.

Max walked through the door a couple minutes after six, his cheeks and lips rosy from the cold weather. He ran and jumped on his bed, letting out a loud sigh.

"Mom, I think I'm in love." I couldn't help the laugh that escaped my lips. That was the last thing I was expecting to come out of his mouth.

"In love?" I asked, tapping on my watch, "after only being here six hours? That's impressive."

"Lindsay is the coolest girl I've ever met."

"Woman, sweetie. Lindsay is a woman."

"Yeah, a woman that loves to snowboard," he smiled. "I'm so glad we came. This is going to be the best trip ever," he said closing his eyes. Holding my robe together, I jumped on the bed beside him smothering him with kisses.

"Maaaa," he yelled trying to squirm away.

"It's time to get ready," I laughed, as he ran to the bathroom. "I've laid your clothes out, let's get a move on."

CHAPTER FOUR

*M*ax and I were ready in no time and heading downstairs, when I realized I'd forgotten my purse; so I sent him along while I ran back to get it. I was in the elevator going back down, when it stopped on the 8th floor. I stepped back against the wall, as I anticipated people getting on. The doors opened, and there in front of me was *Hayden*; slightly older and even more handsome and debonair in a black tuxedo pants and a white jacket, but I knew for sure it was him. I couldn't move as he seemed to be stricken by the same temporary paralysis, so we just looked at each other, and as slowly as the doors had opened, they closed.

Hayden. He's here? Shit! Was he the man at the elevator this afternoon? Why was he wearing a tux? Is he with the Weiss family as well? I needed to get out of here. Max and I couldn't stay. Oh my God, Max. I wanted to get out of that elevator. I needed air, as I frantically pressed the 'L' button and as soon as the doors opened, I flew out into the lobby; my eyes wild.

"Glory," I heard someone call. It was Edward and Harriett. They walked towards me as I looked around for Max.

"My goodness, you're an angelic sight," Harriett said. "You look absolutely stunning."

"Thank…thank you," I mumbled, holding my breath as the elevator behind me opened.

"Are you alright? You look like you've seen a ghost," Edward said, searching my eyes in concern. Pull yourself together damn it!

"No, I'm fine. I've just misplaced my son," I said with an awkward smile.

"Oh, he's already inside," said Harriett. "Let's head in," and with that she walked into the function room.

Turning his attention to me, Edward wrapped his arms around my shoulders and pulled me close, whispering in my ear, "She loved it! She couldn't believe I remembered," he added with a small chuckle.

"That's great." A tight smile was plastered across my lips, as he let me go and ran to catch up to Harriett.

"You've worked your way up," thundered a deep voice behind me. I closed my eyes as the realization hit, that I couldn't run. "What the hell are you doing here with my father? Don't you realize he's a married man and my mother is in the next room, or don't you even care about things like that?" I turned to find Hayden standing with his arms folding across his chest. His eyes were ablaze with anger as people began looking in our direction. *Father? Edward was Hayden's father? I was feeling faint.*

"You don't...understand," my voice cracked as I turned away, determined not to make a scene.

"Of course I understand. You're sleeping with my father and have the audacity to do it so openly. Necking in the lobby and hugging as soon as my mother turns her back? I saw you with my own eyes!" he barked grabbing my arm and spinning me around to face him.

"You don't know what you're talking about," I said through clenched teeth. "Now take your hands off me," I said snatching my arm away and storming into the room. My eyes were searching the crowd for my son.

"Over here mom," yelled Max waving his arms. He was already seated at a table close to the front with Jeff, Clay, and a few people I didn't recognize. I slipped into the seat between Jeff and Max, just as Edward started tapping on the microphone at the podium, asking everyone to take their seats.

Leaning into Max I whispered, "We need to leave right now!"

He turned and looked at me, then replied, "Leave? Why? What's wrong?"

"Please don't ask me any questions. Let's just go."

"Mom we can't leave right now," he said looking at me in confusion. "Sssh."

"Don't shush me Maximus. We need to leave now!" I could feel Jeff pulling on my arm to quiet me.

He leaned over to me, "Glory, what's wrong, you're shaking like a leaf?"

"Nothing," I said straightening up in my chair as Hayden walked in and sat a couple tables over from us with his parents. Jeff waved to him. He hadn't taken his eyes off me. The Weiss' were his parents. All these months, and I never thought to ask the names of their children, not that it would've mattered.

Edward welcomed everyone and then Harriett stood up to go over the agenda for the week. They had a lot planned and were expecting the best year ever. I tried to ignore Hayden, but he was looking at me with obvious disgust. How could this happen? Everyone was laughing at something Edward said but I couldn't concentrate, I couldn't think. Max slipped his hand in mine and gently pulled me towards him.

"What's wrong? You don't look so good," he asked, there was concern in his eyes as he reached up and touched my cheek. "You're sweating."

"You're right; I'm not feeling very well. After they're finished with the welcome you can bring me up to the room."

"All right," he said squeezing my hand.

"On a separate note," Edward was saying, "this has been a stressful and exciting past few months for Harriett and I, between Hayley expecting our very first grandchild." *PANG,* "Hayden finally getting engaged," *DOUBLE PANG.* Were those real chest pains? Am I having a heart attack? I'm a cardiologist I should know. I had the urge to scream. "And my recent recovery," at our table alone heads started to turn to Jeff as people asked recovery from what. "The bottom line is that we're happy to be here, and you're here because you're all special to me and my family; so let's enjoy the next ten days." The room erupted in applause and cheers as Edward and Harriett kissed, and then sat back down. The band picked up exactly where they'd left off, and the waiters and waitresses jumped into action.

Turning to Jeffery, I said, "We're going to head up. I'm not feeling very well."

"Head up? You do look a little pale. Let me help you," he said as both Max and I stood up.

"No that's fine, you stay. Max and I can manage."

"Max *cannot* manage you alone. Let him stay and I'll bring you up."

"No Uncle Jeff, I'll stay with her," Max said with some defiance, taking my hand. That's my boy!

"Glory, Max," Harriett was calling us over to their table. Shit, shit. I tried to pretend I hadn't heard her, stepping around Jeff, but she called us again.

"Mom, Mrs. Weiss is calling us. We should tell them you aren't feeling well, in case they miss us."

"You're right," I said straightening my shoulders as I walked towards their table. I thought for sure my knees would buckle.

"Everyone, may I present the talented Dr. Glory Strair and her wonderful son Maximus," announced Harriett.

"*Glory? Doctor?*" asked Hayden his eyes dancing between Max and I, not trying to hide his confusion or disbelief.

"Yes," said Edward, "she's my cardiologist and surgeon."

"Surgeon?" asked a pregnant woman, who I assumed was Hayley.

"Yes, she's the reason I'll be around to see my first grandchild," Edward added with a smile.

"Dad are you sick?" It was obvious she was worried.

"Not anymore, thanks to Glory. I had open-heart surgery about three months ago and came through with flying colors," he announced. There was shock all around as everyone started asking questions. Hayden's eyes still hadn't left mine.

"Mr. and Mrs. Weiss," Max interrupted, raising his voice over everyone else's, "My mom isn't feeling well, so we're going to head up."

"Aww, I'm sorry to hear that," Harriett began. "You work so hard at that hospital; your body is probably going into withdrawal. Son, why don't you help them upstairs," she said turning her attention to Hayden.

"N-n-no, that's fine. I really think I'm just a little tired. It's nothing but a headache." My smile was weak, but I hoped convincing.

"And I'm sure having you traipse through that perfume shop didn't help," Edward added in an apologetic voice.

"Edward you had Glory buy the perfume?" Harriett asked with a laugh. "You were in on this gift too?" She had turned to playfully frown at me.

"No, no," I said as I took the opportunity to explain what happened in hopes that it would clarify things for Hayden. Everyone at the table, except Hayden, was in stitches as I told the story and Edward finished up with how he had to sniff my ear to figure out which perfume it was. Perfect! If that didn't prove to him that I wasn't sleeping with his father, then nothing would.

"Well you got it right and I love it," Harriett said, giving Edward a kiss on the cheek. "Are you going to have Max come back down?"

"Uh, no," I said, "I wouldn't feel comfortable not being here to watch him."

"Don't be ridiculous, you know he's no trouble, plus there are a couple kids his age around to keep him company," Edward said as he pointed around the room at a couple other boys.

Max's eyes lit up for a second before he said, "That's ok. I'd rather stay with my Mom, if she needs me."

"Your Mom needs her rest. Edward's right," Harriett added. "Why don't you put her to bed, then come back down for some dinner and run around with the other boys your age."

"May I Mom?" It was clear he didn't want to leave. "Pleeeaaassseee."

"I have a better idea. You come with me and I'll grab some headache medicine, and then come right back. I'm sure I'll feel better in a little while." The last thing I wanted to do was leave him alone with Hayden.

"I think Mrs. Weiss is right, and you need some rest. You never get sick and just now when you came in you looked *really really* sick. I'll help you to bed and then I'll come back."

"Fine, but make sure and watch your manners," I said, kissing him on the forehead. "I'll see you all in the morning for breakfast."

"Someone should still go with you two," Hayden added, getting up from his seat.

"That really isn't…"

"I insist," he said firmly taking me by the elbow.

"He's right Mom. I don't think I can lift you if you passed out on me," piped in Max with a little laugh.

"It looks like I'm out numbered." My frustration was clear. "Good night everyone."

As we walked into the lobby Jeff ran out. "Are you going to bring her up?"

"Hey Jeff. Yeah I have strict instructions from my mother to help the good doctor up to bed," the sarcasm was dripping from his voice.

"Good, I'm glad she listened to someone. I hope you feel better Glo." The moment Jeff called me by my nickname I felt Hayden's body stiffen next to mine.

"I'll be fine. See you in the morning."

"Glory?" someone else was calling me. You've got to be kidding me, I thought as I turned to see Eric.

"Hello Eric."

"Hey Jeff, Max, what's up H?" Turning his attention to the others he looked from me to Hayden. "You two know each other?"

"Yes…"

"No…" I replied at the same time, everyone looking at us with questioning eyes.

"My mom isn't feeling well, so Mr. Weiss' son volunteered to help me take her up to our suite. We should go." Max was trying to lead me away, but Eric stepped in front of me putting his hand against my cheek. I immediately saw Hayden step back.

"You really don't look well, let me help you. H, I've got it from here," he said slipping between myself and Hayden. Max wrapped his arm around my waist as we walked to the elevator. Eric *and* Hayden? This was going to be a long ten days.

Once we got to my suite Max took my shoes off while Eric looked for some headache medicine. "All right you two, I think I can handle it from here," I said with a little smile. "You can head back down."

Max walked over to me and gave me a hug and a kiss. "Please try to get some rest. This is supposed to be a fun trip, but tomorrow if you still want to leave, we can." He could never know how much I loved him.

"Okay," I said returning his hug, "put your room key somewhere safe."

"I will. Are you coming Mr. McNair?"

"Uh, not right this minute. I wanted to talk to your mom."

"She really needs her rest." The annoyance was already creeping into his voice.

"I promise I won't be long."

"*Humph*, good night." Once he was gone Eric turned his attention back to me.

"Are you sure you're alright? You really look quite pale. I can stay with you, if you like."

"Thanks, but I'm sure I'll be fine."

"I've missed you so much." He took my hand and brought it to his lips.

"Eric, please don't. I've told you this isn't going to work," I groaned, gently pulling my hand away. "I don't want to hurt you, but I really just want to be friends."

"But why? Everything between us seemed so perfect. The night we shared." Was he talking about the worse night of my life? I had to wonder if we were even at the same address that night. We didn't make love, he satisfied *his* needs, he was a selfish lover and thinking back on it, I found myself becoming angry. I was disgusted that I went along so willingly even though I didn't want to do it. Something so special and intimate, and I did it just because; that was stupid of me. And then for it to not even be fulfilling was a double whammy.

"I'm sorry, I really am, but I can't do this. Like I told you before, we can be friends, but nothing more. Please try to understand and respect that."

"I'll respect it, but I can't understand it."

It took some effort, but once I told him I really didn't feel well for the umpteenth time, he left, promising he would check on me a little later. I couldn't believe what had just happened. My mind was still trying to grasp the fact that Hayden was here. He actually existed.

~

My eyes hadn't left the door as I waited for Max and Eric to come back down from Glory's room. Everyone was mingling as the first course was brought out. My mother was talking to me, but my mind wasn't there. Max had just walked through the door and I didn't waste any time excusing myself as I joined him at his table. Ignoring the curious glances from Jeff, I ask how Glory was.

"I'm sure she'll be fine," not hesitating to start cutting into his salad. "I've just never seen her look that way. I'm always telling her she works too hard, but I guess she's doing it for me," he said with a worried smile.

"Don't worry Max, I'm sure it's just a mixture of fatigue and jet lag," I chimed in, knowing full well that it was seeing me that had made her physically sick.

"She needs to get some rest though. I hope Mr. McNair doesn't stay up there all night," I could tell he was upset.

"I didn't know Eric and your mom were friends," I lied. Thankfully Jeff and Clay had finished their salads and had gotten up to mingle.

"That's the thing, I think he wants to be more than friends, but my mom won't have it." He opened his eyes as though he didn't mean to say so much. "Please don't tell her I told you that, she gets very upset if she knows I'm talking about family business outside our home," he said, his eyes pleading with me; I knew I liked him instantly.

"I won't breathe a word of it," I whispered back. "It's amazing to me that she's even single."

"I know, that's what I've been telling her. My friends at school think I have the hottest mom, which is kind of gross when you think about it, but I guess I should be proud. I'm always telling her how beautiful she is and that she should go out more often and not work so hard. Unfortunately, the one time she took me up on my offer to date someone, she brought Eric home." I was trying to contain my laughter as he rolled his eyes. "Your mom made up some excuse about having extra ballet tickets and gave one to my mom and the other to Eric. I mean he's nice and all, but I don't like him. I just want her to be with my Dad." Again his eyes opened wide as he realized he'd once again said way too much. So she *was* married, I thought.

"Any man that could divorce your mother would be crazy in my eyes, but I'm sure she and your Dad will work things out." I knew it was slick but I had to find out as much about her as I could.

"They were never married. He doesn't know about me. *I* don't even know who *he* is," he retorted and I knew then he didn't appreciate my comment. Now my mind was spinning. Max didn't know his father? His father didn't even know about him?

"I'm sorry. I didn't mean anything by that. How old..." I began, but was interrupted.

"Hayden," my father joined us, "how's Glory doing?"

"Umm, I'm not sure. Eric brought her up."

"Oh," turning to Max with an apologetic smile he said, "you can blame that on my wife. She's always playing match maker. I told her not to invite him, but she insisted." So my Dad wasn't fond of the match either, that was good to know.

"That's ok, I'm not worried," Max replied. "It's pretty impossible to get my mom to do something she doesn't want to do." We all laughed, although inside I was hoping that was true.

"I'll catch up with you boys later." My father turned away as my mother was beckoning him from a few tables over to join her. Once again it was just the two of us.

Max was finishing up the last of his salad. "Did I just hear Mr. Weiss call you Hayden?"

"Yes, that's my name."

"That's weird because its mine too. I guess I've never really heard anyone else with that name." I felt the pressure building between my temples.

"I thought your name was Max?"

"It is, *Maximus Hayden Strair.*" My frown deepened. It couldn't be - as I searched his eyes. He couldn't be my son, could he?

"How old are you Max?"

"I'll be twelve next week, February 14th. Mum calls me her love child." My God!

"Tell me about your Dad," I pressed, trying not to come off too pushy.

He was hesitant. "I really can't. My mom doesn't like people to ask about him and if they persist she says I'm to send them to her. So if you have any questions, you'll have to ask her. I've already said too much."

"Oh believe me, I will," I responded under my breath.

We talked a little longer until I saw Eric come back down. He didn't look pleased at all, which was fine with me. I waited until dinner was served and excused myself. Minutes later, after using some bogus excuse and a couple compliments directed at the young receptionist, I had Glory's room number and was on my way up in the elevator.

CHAPTER FIVE

$\mathcal{I}$ was sitting on the floor in front of the fireplace crying my heart out, wondering how I was going to deal with Hayden, when the sudden knock on the door startled me. Jesus, Eric was persistent. I quickly wiped at my eyes. The last thing I wanted was for him to think I was crying over him. I walked up and placed my forehead against the door, closing my eyes.

"Eric, please…not now," my voice cracking unintentionally. "I can't do this with you and talking about it more isn't going to help. I just want to be friends. Please… go away…I really don't feel well."

"This isn't Eric," came the deep voice on the other side of the door, and I instantly recognized it as Hayden's. I snapped my head away as I peered through the peep hole, after the fact.

"Waa…what do you want?"

"Isn't it obvious? I want answers," he said gruffly. "Now open this door."

I turned the latch and opened the door slowly. He just looked at me for a moment and then walked past me into the room without even a sideways glance. Why were we so angry with each other? I'd played this meeting out so many times in my head and nothing was going the way I planned. He seemed so disgusted with me. I thought…I don't know what I thought, but this isn't the reaction I was hoping for. Maybe I was expecting him to look at me the same way he did so long ago. When we went to sleep that night everything was perfect and now…and now, I just didn't know anymore. I guess deep down I wanted him to meet *Glory*, but he only saw Glo and that's why it was so easy for him to believe that I was sleeping with his father. My mind was spinning. We were silent for a long time. I could hear my heartbeat pounding in my ears. He was standing with his back to me, the lines of his shoulders straight from his rage.

Finally, he began, "I'll start by asking you two questions and for right now all I need are yes and no answers," he was still looking out the window. "Were you ever a prostitute?"

I let out a long sigh, this question I would gladly answer. "No," I replied quietly. He took one hand out of his pocket and curled it into a fist at his side.

"Is Maximus my son?" How could he know? I was silent, standing there with my eyes closed, trying to figure out how I could turn back the hands of time so that I had never met the Weiss', but most importantly that Max and I never came to Colorado. "Is Max my son?" he asked again, his voice steady.

"I..."

"Yes or no, damn it!"

"Yes," I whispered, as he brought his fist up to the window, almost in slow motion and pounded it against the glass. I jumped, but wasn't afraid. I should've lied, but couldn't.

"Can you explain any of this?" the muscle of his jaw jutting out as he obviously grinded his teeth.

"There's nothing to explain," I replied quietly. He turned to face me, the anger burning behind his eyes, making me cringe as he took one step towards me. He was furious.

"How can you say that to me? How? Explain how a *virgin* ends up at a party with eleven prostitutes!" *He knew.* "Explain to me why you left the way you did. Explain to me why I searched and never found you, but the minute I gave up and convinced myself that it never happened, and asked another woman to marry me, you show up! Explain to me why you didn't try to find me after you found out you were pregnant! *Explain it to me!*" He was yelling, his voice angrily bouncing off the walls.

"Please don't yell." My head was throbbing.

"I will yell if I want to God-damn it! Now start talking." My tears came then as I tried to gain my composure and explain to him what happened; he just stood there watching me.

"I didn't mean for any of it to happen. My Aunt Miranda, the one in the red dress, ran a small escort service at the club. The night of your party one of her girls called in sick and she needed someone to fill in. She had no one else so she begged me to come and promised that I wouldn't have to do anything. I'd never done anything like that in my life. I spent most of the night hiding by the pool." I took a deep breath, "When I saw you leaving, I thought it was my only chance to get out of there, so I asked you to bring me with you. You know the rest."

"*Noooo*," he drawled sarcastically. "*I don't know the rest.* How could you do something like that and let me believe you were a prostitute?"

"Listen, I never thought I would see you again. I was enjoying your company; I'd never met anyone like you. I made the decision not to tell you the truth. I made a mistake alright? There's nothing else I can say."

"How old were you?" he asked. I didn't want to answer *that* question. "How old were you?" he repeated.

"Almost eighteen."

"Jesus Christ! *You were seventeen?*" he growled running his hand through his hair. "Why would you do something like that? Why did you leave without saying goodbye? Why didn't you take the money? You left me with so many questions."

"I knew the minute you woke up and saw those sheets, you would know I had lied to you. I didn't want your money, I never did. It was my choice to stay with you that night and make love to you. I wanted it just as badly as you did. Nothing else mattered! I wasn't thinking straight. Up until that point, my life had been relatively uneventful, except for the death of my parents."

"So you thought screwing a stranger six years older than you was fun?"

"No. That's not it! I was leaving for college in the Fall and thought I would do something wild, since the next eight years I wouldn't have room for fun. That's all. My getting pregnant wasn't a part of the plan!" Now I was the one yelling.

"So you did have a plan?"

"No God-damn it I didn't have a plan. I *planned* to have one drink, I didn't *plan* anything else. *You're* the one that begged me to stay. *You're* the one that wanted the *full* experience of Glo. I didn't know how to refuse you. I didn't want to refuse you. Please believe me."

"How can I believe anything you say? Was anything you told me that night the truth or was it all a part of your big lie and Glo's début? Your parents, their deaths?" That accusation hit a nerve; a very painful nerve.

"Listen to me, the only part of that night that was a lie was me leading you to believe I was a prostitute. Everything else was… everything else was *me*."

"It wasn't *you, Dr. Glory Strair*, it was *Glo*. You were acting, faking, pretending, whatever it is they call it! No matter what you say, that's what you were doing." My tears came anew, as it was clear now that I'd hurt him.

"I don't know what to tell you. I had never been with anyone else as Glo or Glory, but I wasn't faking! I don't even know *how* to fake it! Yes I led you to believe that I was an experienced prostitute. Yes, I had to *act* like I was super confident as I stood naked in front of a man for the first time in my life. Yes, I had to act like I knew how to kiss and do everything else, but that lasted all of five minutes before I became so…so overwhelmed…that I didn't have to pretend any more. I *wanted* to kiss you as passionately as I did. I *wanted* to be a willing and obedient lover. I *wanted* to please you. That's why I left the way I did, because after what we'd shared I couldn't pretend anymore. I was a poor eighteen - seventeen year old girl praying, against all odds, to get into an Ivy League college and become a doctor. You were… you were everything I wasn't. If I'd stayed it could've destroyed you. Can't you see that?"

"But…it was your first time. You should've told me; better yet you should've stopped me." He took another deep breath and began pacing. "I knew it. The instant I talked with you I knew you weren't like the other girls. And then when we were making love, the moment I was *with* you I thought I felt something, but pushed it to the back of my mind telling myself that I was crazy. When I woke up and saw the sheets it just confirmed it. I would've been gentler or…" his voice trailed off as he again ran his hand through his hair and let his head fall back against the window.

"Hayden, it was perfect. You were perfect. Don't you realize that if I felt the way you thought I did, I would've taken the money? Seven thousand dollars was more money than I'd seen in one sitting. I didn't want your money. I had no regrets. If I had to do it again…I wouldn't change a thing."

"Even after you found out you were pregnant?"

"Even after. Max is everything to me. I can't imagine my life without him. Whenever I thought about quitting all I had to do was look at him. I have no regrets."

"*None*?" his eyes were probing mine. I knew what he was asking?

"None," I lied.

"Does Max know?"

"Know what? He knows that I met his father at a party. He knows I don't really know a lot about who his father is and that even though it wasn't planned, he was my biggest accomplishment. Nothing has to change," I was starting to panic again. "Do you hear me? *Nothing* has to change. You're going to get married, and Maximus and I are going to go on with our lives."

"Are you serious? *Everything* has changed. He's *my* son as well. I will not pretend that he doesn't exist or that night twelve years ago never happened. I've done enough pretending to last a lifetime. If you want we'll tell him together, but either way he's going to find out. I've already missed twelve years of his life and I don't intend on missing another second."

"Do you hear what you're saying? What about your fiancée and your family? Your parents? They won't accept this."

"What about them? They have nothing to do with this and I don't care if they don't accept this. I can't believe what *you're* saying to me." My world was crumbling as I sat on my bed with my head against my knees. He came and sat next to me and I instinctively moved over; he was too close. "You don't really want me to just walk away do you?" I couldn't breathe, I couldn't think. I was becoming acutely aware of the bed we were sitting on, how incredibly handsome he looked in that tux, and my unresolved need to feel like a woman again. "Are you really sitting here, wishing that tonight never happened? You mean to tell me you haven't thought about me at all during the past twelve years?" There was a painful knot in my throat where a blatant lie was beginning to form.

"I *do* want you to walk away. I *do* wish tonight never happened and I never, ever dwell on the past. And you were definitely in my past." I hadn't taken my eyes off the fireplace as I sat there hoping that he fell for it.

"I don't believe you. Look me in the eye and tell me what you just said! Tell me you don't regret leaving me."

I jumped off the bed as though someone had pinched me. "I don't have to look you in the eye, and you don't have to believe me. Please just get out!"

"I'm not leaving until I have all the answers I came here for," he growled defiantly. "If you wanted to deny me, that night and what we shared, why did you name him Hayden?"

"For obvious reasons, because it was the name I knew his father by." He let out a long sigh as he fell back onto the bed. "Please go…I don't want to hurt you." My voice was soft and uncertain. I knew in my act of desperation I was bound to say something that I couldn't take back.

"You don't want to hurt me? You're unbelievable." He was looking at me in utter amazement and again, I'm not sure if it was even possible, but the room was filled with deafening silence. Then his features changed. "I'm sorry… this is just so much. I really can't be upset with you," his tone softening. "It's not like you knew Hayden was my real name, in which instance you could've gotten Harvard's yearbook or something and tried to find me. We were both in the dark. I can't believe any of this is happening, and that you're here. He's my son as well Glory, and I want to be involved in his life. The bottom line is you're going to have to share him now."

"I can't," came my choked reply, the tears silently rolling down my cheeks.

"Then I'm sorry, but you don't have a choice. You *will* share him because I'm not going anywhere. I'm here to stay," and with that he stood up and walked out the door.

~

My mind was spinning as I left her room. *Dr. Glory Strair*, her name was Glory. She was only seventeen. I had a son, *Maximus Hayden Strair*. It was amazing how much things could change in the blink of an eye. How could she really expect me to go on as though nothing had changed? If only she knew how that night had turned me inside out and tormented what little hope I had for any perspective long term relationships. Waking up to find her gone and money still there, her note, and the sheets; my mind was in shambles. For years after our rendezvous, being or talking with any other woman was torture. I kept on doing involuntary comparisons of everyone to a woman I'd only known one night, one perfectly beautiful and unforgettable night. Seeing her just now was exactly what I needed to put my life in perspective. As I walked back into dinner I saw Max in deep conversation with my father. I couldn't wait to tell them, I didn't care what anyone thought. I had a son. I walked up and immediately he turned his attention to me.

"Are you okay?" Max asked as though he could see my internal chaos.

"Yes, I'm fine."

"Well, I'm going to introduce myself to those kids over there, so see you later," he said heading over to the Nealand twins.

"That there is a great kid," my Dad was saying as he walked away, "and boy does he love his mother. It's weird, but there's something about him that reminds me of you when you were a kid. All I have to say is that the man that left her must have been a fucking idiot. He didn't deserve her," he said with some degree of disdain. "Jeff was telling us about all the shit she's been through, trying to get where she is, and it just breaks your heart. She really is an amazing person and a fantastic doctor." He paused as though he was waiting for me to say something. "Do you know why your mother and I took a liking to her?" I shook my head. "She's a fighter Hayden. You wouldn't know this, but Jeff was on his way to do *my* surgery when he had the accident; and we had to choose between letting a very green Dr. Strair perform my open heart surgery, or the well-seasoned prick that neither your mom nor I liked." I was listening intently to what he was saying, because I was genuinely interested in how they'd met.

"Jeff came in bleeding like a stuck pig and told us what happened and that there was a surgeon that was just as good as he was, if not better, who was ready and willing to do my surgery. The only thing was her age. He said he would let us meet her and if we weren't comfortable, then Dr. Nolte would do the surgery the following day; but in his opinion this woman was better."

He went on and told me that when she walked in, my mother mistook her for a nurse's aid, since she didn't look a day over eighteen. And Glory must've been so nervous that she knocked over anything standing straight up between the door and his bed. He was laughing as he recalled the thought.

"But Hayden the minute those mishaps happened, you could visibly see her wipe them from her mind as she squared her shoulders for the challenge." Yes that sounded like the Glo I remembered squaring her shoulders when I implied she couldn't possibly know any of the literature we were studying. I smiled inwardly. "I put up a good fight, but she remained confident and stood her ground telling us every reason why she was the best person to do the surgery; still remaining respectful. Up to the very second I told her she could do the surgery, my mind was screaming Nolte, but my heart and mouth were saying yes to her." He added that my mother wasn't happy initially, but thankfully, he came out with flying colors. "Glory stopped by everyday, sometimes twice, and I knew it had nothing to do with who I was or knowing Jeff; but it was because she cared. She did it for all her patients, and we fell in love with her from that moment on."

"What about Eric?"

"Your mother has been playing match maker from the minute she found out Glory was single, and for a while she was dating Eric. Seeing her alone and struggling makes you sad, but I know things are getting better for her now that she's taken over for Jeff. She has to fight for everything because those bastards she works with won't give her anything easily. I know because Jeff told me, and because I've seen her in action at the hospital. She's a good woman and some dumb ass left her pregnant and alone, not knowing the potential he had lying next to him. Oh well, you live and learn, and if Harriet Weiss has anything to say or do about it; she won't be single for much longer."

I don't know why, but I was becoming angry again. Is that what people were going to think of me, that I'd abandoned them? I abruptly excused myself and went outside for some air.

For the past couple of months, Eric had been talking about this phenomenal woman he'd met. She was beautiful, intelligent, and financially stable, with a young son. In passing when I'd asked about her, he'd told me he thought she was the one. I never thought to invite them over to dinner. He made it seem like they were much more than friends. Eric and Glory? Oh no, I couldn't handle that. At least I was being honest with myself. Eric was a friend and a close colleague, but he couldn't have the woman of my dreams and my son too.

I know this is a typical "guy thing" to do, but I couldn't help visualizing him with her. She was a wonderful lover. I was jealous of what they'd had, no matter how brief. It was a lot longer than my one night and for that I hated him. I was angry that Glory had taken the endless possibilities of *us* away from me, leaving the way she did; but how could I blame her? She didn't know my real name and for all she knew, I believed she was a prostitute. I'm just happy she kept our son, she could've aborted him in order to focus on school and her career, but she didn't. For that, I would be eternally grateful.

As I stood out on the balcony watching the snow fall, I thought back to that night in Las Vegas and how she felt, writhing and moaning against my warm flesh. She was so willing to do everything I asked of her and doing it extraordinarily well. Her body was soft and yet there was a firm thickness to her that made my mouth instantly water. Her tightness was indescribable as she fit my member like a glove and with relative ease, or should I say minimal discomfort, given her condition. I had been with many woman, who were unable to bare my entire shaft to the hilt, unable to push pass the brief period of discomfort, to the endless hours of decadent pleasure waiting for them. So that act alone was impressive on her part. *A virgin?* Having my suspicion confirmed was unnerving. Knowing her real age was surprisingly upsetting. Remembering her enthusiasm toward my requests and the breathtaking performance she'd graced me with, made everything else irrelevant.

Closing my eyes I could see her like it had happened only moments before, biting her lower lip, her eyes tightly shut as she gently embraced my full length gasping for air upon completion. She was gazing at me so intently when I moved within her, touching that forbidden spot deep within her and feeling the shudder ripple over her body, hearing her scream out in ecstasy, kissing and biting the meaty part of my arms. Our fingers were interlaced above us, as I could remember kissing each one of her knuckles tenderly. I'd never done that to any of the other women I slept with. Kissing knuckles? Yeah right. For me it had always been about rocking their world and placing myself at the top of some list as the best lover they'd ever had. It was about stamina and the number of orgasms in one session; it was about knowing at any time if I wanted to have them again, they would drop everything to oblige, whether we were in a relationship or not. That wasn't my goal the night I slept with Glory. Frankly, I didn't have a goal other than to experience her completely. Although, if anyone asked, I would've told them it was the best sex I'd ever had. I thought I'd done everything to rock her world that night in Vegas, but still she was able to walk away and never look back. That was a first *and* a last for me.

Things with Glory were so different. The memories I tried for so long to forget were coming back. And there in the chill of the Colorado night, my body became hot and painfully swollen. I was dying for a taste of her on my tongue. I wanted her again.

It took almost half an hour for me to get my thoughts and body under control. I saw Hayley come out on her cell phone, and she was obviously upset.

"What's wrong?" I asked once she'd snapped the phone shut.

"Nothing," her tone was stiff.

"Don't tell me anything. Who was that on the phone? Brian?"

"Yeah. He missed his flight so he's going to fly up with Lisa on the jet, tomorrow evening."

"Okay and what's wrong with that?"

"Nothing," her tone still hadn't changed.

"It's obviously something, so stop saying that. What's bothering you, the fact that he missed his flight or that he's coming with Lisa?"

"Quite frankly, both," and with that she marched off.

My sister and I had always been close even though we were three years apart, but ever since she found out she was pregnant, it seemed as though she was always mad at me about something. Both her and Lisa had been the best of friends growing up and she was actually the one that had introduced us. Then their last year of college something happened and she's hated Lisa ever since. No one knows what happened between them, but I know Hayley definitely was not thrilled when I proposed at Christmas, rolling her eyes and storming out of the room. I've confronted her about it and asked Lisa, but they never answer me. Hayley and Brian had been together since my sophomore year of college. They seemed to be very much in love, but Brian refused to bite the bullet and commit, which resulted in my sister breaking up with him the January before our graduation, her junior year as an undergrad. After that, they had more of an on and off relationship than Lisa and I, if that was even possible. I'd come to the conclusion that she and Brian were having problems, and she was taking it out on Lisa and I. *Lisa and I*, God that sounded so wrong. What would she think when I told her about Max? Did I even care what she thought? I should, but I didn't. Everything was different now.

Everything.

I went back inside and for the rest of the night my eyes kept trailing to Max as I watched him interact with everyone around him. My father was right, he was an amazing kid. It was close to midnight when everyone started to make their way to their rooms. I caught Max at the elevator.

"Hey, Max,"

"Hi Mr. Weiss, that was a nice party wasn't it?" I realized he had his mother's smile.

"Yeah, if there's one thing my mom does well, it's throw a party," I added with a laugh. "Listen, I was wondering if you and your mom would like to join me for lunch tomorrow." I had no intention of waiting for Glory to make the first move.

"Umm, sure I wouldn't mind, but I'll have to ask her. What time were you thinking, because the twins and I wanted to head out early?"

"I'll talk to your mom, and we'll meet in the restaurant around one for lunch. Is that alright?"

"Sure."

That night I tossed and turned. Every time I closed my eyes I saw her, naked and exquisite in front of me. My body ached for her. She could quite easily be the most beautiful woman I'd ever laid eyes on, and seeing her in that dress tonight in the elevator did something to me. When I saw my father in the lobby earlier I thought it was her, but told myself it couldn't be. Then when I thought I saw them hugging outside the dining room, something in me snapped. Tomorrow I would get to see her again, I thought. *Tomorrow I'd have another opportunity to make her regret not giving me a chance.*

CHAPTER SIX

*M*ax left bright and early this morning, but not before he mentioned that Mr. Weiss' son had invited us to lunch at one o'clock in the restaurant downstairs, and he thought he was a nice man. I cried all night, getting up to go into the bathroom when I felt I was too loud, not wanting to wake Max. It was a little after eleven when the phone rang.

"Hello."

"Are you feeling better this morning? We missed you at breakfast." It was Hayden's deep slow roasted voice on the other end. My stomach fluttered. His was the last voice I wanted to hear so early in the morning after the dreams I had all night.

"I'm better, just not in the mood for breakfast."

"I'm not sure if Max mentioned it, but I was hoping we could all meet for lunch today and talk about everything."

"He did mention it, and no we can't meet for lunch. *I* am going to tell Max on my own time…"

"What if your *own time* isn't what I have in mind?" He asked cutting me off. "You don't understand do you? *I DON'T WANT TO GO ANOTHER DAY WITHOUT HIM KNOWING!*" He yelled, forcing me to pull the phone away from my ear.

"There's no need to yell at…"

"There *is* a need, especially when you don't seem to understand or appreciate the *need* I have to be involved in my son's life."

"I am not saying I don't want you to be a part of his life. I just need time."

"Well I'm sorry, but you can't have it! You've had twelve years and in that time I'm sure you must have thought of how you would tell me if we ever ran into each other again. Well here's your opportunity. The dining room at one, or I'll tell him myself!" CLICK.

Jesus Christ, he was an obnoxious bastard! It was obvious I wasn't going to be able to change his mind, and there was no way I was going to tell my son in a crowded dining room that Hayden Weiss was his father. I had no idea how he would take it. Moments later, I was on the walkie-talkie telling Lindsay that Max had to come back to the hotel. After he whined and complained, I told him I expected him back within the hour. I had a bath and was zipping up my boots when he walked in, his mouth pouting a mile away from his face.

"Don't be upset, you'll be back out there in no time."

"Yeah mom, but lunch isn't until one. The twins were just about to show me some cool flips."

"Flips? I don't even want to know," I said rubbing my temples. "Come sit by the fire with me. I need to talk to you." I held out my hand for him and with an exasperated look on his face, he joined me.

"What's up?" he asked squeezing beside me in the oversized leather chair. I took his hand and brought it to my face, liking the feel of his cool skin against mine.

"You're so cold."

"I'm fine mom, tell me what's wrong," he said as he took his hand from my face and brought it to rest on his lap.

"Meu amor, sabe quanto amo-o…"

"Mom, Mom, please not in Portuguese. Talk to me in English please." When he was younger I could never get him to speak in Portuguese, he would always revert back to English, even though he understood most of what I saying; he would never speak it.

"Okay, okay," I said with a nervous laugh. "My love, you know how much I love you, right?"

"Yeah mom I know, what's this about? I'm getting worried, just come out and say it. It's not like you to beat around the bush."

I took a deep breath and began, "Last night I saw your father."

"What?" his eyes were wide. "Where? Here? When did you… why didn't you tell… Wait, he's here in Colorado? Is that why you weren't feeling well?"

"Sssh, calm down and listen. Do you remember how I told you I met your father?"

"Yeah at a party, you thought he was charming and…"

"Yes at a party. I'd gotten a ride with him back to town and ended up staying with him for a drink at his hotel, you know the rest."

"Mom, who is he?" I paused, trying to swallow the tightening in my throat.

"Hayden Wei…"

"I knew it! I knew it!" he was yelling and jumping up and down. I couldn't believe it. "This is so cool! He is so cool! Does he know? Is that why he wants to meet us for lunch? Is he happy? I knew it was weird that his name was Hayden as well. When I was talking to Mr. Weiss, he said something about me reminding him of his son. Do the Weiss' know too?" he was asking a million questions a minute, but even more amazing to me was his excitement. "Do you know he runs one of the top investment banks in the country, and he loves Math, just like me?"

"Yes I knew all of that," I said with a soft voice. I couldn't quite get over his reaction.

"You knew?" his eyes were wide.

"I mean I found out last night! I had no idea Edward and Harriett were your father's parents."

"Is this why he wants to go to lunch?"

"Yes, he's thrilled and doesn't want to waste another second getting to know you."

"Omigosh, this is a dream come true!"

"You're happy about this?"

"Of course I am. Why? What's wrong, aren't you happy? Isn't this what you wanted?"

"What?"

"You know…to see him again, for us to be a family." I got up then and walked to the window, running my hand through my freshly blow-dried hair. "Mom?"

"Sim encantador," *yes darling*.

"Isn't this what you wanted?"

"Yes and no. I did want to see him again and deep down I guess I did wish we could be a family; but he's engaged to be married. So, as much as he wants you to be apart of his life, there's no room for me."

"Yes there is."

"No there isn't, and that's what I need you to understand before we meet him today. There is *no* us. He is *your* father, and I'm happy that he wants so badly to be apart of your life, but there is no us. His family doesn't know, so after we have lunch, I'm sure he'll speak to them before dinner tonight. I need you to promise me that you won't talk about me. He doesn't have to know that I don't date much, or I've been single all your life. It's none of his business. Do you understand me?"

"I get it," he said turning me from the window to face him. "You don't want him to know you still love him."

"What?" I asked, pulling away. "Não seja ridículo. I hardly know the man."

"I'm not being ridiculous. I think you know him better than anyone else." Sometimes it amazed me how quickly he picked up on things. "I'll be ready in a jiffy," he said turning away from me, but not before I saw the tears in his eyes. He was so happy.

Hayden was waiting in the lobby in front of the restaurant, pacing back and forth. I could tell he was nervous. Max hadn't stopped biting his nails since we got on the elevator. He was nervous, too. I gently took his hand from his mouth and told him everything would be alright. He just smiled. Hayden looked up and saw us coming, and Max immediately took off and jumped into his arms. I was shocked and so was he, but his rigidness quickly disappeared as he embraced Maximus. Nothing else mattered to me at that moment. My heart was full and finally my birthday wish had come true. I walked up to them and gently put my hand on Max's shoulder, and I could feel him crying. His soft sobs tugged on my heart strings because even when he was sick or in pain, Max refused to cry. Now here in the open, without a care in the world, he cried in his father's arms. My tears were at the brim of my eyes, but I refused to let them fall. They finally pulled away from each other, wiping at their eyes. Hayden seemed so happy, how could I even imagine taking this away from him and pretending like it never happened?

"I guess I don't have to ask if your mom told you," Hayden said with a smile.

"No, you don't have to ask," Max replied with a little laugh. Looking at me Hayden mouthed "thank you" to which I only shrugged. I wanted to hug him and have him hold me the same way, but he could never know that.

"Are you happy about this?" Hayden asked searching Max's face with those liquid dark eyes that seem to pierce through your soul.

"Are you kidding me? I think I'm as happy as I've ever been!" Max announced with a smile. Ouch. I don't know why and know it probably shouldn't have, but that hurt. Grow up Glory!

"I was thinking maybe this restaurant isn't the best place for us to have lunch, do you want to go out to another one? There's a great Italian bistro the next town over, and I'm sure it's a lot more private."

"Umm…" I began.

"That sounds good, doesn't it Mom?" Max responded, his eyes wide with excitement. I agreed and shortly after notifying the bellboy, the valet brought Hayden's Range Rover to the front, and we left for lunch. I was thankful for such a spacious interior, sitting in the front seat beside Hayden. I was hoping it would feel like I was a mile away, but it didn't. He and Max talked the first twenty minutes to the restaurant, from math to snow boarding, to school and girls. I just kept quiet, enjoying listening to Max talk about his life. There were so many things going through my mind as I looked out at the endless sea of billowing snow covered mountains. It was the touch of Hayden's hand on my arm that brought me back to reality.

"Why are you so quiet?" he asked, glancing back and forth between my face and the road.

"Uh, no reason. I have a lot on my mind," I said looking back at Max who was now enthralled with one of his video games, headset and all. "I'm sorry; how far is this place we're going?" I had to get out of this car.

"Not very, maybe another five minutes or so. Is driving with me so unbearable? The last time we were alone in a car, I remember you found it very pleasant." His face was sullen as though my reaction to him was hurting his feelings.

"The last time we were alone in a car, I really needed a ride, so I would've said anything you wanted to hear." *Stop it Glory!* What the hell's wrong with me? I kept saying all these hurtful things that couldn't be further from the truth.

"Really? Are you saying you didn't enjoy our conversation?" he poked, oblivious to the fact that I meant to hurt him with that comment.

"That's not what I'm saying. I just don't want to talk about this anymore" I said bluntly, looking back at Max who was still clueless to what was going on up front. The silence that followed had become uncomfortable, so I asked, "Have you thought about when you're going to tell your family?"

"I wanted to do it tonight before we head down to dinner."

"Ok, fine. Do you need Max and I to be there?"

"I would like to have you both there, yes." Why did I ask? I should've known what he was going to say.

"Alright," I said turning my attention back out the window.

"You haven't changed a bit," he said still looking at me. And like it did so long ago, my skin became warm under his gaze.

"I beg to differ," I replied stiffly, "I think I've changed a lot."

He ignored my tone and continued. "Do you want to hear something interesting?" I didn't answer. I didn't want to encourage him. He didn't know how hard it was for me to be so close to him. We were apart and yet so painfully close. "I passed that Advanced Literature final with 91%. The professor was astounded." I couldn't help the smile that played across my lips.

"Really? That's great!"

"Yup, your advice really worked." He was smiling, not taking his eyes off me. His teeth were perfectly straight and his lips, oh those lips. I remember how they felt on my body, like it was yesterday. They were warm against the sensitive flesh of my womanhood. His tongue was firm, yet so soft as it entered me. I had to blink my thoughts away.

"Please watch the road," I said, shifting in my seat, embarrassed by the unfamiliar contractions I was having in my lower abdomen. The visions were as clear as the Colorado skies behind my mind's eye. I could almost feel his muscles and smell his intoxicating cologne. The spasms between my legs increased as I tried desperately to think of something else. It was almost as though someone was holding my womb in the palm of their hand, and like you would a dying heart, gently and firmly squeezing it. One pump. Two pumps. Threee-e-e-e pumps. Oh God, I think I wet myself, or was that something else? I was mortified as I felt the new moisture between my legs. He hadn't even touched me and…and…I *had* to get out of this car. Thankfully, we were pulling into the restaurant. I think my door was open with one foot out before he put the car in park.

"Jesus Christ, Glory, you're going to get yourself killed. At least let me park the damn car!" he was yelling, but I was off, slamming the door as I trudged through the snow.

Once we were seated, Max and Hayden delved deep into conversation. Max wanted to know everything about him, from whether he had any other children, to his business, and college experience. Hayden wanted to know where we lived and wasn't too happy when he found out we lived about forty-five minutes from each other. He asked about school, his friends, the sports he played, his favorite foods. Max was telling him how I only had a few pictures of him as a baby, but when we got back to New York he would have to come over and see them. He was right, in all these years I only had a handful of pictures of Max and the majority of them came from other people.

I tried to be excited about what was going on, but I couldn't. I was glad Max was happy, but I was also slightly envious and hated myself for it. I wanted Hayden as well, but I would never have him again. I sat there silently in my own little world of "what ifs" and "why didn't I's." It was Max raising his voice and tapping on my arm that brought me back to earth.

"Mom, Mom!" he was looking at me with a worried look on his face as was Hayden.

"Yes, yes Maximus. You don't have to yell," I answered, squinting my eyes at him.

"I do have to yell when you're sitting right next to me and don't answer me after I called you three times."

"I'm sorry," I said trying to give him my best smile. "My mind was in another world."

"Well come back to our world," he said looking between Hayden and myself. "The lady wants your drink order." Looking up, I saw the waitress with an impatient look on her face.

"I'm sorry; umm…I'll just have a water please. Thank you." She quickly jotted it down and walked away.

"Mom, you aren't asking Dad…" he stopped then, the look on his face was priceless. "Wow, I've never called anyone that," he said with a broad smile.

"And I've never been called that," Hayden said reaching over and squeezing his shoulder. They were like two pigs in mud, basking in each others presence. "It sounds nice," he added.

"Yeah it does - a lot better than I thought it would. It sounds perfect," Max affirmed. "So Mom, I was saying that you aren't asking Dad any questions. Isn't there anything you want to know?"

"Now that you mention it, I guess there are a few things I should ask. Have you set a date for your wedding?" Max was not happy that I brought up Hayden's wedding. I wasn't too involved in their conversation, but it was obvious to me that Max was skirting that issue. They both were. "Well?" I pressed.

"Umm," Hayden seemed uncomfortable as well, "we haven't really set a date yet, the engagement only happened a couple months ago."

"But you must have some idea of when you would *like* to have it?" I pressed again.

"Actually I don't, I honestly haven't thought about it," aggravation creeping into his voice.

"Does your fiancée like kids? Do you think she'll have any problems with Max or this situation?"

"I'm sure she likes kids, but I don't know how she's going to react when I tell her. I don't think that's something one can gauge." Turning his attention to Max he said, "A lot has changed in one day. I need to reevaluate *all* aspects of my life. Once Lisa flies in tomorrow, we'll discuss it, but I'm sure she's going to love you."

"Wow, so you guys *did* get together even after you broke up," I stated matter-of-factly. *Lisa.* "Although, now I have to ask if you were ever broken up at all?" Anger flickered behind his eyes as he glared at me across the table.

"Mom, what are you talking about?" Max asked.

"Nothin…"

"How did you know about Lisa?" Hayden interrupted.

"What do you mean how did I know about Lisa? You told me about her!"

"No I didn't! When you asked if I had a girlfriend I told you "no" that we'd just broken up before I came on my trip. I never told you her name." Shit! He was right. Damn I'd put my foot in my mouth. I knew her name from when he was talking to the blonde man by the pool.

"Either way," I said through a fake smile, "it's not important. And this probably isn't the best place to talk about it," pointing my chin in Max's direction. I could tell Hayden didn't like it one bit, but he dropped the subject.

The rest of the afternoon was pretty uneventful, with Max and the new found hero of his life, deep in conversation and me adding my tidbits when my son pinched or kicked me under the table for my lack of involvement. It was funny seeing them interact. They both ordered the same thing, with no onions or croutons on their salad. Max chimed in that he hated uncooked onions and croutons to which Hayden added that he did also. That made them both laugh, finding such silly things that they had in common.

It was almost four when we headed back to the resort. On the way Hayden called his mother and father; told them he wanted to talk to them in their room before they went down to dinner, and asked that they let Hayley know as well. His mother pressed for more information, but that was all he said. I was scared out of my mind. What would they think? I mean, in a way I was thrilled because over the past few months Max and I had grown very fond of them, and I knew they liked us, but this was going to be completely unexpected. I was more worried about what Harriett would think of me. I had a hard enough time getting her to warm up to me the first time around.

"Glory, when we talk to my parents tonight, how do you want to tell them we met?" Hayden asked once he hung up the phone. I snapped my head around to make sure Max wasn't listening and thankfully, he had his headset on, and had fallen asleep against the window. "Don't worry, I checked in the rearview mirror before I asked," he said with a hint of an attitude.

"What do you mean? We'll tell them exactly what I told Max, they don't need details. It's not very far from the truth, but we will obviously leave out the part about you thinking I was prostitute," I whispered. "Either way, whatever is said tonight will only portray me in a less than favorable light and you as a macho stud; I've already resigned myself to that fact," I added with some degree of disdain. He looked apologetic, because he knew what I'd just said was true, but he said nothing.

Maybe it wasn't such a good idea that Max came to that meeting as well. I mean it's a known fact that the sexual relations of men and women are viewed differently. Tonight I would be thought of as the whore, loose and irresponsible, and he will be the typical man sowing his royal oats – those perceptions cannot be avoided. The bottom line was that I really had no idea how they would take the news. All that mattered to me was that deep down my son knew I was a good person. Continuing to be Edward's doctor may be difficult, but I would understand completely if he would prefer to see someone else.

"Hayden?"

"Yes Glo." His calling me that caught me off guard. I had to pause and think about what I was going to say.

"First of all, please don't call me that. Second of all, I'm thinking it may not be a good idea having Max come to the meeting with your parents tonight." He opened his mouth to say something, but I cut him off, "I think we should talk with them first, and then call Max down."

"Alright, that's fine," he said looking straight ahead. He looked upset, but more sad than angry. I wanted to know what was wrong, but wouldn't dare ask. I was probably the problem. I'd been giving him attitude since last night, and now maybe he was the one that was sick of me. After a few more minutes, I couldn't stand the silence. Typical woman, I created the negative atmosphere, and then couldn't handle it when he gave me a taste of my own medicine.

"I hope my earlier "macho stud" comment didn't offend you," there was a smile in my voice.

"Uh, no, I don't offend easily. Everyone has a right to their opinion," he added with the smallest of smiles, obviously recognizing my reference to our first conversation in Las Vegas.

"Good." After a slight pause I began, *"My mistress' eyes are nothing like the sun; Coral is far more red than her lips' red."*

"Shakespeare. Sonnet 130," he said, laughing after I burst into applause.

"Excellent!"

"Yeah, I had the best tutor. All she needed was one night to turn me into a sonnet quoting fool. She was worth every penny…"

"Priceless even," I said in a more solemn, voice finishing his sentence, the reality of my situation setting in once again, as I put my chin in my palm and gazed out the window. The cramping in my lower abdomen had returned.

How could he have such an affect on me? I knew then, even though he hadn't touched me that I would never get him out of my system. God help the man that attempts to make love to me next, he has a lot to live up to. Maybe that was my problem with Eric; the fact was that all men aren't like Hayden. So waiting around for it may be like waiting for a blizzard in Barbados. I just can't bring myself to believe that what Eric and I had was acceptable, it can't be. He didn't even attempt to see me naked, that couldn't be normal could it? I don't know anymore…he really was a nice man, maybe I needed to give him another chance. No, what I *needed* was to get over Hayden Weiss and maybe Eric was the distraction I needed. Shit, my mind was a mess; the whole point of a distraction would be to have someone who could take your mind *off* your current situation. There was no way in hell Eric could ever take my mind off of Hayden. Although I didn't have a lot of experience in the sack, the one thing I knew for sure was that on a scale of one to ten, Eric was a negative infinity, *plus* one. I would have to find someone else. Maybe it's time I took up skiing with my own personal ski instructor. I'm sure those people had flings all the time. But did I *want* someone who had flings all the time? Ahh, this would need more thought.

It was only after the doorman opened my door that I realized we were back at the resort. Max was stumbling out of the back seat still drowsy from his short nap, when Eric rushed out the front door, almost as though he'd been waiting for me.

"Where have you been?" He didn't yell, but asked in a loud enough voice to attract some attention from passersby.

"Excuse me?" my brows furrowing.

"I've been looking for you all day? Where's your cell?"

"Oh, I left it in my room. Why were you looking for me? Is something wrong?" That's when he noticed Hayden walking around the front of the car after giving the valet his keys. He was looking from Hayden to me and back again.

"Where were you?" he asked again, ignoring Hayden completely. Was he really angry with me? He was milliseconds away from pissing me off royally. I had enough on my mind with out his pigeon-brained tantrums.

"It's none of your business," snapped Max.

"Maximus Strair," I pulled his shoulder as he tried to walk away. As much as I wanted to say the same thing to Eric, Max didn't have the right and it was rude of him. "There's no need to be rude, now apologize to Mr. McNair!" His arms were folded against his chest and in a lower more deliberate voice I said, "Apologize."

"I apologize," Max said looking at his feet, "that was rude of me." I had embarrassed him in front of Hayden, but I didn't care.

"Come on Max. Let's hit the slopes before dinner. See you guys later." And snaking his arm around Max's shoulders, Hayden and Max walked away.

"What the hell was that all about?" growled Eric once he thought they were out of earshot. "What were you doing with Hayden Weiss?"

"Eric, lower your voice," I said through my sweetest smile walking towards the front entrance, but he grabbed my arm, yanking me around. The milliseconds had long since passed.

"Answer me! What's going on?" his voice louder than before. I pretended as though I could barely feel his fingers digging into the sensitive skin under my arm, stepping into his body with a stealth grace.

Tiptoeing up to him, in a low, deliberate voice I whispered against his ear, "Take your hands off me. Have you lost your mind?" He tried to pull away, coming to his senses, but I now had a fist full of his sweater, keeping him close to me. Anyone looking at us would see a woman nuzzling in her partner's ear. "Don't ever put your hands on me again, do you understand me? Max is a child, so coming from him it's inappropriate, so *I'm* going to tell you. Mind your own fucking business. What little hope there was of us ever being in a relationship, *you* just crushed when you put your hands on me!" And snatching my hand away I stormed off. I was holding my breath hoping that he fell for my display. Once I was out of sight in the elevator, I let out my breath and a monster laugh. Thank God. He just made it so easy for me to walk away from him without feeling badly about it. Jerk!

CHAPTER SEVEN

Max came back to the room just after 5:30 and said that Hayden would meet me in his parents' suite at six.

"Did you guys have fun?" I asked fixing the wide neck of my pink cashmere sweater as it fell off my shoulder.

"A blast! Dad even tried the snowboard. He was pretty good too. You see, I told you it would be fun if you just tried it."

"Well I'm glad you had fun."

"You look pretty," he added, giving me a complete once over.

"Thanks, but don't just stand there staring at me. Come and help me with this." "Ooohhh, you're going to wear the pink pearls?"

"I figured since I'm wearing this pink sweater with the grey pants, the set would go nicely." I was putting in the last stud as he reached for the necklace.

"You look beautiful, and I'm sure Dad will think so as well. Move your hair." I ignored the comment about Hayden and bent down swinging my braid over my shoulder as he clasped the necklace around my neck, and then the bracelet.

"Alright, how do I look now," I asked doing a little twirl.

"Good, really good. I just don't like your hair." He went on to say that he preferred it open and that the loose French braid I did made me look like a teacher. I ended up undoing it and wearing my hair open as requested. We talked a little while longer until it was six, and then I told him to hurry and get cleaned up. He should come up to the Weiss' suite around quarter to seven. I turned to walk away, and Max pulled my arm to tell me something. Unfortunately, he pulled it in the same place a bruise was forming from my earlier run in with Eric, so I flinched.

"I'm sorry, did I hurt you? What's wrong?"

"Nothing, I hurt my arm this afternoon," I lied.

"Did *that* happen when Mr. McNair grabbed your arm?" he said motioning to my arm, his arms in turn folded angrily across his chest.

"How did you…"

"Dad and I saw him grab you just before we got on the elevator and I had to beg him not to turn back. You should've seen it. He wanted to kick Eric's …you know what."

"Don't you dare say it," I said with smile, happy that he didn't say what I thought he was going to say.

"I didn't say anything," he protested. "Anyway it was great. He didn't relax until I told him you could take care of yourself."

"Awwh, thank you sweetie," I said rumpling his hair. "It's nothing, really. Now what were you going to tell me before?"

"I was going to tell you that I love you and that even though I have my dad now, nothing between us will change." I dragged him into my arms. I needed so badly to hear him say that. My tears came then, as I hugged and kissed him. He just held me.

Once I pulled myself together it was almost 6:15 so I hurried up to the Weiss' suite. Hayden opened the door almost as soon as I knocked. I apologized for being late, and he made a joke that he thought I'd stood him up. He'd spent the last fifteen minutes trying to keep his mother at bay.

"Do you want to start or should I?"

"Hayden, who's that at the door?" I heard his mother call from the sitting room. I thought my suite was fairly large, but theirs was huge.

"It's Glory, we're coming," he responded. "Well?" he asked in a lower voice.

"Umm, why don't you let me begin and feel free to jump in at anytime, if you disagree with what I'm saying, alright?"

"Sounds like a plan," he said. I closed my eyes took a deep breath and followed him into the large room. There were hugs and kisses all around from his parents although they seemed a little perplexed that I was even there.

"We weren't expecting you," Edward began. "Are you involved with whatever it is that Hayden has to talk to us about?"

"Yes, I am."

"You look absolutely gorgeous, as usual, my love," Harriett was saying. "Are those pink pearls?"

"Umm, yes, but why don't you all have a seat so we can get started." I was thinking that the last thing I needed was Edward having a heart attack at the news. When I realized Hayden was still standing beside me, I asked him to have a seat as well. I was already nervous and his towering over me wasn't helping. Once everyone was seated and looking at me with questioning eyes, I began.

"There is no easy way to say this, so I'm just going to say it. Here goes. Last night wasn't the first time I met your son. We actually met at a party hosted by my Aunt, almost thirteen years ago, when he came to Las Vegas before his graduation." I took a deep breath, thankful there weren't any interruptions up to that point, only looks of puzzlement. "I would love to say that there was excessive alcohol involved, but I honestly can't. That night we made a mutual decision to spend the night together." Hayley was brimming with intrigue, while Edward and Harriett just looked back and forth from me to Hayden and back again. "We didn't know each other's names, which was something that I wanted, thinking I would never see him again. And until last night, I hadn't. I'll make a short story, even shorter. Two weeks before I started Yale, I found out I was pregnant with Maximus," I paused then as the realization of what I was saying started to sink in around the room. "Max is Hayden's son" I blurted out. "His full name is Maximus Hayden Strair." Harriett was covering her mouth in obvious shock, and Hayley looked surprisingly happy.

The silence didn't last long as they immediately began with questions about Max and what we were going to do; if Max knew; and what our plans were. Harriet didn't have as much to say, but she was now looking at me sideways, as if trying to put together if I'd known all along. She asked if Jeff knew, and I reiterated that *no one* knew, Max only found out himself this afternoon.

Edward is the one that asked the near lethal question of what an eighteen year old girl was doing at that type of party, and if Hayden knew my age. I told him since my Aunt was the hostess, she was short-staffed that night and asked me to fill in. At that point he sent a stern glance in Hayden's direction. I told them, in his defense; that Hayden thought I was much older. I wasn't feeling well half-way through the night, and once I saw him leaving, I begged for a ride; making it clear that he in no way took advantage of me.

"It was a long ride back to city," Hayden added, "and enough time for me to become completely enthralled by her. We ate and talked the night away, then she was gone before I woke up the next morning." My eyes turned to slits then, since he could've obviously left that part out.

"Please don't take this the wrong way, but had I known Hayden was your son I would never have come here," I said, when I started getting the obvious "why-did-you-leave" looks.

"But why?" asked Harriett. "Didn't you want him to find out he has a son? I would think you would be thrilled about this," she didn't sound upset just surprised that I would've said something like that, but I was being honest.

"It's not about him finding out. I just would rather him not find out like this. Thirteen years is a long time. I was heading down to dinner last night, the elevator stops on the 8th floor, the door opens; and there he was, standing in front of me! I almost fainted. I think I made myself physically sick from the initial shock, but that's beside the point. Max is thrilled and so is Hayden. So in the end, that's all that matters."

"That's not all that matters! What about you?" Hayden asked in a deep voice walking away from me, towards the French doors that lead to the balcony, his hands buried in his pockets. "How do *you* feel about me?" I was completely dumbfounded that he would ask me something like that in front of his family. Was he baiting me? I mean, he was engaged to be married. How did he expect me to feel about him?

"How I feel about you doesn't matter! You're my son's father, and I'm glad you want so much to be a part of his life…" he cut me off.

"But if it were up to you, would you have preferred not seeing me at all and going on without me being in his life?"

I was becoming uncomfortable. They were all staring at me, and he still hadn't turned away from the window to face me during his verbal onslaught.

"As I said before, I'm happy that Max is happy. How I feel about you does not matter. You will be married soon, hopefully, and all that will matter then is that your wife treats both my son and I with respect. That's it. Now if there's something else you're fishing for, then come right out and ask me. Don't try to throw me under the bus in front of your parents. What do you want from me?" I was livid. He turned to face me now, his eyes dark with anger like they were when he saw his father hug me.

"I want you to tell me how you really feel and not what's politically correct! I *want* to hear that deep down you missed me, and that you've at least thought about me periodically over the past twelve years, or that you wanted to find me and be part of my life. For us to try be a family. I want to hear that given the opportunity to find me you would have. I want to hear that for the past twelve years, it wasn't easy for you to just forget about me and sweep that night under a rug. I want to hear that you wished I was around!" he was yelling, his voice wrought with emotion as he walked towards me. Was it me? Did he not see the three other people sitting in the room staring at us in total amazement? Did he not care? I couldn't think, again having flash backs of his naked body on top of mine. Then standing in front of me, he lowered his voice, "I want you to say that walking away was as hard for you as it was for me to wake up and find you gone. *I want you to tell me how you really feel!*"

I think my body was physically shaking as I stared at him. No one in the room spoke. My eyes darted over to Harriet, who was now uncomfortably playing with the mink scarf looped around her neck as though with each minute and every word it was becoming a tight noose around her slender neck. I couldn't believe what he was saying.

"Since last night, you've talked to me with such disregard, as if *I* was the problem, and *I didn't* have a right to want to be a part of Max's life as much as I did. As if *I* was the one who walked away. Do you wish last night never happened; that you still had Max all to yourself in your perfect little world?"

"What do you want me to say?" I asked in a barely audible voice, very much aware of his parents and sister being in the room. "You're about to be married...We shared one night...I was young and *stupid*..."

"Stop using my engagement as an excuse! I'm asking...please."

"Asking what? Why here?" looking around as my tears fell. "Why would you ask me this *here* in front of your family? You're about to marry another woman. What the hell do you want me to say? Why does it even matter? The fact of the matter is you don't know me, and I barely know you. Do you want to hurt me or embarrass me? Because if that's what you wa..."

"No, no, I don't want to hurt you, but I figured with my family here it would be harder for you to lie to me." He was right. It was hard enough trying to lie to him with his eyes piercing right through me, but trying to lie with six extra eyes doing the same thing, was damn near impossible.

"How I feel doesn't matter," I repeated softly, as he closed his eyes in frustration. "It's a little too late to ask me what I want. Max is so happ..." I began, but again he cut me off. His family just sat there, not saying a word, soaking it all in.

"Would you rather if we went back to being figments of each others imagination?" He was relentless. He wouldn't drop it, but kept on asking over and over how I really felt. I was becoming nauseous.

"Hayden I'm happy you're going to be a part of Max's life, that's the way it should be."

"You're full of shit! Why don't you just admit that you wish you could turn back the hands of time and never come here. Never see me again..."

"Hayden that's enough!" interjected his father when it became apparent he wasn't letting up, and that I was close to a physical breakdown. Edward stopped him in the nick of time, since I was convinced I would've spilled my guts in the next second; telling him how much I loved him, that I wanted him so badly it hurt, and that without Max, the past twelve years would've been unbearable.

"You're right that is enough," he said and wiping his hand across the lower part of his face, he turned away from me. "Forgive me. I don't know what I was thinking, expecting that *she* would be honest with me." Almost on cue there was a knock at the door and he walked away to answer it. Why did that hurt so much, him walking away from me, him implying I was some type of dishonest person? He was slowly but surely breaking down my will to build a wall around myself. I didn't want to hurt him, but I was and why? I didn't even know. I guess I didn't want to appear as weak and as whipped as I felt.

Over the past twelve years I had made excuse on top of excuse for why I wouldn't date or have physical relationships with men; from school, to work, to Max, to work again, when the reason all along had been the fact that I was waiting. Waiting to one day run into the man that had truly made me into a woman, the man who brought me out of myself. The man I loved.

"Glory, Glory," Hayley was calling me. "Come sit down, you look like you are going to topple over any minute." She was right, I was shaking. I cut open people's chests and hold their hearts in my hands. I was always in control, but for the past two days I've felt so feeble, like I couldn't handle the stress. I couldn't handle Hayden.

"Uh, no, I'm fine," I mumbled straightening my shoulders as I tried to regain my composure.

"Glory it's all in the past. It's shocking and completely unexpected, but I hope you know we're thrilled about this. No matter what goes on between you and Hayden, you are now a part of our family; you have been since the surgery. Everyone makes mistakes. It will all work out in the end. You're an amazing wom…"

Edward became quiet as Max walked in. God the resemblance between them as they stood side by side was striking. Harriett and Edward immediately jumped up and embraced Max, who gladly returned the hug, followed by Hayley. Hayden did the formal introductions, calling them his Aunty and grandparents.

"Seeing you two together it's a wonder why we didn't notice the resemblance before," Harriett was saying as she tenderly placed her palms on both Max and Hayden's cheeks. Max was looking for me. I could see him trying to look around the small circle of people, so I quickly wiped away my tears.

"Where's Mom?"

"I'm right here," and he smiled when I stood to my feet. "You look very handsome," I said, fixing his tie.

He took my hand away, "I know you're worried, but this is going to be so perfect. Wait, you'll see." The happiness was just radiating from him. I looked over as I noticed for the first time that both Harriett and Hayley were crying as well.

Harriett was talking about throwing a huge party for Max's birthday next week and announcing it then. Max was fine with that, but neither Hayden nor Hayley saw any reason to wait, especially when all the family was already here at the resort. So it was decided that after Lisa's arrival and Hayden talked with her, they would make the announcement. Harriett still wanted to do the party, which everyone thought was a great idea.

After a few more minutes, we headed down to dinner. I sat in the same seat I did the night before, but Max had joined his father's table. I ignored a joke Jeff made about Max moving on to a 'cooler' table. Eric had made several attempts to talk to me throughout the night, but was met with a cool silence. I was in a bad mood, my arm was throbbing, and my son hadn't said more than ten words to me all night. He was enthralled with his *new* family. I was miserable, trying my best to be a good conversationalist, when all I really wanted to do was go to sleep, then wake up and have this all be a terrible nightmare.

I got up to stretch my legs and walked over to the bar and started up a conversation with some of Hayden's cousins who were enjoying the couples on the dance floor. I had to admit, this family knew how to have fun, and they all seemed to get along so well.

Rosie was the big-boned first cousin and April was her sister, boy could those two talk. I couldn't get a word in edgewise, but I didn't mind since they were giving me the scoop on everyone in the family. I wasn't in a talking mood anyway. They filled me in on who was married to whom; how many kids they had; who was divorced, and who should never have gotten married in the first place. They were quite funny. None of them seemed to like Hayley's husband or Lisa for that matter. Adding they didn't know how Hayden and Hayley could have such poor taste in partners, knowing they could have had the pick of the litter. That's when *he* walked in; I could hear the small gasps all around my little area. *Omigod he's here; God he's gorgeous; He doesn't count as family does he? No, he's not blood.* Immediately there was a flurry of activity, compacts coming out, smoothing of dresses and trips to the ladies room.

I leaned into Rosie to find out what was going on, and she gladly told me that the good looking specimen who had just walked in was Michael Beckford, the stepson of Edward's cousin's new wife. Ooh, that was mouthful. Basically this woman married Michael's father, who later died. She then remarried a couple years later to Edward's cousin, Walter. Michael apparently didn't have a good relationship with his biological mother so he was adopted into the Weiss family. He was the hot item at the last two winter getaways, and the single ladies in the family were eager, since he recently became an available bachelor. She leaned a little closer to my ear and said Hayden was off limits, so they had to take the next best thing. Rosie wasn't wrong; Mr. Beckford was definitely pleasant to look at. What did the nurses at work call men like that? Aahh yes, eye candy. Yes indeed, Michael Beckford was definitely that - eye candy, and looking around it was fair to say we all had a sweet tooth.

Rosie and I talked a little while longer and then I decided it was time to hit the sack, since I didn't get any sleep the night before. I ambled over to Max at the head table, still knee deep in conversation with Hayden and slipped my arms around his neck, kissing his cheek.

"Remember me?" I asked with a little laugh. "I think I'm going to head up. I didn't get much sleep last night. Will you be alright?" Almost immediately there were protests from the Weiss's about my early retreat.

"You're heading up already?" Max whined, reaching back to hug me awkwardly as he tried to return my kiss. "You didn't even dance, and you *love* to dance," he announced with a chuckle.

"Oh no, not tonight. I want you to try and head up a little earlier. Coming to bed at midnight and then getting up at six, is going to take a toll on you, alright?"

"Okay Mom."

Then raising my head and looking at everyone around the table for the first time, I said good night.

"I'm sorry, I don't think we've met," announced Michael Beckford, standing to his feet at the far side of the table, he reached across the center to shake my hand. I hadn't even noticed him there. "I'm Michael Beckford."

"Glory Strair," as I leaned between Max and Hayden to take his hand, very conscious of how close my breasts were to Hayden's face. "I'm a friend of Edward and Harriett, and this is my son," I added using my other hand to smooth Max's hair.

"Wow, you have a son this age? You don't look a day over twenty," he said still not letting go of my hand.

"Well, she's actually thirty," Max added in a gruff tone, making it clear right away that he didn't like Mr. Beckford one bit. I couldn't seem to win with this kid.

"Yes, thank you Max for the clarification," I chuckled as the table erupted with laughter except for Max and Hayden. "Well Mr. Beckford, it was nice meeting you." I was trying to release his hand, but he wouldn't let go of mine.

"Will you be joining us on the winter walkabout tomorrow?" I was becoming uncomfortable since everyone at the table had now stopped talking to listen to our conversation.

"Umm I'd forgotten about it, but I don't have anything else planned, so I don't see why not."

"Great," he said and then didn't say anything else for a long while. He just kept looking at me, holding my hand as though he was in a daze.

"Mr. Beckford?" The color was walking up my cheeks.

"Please call me Michael."

Hayden cleared his throat. "Umm, Michael? I think Dr. Strair's arm is attached to her body and according to the laws of physics, she can't leave without either," he said through a sugary smile and made an obvious glance at our hands. Michael immediately let go, released from whatever trance he was in. I continued to turn a shade of purple.

"I'm sorry…I … uh."

"There's no need to apologize. Good night everyone." That poor man was falling all over himself, much to the amusement of everyone else at the table, and he didn't seem to care. I could almost read Harriett's thoughts behind those icy blue eyes. Giving Max a final kiss I walked away. Rosie met me at the door, catching me completely off guard.

"Did I just see you shake hands with Michael? What did he say?" she asked dragging me outside with her. I had to laugh at the face she was making.

"Rosie, it was nothing. He introduced himself and asked if I was going to the winter walkabout tomorrow, and I said I thought so; that was it."

"So *he's* going to the winter walkabout? Why can't gorgeous men like activities that don't include walking miles in the freezing cold?"

"I don't know, but you should come and keep me company. It'll be fun. I'll see you at breakfast. I'm dead on my feet."

"Oh I'll be there, I may whine and complain all day, but I wouldn't miss it for the world," she said bringing her hand to her chest in dramatic fashion, batting her eyelashes. I couldn't help bursting out with laughter again.

I got up to my room and with a running start from the door, jumped onto my bed. I was exhausted. I had only been here one day and already I felt emotionally drained. I closed my eyes and as usual, dreamt of Hayden.

CHAPTER EIGHT

I'm not sure what woke me, but when I looked at the clock it said 2:34 am. I glanced outside and the midnight blue sky was sparkling with millions of stars. I rolled over, realizing that someone had removed my boots and put me under the covers. My Max, I thought with a smile. Across the room I could see him sleeping soundly in his bed. I couldn't fall back to sleep so I decided I would go for a swim. That was the good thing about medical school; you learned to feel completely rejuvenated after only a few hours of sleep. One of the things I found appealing about this place when I looked at the brochure was the 24 hour outdoor heated swimming pool. I quietly slipped on my new designer bathing suit and wearing my furry UGG boots and terry robe, I went downstairs.

There were surprisingly quite a few people up and about, not including the resort staff, but thankfully no one was outside by the pool. The steam from the pool was billowing a couple feet high, urging me under its thick foggy blanket. I quickly stripped and dove in, not wanting the chill to reach my bones. Damn, it felt good. I did a few laps, played around and then did a few more. My eyes were starting to bother me and I wished I'd brought my goggles. I swam over to the edge of the pool where I'd left my folded towel, and with my eyes closed, I felt for it, but it wasn't there. I tried to squint, but my eyes burned like hell. Did I make a mistake? I could swear I put it at this end of the pool. Wiping at my eyes I finally managed to open them to find Hayden sitting on the lounge chair with my towel draped over his lap. His hair looked completely disheveled, like he'd just rolled out of bed, but he was still wearing his clothes from dinner, his tie loosened around his neck. He was so gorgeous. The fluttering in my stomach was soon replaced by the return of that unbearable cramping in my lower abdomen.

"Were you looking for this?" he asked, trailing the rim of his coffee mug with his long beautiful fingers as he tapped my towel with his other hand. I remembered those hands and how they had maneuvered my body with such precision, knowing exactly how and where to stroke me. With hands like those he could be a surgeon as well. I had to physically shake my head to stop the thoughts that were running through my mind. "Was that a no?" he asked raising his eyebrows.

"No, that wasn't a *no*. What are you doing here anyway?" I asked, again rubbing at my eyes as the stinging returned.

"I couldn't sleep."

"And what, you just happened to find your way down to the pool at three in the morning?" my voice dripping with sarcasm. "Give me my towel."

"I didn't come down here to fight with you Glory," he said walking over to the edge of the pool. I held my hand out for the towel, but he ignored it stooping down in front of me. Taking the edge of the towel he folded it and gently wiped my eyes. "Better?" I would never admit that they were, so I remained silent. "Why do you hate me so much?" Hate him? How could I ever hate him?

"I don't hate you Hayden and…and I'm sorry if I've made you feel that way."

"You sure as hell could've fooled me!"

"It's just…you don't understand. I've tried for so long to pretend…," I stopped myself letting out a long sigh. He could never understand how hard this was for me. "Why did you come down here?" I asked again taking a few steps back from the edge of the pool as though I thought the steam would hide me from those eyes.

"You can't tell from here, but my room is on the 8th floor and I was having my fourth nightcap on the balcony when I saw you," he stood up pointing towards the rooms of the resort. "Since you were the reason I couldn't sleep, I figured I would come down here and have you be the reason I stayed awake."

"Why did you do that to me tonight, in front of your parents? What were you trying to prove? If you wanted to hurt me, you succeeded."

"I told you already, all I wanted was for you to tell me the truth. I didn't want to hurt you."

"Hayden, because I'm not saying what you want to hear, it doesn't mean I'm not telling you the truth."

"Alright, let me go about this another way since I don't believe you. Did you ever regret leaving me the way you did?"

"No," a blatant lie, but an answer nonetheless. I let out an exasperated sigh, running my hands through my wet hair. I waded a little further out in the pool and felt hidden by the steam, which made talking to him so much easier. I didn't feel as though he could see into my soul with those eyes of his. "Hayden you thought I was a prostitute and I wasn't. You also thought I was this experienced lover and I certainly wasn't. I tried to talk myself out of spending the night with you, telling myself that there was a big difference between good conversation and good sex and because I'd successfully made my way through my conversation with you didn't mean I would be as successful with the latter, but it didn't work. I couldn't tell you that morning because I thought you would've been upset."

"How could I be upset, when you effortlessly gave me the most beautiful night of my life?" *I could feel my heart pounding and the sensation of its pulse reverberating between my legs.*

"That's easy to say now, but if you'd known then that you'd just taken the virginity of a seventeen year-old girl, a couple weeks before finishing grad school, with your entire life and career ahead of you, I'm doubtful that you wouldn't have been upset or disappointed. Better yet, furious."

"Maybe, but you stimulated my mind *and* my body in ways I had never imagined. I honestly thought I was the one who had disappointed you."

"Are you mad? Disappointed? Me? Never! Is that really what you thought? I mean I left the note and I thought that said it all."

"Yeah, but no one shares what we shared and then never sees the person again, at least not with me. I had every intention of waking up that morning and telling you my name, address, social security number, bank accounts," we both started to laugh then. "I went to sleep thinking that I could change you. I don't know anymore…I just feel as though I may have pressured you in some way. The fact is you made all the decisions for me and took my options away when you left the way you did. I had no say in the matter." There was sadness in his eyes that tugged at my heart strings. I stepped forward then, because this time I did want him to see into my eyes.

"Listen to me. I wanted to leave because I didn't think I could fool you much longer. I thought if you knew how old I was, or how poor I was it would've ruined what we'd just shared, but every fiber of my being wanted to make love to you that night. You didn't pressure me at all. I wanted it. I wanted you," I sighed again. "You don't understand…I've tried so hard to pretend it never happened, that you really didn't exist, that the night we shared was some figment of my deprived imagination and Max was some amazing gift from God."

"Believe me, I understand completely, but I have to ask. Did you think about me at all…," I cut him off.

"*Everyday,*" I whispered stepping back again. "I can't look at Max without seeing your face. Even now, I can close my eyes and relive what we shared over and over and over again, like it was yesterday - *every touch, every kiss, and every endearing whisper.*

Honestly? I certainly tried, but I couldn't forget you. So yes I do think about you, everyday."

"Do you really wish you'd never see me again?"

"No and once again I'm sorry if I made you feel that way…I guess I would've liked it to be on my own terms. Yesterday or the day before rather, was hard for me. I wasn't prepared, seeing you was such a shock, and then the fact that you thought I was sleeping with your father, it just brought everything back. I wanted to be prepared. I replayed our meeting so many times in my head and it was always the same – on my terms. Then to find out you were engaged, was a bitter pill to swallow." I ran my hand across my forehead and left it there, exactly where I could feel the pressure building. "I have to tell Max to be realistic. He's thinking that we're going to be one big happy family and we aren't. If I had my own way I guess I would want us to be a family, the way my parents were, so in love and happy. But that doesn't happen to everyone and I'm fine with that." He was silent, his eyes closed as he ran his hands back and through his hair grabbing handfuls of it.

"Glory I told you last night and I tried to tell you again today that everything is different for me now. Everything. My life can't - won't go back to the way it was; and I hope that now I'm here, yours won't either. Right now I'm reevaluating *every* aspect of my life. So much has changed to the point that I don't want to marry…" he began.

"Ssshhh, please don't say it. Please don't say another word… we've already said too much." Walking forward I put my hands flat against the edge of the pool I pulled myself out of the water. The cold air quickly took away the heat from my body and I could feel my nipples grow painfully hard. Hayden just stared at me, like the night I stood naked in front of him, he admired every mole, each curve, from my head to my feet. Then his eyes became dark with anger as he stepped towards me, his brows furled. His rage instantly began to radiate from his body like heat from an explosion. I took a step back

"What's wrong?" Taking my wrist he lifted my arm. Shit, my arm! Eric! I quickly snatched it away, bringing it across my chest and putting my other hand over it.

"*Son-of-a-bitch!* Max told me he hurt your arm, but I had no idea…"

"It's not as bad as it looks…" I said reaching for my robe.

"I knew I should've gotten off that fucking elevator…" he was pacing back and forth. Max was right, he was pretty upset.

"Hayden, I take 1500mg of iron a day, you could sneeze on me and it would leave a bruise…"

"I should really kick his ass!" I walked forward and put my palm against his shoulder.

"No. Please… don't. I dealt with it," once again there was silence. My hand was warm against the cool material of his jacket. I was touching him. We were too close. He was too close. I had to leave before I did something, I really wanted to do. I wanted him so badly it hurt. It physically hurt.

One pump, two pumps, threee-e-e-e.

Snatching my hand away I said, "It's late I should really get back upstairs. I'm glad we got the chance to talk and hopefully you got some of the answers you were looking for. I'm really sorry for how I've been acting towards you. I'm not like that and I…"

"I know, I know. I'm glad we talked as well. I feel a lot better about this, about us, I mean about Max," we kept looking at each other. "Good night Glory."

"Good night Hayden," and wrapping myself in my robe, I grabbed my boots and ran upstairs.

CHAPTER NINE

After Glory left I took my time heading up to the room, collapsing on my bed while I thought of all the reasons why I didn't want to marry Lisa. I had proposed to her for the wrong reasons to begin with and now the thought of going through with the marriage seemed like an even more dreadful idea. Lisa was…Lisa was familiar. My family knew her and I knew her. She came from good stock and ran a great advertising firm, not to mention her good looks. She was always the one at school and in college that all the girls envied, a natural blonde with legs that went all the way to heaven. Her junior year of college, against my wishes, she had her breast done, going from a 36 B to a 36 DD which led to one of our several breakups. She was a beautiful woman and she knew it. I was never the jealous type because deep down I guess I never really cared if she left me or not. Plus it wasn't hard to please her. On any occasion when I had to buy her a gift, it never took much thought. I could send my assistant to any expensive store to have her pick up something, anything, and Lisa would love it, jewelry, furs, cars, bags, a couture wardrobe anything was fine, as long as Lisa knew it was expensive. She was superficial and proud of it. She was everything I detested in women, but yet I stayed with her.

I remember when I returned home from Las Vegas, my mind was in shambles thinking about *Glo* and Lisa wanted to work things out with me. Finally after a few months, I decided we would meet for dinner at my house and on a piece of paper we had to write why we wanted to be with the other person. She thought it was the dumbest idea, but once she realized it was the only way I would have dinner with her, she agreed. I should've known when I stared at a blank piece of paper for five hours that it wasn't a good sign. Then I thought of Glo and the night we shared and all the reasons why I wanted to be with her that weren't physical and after ten minutes I had a full page. Needless to say, Lisa was completely blown away by my list, so much so that we ended up having sex right on my dinner table. When we were finished I asked for her piece of paper and after much resistance she finally handed it over. What I read was another blaring sign that she was not the woman for me, but I ignored it. It read:

Why do I want to be with you?

Because-you're *THE* Hayden Weiss

I was mad that she couldn't find anything else to say, and then she took me in her warm mouth to show me why she wanted to be with me; the intense will I had to stay angry at her quickly disappeared. That was another thing Lisa was very, very, very good at, using her body to get what she wanted and even though she was extremely skilled in that department, there was something about being with her that could never compare to what I had with Glory. Later that night, after we were exhausted from having sex I had to silently remind myself that I couldn't find one reason to stay with her either and that it took thinking of another woman to put words on the paper.

Everything was different now. I couldn't wait until tomorrow night to talk with Lisa. I had to do it now. I dialed our home number and she picked up on the second ring which surprised me because she was a heavy sleeper.

"Hel…lo."

"Uh Lisa?"

"Hay…Hayden?"

"Yeah, I'm sorry to call so late, but I have something important to talk to you about and it can't wait until tomorrow night."

"Uh…okay." I could swear she was whispering to someone. She was shushing them or saying stop.

"Did I wake you?"

"Uh no, no…I was up packing a few extra things; this really isn't a good time. Are you sure it can't wait until tomorrow morning?" She was lying.

"I'm positive. Are you alone?"

"Yes of course I'm alone; it's the middle of the night. You probably heard the television. I'm sorry baby it's been a long day. What did you want to talk to me about?" Then I heard a door close as though she'd left the room. She was definitely lying.

"There's no easy way to say this so I'm just going to come out with it. I found out on Friday that I have a son."

"What? A son? Where in Colorado?"

"Umm yes. I mean no, it's a little complicated so let me just tell you what I know right now. When I went to Las Vegas for my graduation I met someone at a party and we spent the night together."

"You had unprotected sex with a woman you didn't know, in *Vegas*?"

"Yes."

"She could've been a prostitute for all you know. *I've* never even had sex with you without a condom and I'm your fiancée for Christ's sake! How could you do this to me!"

She was right about that. Lisa and I had definitely our issues and even though she thought things never got back to me, there were several rumors about her sexual promiscuities. Whenever we broke up she would sleep with people to get back at me, but it never got the reaction she was hoping for.

"Lisa you need to be quiet and listen to me. First of all I did nothing *to* you! We weren't together at the time and I've never had any, and I mean any problems with my tests. She wasn't a prostitute. A long story short is that she got pregnant, we didn't even know each other's names and she had our son."

"Our Son? I don't believe what I'm hearing. She had sex with a man whose name she didn't even know and you're telling me she isn't a prostitute?"

"Yes that's what I'm saying and he is *our* son. She's now a cardiac surgeon in New York and just happens to be the doctor that performed Dad's heart surgery?"

"Wait, wait Edward had open heart surgery? This is too much. What the hell is going on up there?"

"I know it's confusing, but just listen to me. I guess over the past few months she's become good friends with my parents and she's also quite close to Jeff and Clay. My parents invited her and her son here for the winter get away, and I ran into her and Maximus last night. She didn't know I was their son and Max didn't know I was his father."

"That's a pile of shit! Don't tell me you believe any of this. I thought you were smarter than this! You actually think that she didn't know you were their son? She set this up! She knew all along and now she probably wants money! Any woman that would sleep with a man she doesn't know and then actually have his child can't be trusted. Do your parents know? Harriett will never fall for this. It's obvious this woman is a gold digger, probably saw your name in the paper and made her plans."

"Lisa I can tell you right now that it's not like that. She didn't even want me to know about Max. I'm the one that put it together when I found out his age and the fact that Hayden was his middle name."

"But I thought you didn't know each others names."

"Yes I know, but it gets a little tricky. We were supposed to give each other fake names, but I gave her my real name instead, that's beside the point. My parents and Hayley already know and they're thrilled. He's a great kid."

"WOW, so you're telling me that you have an eleven year old son."

"Yes, Maximus Hayden Strair"

"Humph, what type of name is Maximus? Wasn't that the name of the gladiator? I still think you should have a paternity test. That slut..."

"Lisa, there's no doubt in my mind that he's my son, so let this be the last time that you bring up a paternity test or call Glory by anything other than her name! They aren't going anywhere, so you need to get used to it. I have a son and I plan on making him a very, very big part of my life." I was yelling, but I didn't care. I didn't like her implications. If only she knew Glory was the farthest thing from a Las Vegas call girl, slut, or a petty gold digger.

"All right, all right, calm down. I didn't mean anything by it sweetie. This is all just a bit much. Listen, if you want we can even give him a part in the wedding."

"Listen, about the wedding I think we should hold off."

"What? Hold off? We have been holding off, for the past ten years. My clock is ticking!"

"Clock? What clock? You don't even want children. Listen, a lot has changed in the past couple days, I just need to organize my thoughts and decide what I want to do."

"Decide what you want to do? Hayden, what are you saying? I don't care about your son. I mean I do! I will love him like he was my own and I promise I won't bring up a paternity test again. Please...nothing has to change. We can still get married in the fall and..." I couldn't help the little laugh that escaped my lips. "What's so funny? Are you laughing at me?"

"I'm not laughing at you. It's funny because that's the same thing Glory said, 'nothing has to change'. But that's what you both don't understand, that everything's changed. We'll talk some more when you get here tomorrow night. I'm sorry I called so late."

"Hayden, I love you."

"See you tomorrow." And with that I hung up and without a moment's hesitation called the security desk.

"Good evening, Archway."

"Geoffrey?"

"Uh, yes."

"Geoffrey its Hayden from the penthouse."

"Yes, hello Mr. Weiss how's the weather up there in Colorado?"

"Not bad, not bad, listen, I need a favor."

"Sure, anything."

"How long have you been on duty?"

"I'm doing the six to six shift this weekend. We're short-staffed because of the vacation week. So I pulled a double on yesterday and today."

"Were you there when Ms. Steller got home?"

"Yes sir, she came in around quarter to eleven this evening."

"Was she alone?" He was a little hesitant as though he knew what I was getting at.

"Yes sir she was." I let out an obvious sigh. Damn it Hayden, you need to relax a little more. I have serious trust issues.

"Oh okay, great, thanks. I'm sorry I called so late. Have a good evening."

"Uh, Mr. Weiss?! Mr. Weiss?!" He was yelling as though he thought I'd hung up.

"Yeah Geoffrey, I'm still here."

"Ms. Steller was alone when she came home, but like clockwork Mr. Rafferty came shortly after and he hasn't left. He also came last night around eight and was still here when I got off my shift at six this morning. He usually comes fifteen minutes to half hour after she does." Brian Rafferty? Lisa was upstairs with Brian? No doubt in my bed! She was sleeping with my sister's husband. "Mr. Weiss, sir, you still there?"

"Yes, yes, Geoffrey, I'm still here. Usually? What do you mean usually? How long has this been going on?"

"Sir I don't want to lose my job."

"You won't lose your job Geoffrey. I own the building, remember?"

"I would have to say about seven or eight months."

"*Seven or eight months?!?*" Once again I didn't mean to yell, but I did.

"Ah, yes sir, that's when I first noticed."

"But when? I'm always home."

"Uh, no sir you aren't and your schedule is pretty much like clockwork. You leave at six in the morning and are gone usually until ten or eleven at night. I've seen Mr. Rafferty show up as early as 6:30 in the morning, or around lunch, or in the evenings and that's on the days you aren't traveling. When you're out of town, like now, he spends the night."

"Son-of-a-bitch!"

"I'm sorry Mr. Weiss."

"Don't be, don't be, you have nothing to be sorry about. Geoffrey don't say anything about this alright?

"My lips are sealed."

"Thank you."

"For what sir? The way I see it I just ruined your life?"

"No, you just saved it. Have a good night."

"Same to you sir."

I hung up, my mind racing. I made one last call, leaving a message on my doctor's voicemail requesting an appointment as soon as I got back. These lab tests would give me some closure.

I laid in bed staring at the ceiling. Lisa has been having an affair with Brian. I wondered if that had anything to do with why Hayley had been treating me the way she was. Did she know? And if so, why was she tolerating it? Probably because of the baby.

Like Lisa, Hayley had majored in communications and advertising in college, but had never gotten a job. She started doing some free lance work for the New York Times and then she married Brian and became a house wife. He was a big time sports agent and did very well, so money wasn't an issue. Son of a bitch! My blood was beginning to boil again at the thought of what he was doing. I swear I'll make him pay for this, not because he's sleeping with my fiancée, because I honestly couldn't care less about that, but because he was my sister's husband.

If I thought I couldn't sleep before, well I definitely couldn't sleep now. I laid awake for hours trying to figure out how I would handle this. Lisa was going to be the easy part, because she'd made it easy for me to just walk away. Brian on the other hand would need some finesse since I knew for a fact that my father insisted he and Hayley both signed a very wordy prenuptial agreement. A prenup that could be Hayley's only saving grace right now and that's why I had to get all the proof I could, to bury Brian for good.

When I could bear it no longer, I rolled over and called Hayley's room. It took a couple tries, but she soon picked up.

"Hail?"

"Yes? Hayden is that you? Is everything all right?"

"Yes, but we need to talk."

"What the hell about? It's barely six o'clock?"

"I need to talk to you now, it's important. Can I come up?"

"What's this about? Can't it wait until a decent time?"

"No it can't. I'm on my way."

"Fine."

My fatigue only hit me once I ran up the four flights of stairs to Hayley's suite. I knocked and she opened the door. Once we were in the sitting area I built back up her fire and we sat down.

"You look like shit! What's this all about Hayden?" Now more than ever she looked like a little girl, sitting with her feet crossed under her. The pregnancy had filled out her face and her cheeks were rosy from the cold weather, but her eyes seemed so sad.

"It's about Brian and Lisa." Her features changed instantly as she became angry.

"What about them? I hope you didn't wake me up out of my much needed sleep to ask me why I was upset that they were flying in together."

"No that's not why I woke you," I took a deep breath. "I woke you up to find out how long you've known they were having an affair?"

"What?" Immediately she jumped off the sofa. "I knew no such thing! Are they? How did you find out?"

"You know they are and that's why you've been so upset with me. I just found out a few hours ago and they don't have a clue that I know." She sat back down with a thud, rubbing her bulging belly lovingly. "I want to help you destroy him."

"Why? What makes you think I want to destroy my husband? You don't even love Lisa, I, however, happen to love my husband very much!" she started to cry then, doubling over as though someone had just punched her in the stomach. I just held her until she'd caught her breath long enough to speak. "That's a lie. I hate him Hayden!"

"Tell me what you want me to do Hail, and I'll do it, but I can't let him get away with this."

"He gave me Hepatitis Hayden and I didn't even know. I found out when I went for my prenatal check up. I don't know how long I've had it because I didn't have any symptoms and it looks as though…it's far gone now…they saw a spot on my liver. They found the tumor at my last ultrasound. They think…"

"Tell me you aren't serious. Hail what are you saying?"

"They think the tumor is small, which is a good thing because it can be surgically removed. If my liver is in good condition, surgical removal is my best chance for long-term survival. They think the baby may be fine, but she'll need to get medicine as soon as I deliver to protect her. If she has it, there's no cure for Hep B." She looked like she was in so much emotional pain, that I wondered why I hadn't noticed before. "How could he do this to me Hayden, to us?

I'm so mad I want to die, but I don't know what to do." She began to wail and all I could think of was how I was going to kill the bastard.

Brian would never have been my choice for my sister, but she loved him and I had to respect that. While we were in college I'd seen sides of him that would rather not have and I honestly hated his guts. He was a filthy dog and I would treat him as such.

"How long have you known about this?"

"A few months now. I tried to talk to him so many times about it, but he never gives me the time of day. So he doesn't even know. I needed someone to blame and since I felt I was doing everything right as his wife, I blamed you. I felt if you would be honest with Lisa, then she wouldn't need to find solace with *my* husband."

"I'm so sorry Hayley. I had no idea…"

"Don't be. I was grasping at straws. If it wasn't Lisa it would've been someone else. For all I know, there was someone else. What are we going to do? I think they've been sleeping together for at least the duration of my pregnancy, although it could be longer."

"How did you find out?"

"I just knew when I saw them together that she was the one. She's a despicable person. I never knew what you saw in her."

"Lisa will get what's coming to her, but I was serious when I said I am going to destroy him."

"How?"

"You let me worry about that. You just worry about you and the baby. I'll take care of everything. Do mom and Dad know?"

"Of course not and you can't say anything, either! This is just so…embarrassing. To have your husband cheat on you is one thing, but when you get an STD, it takes the humiliation to a whole other level. Even at my doctor's office I feel as though they look at me differently. I don't want mom and Dad to know." She was getting flustered and her hands were shaking.

"Ssshh, don't worry I won't say a thing, but I need you to go on as though nothing has happened when they come in tonight. I'll keep you posted."

"Fine. Don't take this the wrong way, but I think you should get tested. I mean…this isn't…Lisa has no problems using her body to get what she wants."

"If you're saying that this isn't the first time she's cheated on me, I know. I don't think I've ever had unprotected sex with her, which is pretty sad when you think about it considering I was about to marry the woman, but I already planned on seeing my doctor when we got back home."

"What do you mean you've never had unprotected sex with her? Never? That doesn't sound right. Are you sure?" she asked with an incredulous look on her face. "You're telling me you've *never* had unprotected sex with Lisa, not even once in the heat of the moment?"

"Not even once," I replied bluntly and it was the truth.

"Hayden the reason Lisa and I stopped speaking in college was because I found out she was pregnant and she was going to have an abortion without telling you. I just assumed the baby was yours and I didn't agree with what she was doing. She never told me otherwise, she just let me assume it was yours."

"What? When was this? I can tell you right now that it wasn't mine. Lisa was pregnant? This is just unbelievable." My mind was racing, but I knew for a fact that I had always used protection with her.

"So it wasn't yours?"

"I don't think so. It couldn't be, as much as she wants to be married into our family, I think she would've jumped at the opportunity to make me marry her. I was never that comfortable or should I say completely trusting of Lisa."

"And yet you asked her to marry you," Hayley said with disgust. "That I just don't get."

"I know…I just…wanted to get everyone off my back, Mom especially."

"Don't worry about it. I know how Mom and Dad can be. Why do you think I finally bit the bullet and got pregnant knowing all the problems Brian and I had? It feels good to finally be able to talk to you about it. It's great that you're paranoid about protection. I know you were always the one with the ridiculous supply of condoms in college. Didn't they call you the Protection King when you were at Harvard? You know I would steal them when you were home…"

"Aaahhh, too much information," I yelled jokingly putting my hands over my ears. "I don't want to know all of that!" She started to laugh.

"Why didn't you use protection with Glory? I mean that's not like you. You two didn't even know each other and you met, in of all places, at a Las Vegas party! *Las Vegas* Hayden? Isn't Nevada like the only state to legalize prostitution?"

"I know, I know, but Hail I swear to God protection was the farthest thing from my mind when I was with her. I was focusing my energy on getting her to stay. I just wanted to talk. And then I became so enthralled that I wanted her to spend the night with me. I wanted her so badly, it hurt Hail. And…I mean all we did that night was talk and even that was turning me on. She was funny…down to earth…and…and you won't understand. I'd never met anyone like her."

"Yes I do. I understand completely. She was probably the only woman you'd ever met that hadn't attempted to jump your bones right away. So what are you going to do about it?" I eased back in the chair so I could look at her face.

"Do about what?"

"About Glory and your son. Are you really happy about Maximus?"

"Happy? I'm thrilled! Honestly, if it had been any other woman from my past I may not feel the same way, but Glory…," I stopped for a moment and closed my eyes. "She's different. I can't begin to explain what we shared that night, because I've never experienced it again. Not even with Lisa," I let out an exasperated sigh grabbing a handful of my hair. "And Max is just plain wonderful. He's everything I would've wanted in a son, you know what I mean? He does well in school, he's polite, and respectful, not to mention handsome as all hell," I added with a smile.

"Do you love her?"

"I don't know. I mean there *is* something there, but I can't say that it's love and not lust."

"Why didn't you take the time and find out? Men! You're always afraid of commitment. Wam-bam thank you ma'am!"

"Me? Oh no, I won't take the fall for this one. When I woke up *she* was gone. *I* was more than willing and prepared to see what developed between us, but she never gave me a chance. I thought maybe the feelings were only flowing one way and that I was mistaken about how special that night was."

"Good. You got a taste of your own medicine, but I can tell you right now after watching you two last night, that those feelings *are* definitely flowing in both directions. She's putting up a good fight though. The fact that she kept your baby says so much." I was glad someone else believed that and not just me.

"I know that's what I keep telling myself. Lisa thinks she's using me for money."

"That bitch would think something like that. When she takes one look at Max's face it will all fall into perspective. Are you really going to leave her?"

"I think I've already left." She rested her head back on my shoulder as I rubbed her belly and watched the sun rise, it felt like old times again.

Once she fell back to sleep I put her to bed, went down to my room, and made my plans. I made a few calls and then called the security desk at my apartment, thankful for the time difference, which meant I caught Geoffrey before he got off. I explained to him that I was having someone come in that would compile all the security tapes from the last eight months and requested that he have access to everything he needed. I assured him he would be paid for any overtime he had to put in, so that shouldn't be an issue. He seemed more than willing, indicating he would do it for free, we both had to laugh. I guess it became obvious that the staff didn't like Lisa very much. Marcus, my security/private investigator, had helped me before when I wasn't sure about certain clients and I trusted his work. He told me all he needed was a couple days to have exact dates and times Brian had come over when I wasn't home. He too seemed more than willing, adding that he would have them followed to the airport; I'd already spoken to the pilot about an extra passenger that was to be kept hidden, so the ball was in motion. By the time I was finished I was completely exhausted. It was after eight when I changed out of my dinner clothes and crawled under the covers.

It seemed like my head was just hitting the pillow when there was a loud knock at the door. Who the hell could that be?

"Who is it?"

"Hayden, its Eric." He was the last person I wanted to talk to right now, since I could still see myself ringing his neck clean off his shoulders for putting his hands on Glory. I opened the door and he strode right in without a word and began pacing back and forth.

"What's up?" like I didn't already know the answer.

"What's going on between you and Glory?" He turned to face me with his hands akimbo.

"Eric, I'm not getting between you and Glory. If you have questions you should ask her."

"I'm not asking her, I'm asking you! She said on Friday she didn't know you, but I get the distinct impression that you two know each other somehow. Tell me."

"We barely know each other."

"If that's the case where did you go yesterday?"

"Listen, correct me if I'm wrong, but I thought you two weren't in a relationship, so what does it matter where we went yesterday?" I asked with raised eyebrows, doing nothing to ease his discomfort. I'd always known he could be obnoxious, but now I was seeing it first hand. I had every intention of fueling his fire.

"It matters because you are almost a married man. It matters because things between us could've worked out if you hadn't interfered…"

"Me interfere? No buddy you're the one who messed up when you put your fucking hands on her – grabbing her like she was *your* property. You messed up, not me! Glory and I aren't involved, we just…"

"We just what?" he pressed.

"We have a history."

"A history? What type of history?"

He wasn't going to let this go. Everyone would find out tonight anyway. "A twelve-year *old* history. Max is my son." The shock was plain on his face, but he didn't interrupt me, so I continued. "I saw her on Friday for the first time in twelve years. At the time we didn't know each others names, and Max certainly didn't know who I was. She told him yesterday and we went to lunch to talk about everything. There! Are you happy now? I'll probably be making an announcement tonight at dinner."

"What? Max is your son? Jesus. This, I wasn't expecting. I mean she told me she and Max's father weren't in a relationship at the time, but I had no idea it was a one night stand?"

I became defensive. "That's not what it was!"

"Of course that's what it *was*. I want to be with her Hayden…" Something about him seemed almost desperate.

"And like I told you before Eric, that's none of my concern. That's between you and Glory, I'm staying out of it." My blood was beginning to boil.

"What are you going to do about Max and Lisa?"

"Quite honestly Eric it really is none of your business."

"I'm tired of people saying that. She *is* my business. I care about her!" he yelled.

"That's not what the bruises on her arm say, asshole," I yelled back. He was shocked that I was so angry.

There was a look of eureka on his face. "You care about her don't you?"

"That's a stupid question; of course I care about her. She's the mother of my son."

"Yeah, whom you haven't seen in twelve years," he retorted.

"It doesn't matter if I didn't see her for a hundred years!" my level of frustration is at an all-time high. "What do you want Eric? Why are you here? Honestly, I don't have time for this. I haven't slept in over twenty-four hours and I'm dead on my feet."

"Help me get her back!" he blurted out. He couldn't be serious. He wanted *me* to help *him*?

"I'm sorry I can't do that," I replied without hesitation.

"Why not?" I turned away and walked to the balcony. It had just started snowing. "I thought we were friends? Jesus you've known me a lot longer than you've known her!"

"Because…" I continued looking out the window, willing myself to remain calm.

"Because what? Because you care about her? Hayden you're getting married, I can take care of her."

I turned to face him. "I don't think you can." If he forced this, he could be pushing our working relationship and so-called 'friendship' out the window, and at this point I was more than willing do that. He was the wrong man for her and if he kept this up, I would tell him.

"And *you* can? Let me get this straight. You spend one night with her and never see her again. That would make her like what - eighteen at the time? I mean she just doesn't seem like the type," he was pacing back and forth. "If anything she seems more like a nun. Think about it; it took me three months to sleep with…"

"Shut your fucking mouth Eric! What the hell are you doing? I don't want to hear any of this, especially when you don't know what the hell you're talking about," I yelled. He had successfully pushed my buttons and pissed me off royally. Now I didn't have to wonder if they'd had sex because he just told me. Asshole! I could kill him right now.

"Don't put up this charade with me Hayden. I know you remember? You would step on anyone to get what you wanted and this knight-in-shining-armor act that you're trying to pull isn't working," his voice was dripping with sarcasm and disgust. "You're a selfish bastard do you know that? What… if you can't have her no one else can? What type of shit is that? Unless you intend on being with both her and Lisa, I don't see your point!" He continued pacing back and forth in frustration.

"You know, the word around town is that you always had to have the prettiest girl and if you didn't, you would find a way to get her. Is that what you're going to do with Glory?" Eric growled. I took a couple steps towards him because I wanted to make sure that he knew I wasn't afraid of him. He'd crossed the line and my temperature gauge was reaching a dangerous high.

"You don't care about her Hayden and you probably never did. Maybe if I was as forceful with Glory as you probably were I could've taken advantage of the situation and gotten her into bed a lot sooner than three months. Care about her?" he practically laughed and the steam coming out of my ears had now officially blinded me. "You didn't even know her name for Christ's sake! She was just another notch on your belt of conques..." That was it!

I didn't wait for him to finish as I planted my fist square across his jaw and felt the teeth shift in his mouth and against my knuckles from the impact of the blow. The pain that radiated up my arm was excruciating, but I curled my fingers into an even tighter ball, hoping he retaliated.

He stumbled backwards into the coffee table in front of the fireplace, sending the bottle of gin from earlier crashing onto the floor. He held his jaw and licked at the tiny trickle of blood at the corner of his mouth, his eyes darkening with rage, to match the intensity of mine. I could see his hands balling into fists at his side and anticipating his next move, I side stepped as he lunged at me, making him lose his balance. He was grappling for the back of the large sitting chair, while my fist rammed upwards into the sensitive area between his ribcage and hip. He howled in pain trying to steady himself. When he finally turned to come at me again, I was ready and waiting. I didn't even have to move much, as he practically turned face first into my fist. The crunch that resulted almost made me cringe, but I quickly had him by his throat and up against the fireplace, pushing his lower back, into the thick wooden mantle. He cried out, but I didn't ease up.

The tone of my voice was somewhere between a roar and a hiss. "Listen, and listen well. I don't care who Glory wants to be with," LIE, "as long as she's happy. But I can tell you right now that person won't be you," I snapped, FACT. He tried to struggle against my body, but I only pressed harder and squeezed tighter. "You got into a jealous fit because you saw her and Max getting out of a car with me in broad daylight. You leave your fucking hand print on her arm where you grabbed her in anger. And now you show up in my room blaming the fact that any chance of a relationship with her is ruined, on me? You've got some nerve! What is it Eric, you don't like to be turned down? Well get used to it, because that's Glory. She doesn't care who you are and what your ego is like, when she walks away, she walks away for good. I know because she did it to me. *She* walked away and I didn't even have to put my hands on her for her to do it," I said with a wicked smile, enjoying the anger that had left his eyes and the fear that replaced it.

"And as for you finding it so hard to believe that I care about her, I do! I don't give a flying fuck if you believe me or not. She kept my son, when she could've just as easily gotten rid of him and that means more to me than anyone will ever know. You don't know me. You know what these assholes around town know, and what you see in the office and the boardroom, but *you* don't know *me*," my grip tightening around his neck for effect. "And don't think for a single second that you do. You had your chance, which was way more than I ever got and you ruined it. Not me, *you*. So if you're looking for sympathy you've come to the wrong place partner. So get the fuck out of my room before I let my anger get the better of me and beat the shit out of you!"

He was sputtering when I snatched my hands away from his neck, coughing and gasping for air. I couldn't care less if he's lost consciousness at that exact moment. He'd crossed the line in a major way. He stood to his feet and backed his way to the door, using his hand to stop the flow of blood coming from his nose.

"Oh and Eric?" he paused to look at me, "Don't ever let her name cross your lips in my presence again, do you understand me? Your resignation is optional, but at this point, strongly advised." He didn't say another word as he stormed out, slamming the door behind him. It took me a few minutes to calm down after he'd gotten me all riled up, but once I did, I shut him out of my mind and crawled back into bed, or so I thought.

Unlike my usual dream of Glo this time I had a nightmare. It started out like all the others with us in bed at the Bellagio making love, our bodies intertwined, hot and sweaty against each other, but once she collapsed in my arms I realized it wasn't me that she'd just made love to. It wasn't my name she'd been calling out. It was Eric. Aaaahhh!!!!

CHAPTER TEN

lmost everyone was at the winter walkabout. I tried to act like I barely noticed Hayden's absence, but I couldn't. Michael Beckford and Rosie did a good job of keeping me occupied though. He was actually really pleasant and easy to talk to. Rosie stayed with us the entire time and made the conversation very lively. Michael indulged her, but it was obvious where his interest lay, and that was with me. Max was on the slopes with the twins and Lindsay, so I didn't have to worry about him giving Michael attitude. Once we got back to the resort, my legs felt like dead weights in the snow boots. Rosie joked that she was going to head to the hot tub so that she could thaw out and asked if I wanted to join her, which sounded like a great idea, but then I remembered my arm, and thought I should stick to midnight swims. I declined, adding that I was ready for lunch and told her I would see her at dinner.

Once Rosie walked away Michael seemed almost relieved, gently holding my elbow to stop me in the lobby. "Would you like some company for lunch?"

"Umm, sure why not. Do you want to meet in the restaurant in thirty minutes or so? I have to get out of these wet clothes." I was smiling and thinking with some degree of excitement that I had just found my distraction.

"Sounds good to me, so I'll see you in a little while then," he replied tossing his room keys from one hand to another. I quickly went to my room had a hot shower and changed. I was brushing my teeth, when I heard the loud chirping of the walkie talkie on the fire place mantle. God I don't even know how to operate this thing. I pressed the button on the side.

"Hello."

"Ms. Strair?" came a woman's unfamiliar voice on the other end.

"Yes, Lindsay?"

"It's Lindsay. I ... we need help ...there's been ...an accident..."

"Accident? What accident? Where's Max? Where are you?"

"I ...can't hear you..."

"Where are you?" I screamed.

"The Slit."

"Is Max hurt?"

"They...fell..."

"Fell where? Who? Who fell?" *Oh God...I have to get to them.* "Tell me where you are Lindsay, I'm coming!"

"We're about ....a quarter mile down Slit... Throat Gulge...Call the ambulance..." *Ambulance? Slit Throat Gulge?* What was she talking about? My tears came then. I was frantic, running for my jacket and my snow boots.

"Lindsay, who else is with you?"

"...twins...Max...me...I think....battery...dying."

"Alright, don't talk anymore. Save the battery I'm coming!"

Once my shoes were on I was out the door and bolting down the stairs, since I couldn't wait for the elevator. I was sprinting to the front desk and almost like a scene from a bad movie; I tried to slow down, since my boots were still wet from the walkabout. I felt myself sliding and my arms were flailing at my sides as I tried to grip the counter, but missed and slipped. All I saw were my feet above me and my arms flapping at my side like some desperate bird. My head hit the floor with a loud thud. I swear I could hear something crack or snap. There were gasps all around, as the staff and lodgers ran to help me. A sharp pain instantly radiated up my spine where my tail bone had hit the floor. I wanted to get up, but for a moment I couldn't move. The air had been knocked out of me.

"Are you alright?" a woman asked as I tried to sit up.

Wincing in pain I told her I was fine, a definite lie. My head was throbbing as was my backside.

"You should stay put," someone else was saying as they pushed on my shoulder to get me to lie down. "That was a pretty hard fall."

"I'm fine! Please... I need your help. My son has had a fall... on Slit Throat Gulge. They're about a quarter mile down. There are four...of them all ...together...Lindsay the ski instructor is with them," I yelled barely able to catch my breath. Immediately there was a flurry of activity and people on the phone as two more managers helped me to my feet and asked me again what had happened and again I explained. When the third person asked, I lost it. "I can explain on the way there," I screamed. "We need to get to them now!"

"Ma'am, right now I need you to calm down," one man was saying in a soft voice.

"*I can't calm down,*" I said through clenched teeth. "My son is hurt and I need to get to him. Now either you help me or not, but I don't have time to explain it over and over again. We're wasting time!"

"Glory?" came a deep voice from behind me. It was Edward.

"Oh thank God, maybe you can help me. Max fell. The twins are with him. They just called me on the walkie talkie, but the battery was dying. I need to get to Slit Throat Gulge. He's hurt Edward!" A crowd was starting to form, but I didn't care. Harriet was beside me as Edward turned his attention to the desk.

"Did you call Hayden?" she asked, her eyes filled with worry.

"No, I didn't. I'm sorry. I just ran out of my room straight to the front desk. Can you call him for me?" I could barely think as my head continued to throb.

"Don't worry. I'll call him."

"Glory? What's going on?" I turned to find Michael. I quickly explained and he joined Edward at the desk. Within minutes we were waiting for snow mobiles to carry us up the mountain.

"Alright, load'em up!" yelled a man in a bright orange ski jacket with matching goggles across his forehead, once the four mobiles were there. "Ms. Strair we'll radio back as soon as we've found them!"

"Like hell you will. I'm going with you!" I snapped, pushing past him into the passenger seat.

"Ma'am it will be best if…"

"Bill we're going with you!" someone behind me yelled. It was Hayden, with one foot in his boot and the hood of his jacket between his teeth as he hopped to put on the other boot.

"H, you know this boy?"

"Yeah, he's my son!" There were gasps all around as the family members and friends there on the winter reunion started to gather in the lobby, looked around with puzzled looks on their faces. Michael was just as shocked, but I couldn't think about any of them just then. I needed to get to my son.

"Alright, let's go!"

Michael was behind Hayden heading to the back seat, but I saw Edward pull him back and whisper something. Michael looked at me with a smile and raised crossed fingers. I wondered why Edward didn't let him come, but right now that was the least of my concerns.

Once we were moving Bill asked, "Ma'am, what exactly did Lindsay say?" I went over the conversation again verbatim. He didn't look very pleased. "The Slit has been off limits for a month or two now," he said over his shoulder, directing his response more at Hayden that at me.

Hayden wanted to know why and Bill went on to say that some ground had given way six to eight weeks ago, and they didn't have time to evaluate it with the busy season starting, so they just blocked it off and put up signs that it was unsafe and off limits.

"Does Lindsay know this?" He knew exactly where I was heading with it.

"All our staff was notified," he replied, turning his attention back to the road. I felt even more ill as I leaned back against the head rest, which I attributed to being literally sick with worry. Then I felt a hand firmly squeeze my shoulder.

"Everything will be okay," Hayden whispered by my ear; it felt good having him there with me.

"I know. I'm sorry I didn't call you myself, but once I hung up with Lindsay all I could think of was getting help."

"It's alright, I understand. I'm just glad I'm here." I knew I was scared, but I felt physically ill. My back pain seemed to be getting worse and the seat in the snow mobile wasn't helping. I felt the urge to close my eyes, but I couldn't because I automatically saw worse case scenarios playing out in my mind, and I didn't want to think like that. Max was going to be fine. I kept saying it over and over again in my head until I looked out the window and saw how far up the mountain we were. *Slit Throat Gulge*? I swore I would kill Lindsay if anything happened to my son. We were stopping.

"Are we here?" I was looking around.

"No, not yet. This is as far as we can drive so we'll have to go the rest of the way on foot. You're more than welcome to stay…"

"No thanks Bill, I'm coming," I said without waiting for him to finish. "I promise I won't interfere."

"Fine let's get going!" He hurried over to his team and announced that most of the sink holes had been flagged, but that he was sure some weren't and we needed to keep an eye out. He thought they were about a mile or so from the location Lindsay gave. I started walking up the path.

"Glory!" Hayden was running to catch up to me. "You can't walk ahead. This can be dangerous; you need to stick with the team." He was smoothing my hair away from my face. There was something in his eyes as he looked at me. "You aren't even wearing a hat," he said with a smile, "here take mine," as he took it off and handed me his cream colored wool scully to put on.

"Thank you."

"There's no need to thank me. Are you cold? Your skin looks so pale?" I did feel a little cold, but who wouldn't considering how high we were. I was grateful for the hat pulling it over my ears.

"I am a little cold, but I'll be fine once I find Max."

"Okay, let's go," and he took my hand as the team swished by us. After we were walking a while the team started calling out for the kids and I took out the walkie talkie to call Lindsay. I tried 'chirping' her a couple times with no luck, and then I got a 'chirp' back.

"Ms…Strair?"

"Yes, Lindsay?"

"No this is Tomas…Lindsay…helping …Timothy and…"

"Honey, we're coming can you hear or see us?" Nothing. "Tomas, can you hear us?"

"Yes…I can…hear…you."

"Bill we must be close, they can hear us."

"Over here!" the farthest team member up front yelled. I started running then, Hayden was beside me. Bill was on the radio calling in our location and the others were pulling out ropes and medical supplies. I looked over the edge and there was a steep slope where anyone could've easily slid down, but there was no way to get back up without someone at the top pulling you. I could see Max and someone else lying on the floor. Lindsay had Max's head on her lap. Oh God!

"Maximus! Max! Are you alright?" I was yelling and Hayden was trying to pull me away from the edge. "Tomas, Timothy, are you both alright? Max? Talk to me!"

"Tim broke his leg!" yelled Tomas.

"Ms. Strair, I think Max is fine!" yelled Lindsay. "He may have a dislocated shoulder, but he's in a lot of pain."

"Max darling talk to me." Bill and Hayden were shouting out instructions for them and one man was already roped up and half way down the incline. Lindsay and Tom were able to climb up when they threw another rope over the side. Lindsay immediately ran into my arms. She was crying. "Ssshh, it's all right," I said rubbing her back. "Everything is going to be fine, we're here now. What happened?"

"I'm sorry…it wasn't my fault. I was taking them to a 'Blue' slope when Tim had the brilliant idea to try this slope. I tried…we all tried to stop him, but he wouldn't listen and took off. We waited a few minutes because there's a point on the blue slope where you can see people coming down the Slit, but he never passed it. We waited a little longer and that's when we figured out something was wrong. I wanted to call for help but Max and Tom didn't want to wait, so we went back. I tried calling you but I wasn't getting any answer until that last time.

"I must've been in the shower. I'm sorry."

"We found him and Max tried to get him, but Tom lost his footing and let Max go. Please don't be mad at him, he was just trying to help."

"I'm not mad. I'm just glad you're all safe!" I heard someone cry out in pain and when I looked, two members of the rescue team were splinting Tim's leg and trying to move him onto the crate to lift him up. Hayden was down there talking to Max. How did he get down there? I wanted to be the one down there. I tried not to be angry. It took thirty minutes to get them both up.

"Mom?"

"Yes darling?" I rushed to Max's side.

"I'm sorry!" his eyes were wet, but he wasn't crying. He looked so pale.

"It's okay. I'm glad you're fine. Broken bones we can fix… anything else…," I started to cry then. "Anything else I couldn't handle." I was kissing his face, his head, arms, chest, when Hayden gently pulled me away. Tim was lying on the ground next to Max and reached over and squeezed his hand.

"Thanks for coming to get me," Tim said and then turning his attention to me and the others he said, "This was all my fault, not Max or Lindsay or Tom's. I'm sorry." Hayden was reassuring him that everything would be fine and we'd all made stupid mistakes before, we just had to learn from them. Once everything was under control and Tim's leg was secured and Max's arm was wrapped we headed back down the mountain. Hayden wouldn't leave Max's side. I was still extremely light headed and nauseous, and if anything it seemed to be getting worse, but I tried not to focus on it.

Once we got back to the resort ambulances were waiting and the kids were rushed to the hospital a couple towns over. Hayden, his parents and I had to drive since we all couldn't fit, with Tom and Tim's parents following us. Hayden and his dad were in the front seat and Harriett and I were in the back. Something was wrong with me, I could feel it, but I didn't know what. I was cold, shivering almost and my head was still throbbing from my fall. The urge I had to just close my eyes and go to sleep seemed to be getting worse. I felt weak.

"Glory are you alright?" Harriett was asking as she rubbed my hands between hers. "You're awfully pale and your hands are so cold?"

"I don't feel well, but I'm sure I'll be fine once I get to the hospital with Max," I whispered fighting the urge to faint. My head was cold and I wondered if I'd gotten snow in my hair or under the scully so I slipped my hood off and took the hat off. Much to my surprise it was soaked with blood.

"My God Glory!   Where's all that blood from?" Harriett shouted, she turned my face towards her and I put my hand at the back of my head and felt the warm sogginess of my blood soaked hair. There were some clots in my hair, but the blood was still flowing.

"Blood? What blood?" Hayden was yelling, trying to keep his eyes on the road and still look at me through the rearview mirror. Edward turned to kneel in the front seat so he could help Harriett. Why didn't I notice it before? As I leaned back against the seat, under my jacket I could feel my sweater soaked where the blood was running down my back. I was so focused on finding Max that I hadn't realized that I was bleeding. I was sweating now as I continued to feel around the back of my head closing my eyes. I felt so tired, so weak.

"Glory open your eyes and look at me!" Harriett was yelling. "Oh God Hayden! You've got to hurry…"

"Glo, Glo, stay awake. Don't do this to me baby! Open your eyes! Baby…" that was the last thing I heard, then everything went black. He called me baby.

CHAPTER ELEVEN

My head was still throbbing although now it seemed to be more localized towards the back of my head as opposed to the all over throbbing I'd experience in Hayden's car. I could barely open my eyes as the bright florescent lights over me made it difficult.

"Mom, mom, it's Max!" He sounded distraught. I could feel him rubbing my hand and kissing my cheek. "Dad, Dad, mom's awake!" he was yelling. *Dad?* Oh right, somehow I was still hoping that it was all a bad dream. I squinted until the bright lights became bearable and then started to look around.

"Glo? It's me Hayden," they were both standing over me. What the hell happened? Why was I in the hospital?

"What's going on?"

"When you fell running to the front desk, you literally cracked your noggin. You were so caught up in finding Max that you barely noticed you were bleeding. You lost a lot of blood," Hayden was saying. He looked so worried. That's right Max, the fall!

"Oh God Max, are you alright? How's your shoulder?" I asked trying to sit up.

"Oh no you don't!" Hayden yelled. "You have to stay put!"

"Mom I'm fine. My shoulder is fine. You, on the other hand, I'm worried about."

"Oh sweetie, I'm so sorry. I didn't mean to make you worry. I… I just didn't realize how bad it was. How long have I been in here?"

"Since yesterday afternoon," said Max. I felt the bulky bandage around my head and immediately became embarrassed. My son had a snow boarding accident and I'm the one laid up in the hospital for tripping and hitting my head. Unbelievable! The doctor came in shortly after and gave me a status report. I got a mild concussion when I cracked my scull and lost a lot of blood thanks to my daily iron regiment. I required some stitches, thirteen to be exact, and there was some swelling, but in the long run there should be no permanent damage. I also had a bruised coccyx, tailbone, which would prove to be the most uncomfortable of my injuries. I would need to take it easy for the next week. The bandage couldn't get wet for 24 hours, and the stitches would dissolve in seven days. The doctor prescribed ample pain meds, but ice, ice and more ice was all he could recommend for my back along with the ibuprofen for the inflammation, blah, blah, blah. I stopped listening when I looked over at Hayden, who was listening intently to the doctor's every word with his arm around Max's shoulders. Even in my current condition he made my body quiver. As usual his thick black hair was disheveled and those dark eyes were definitely tired. Max was asking about restrictions on activities when the door opened and in walked Michael.

"The minute I leave to get coffee, you wake up?" he said with a smile. I was surprised he was even there. He leaned in and kissed my cheek. Whoa…did I miss something? I never had lunch with him. Did I?

"Umm, I'm fine really. I hope you didn't waste anytime waiting around here? It was just a little cut." I was embarrassed that he was so affectionate in front of Max. Hayden's face didn't change much, but his eyes told another story. He didn't like my interaction with Michael.

"It wasn't a waste of time," he said, and peering around my head added, "and that's more than a little cut. I needed to know you were alright." He was tenderly rubbing the back of my hand. I pulled away nervously and turned my attention to the short doctor staring at me.

"Dr. Smith do I need to stay here much longer?" I was eager to get out of my johnny and back into normal clothes.

"No. I want to check a couple more things and then you are free to go."

Those couple things took another two hours so it was almost three when we got back to the resort. Thankfully the bulky pressure bandage had been replaced by a smaller, not so noticeable one, so walking in public was fine. Michael wanted to go with me up to my room, but I insisted it wasn't necessary and that I would see him at dinner. Hayden stopped to speak to a manager at the front desk about something so Max and I went ahead to the elevator.

Once the door closed he asked, "Are you feeling alright?" just as I leaned against the wall and closed my eyes.

"Yes I'm fine, just a little tired I guess. How about you? How are you feeling? Did you stay at the hospital all night?" I moved a long curl away from his forehead.

"That's what I wanted to tell you before dinner. Dad's fiancée Lisa is here and she isn't thrilled that Dad refused to come back to the resort last night, on her first night here," he said with a twinge of satisfaction in his eyes.

"Really? Have you met her?" I questioned.

"Nope, not yet, but I can tell already that I don't like her." I couldn't help the tiniest bit of pleasure I felt hearing him say that, as we got off the elevator and walked down the hall towards our room. "Mom?"

"Yes love."

"I don't think Dad loves her."

I walked in and kicked off my shoes, heading for the bathroom. "Max I want you to stay out of it do you hear me? It's none of your…"

"Mom I know it isn't any of my business. I was just telling you. Jeeeze! I thought you would want to hear that, since you've been using the fact that he's marrying her as an excuse not be with him." Now he was becoming much too smart for his own good.

"Well you're wrong, and I don't want to hear anything about it. I don't care!" LIE. "Contrary to what you may think, I don't want to be with your father!" Another lie. I was on the express elevator straight to Hell after this weekend.

"Fine, I won't say anything about either of them again," he walked away with a pout.

"Alrightie then. Now I feel gross, so I'm going to take a shower."

"Remember you can't get the bandage wet."

"I remember Dr. Strair, Jr," I added with a laugh.

"Will you be fine if I go and see how the twins are doing? Tim came back last night."

"Umm sure. You're staying in the hotel right?"

"Yeesss mom," he drawled.

"Don't yessss mom me, Mr. Slit Throat Gulge," I said playfully hitting him on his arm. He started to laugh then. "I can't find my key, so don't forget to take yours that way you can get in. If I fall asleep, I don't want to have to wake up to get the door…I'm exhausted. I want to at least get a couple hours rest before heading down to dinner." He kissed me goodbye and then I got in the shower, letting the hot water pound against my body. My back was killing me, directly above my bottom was extremely sore, swollen, and tender to the touch. I just couldn't believe how much damage my fall did. When I got out and turned to look at myself in the mirror, I was shocked at how badly bruised I was. You would have thought I was the one that fell down the side of a mountain. Damn iron tablets! I looked like Barney's twin sister or like I got beat up by a giant eggplant. I gingerly slipped on my panties and snapped my bra around my waist to put it on as I walked out of the bathroom.

"How was your shower…," I was shocked as I faced Hayden in my underwear and exposed breasts. I wanted to move, but couldn't. I wanted to wrap myself in a towel, but couldn't. I wanted to say something, but couldn't. I was accustomed to having my own master bed and bathroom so privacy was never an issue, plus I knew Max was gone.

When it became obvious that I wasn't going anywhere he quickly turned away. "I'm sorry. I saw Max…by the elevator and he gave me his key… since you were in the shower. I'm sorry…I should've yelled to let you know I was out here…I was going to build you a fire and make sure you were all set…I brought you some ice. I can leave if you want me too," he was rattling off the words quickly with his back still turned to me. I couldn't answer. "Glory?" he said a little more loudly. I snapped out of what trance I was in and silently rushed back to the bathroom and put on my robe, pretending like it never happened. I didn't say anything, convincing myself that talking about it would only make it worse. When I walked out he had his hands stretched in front of him against the fire place mantle with his head down.

He turned around when he heard me come out of the bathroom and our eyes locked. "Thank you for all your help. I mean with Max and bringing me to hospital and so on. Max told…"

"You don't have to thank me. It was nothing. You scared…" There was a knock at the door and I abruptly turned away from the intensity of his gaze.

"Who is it?"

"It's Jeff and Clay." I fixed the front of my robe and opened the door. Clay went to swoop me up in his arms, but I backed away commenting that my back was killing me. They were going on and on about being so worried when Jeff noticed Hayden by the fire place.

"I'm sorry Hayden, I didn't know you were here. Were we interrupting something?" Jeff asked with a devious smile.

"No, not at all. I … I was just about to leave. Max went to visit the twins and I …well I just wanted to make sure Glory was comfortable and got some breasts…I mean…I meant rest," I could tell he was mortified as I saw the blush creep up his neck to his cheeks. I smiled inwardly at the thought that he was still thinking about my breasts. "I'll see you guys at dinner," he rushed, hurrying towards the door.

"Definitely," I said with a small smile. "Thanks again Hayden." And with that he passed us and walked out the door.

Clay and Jeff just kept looking from me to each other until they finally burst out with laughter. "Do I even need to ask what just happened?" Jeff asked between laughs.

"It's not what you think!" I too started to blush, shoo'ing at them with my hands as they followed me over to the sitting area.

Jeff was the first to cut to the chase. "There's a vicious rumor spreading around this resort."

"Do you care to shed some light?" Clay added.

"Is Hayden really Max's father?" Jeff pressed jumping right into the gossip as he got comfortable on the sofa. God I'd forgotten how nosey these two could be. In the beginning of our relationship they were worse, but as time went on they realized that I didn't like 'man-questions' and backed off. This time an explanation couldn't be avoided. I took the next half hour and told them the full unedited version of how I met Hayden. I trusted Jeff and Clay completely, plus he knew about my Aunt Miranda's business, just not of my involvement, so it wasn't difficult for me to tell them what I'd done. Once the initial shock went away, all he could say was what a small world it was and that he couldn't believe how all this time he was so close to me and it never came up or that I never met the Weiss' or Hayden for that matter.

"Do you love him?" I couldn't believe he'd gone straight to the big question like that and for the first time in four days I was compelled to tell the truth.

"Yes, but if you tell anyone I'll deny it till I die. He's about to marry someone and Max is already getting his hopes up." I was frustrated and for the first time completely unhappy. I don't know who I was kidding, but I wanted that man more than I'd wanted anything before in my life.

"I can tell you right now that he isn't going to marry Lisa Steller," Clay interjected with some degree of disdain.

"Why does everyone keep saying that? He wouldn't have asked her if he really didn't want too."

"Because it's the truth. Hayden has turned a blind eye to all her transgressions for far too long and the time is fast approaching when he'll leave that tramp high and dry! She has more issues than a newsstand. He doesn't love her and he never did…"

"Maybe seeing you was what he needed," Clay interjected. We talked, or should I say they did most of the talking, as I continued to periodically shoot down their theories of Hayden and Glory together forever out of the sky. I knew I wasn't fooling them as I silently hoped that one day we *would* be one big happy family and live happily ever after. I just didn't want to have anything to do with him leaving Lisa. He would have to do that on his own, my conscience couldn't handle being the cause of their break up.

It was after five when they left so I could get some rest before dinner. Clay made a joke that they would leave me to get some breasts and that just ignited another eruption of laughter, but they finally left. I had no luck trying to sleep, since everyone and their mother called to see how I was feeling, Michael, Eric, Rosie, the Weiss', Hayley, and the Nealands'. I was doing a great job of staying ahead of my pain, but thought I should ice my back to help with some of the swelling. Max came up from visiting the twins around 6:30, but was in the shower getting ready for dinner, so I decided to walk down the hall and get some more ice, since I'd already used the bucket Hayden brought earlier. *Hayden, Hayden, Hayden*...he enveloped my thoughts, which just made me want to pursue things with Michael even more. He was moving on with his soon-to-be wife, so why shouldn't I? I mean Michael seemed nice enough and definitely had sex appeal from what I'd learned from Rosie, so it was safe to say that if given the opportunity he could most certainly distract me.

I opened the first door I came to and immediately came face to face with a man and woman in a compromising position in the throws of having sex. All I could see of the woman was a pile of blonde hair, since her face was buried in a stack of folded towels. Her black halter sequined dress was yanked up around her waist and her bottom lifted up in the air as she stood on one foot with her left knee up on the counter. Her lover was in a black suit with his trousers and briefs dropped around his ankles standing behind her with one hand on her left hip and the other hand firmly holding her thong underwear in place off to the side of her bottom. I could tell they were at a critical point from the look on his face and the noises she was making when I entered. When the door opened it took a second, which seemed like an eternity, for him to stop what he was doing and look up at me in complete shock.

"Oh God, I'm sorry...I was looking for...for the ice machine," I said quickly closing the door and biting my bottom lip to stop the laugh building in my stomach. I looked up and the sign on the door read 'LINEN CLOSET' and the door next to it said 'ICE AND VENDING MACHINES'. I wanted to kick myself for being so careless, blaming it on my thinking about Hayden as I hurried to fill my ice bucket, but then I thought, what the hell are they doing screwing in a linen closet anyway? They're staying in a hotel for

Pete's sake that's the point of getting a room isn't it, I thought in disgust. I hurried back to my room before they came out, regretting my brisk walk when I felt my back start to literally throb.

"Mom, where did you go? Are you alright?"

I closed the door. "I'm fine. I went to get more ice and…I think was walking too quickly down the hall." He was upset, arguing that I should've let him go as he struggled to button his shirt with his one good arm, so I helped him. After I assured him that it was fine and told him to head down without me. It would take a while for me to get ready since I wanted to keep the ice pack on for twenty minutes, so I would probably be a little late getting to dinner. After ten minutes of him protesting, he finally went down without me. Once I iced my back and drugged myself, I felt much better so I freshened up and heading down the elevator by eight. Tonight I elected to go with a simple ivory pants suit and gold shoes sporting a low and appropriate 'baby-doll' heel. My filthy hair was tucked into a tight chignon at the base of my neck.

As soon as I entered the dining room, heads started to turn and I was sure the announcement about Max had already been made. For the first time in my life I was embarrassed, not of Max, but of the situation and how others now perceived me. I felt I had gone from being a fantastic doctor with a wonderful son, to the woman who got pregnant on a one-night stand with Hayden Weiss, but happened to now be a doctor. Rosie was the first to run up to me to see how I was feeling and officially welcomed me to family. She said we would have to talk later, which meant she had some gossip for me. I had to smile as she lowered her voice like everything she was saying was top secret. She gave me a genuine hug, kissed my cheek and hurried off once we made plans to spend the following day together. I was stopped by a few more people before I made it up to my table, all concerned with how I was feeling. My seat beside Jeff was taken so I ended up sitting with my back to the Weiss' table. I had barely sat down when the twins' parents came over to thank me for all my help and to praise Max for going back to help Tim, pretty much reiterating everything they'd said when they called up to my room. They added that the boys had been raving about Max since Friday, so they were hoping once we got back to New York we could all get together. I told them it wouldn't be a problem. Max came back to the table from wherever he was and gave me a huge hug. The wait staff was just bringing out the main course when I leaned into Clay and asked how the announcement went. He said it hadn't been much of an announcement since the shit kind of hit the fan yesterday with

Hayden's declaration in the lobby before we left to find Max - *his son*. He said for the most part everyone was thrilled, commenting on Max's looks and all the good things they'd heard about you. I felt a little better, but I was still uncomfortable. It seemed like I was the center of everyone's conversation, from the looks I was getting and the impromptu walks pass my table.

Dinner was wonderful as usual and went without a glitch. The majority of the guests had already left our table and were heading for the dance floor, when Jeff started making trouble, scooting over to the empty chair beside me.

"Aren't you going to go over and introduce yourself to Lisa?" he asked with a sideways glance.

"Uh no!" I replied through clenched teeth. "Are you mad? Why, do you think I should?" I questioned.

"I don't know, although I may be inclined to say yes, knowing the type of person you are," he paused for a minute and looked up. "Well it doesn't look like you'll have to do that after all since they're coming over."

"Coming over where? Here?" I asked immediately planting a fake smile across my face.

"Yes…" He became quiet when Edward stepped up to hug me.

"Glory, you must have slipped in under the radar. We didn't even see you come in," he said squeezing my shoulders. It hurt like hell, but I didn't say anything.

"Well it certainly didn't feel that way," I said with a smile. "It felt as if everyone's eyes were on me!"

"They were probably looking at how beautiful you are," Max said with a straight face, while everyone else laughed. That boy really knew how to drop one-liners that grabbed everyone's attention into a conversation.

"Thank you dear," I said reaching over to pinch his cheeks. "That's why I pay you the big bucks. Flattery will get you everywhere Mr. Slit Throat Gulge!" Again there was another eruption of laughter.

"You're never going to let me live that down are you?" he chuckled.

"Probably not!" I said with a smile. Everyone was still laughing. Hayley was the one that ended up bringing us back to reality.

"Glory we're being rude. Let me introduce my husband Brian Rafferty and Hayden's fiancée Lisa Steller, the last of the Weiss family left for you to meet." I stood up to greet them looking around for the first time; the shock that played across my face was obvious at once. I immediately recognized her blonde curls, black sequined halter dress and his face. Brian and Lisa had been the couple in the linen closet!

CHAPTER TWELVE

*B*rian was holding out his hand to shake mine, as was Lisa, but I couldn't bring myself to shake theirs. *I* unfortunately knew exactly where their hands had been.

"Mom?" Max was nudging me.

"Glory are you all right?" Harriett was asking.

I think Brian was the first to put two and two together when he saw the look on my face. He recognized me as well, although there was something more familiar about him than the fact I'd seen him less than two hours ago with his pants down having sex with his soon-to-be sister-in-law. I had seen him before tonight, but I didn't know from where. He quickly dropped his hand, but Lisa still had hers outstretched, I could tell the stupid wench didn't know who I was. Oh yeah, that's right she was too busy stuffing her face into a pile of terry cloth!

"Mom, umm I think Ms. Steller is trying to shake your hand," Max tried to say as discretely as possible.

"Thanks for pointing out the obvious dear," I mumbled under my breath, noticing the room had quieted down significantly. I continued to blatantly ignore her outstretched hand, looking her straight in the face. "So let me get this straight. You're Hayden's fiancée, soon-to-be sister-in-law of Hayley, right?" She snapped her arm back to her side, when it became painfully obvious I had no intention of taking it, and not waiting for her response I continued turning my attention to Brian, "And *you're* Hayley's husband and Hayden's brother-in-law. Do I have that right?" He was becoming uncomfortable as I saw the beads of sweat start to form on his upper lip. His eyes turning to slits as he glared at me. If he could've ripped my head off right there he would have.

"I can tell you right now that it's not a good sign when you can't even shake the hand of your son's father's wife!" Lisa snapped as she stood with her hands on her hip and a look of disbelief across her face. Her eyes were like daggers, but that didn't faze me. My Aunt had often tried the glaring tactic with me, but it always failed.

"Fiancée!" I snapped back for clarification. "You aren't married yet. And you're right; it is a bad sign, but a sign nonetheless!" Everyone was appalled and looking from Lisa back to me. I could feel Jeff pressing into the back of my thigh. What was I doing? Let it go Glory, it's none of your business, what do you care who any of them are sleeping with. But his wife is eight months pregnant for

Christ's sake. Dirt bag! Brian was obviously still the one with a functioning brain, who tried to change the subject.

"Maybe this isn't the place..." Hayden began, but Brian interrupted him.

"Do I know you from some where; you seem very familiar to me?" Wrong question ass-wipe!

"Yeah, I think we met by accident a little earlier in the linen closet!" Then it was like light dawning over Marblehead as Lisa's eyes became wide with the realization of who I was. "Max give me your room key!" I snapped and once he put it in my hand I stormed off.

These people were unbelievable. He was actually sleeping with his brother-in-law's wife? I think I was still in shock as I waited for the elevator back up to my room, impatiently pressing the 'up' button when Hayden ran up beside me.

"What the fuck just happened in there!" he growled not trying to be discreet. "What's going on with you? Am I missing something?"

"Nothing's going on, ask your wife and your brother-in-law," I snapped. "Devo ter à esquerda aqui quando tive a possibilidade!" I continued grumbling under my breath.

"What? What are you saying?"

"I said I should've left here when I had the chance!" Why was I so angry? Why did I even care? Because she was hurting the man I loved, that's why. Because I would kill for what she had and she was screwing another man! I had to get away from these people. I had to get my son away from them. I was pressing the button again. "Damn it, hurry up!" I said as the tears began to painfully form in my throat. I was directing my anger at the elevator as I leaned into the button.

"Glory, calm down. Please tell me what's wrong." He was gently pulling my hand away, looking at me with those eyes; those eyes that made me melt inside, and almost on queue the elevator in front of me opened and I rushed in leaving him alone in the lobby. What was wrong with me? I could feel the tears burning my eyes. You know how you feel when you're so mad but can't do anything about it? All I could do was cry, as I shook uncontrollably. It had only happened once before during my residency when I had the urge to punch the lights out of a sexist attending physician on staff at the hospital. He'd said the wrong thing to me far too many times, constantly overlooking me for cases, and belittling me in front of staff and patients. I was crying so hard I couldn't even see to swipe the key to my room. I just felt so helpless. I had grown accustomed to being in control of all aspects of my life, but over these past four days, my self control seemed to be snatched away from me.

My night with Hayden in Las Vegas had been the last time I felt like I wasn't in control of a situation, even though the experience made me stronger and more confident. I had always known that boys found me attractive, but after that night with him and the way he looked at me, I knew that contrary to the way my Aunt had always made me feel and treated me, that I was a desirable woman who didn't need to hide behind school ever again.

When I found out I was pregnant, my world should've, but didn't come crashing down. There wasn't even a blip on the screen of Glory Strair's life. Maybe God knew that deep down inside I was lonely. My pregnancy simply wasn't an issue, I would deal with it. Everything happened for a reason. Even if it took fifty years, I would become a surgeon. I had lost both parents at a relatively young age and never felt the way I was feeling right at this minute. Between seeing Hayden again, Max's near death experience, my aching body, and what I'd found out tonight about Lisa, I was completely overwhelmed. I needed to get back to my element. I needed to go home. I needed to save lives and feel like Dr. Strair again, as opposed to the girl that got knocked up by Hayden Weiss. I collapsed on my bed, ignoring the pain that consumed my body once I did so. There was a knock at the door.

"Go away!"

"Glory it's Jeff, open the door!"

"No Jeff, please go away. Not now, alright? Not now." There was some silence as though he was measuring the degree of seriousness in my voice.

"Alright dear, I'll leave you alone for now."

The message light on my phone was flashing and I inched over to retrieve it, my back willing me to stay put. My prayers had been answered one of the messages was from Becca telling me that one of my patients needed surgery and wouldn't consent to having Dr. Nolte do it. She wanted me to call and convince the patient that he was more than capable of performing the surgery. Like hell I would, I had my out. The only thing was that I knew Max wouldn't be happy; and as many issues as I was having with the entire situation, I didn't have the right to take this experience of being with his father away from him. I knew Jeff wouldn't mind watching him and with Hayden here, I'm sure he would be fine.

The other message was from Eric apologizing for his behavior and telling me something had come up and he had to head back to the city. I hung up and called Becca at home, telling her I would be back in the office by tomorrow afternoon and to try and schedule an OR when she got in. She didn't hide how upset she was that I was coming back after only a few days, but I couldn't care less how mad she was. I abruptly hung up and called the front desk asking if there were any adjoining suites available next to Jeff's room and luckily there was. After my fall, I think they were trying to be as accommodating as possible. I would propose to Max that he stay by himself in an adjoining room from Jeff's. There was another knock at the door as I hung up from with the front desk.

"Yes!"

"Mom it's me!" I was glad it was Max, I gingerly walked over and opened the door. "What happened down there? Are you okay? I mean she doesn't seem like the nicest person, but you were downright rude." He began rambling on and on as soon as I opened the door, but I had already turned away, dragging my empty suitcases out of the closet, and tossing the largest one on Max's bed. "Where are you going? What's the suitcase for?" I could tell he was getting more upset by the minute. "Mom, answer me. I don't want to leave!"

"You aren't leaving Max. I am. I got a call from the office and they need me for a case…"

"What? That's a lie, you just want to leave."

"No it isn't! Becca called a little while ago. I just got off the phone with her at home."

"Why can't they find someone else to do it? You aren't the only surgeon in the world you know! I'm sure if you told Uncle Jeff he could put a call in. I mean…you've only been gone three days and they call you already! This is our real first vacation ever…"

"I know, I know, that's why you're going to stay. I've arranged for you to stay in an adjoining room from Jeff and Clay, and with your Dad here I'm sure you won't even miss me." I pretended to busy myself with emptying the dresser.

"Of course I'll miss you! Do you realize my birthday is next week and for the first time since I can remember, you have the opportunity to spend it with me and you won't?"

"I do realize next week is your birthday and we'll celebrate once you get back to New York. Your Dad and grandparents are going to throw you a huge party…."

"Don't you want to be here for any of it? You don't understand…"

"Max, you don't need me here. We'll do something together when you get back!"

"You're running! That's what this is all about. You can't handle being so close to Dad, so you're going to run away. And you preach to me about quitting?" It wasn't what he said as much as how he said it that made me stop in my tracks.

"Pardon me? Max, I suggest that you stop right there before you say something that gets you in serious trouble." My head was killing me and I honestly didn't have the energy to get into it with him right now. "You're right...I *can't* handle this. So much has happened in the past few days that I honestly feel completely overwhelmed. I don't want to be here. I don't want to be introduced to Hayden's fiancée and pretend like everything is alright. I don't want to spend the next two weeks avoiding Eric. I want to go home. Now, all of that being said, I still know how much being with your father means to you, so that's why I want you to stay. I trust Jeff..." there was another knock at the door. "*Jesus Cristo!*" I said through clenched teeth. "Who is it?" I yelled, not trying to hide my annoyance.

"Glory it's me. Hayden." Before I could answer Max had already turned around and headed to open the door.

"Great, come on in!" I mumbled rolling my eyes. I continued putting clothes in my suitcase, trying to seem as though I didn't care that he was there.

"What's going on? Where are you going?"

"She's leaving," Max grunted.

"Leaving? Why?" I didn't answer and continued what I was doing, until he walked up behind me and gently turned me to face him. "Why are you leaving?" I hated being so close to him. I couldn't think. I hated the fact that he sounded so sincere. I squirmed out of his arms and walked to the closet. The sensation of tingling skin where he'd touched me still remained.

"They need me for a case at the hospital," I said nervously.

"Bullshit! You've only been here, what three, four days?" he protested.

"That's what I told her," Max interjected.

"Listen, both of you, I've already told Max that he can stay. I've gotten him an adjoining room next to Jeff and Clay. I don't want to spoil your time together. You two should be spending as much time as possible together anyway, without me lolly-gagging around, cracking my skull and such," I added with a weak laugh.

"What about Max's birthday?"

"She said that we would do something together when I got back to New York," Max said, each word was thickly coated with his attitude.

"Glory please don't leave. I feel terrible that I've made this trip so unbearable for you. I promise I'll …"

"This has nothing to do with you," I lied. "The only reason I'm leaving is because they need me at the hospital, so don't you think for one minute this has anything to do with you! I really don't see what the problem is, aren't you glad Max is staying?" I asked, switching the focus away from me.

"Of course I am. I just…I don't want you to leave is all."

"Well I'm sorry, but don't worry, you've got Lisa here to keep you company," and turning my attention to Max I said, "You can always come back with me if you don't want to stay."

His frown deepened and the tears that were threatening to fall finally did.

"Oh I want to stay. I just can't believe you're going to run away. I didn't want to picture you like this. For once, just once in my life, I want you to prove to me that I'm as important to you as you keep saying. You say everything you do is for me, but that's a lie. You can't prove it because it isn't true." I think I physically cringed from the bitterness in his tone. He was crying and screaming hysterically as Hayden tried to stop him, but he just kept talking.

"It's for *you*; it's always been about you, being the best student, the best resident, the best doctor, and the best surgeon. It's never been about being the best mom. Not once has it ever been about me and what I want! If you want to leave, then go. I don't care anymore at least now I have someone who really cares about me and can give me the attention I deserve. I'm going back downstairs to leave you to your packing." He stormed out of the room, with Hayden calling after him. I was dumbfounded.

On any other day what he'd just said would've crushed me, but not today. I was too focused on the task at hand for my feelings to be hurt. It really didn't matter how mad he was at me. I couldn't stay.

"Please don't do this," Hayden was saying as he let the door close. "You have no idea how much being on this trip with you means to him. I know you and Max don't get the opportunity to go away much. I promise I won't call or bother you again and we can even set up times when Max and I get together."

My vocal cords were tight with the tears I wouldn't dare let fall as I hissed at Hayden. "And like I said before, my leaving has nothing to do with you. Don't think for one minute that because you've spent *two whole* days with us that you can presume to know anything about our family and how much this trip means to Max. I can't… no, let me rephrase that, I *won't* stay here! Now you can do one of two things, either take advantage of this great opportunity for you and Max to have some quality time together and bond, *or* you can let him come back with me. It's that simple. He'll be mad for a couple of days, but I'm sure he'll get over it. What will it be?"

"He can stay." His voice was barely audible.

"Good, now if you'll excuse me I have some packing to do." I had already turned my attention back to my packing as I heard him open the door. There was a pause. My heart was breaking into countless little pieces. I had no idea what I was doing or why I was so angry with Hayden when it was really Lisa and Brian that were the problem; or was it really *me* that was the problem?

"You know, never in a million years would I have thought this would be how our first interaction with each other would be like; especially after all this time apart and what we shared. I've never experienced *anything* like what you and I had together in Las Vegas, and you say you don't regret it, but you've done nothing to make me think otherwise." Sadness coated his every word. "This isn't my fault Glory. I fell into this just like you did, but I'm trying to make the best of it. I *want* to make the best of it." By now I couldn't move. My heart wouldn't let me put a single article of clothing into the suitcase, it hurt so much. I still couldn't face him.

"You were right; you *are* a completely different woman from the one that laid in my arms that night. You listen to people's hearts on a daily basis and you save lives, but you stopped listening to *yours* a long time ago." I could feel my body tense up with each word that came out of his mouth. "What's unfortunate is that you've failed to realize that your relationship with Max is slipping away in the process. And maybe that's partly my fault, since you had Max to think about and couldn't focus on *your* personal wants or needs for such a long time. So for that, I apologize." His breath was raspy as I hear him trying to control the emotions. "Being a single parent isn't easy and I'll never pretend to understand what the past twelve years have been like for you. I don't know what you're running from or running to, but I hope you find it because as God is my witness, I am not going anywhere. You will just have to find a way to tolerate me. I don't know what I have to do to prove to you that it doesn't have to be like this. But maybe this is the way you want it, in which case I'll respect that." He paused and I thought for a moment he'd left, as my shoulders slumped forward.

"Max is wrong. I think everything you've ever done in your career and otherwise has always been for him and making *his* life better. You didn't want him to have to struggle like you did, so you sacrificed your time to be the best you could be and no one in their right mind will fault you for that. But this right here, what you're doing right now isn't about Max, it's about you and I'm really sorry that it has to be like this," and with some degree of finality he silently closed the door.

He was gone and my heart truly ached as I let the tears pour out of me.

CHAPTER THIRTEEN

The day Glory left, I made it a point to avoid the lobby until I was sure she was gone. I felt terrible because even with Max there, I was still miserable at the thought that she wasn't. But I did a good job pretending to barely notice her absence, spending most of my days with Max and avoiding any remote chance of being intimate with Lisa.   She wasn't pleased, but all I needed was a couple more days before I would have all the information that I needed to bury Brian for good and her right along with him. Hayley was having a harder time. I had seen her brushing him off when he tried to kiss her or touch her stomach. It was taking every ounce of my will power not to attack him and rip his heart out right there in the snow. Hail was right, now that I knew they were sleeping with each other, the signs of their infidelity just seemed to jump out at you. His hands would linger on her back or arms if they were talking or if he was helping her to her seat. Lisa's body was familiar with his touch. At one point when he thought no one was looking, I could swear I saw him lean over, pretending to tell her something at the dinner table, and take her earlobe in his mouth. Bastard!

I made it clear to Lisa the night she came in that I didn't want to talk about the engagement; we could discuss it later in the week once I had a chance to put everything into perspective. I wanted to bide my time so I could get the proof, pictures, video, etc that I needed to crush them. Just like I anticipated, she was obedient. I knew the *last* thing she wanted was to lose me, but it was already too late. The secret passenger on our plane apparently got more than enough photos to last a lifetime; they gave new meaning to the mile high club. The plane wasn't fully in the air before those two closed themselves off from the crew, stripped their clothing off, and had raw *unprotected* sex on every surface of *my* plane for the duration of the flight. Thinking about it made my stomach queasy.

Thankfully my P.I. was on the right side of the door to see was what going on. They had close to eleven months worth of security video from my building so denying it was out of the question. Eleven months!   I think I was still in shock. I had them hook, line, and sinker.

After Glory left the resort I questioned Lisa about what Glory mentioned the night before about a linen closet, but she said she had no idea what Glory was rambling about and that the entire exchange just reiterated the fact that she was crazy. But I knew differently. Something had upset her; I could see it in her eyes at the elevator, but what? That bothered me for the first day or two and then I had to redirect my thoughts to the tasks at hand.

My lawyer was in the process of reviewing Hayley's prenup and assured me everything would be in order. I was to collect all the physical proof I could and bring it to his office on my return to the city, at which point we would arrange a meeting with Brian. I would have all the paper work and supporting documents when we got back to the city. A large fully furnished four bedroom penthouse apartment was being decorated in one of my newer buildings while Hayley and I were in Colorado for us to move into once we got back to New York. My things were being moved out of my current apartment and Hayley's things were being brought over from her house. The wheels were in motion. Both Lisa and Brian were here so they were clueless as to what was going on. There was no way in hell, once this was over, that I was going back to my old apartment or that Hail was going home with that rat. This living arrangement would be even better since the new apartment was closer to Glory and Max.

I filled Hayley in on Friday evening before we left and after the initial shock of everything sank in, she was ready to sign the papers on Monday and walk out of his life forever. I was looking forward to 'taking care' of her. The past few months had been uncomfortable for me since I didn't know why she was so upset with me, but now I felt as though things were almost back to normal. My parents would have to find out, but that was also a part of my plan. Once my father finds out about Brian's promiscuities, he might as well move to another continent, because he would be finished in New York, and on the entire east coast for that matter. Hayley was fine with Brian's demise as long as no one found out about her 'condition'.

I had to play it safe with both Lisa and Brian; they were sneaky people, although not quite smart enough. I didn't want them catching wind of my plans before the right time.

I also needed to keep my eye on Michael Beckford. I knew he was asking around about Glory and I'd caught him talking to Max a couple of times, but he made his father proud by being as tight-lipped as a nun in a strip bar. The moment he introduced himself to her at dinner, I knew he would be a problem. Confirming my suspicions, my favorite cousin Rosie told me he wanted Glory's telephone number and to know where she hung out. Hung out? She was one of, if not the best, cardiac surgeon in New York, and he wanted to know where she *hung out*? That only reiterated my previous assumption that he'd always been a party-going socialite, living off of his daddy's money. Don't get me wrong, he was a cool person, but I had a pet peeve about able-bodied individuals who refused to work and he was definitely 'able-bodied'. Eric was out of the picture and Glory was now available, and I wanted to keep it that way. For Michael's sake I hope he didn't interfere.

CHAPTER FOURTEEN

$\mathcal{N}$o one tried to hide their disappointment that I was leaving the resort early. Max disappeared before I left that morning and Jeff was furious, threatening to make me take a mandatory leave from the hospital if I kept this up.

The Weiss' were also upset making it clear they didn't approve of how I'd handled my introduction to Lisa and Brian. But what could I say to them? How could I explain what I'd seen? I listened and I apologized, offering no reason for my behavior. And although they were angry, they didn't give me a hard time about it.

I left without seeing Hayden, which was probably for the best since I hated how I had behaved towards him and the things that were said.

Once I got back, Max and I spoke daily. He seemed to be having fun and looking forward to his party the following week, but I could tell his disappointment was still there. It didn't take much to fill my days at the hospital and I knew my patients were truly grateful that I was back. As usual, I threw myself into work taking on extras cases in the emergency room when I could. I worked through the persistent pain in my back and constant dull headache until I barely noticed them anymore. I did everything I could not to think about Hayden, but nothing helped. I wanted to ask about him whenever I talked to Max, but I held back and he never volunteered any information either. Max could be just as stubborn as I was.

For his birthday I decided I would send his two friends, Patrick and Rory, down with their parents for a couple days, that way he would have some of his old friends there. Their parents were also thrilled since that resort was fairly exclusive and reservations were only granted to past guests and their referrals, that's where the Weiss' came in. When I asked Harriett about them coming, she also thought it was a great idea, so we were all set. I had my gift of new snowboarding equipment and attire, along with a funny t-shirt that read 'I MADE IT HALF-WAY DOWN SLIT THROAT GULGE!!!' delivered to the resort. Harriett said she would make sure they were wrapped and delivered to Max in a timely fashion. I called him early that morning to wish him a happy birthday, but he had already left with Hayden, who had a huge day of events planned for Max and his friends. Once again I could feel my green monster rearing its ugly head, but I had made my bed and now would have to lie in it. There was a knock at my office door jolting me back to reality and away from the thoughts of the last two weeks.

"Come in." It was Becca. "What's up?"

She had made it quite clear that she was mad at me for coming back and was giving me the silent treatment for the past two weeks. But like I said before, I couldn't care less. I was accustomed to people not liking me or being the only one in the room with no one to talk to. It had been a long time since I'd been in that position, but I was no stranger to it, nonetheless.

I was close and friendly with all my staff, but I would have to say I was closest to Rebecca since we were both single parents. I understood why she was upset and I wish I could talk to her about this whole ordeal, but I was her boss and I just didn't feel comfortable.

"I called over to the ER like you requested and they don't have any cases lined up and even if they did, they have two cardiologist on call. So you can go home tonight," she said matter-of-factly.

"Ummm, I guess I'll have to. Thank you. Have a nice weekend." I turned my attention back to my computer screen, even though I had been looking at the same page for the last hour.

"Dr. Strair…Glory, can I talk to you for minute?" She stepped further into my office and closed the door before I could respond.

"Of course you can. What's going on?"

"I was hoping you could tell me. I don't know what's going on with you, but you're going to run yourself into the ground." A deep frown began to form on her brow, "You know, up until last week I would've said to anyone that we were friends…"

"We are…" I quickly interjected.

"Then listen to what I have to say as a friend and not as an employee. You are, without a doubt, one of the best surgeons in this hospital, everyone knows that. But in an effort to run from whatever you're running from, you're letting this practice consume your life! You're hiding behind it." Now standing beside my desk, she took a deep breath and continued, "Number one - You're setting a bad precedent for your patients and ruining things for the other doctors at this hospital when you come to your patients' beckoned call, knowing full well that no other physician would do it. On one hand, the patients see how dedicated you are to them but on the other hand, your actions undermine the efforts of the other doctors, and that's not fair. The other doctors trust you with their cases when they're away, but it doesn't look as though you can do the same. Number two - you need to go home, this office has been your bedroom and dining room for the past week and a half and don't think for a minute that the staff haven't noticed. You have a son that's growing like weed and you're missing it."

She paused and took a deep breath then started again. "Now I know you don't have a lot of people close to you, but I would hope that you feel comfortable enough to talk to me, if you need to." Looking around the room, she said, "This isn't healthy Glory. Do you want to tell me what happened in Colorado that has you all tied up in knots, not wanting to face anything outside these hospital walls. I really want to help you. Is Max alright?"

"Max is better than alright," I choked. "I'm sorry if I've been hard to work for lately. I've just had a lot on my mind."

"It's alright. We've worked together now for six years and in all that time you've been an absolute joy to work for and a good ear when I needed it; now it's my turn to be that ear you need. Talk to me." She pulled a chair close to the desk.

"Do you remember the Weiss's?"

"Of course I do. They were the ones who invited you to Colorado weren't they? You operated on Edward."

"Yes. I'll make a long complicated story, short and to the point…"

"Don't. I don't have to be anywhere in particular and everyone has already left, so you can talk to me all night if you want to."

"Really? You don't mind?" I asked as she pulled her chair even closer to me, making me feel more at ease.

"Really. It's about time you cried on my shoulder. For years I've been the one complaining and crying about school or Jared or his father. It's your turn,' she said with a smile.

I took her up on her offer, one hour and a box of tissues later she knew everything, including why I left the resort.

"Wow…I mean…wow!" She was massaging her temples as she closed her eyes.

"I know, I know …tell me about it right?" I said blowing my nose. "Now do you have any pearls of wisdom?"

"I have a couple, but I guess the first thing I need to know is if you love him. Do you think he's the one you're meant to be with for the rest of your life?" she asked, searching my eyes for an answer.

"I do love him and I can't see myself being with anyone else, but I'm scared. I've really only spent one night with this man and I don't want this decision to be based solely on phenomenal love making."

"I agree, so you're going to have to get to know him some more."

"But he's engaged to…" she interrupted me abruptly,

"Listen, from what you've told me about what everyone has been saying, and based on what you saw, there is no way in hell he's going to marry her. So the only thing you need to focus on is if you want him or not."

"I do, more than I care to admit."

"Then it's simple, while you wait for things to unfold between Hayden and Lisa go on a few dates with someone. That way it doesn't look like you have no social life at all. Besides, if he feels the same way, which I think he does, then seeing you date someone else may hurry up whatever he plans on doing with Lisa. If it doesn't go as I suspect it will, at least you will already be dating someone," she added with a little laugh. "There is more to life than this practice Glory and you need to start acting like it. I know you have a ton of responsibilities, but you're young and Max is right. We'll start with finding a date, which shouldn't be hard for you, but the bottom line is you need to get out more!" She was playfully swaying her hips from side to side and winking. "Do you know what I mean?" Wink, wink.

"I have an idea," I responded with a laugh. Soon after that we had what sounded like a promising plan. She was right all I needed to do was find that 'someone'. I hugged and thanked her for listening and giving me advice. She'd been through enough things with Jared's father to have quite a few tricks up her sleeve. It felt good to talk to her. Actually, it felt good just to talk, instead of keeping all my feelings bottled up inside.

"So what are you going to do this weekend?" She was slipping on her coat.

"I think I'm going to take it easy and actually relax this weekend. Maybe do some shopping or something."

"That sounds great! So I'll see you Monday afternoon then, since you have those two cases in the morning."

"Yep, Monday afternoon," we hugged again and she left.

I was able to actually do some work on an article I was writing before I headed home. Talking about my life actually made me feel a lot better. My thoughts didn't seem as selfish when I heard them out loud; up until that point, I didn't realize how unhealthy it was to keep all my feelings bottled up inside. But it wasn't like I could talk to Max about my feelings.

I pulled into the garage at home and turned the car off, closing my eyes. I missed Maximus. I think this was the longest we'd ever been apart. I could hear the phone inside the house ringing so I quickly got out and ran inside. The answering machine was already on, but I picked up anyway.

"Hello?"

"Uh Glory?"

"Yes, this is she. Who is this?"

"Umm, this is Michael Beckford, you know from Colora…"

"I know exactly who you are."

"I'm sorry to call so late, but…"

"That's fine, but how…how did you get my number." I was guessing Harriett Weiss.

"I…umm…I begged Harriett for the past two weeks and she finally broke down yesterday. If this is a problem I'm really sorry. I just…I just couldn't wait until we bumped into each other at the next family function." I had found my 'someone' or should I say, my someone had found me.

"It is a little surprising Michael, but I'm not upset. Is there something I can do for you?"

"Yes there is. Have dinner with me." He was direct and I liked that.

"That seems easy enough, how about you give me a call when you get back in town and we can arrange something."

"I am back, so how about tonight?"

"To…tonight? You're back?"

"Yes, I flew in this morning."

"Well I literally just walked through the door from the hospital and honestly it's been a long eight days for me. I planned to relax this weekend, before Max comes home on Sunday night."

"You could still relax. Let me cook you dinner. I could have my driver pick you up and bring you to my house, that way you wouldn't have to drive."

"To be honest…I…I'm not comfortable just coming over to your house. It takes away a lot of my control over the situation, plus I don't know you that well," I said matter-of-factly.

"I can understand that, so what do you suggest?" I was silent for moment as I looked at my watch. I hadn't eaten since lunch.

"Do you like sushi Michael?"

"I do."

"Its 8:30 now; would you like to meet at Sushi Samba on Seventh Avenue around 9:30 for a late dinner?"

"That sounds perfect! Take a cab, that way you don't have to be on the road too late tonight."

"How late do you plan on us being out?"

"I don't know. I guess I don't want your having to drive home to be the reason why the night is cut short."

I couldn't help but laugh. "At least you're honest. I'll see you at 9:30."

"Glory, you sound like you're smiling. Are you?" Now I really couldn't help the large grin spread across my face.

"I am, why?"

"Because I want to make you smile. I get the distinct impression that opportunities where you smile are few and far between."

"Well you've succeeded. I'll see you in an hour."

I was showered and dressed in twenty minutes and fixing my makeup. For the first time in my life I wanted to knock a man's socks off with the way I looked. I didn't want to be overly sexy, but I did want to make the night worth Michael's while. He had stepped out on a very thin rope when he got my number from Harriett and actually called, but tonight I wanted to make him glad he'd taken the chance.

I opted for a black cashmere sweater dress that accentuated my figure and apple bottom. I accessorized with a wide braided belt, matching purse, chandelier earrings, and black knee-high leather boots. The belt hung on the curve of my hips and added just the right amount of eye-catching appeal to the ensemble. Taking a final twirl in the mirror I saw my mother looking back at me. Growing up my Dad always told me I had a combination of my mother's rare beauty and my grandmother's ornamental loveliness. Right now I was especially thankful for the thick fullness I'd inherited from my grandmother, Althea Strair. I never met the hearty single mother, who cleaned houses during the week, sang in the church choir, and raised my father single-handedly, but I'd heard so much about her before my parents died. They said all my grandmother had to do was walk in a room and her face made the conversation stop. She was big-boned, but no one seemed to notice anything below her neck.

My mother, who had also lost her parents at a young age, loved her mother-in-law and made sure Althea was able to make the trek to Brazil a few times a year and vice versa up until she died when I was almost two. My parents managed to travel to Harlem a couple times a year when I was still a baby before she died. They gave me so much in the little time they had with me. Because of them I was the person standing in front of this mirror.

I spread both palms over my back side and looked at myself over my shoulder in the mirror one last time. I closed my eyes and immediately saw Hayden's face, those eyes. My flesh was becoming warm at my thoughts. He had been in my life all of four days and I missed him already. The persistent cramping returned. Turning away with my coat strewn over my arm, I went to meet Michael Beckford for dinner. I welcomed the distraction.

CHAPTER FIFTEEN

I saw him the moment I walked into the restaurant, sitting at an elegant table over in the corner. A few looks were sent in my direction, but I kept my eyes on him as I walked up.

"Good evening." I smiled with what I hoped was a captivating smile.

"Good evening Dr. Strair. You look beautiful as usual, please sit," he said standing to his feet as he pulled out the chair beside him and helped me to my seat.

"Thank you, but please call me Glory. You sound like one of my patients when you call me Dr. Strair. Besides, I thought we were past that stage, you know with you seeing me in a johnny and all." I laughed, in what was almost a girlish giggle, and it sounded foreign to me. Was I flirting? Becca would be proud.

"I guess you're right, we are past that stage. Thank you for meeting me on such short notice," he returned my smile. He was indeed an extremely attractive man. Rosie would probably slit her wrist right now if she were here, I thought with a smile.

"Don't thank me, it was my pleasure. I needed to get out."

"Well I'm glad I took the chance calling you. Can I offer you some Sake?"

"Yes please." There were two bottles perched in chilled holders at the end of the table.

"I wasn't sure which you would like so I had a bottle of both brought out. What do you prefer, amakuchi or karakuchi?" It took a split second before I figured out what he was asking. There are two basic tasting terms for sake or rice wine, which are sweet or dry.

"Amakuchi please, I prefer sweet sake," Michael smiled and poured me a glass. "Thank you." The waitress came to take our orders, but I wasn't ready so Michael offered to order for me, which was fine. He didn't seem as nervous as he did that first night I met him. Somehow tonight there was a quiet confidence about him that I liked. "How did you leave things in Colorado?" I asked taking another sip of my sake, yet keeping my eyes on Michael.

"Things were great although I wanted to leave the moment I found out you were gone. You didn't even attempt to say goodbye." I was a little taken aback by his directness, but again I found it appealing.

"I know, I'm sorry about that, but I had to leave. They needed me for a case at the hospital and quite honestly I was completely overwhelmed by the situation in Colorado."

"I could see how that could happen. It must have been hard just bumping into Hayden like that, as I'm sure it was just as hard for him to find out he had an eleven year old son." "You seem *very* informed. Was there a lot of talk after I left?"

"There was a lot of talk *before* you left, but not about what you may think. People were genuinely shocked, but at the same time, happy for Hayden. It's obvious you're a wonderful mother and a fascinating woman, so that made the pill of the surprise easier to swallow. Max is a great kid and I think for the most part everyone knows that." His words seemed genuine.

"I really needed to hear that Michael, thank you. I knew I shouldn't be, but for the first time in my life I guess I was embarrassed and wanted these people to think highly of me..."

"Believe me, they...we all do. The drama that followed you leaving was centered more around Lisa and Brian, than you and Max. Anyway, let's not talk about it anymore for now. I want to find out about *you*. This is supposed to be a relaxing night, remember?"

I wondered if Brian and Lisa had been found out or maybe Hayden had finally broken it off. I couldn't even entertain those thoughts or else it would consume my entire evening and my date with Michael would go downhill relatively quickly.

"Yes I remember. You're right let's talk about something else."

And talk, we did. It was almost midnight when I realized the restaurant was almost empty. I'm not sure if my life was just that interesting or he was just a great conversationalist drinking up each word that came out of my mouth. Things had gone surprisingly well. I wasn't sure what to expect, but the evening was better than anything I'd prepared myself for. Although, if he thought for a second that I hadn't noticed all the looks he was getting from the females in the restaurant he was mistaken. A few actually had the nerve to stop by and say good night, which I thought was a little rude, but that was just me. He was there with another woman for Christ's sake. Don't come over! I did a great job pretending like they didn't even exist. If they were old friends or lovers I would never know the difference since none of them held his attention for longer than the moment that they appeared. He wasn't rude or even dismissive, just uninterested. He paid the check and we walked outside. The freezing wind blew across my face as I pulled my warm shearling coat tightly around my shoulders against the cold night air.

"Did you take a cab like I suggested?" he asked as a black Mercedes pulled up.

"I did. Is this you?" I motioned towards the car.

"No, this is us," he said with some degree of pride, taking my hand. He would learn very quickly that things like this didn't impress me. "Come, let me take you home." As we talked more on the ride home I found out that he was quite fond of the Weiss family and appreciated how easily they had welcomed him after his father died and his step-mother met Walter. I was tempted to ask how old he was since I wasn't sure, but refrained. I didn't think I could handle it if he was too much younger than I was. After some time we pulled up in front of my house and I immediately became nervous. "You have a lovely house." I wouldn't invite him in, so he would be disappointed if he was expecting me to.

"Thank you, I've been trying to put a little love into it here and there when I have the time." He was staring at me, and I knew then he wanted to kiss me and I immediately had a feeling of déjà vu, except the man was Eric. If he did indeed want a good night kiss he would also be disappointed in that regard. "Michael I had a wonderful evening," and reaching for my purse between us I said, "hopefully we'll see each other soon."

"Sooner rather than later?"

"Yes."

"How's tomorrow?"

"Tomorrow when? Tomorrow as in today, or tomorrow as in Sunday? It *is* after midnight you know." Again there was that girlish giggle, that was frankly starting to annoy me, but I couldn't help it.

He took my hand between his. "Tomorrow as in today."

"I'm not sure. I haven't been home in almost two weeks and I wanted to do a few things around the house before Max comes home on Sunday. I think my luggage is still in the hallway from Colorado, which is pretty pathetic seeing that I've been back for almost two weeks."

"Well is there anything I could help you with?"

"No, that's not necessary..." He wanted to help me clean my house?

"I want to see you tomorrow Glory and if possible the day after that, and if possible the day after that. Do you get where I'm heading with this?" His voice had dropped to a low rumbling whisper as he gently massaged my hands. I couldn't help the warmth that crawled up my neck to my cheeks. I'm sure his driver could hear us. I was blushing.

"Michael I…"

"Is there a problem? Are you seeing someone?"

"It's a little too late to ask don't you think?" I laughed. Becoming serious again I answered him. "No. I'm not seeing anyone, but I do have a lot going on right now, and with that being said I would still like to see you again. Maybe if I get through with everything I have to do today we could have dinner again tonight."

"Please try. Here take my number," he said reaching into his jacket pocket and withdrawing a preprinted card with his personal cell and home numbers. I'm not sure why, but it bothered me that he had *preprinted* cards with his private numbers on them. Not like a business card or anything, but for personal use. Ummm, maybe there was another reason he was getting all those looks in the restaurant. I made a mental note.

"I'll try," I replied taking his card and reaching for the door. "Good night Michael."

"Good night Glory." I waved from the steps as he drove away, my exhaustion hitting me almost immediately. My clothes were off as soon as I got in the door and I was in bed fifteen minutes later.

Max called around ten that morning waking me up. He called the hospital first and was shocked when they told him I was home. I told him I missed him and couldn't wait to see him tomorrow to which he laughed, adding that he missed me as well. He wasn't sure when he would be home. We talked about everyone except the one person I *wanted* to talk about, his father. Our conversation ended up being cut short when Jeff told him the twins were waiting for him downstairs in the lobby. Once Jeff knew he was talking to me, he wouldn't let him hang up the phone. Max left and Jeff spent the next hour filling me in on the huge blow out between Lisa, Hayley, Brian and Hayden. Needless to say the general assumption was that the engagement would be called off and there was plenty of speculation that Hayley was filing for divorce. I took the opportunity to then tell Jeff what I'd seen the night before I left the hotel. He wasn't shocked, but couldn't believe they had the audacity to do it while away with the family.

"Jeff seeing them together like that and then being introduced to them was the cherry on top of a *very* large sundae with multiple scoops of frustration. I had to get out of there. You understand that don't you?"

"I understand and it definitely puts your reaction into perspective. They had better be careful. I don't know who is worse, Edward or Hayden, but I wouldn't want to cross either of them." I was silent for a moment letting it all sink in. "How are you really holding up?" he asked.

"I'm fine. Actually, I'm better than fine. I went out on a date last night."

"A date? Wow." Some how he didn't seem as excited as I thought he would. "Do I know the lucky gentleman?"

"As a matter of fact you do. It was with Michael Beckford." I'm not sure what he was eating or drinking but at the mention of Michael's name Jeff began coughing and sputtering as though he was choking. "Are you okay? What the hell is going on over there?"

"*You* went on a date with *Michael Beckford*?"

"Yeeeesssss I did. Is there a problem? Why do you seem so surprised?"

"Oh believe me Glory, I'm not surprised. It was clear to anyone with eyes that he wanted you from the moment he laid eyes on you at dinner. I guess he moved a lot quicker than I anticipated. I wasn't even aware he'd left the resort," he let out a nervous laugh.

"It's not like that Jeff. It was only dinner."

"Dinner or not, I want details." I told him there were none to give and that we would likely be having dinner again tonight.

"Are you sure you know what you're doing?"

"What type if question is that? I mean…I think I do," I replied defensively.

"*You think you do*." His sarcasm coated each word. "And what exactly do you *think* you're doing Dr. Strair? Honestly."

I took a deep breath. "I'm trying to forget Hayden Weiss, at least for the time being. That's what I'm trying to do! I don't want him to think I'm lonely and hooked on him. Plus, I thought for sure you of all people would've been happy about me dating."

"But you are hooked on him!" Jeff announced completely ignoring the last part of my statement.

"Yes, but he doesn't need to know that. Things are different now. I can start going out more and giving myself the attention for once. Michael seems very interested in me. What's wrong with that?"

"Nothing's wrong with that sweetie, but if you know Hayden is the man for you then why are you going to waste time with Michael Beckford."

"That's the problem Jeff. I *don't* know that Hayden is the man for me. Quite frankly I don't know him at all." I was becoming upset. "I spent one night with the man, *one night*. These feelings in the pit of my stomach can't be the end all, be all. They just can't be. And it's stupid for everyone to imply that they should be."

"What's wrong with wanting him Glory?" I couldn't believe I was that transparent. "Why are you fighting this?" Jeff pressed.

"Because…," I could barely even hear my own voice, "because he can't know he had this affect on me Jeff. It's embarrassing for Pete's sake. One night…that's all it took, one night for him to turn me inside out and place himself on the seemingly unreachable pedestal of 'Glory Strair's expectations in men'. I'm stronger than this Jeff. I feel so weak when it comes to him!"

"Is that what all this is about? You not wanting to appear weak for wanting this man? Glory has it ever occurred to you that he may feel the same way?"

"Yes, briefly, but I can't dwell on it. He's engaged and until he isn't I have to pretend that these feelings don't exist, for my own sanity if not for anyone else's. I'm the one that's been alone for over a decade, his life has gone on without a hiccup," the thought of him being with countless women after our encounter made me ill. "Don't worry I explained to Michael that I have a lot going on right now, plus we've only been on one date, it's not like we're sleeping together or anything like that."

"Don't speak too soon, from what I've heard about Michael Beckford that may not last very long. He's accustomed to getting what he wants and it sounds as though he wants *you.* He eats women like you for breakfast, lunch and dinner!"

Needless to say neither of us were very pleased with each other once we finished our conversation. It was obvious that Jeff wanted me to at least appear to be available when and if Hayden did break things off with Lisa and that's just not something I was willing to do. Call it a 'female' thing, a 'pride' thing, call it whatever you want, but I would not be caught dead *waiting* around for a man. And even if I *was* waiting, he didn't need to know that. If anything, I would use Michael to get some much overdue experience with members of the opposite sex and deal with Hayden when and if the time came.

I did, however, take Jeff's piece of information about Michael's conquests and tuck it to the forefront of my mind, making another mental note. I would not be a notch on his, or anyone else's, belt. He was sexy, but not *so* sexy that I planned on making the same mistake I did with Eric. I had no intention of being played. I was inexperienced in this regard, but far from being stupid.

~

I was not a happy camper when I hung up the phone with Glory, point blank, I was worried. She had been like a daughter to me since I first heard about her from my close friend, the dean of Yale's Medical School; I had actively pursued her to join my team at the hospital. We hit it off right away and almost immediately she became a gem in my eyes, although she never gave me the opportunity to play favorites. It was a known fact that she had the potential to be the best surgeon in the hospital and that put her on the imaginary hit list of several of the tenured doctors and staff like Nolte and Everton.

It never ceased to amaze me how she juggled being a fantastic physician and surgeon as well as doing such a commendable job raising Maximus. Unless you knew her personally the fact that she was a single parent was invisible. She kept those two lives very separate but gave each one her best. I know Max would disagree, but I knew first hand things could be worse. My mother had slaved to give me the kind of opportunities Glory gave Max and I wouldn't allow him to down play how much she'd done for him and the sacrifices she'd made.

We had known each other almost two years before I met Max for the first time, and that initial meeting was all it took for Clay and I to adore him completely. As we became closer she opened up a little to us, but I always felt she'd been holding something back. Her eyes hid a story that had never been told. Max's father was never discussed at length, until last week when she told us the full story and in that instant things became so much clearer.

Glory and I had the type of relationship where we could talk about almost anything, from work to Max or my relationship with Clay. She was always willing to offer advice and vice versa on the rare occasions that she was willing to talk about a problem. The subject that seemed to make her most uncomfortable was her personal life. One of the hardest things for me to witness over the past nine years was seeing her so alone. She never dated and always came alone to work related functions, in essence becoming the envy of everyone at the hospital and the object of desire for most of the single male staff, physicians, nurses, and techs alike. She didn't take kindly to my interference in that regard, with our relationship nearly being ruined the last time I set her up on a blind date.

I think what made it even more difficult was how seemingly perfect she was. Aside from her extraordinary beauty, she never mistreated her patients, staff, or colleagues, even when they deserved it. People loved to work for her, bending over backwards at any request because they knew in an instant she would do the same for them. But I knew now that she wasn't perfect and that something was missing in her life. My accident changed the path of my career and ultimately my life forever and even though I missed being in the operating room, it presented me with an opportunity I probably wouldn't have gotten, to give Glory a significant push up a very bureaucratic ladder. I knew I could never operate on patients again and all I had to do was get my loyal following of patients to see in her what I'd learned moments after meeting her – that she could be the best thing that ever happened to our hospital. From a professional stand point the opportunity I'd given her was invaluable, but on the personal front she would have to make that journey on her own. Fooling around with Michael wasn't the answer and running away wasn't either. At some point or another she would have to face that fact, let go and love.

I hadn't stopped kicking myself since I'd found out about her and Hayden. All this time he was so close and I never thought to introduce them, probably due to the fact that outside the hospital Glory barely had time for Max, let alone herself, and declined invitations to my parties because she was usually working or covering so that the other physicians could attend. I wanted her to be happy, she deserved it. Michael Beckford couldn't even begin to comprehend what he had and I wasn't sure Glory's naivety would stand up to his expert charm. I firmly believed that if she pursued things with him, she would be making a big mistake. Her future lay with Hayden Weiss. She couldn't have picked a more perfect man, although until Glory, his choice in women left much to be desired. Beauty was never the problem, but their personalities were. The emotions on his face, the day we walked in on them in her room, were as plain as day to a blind man. He loved her and in all the years that I'd known him, I'd never seen him look at Lisa or any of his conquests the same way. I just hope he moved quickly or else he may lose the best thing that ever happened to him.

CHAPTER SIXTEEN

*A*round two o'clock I was convinced I could finish cleaning in time and would be able to have dinner, so I called Michael. After throwing out a few suggestions we decided to venture out to this new Latin club/restaurant called La Tortuga. Michael would pick me up around seven-thirty. I hadn't been dancing in eons, literally, not since I left Brazil as a teenager. Apart from running errands around my Aunt Miranda's club, I'd never been to a nightclub just for fun. My mother was a romantic, so next to poetry and sonnets, she loved music and dance, taking the time to teach me all the local dances, much to my father's dismay. Some of the movements could be very sensual and I already looked much older than my thirteen years. The dancing only made it worse, with me standing out like a strawberry in a bowl of blue berries at the weekly village parties. I loved every minute of it, so I was looking forward to my night of good food, dancing, and music with Michael.

I painted on a knee-length backless fire engine red satin dress. It had a textured lattice-type, interwoven panel right down the front, which only added to the eye catching appeal. Gravity had pulled most of my bruising down onto my bottom and the once dark purple plaques had now been reduced to faded yellowish green bruises, so they were perfectly hidden by the deep scoop of the dress that began just above my bottom. Wearing this would definitely make heads turn, but I didn't have anything else that screamed Latin flavor like this dress. The matching shoes were the piéce de la résistance as I wrapped the satin straps around my ankle ending in a perfect little bow on my shin. My hair was curly and wild, but in this instance very fitting. I was walking downstairs when the phone rang and I assumed it was Michael telling me he was outside.

"Hello?"

"Dr. Strair?" It was a man's deep voice, but not Michael's.

"Yes this is she. Who is this?"

"This is Brian Rafferty." My heart rate increased ever so slightly as the thought immediately crossed my mind that I was going to kill Harriett Weiss for giving him my number. What the hell did he want?

"How did you get my number?"

"You know, it was really bothering me in Colorado that I couldn't place where I knew you from. Aside from our little run-in in the linen closet I felt we'd met before and a face like yours is not one that can be easily forgotten." He was right, from the moment I saw him with Lisa there was something familiar about him, but I couldn't place it either. Then once I found out who they were I hadn't given him a second thought.

"How did you get my number?" Again he completely ignored my question and went on.

"Then it hit me once I overheard the full story of how you met Hayden…doctors probably make a lot more money than prostitutes. Do you prefer to go by Dr. Strair or Glo!" I almost dropped the phone, but I held my composure.

"How much more did Hayden out bid me by that night? If my memory serves me correctly I went from three hundred to one thousand dollars and you still refused me! How much did Hayden buy you for? How much did Max cost? Maybe if I wasn't so cheap *I* could've been Max's daddy…"

It was him. It was really him. The man who grabbed me outside before I left with Hayden. Hayden told him my name?

"What do you want?"

"How do you think everyone would take it if they knew how you paid for medical school? How would Max feel knowing that the difference between his daddy and the next man, was a couple hundred dollars?" I felt dirty. My secret was out and the worst person knew.

"Você bastardo! You bastard! You don't know what the hell you're talking about so I would think twice about calling me with idle threats."

"Idle? Oh no beautiful I know exactly what I'm talking about and unless you convince Hayden to back off and talk his sister out of divorcing me, then everyone and their mother will know exactly what I'm talking about!" Was he really trying to blackmail me into staying married to a woman he obviously didn't love and was cheating on?

"I can't do that. It's none of my business."

"Then you should've thought twice before opening your mouth about what you saw!"

"What I saw? I didn't say anything to anyone about you and Lisa. I left!"

"Well Hayden found out…"

"He didn't find out from me. Maybe if you two had been more discreet this wouldn't even be an issue."

"I don't care! Fix it or I swear to God I will go to the Weiss', Dr. Bruckheimer, Max, or anyone who will listen, with your not so favorable history." Everyone else I could handle, but Max? I couldn't bear it if he found out the circumstances under which I met his father.

"Don't threaten me Mr. Rafferty. You've made your bed, now lie in it! You have no proof!" ***BEEP***.

"I don't need proof. The implication is enough." ***BEEP***. My phone continued to beep. Michael was calling.

"Max will be the laughing stock of St. Bernard's if you don't do what I want and convince Hayley to give me another chance!" He knew Max went to St. Bernard's? God, how much more did he know about us?

"I have nothing more to say to you." And with that I hung up. My chest hurt as I tried to pull my thoughts together and stop from shaking. The phone was ringing again.

"Hello?" I snapped.

"Glory? It's Michael, I'm outside. "

"I'm on my way out." I hung up abruptly. My mind was spinning.

~

Snapping my cell phone shut, I chuckled openly. Did she really think she could threaten me? She was a prostitute for Christ's sake! A 'nobody' who thought she could get away with this. I didn't realize how hard I was squeezing my cell phone until I heard the casing start to crack in my hand. My blood was surging through my veins as I tried to calm down, but it wasn't working. This was the worse thing that could happen right now. I needed the Weiss' more than they could ever know and I had to show them that I wouldn't just roll over and let them destroy me. Things were perfect before Glory Strair showed up, and if she expects me to believe she had nothing to do with Hayley finding out about Lisa, then she had another thing coming. If Hayley divorced me because of my affair, and actually had proof, she could take everything I owned, including my reputation. As it stood most, if not all, of my clientele hopped onboard because of my connection to the Weiss family; they were a powerful and well known family. Edward had introduced me to half of my original clients and the spin-off from that was invaluable. And he knew it.

That pre-nup was the stupidest thing I'd ever done, but he wouldn't have it any other way and I needed to get into her family. I had worked and cheated my way too far, for too long to have them

take it all away because of a super lay, and Lisa was definitely that -
a super lay. I'm not sure what I found more rewarding the
impeccable screw that she was, or the fact that she was Hayden's
screw originally.

I saw how he'd looked at me in Colorado and knew he had every
intention of burying me alive and I'd be damned if I gave that cocky
bastard the satisfaction. If they did, it would be over my dead body
or Glory's.

For as long as I'd known him, Hayden always got what he
wanted – women, jobs, connections, anything he laid his eyes on, at
one point or another became his. Not this time. If I couldn't be with
Hayley he certainly couldn't have that two bit whore. She was a
softie I could see it in her eyes and hear it in her voice. It wouldn't
take much to convince her to talk to Hayley and fix this. And as I
looked at the pictures of the recent PTO gala I'd printed off the web
of her and Max from his school's website, I knew I would take
pleasure in forcing her to do what I wanted. She'd refused me once
before, but I wouldn't let that happen again. I couldn't. She was
nothing but a slut, who got cleaned up, and soon everyone would
know. I would have a piece of all of Hayden's women and take pride
in it. He wasn't better than me and soon Glory would know and *feel*
it. I would make them both pay for underestimating me. If she was
the only proof they had of my affair with Lisa, then I hope they had a
back up plan, because Dr. Glory Strair was about to have a sudden
case of amnesia.

The thought alone of making her do what I wanted gave me an
instant hard on and I decided we would meet face to face sooner
rather than later. We had some unfinished business to take care of.

~

The first hour out on my date with Michael was rough because
my thoughts were inundated with the call from Brian Rafferty and
what I should do, but as usual Michael did a great job of taking my
mind off the issues at hand and I managed to have a blast. Dinner
was wonderful and after finishing an expensive bottle of Miguel
Torres's delicious Spanish wine we made our way over to the night
club.

The minute we crossed over the bridge that led from the
restaurant to the club, we could feel the bass pounding in our chest.
The rhythmic sounds of the guitar and drums willed us to the dance
floor. Michael danced to the first few songs with me, but then

perched himself in the VIP booth and watched me dance the night away. A few men attempted to join me, but I politely shoo'd them away. I danced until my thighs and waist were literally burning, not to mention the soreness in my back, but I ignored them. I was having too much fun. It wasn't difficult to remember the movements and get back into the groove, but dancing as a pre-pubescent teenager and then at thirty were two different things. This time around there was significantly more gyrating and pelvic thrusts involved.

Michael hadn't taken his eyes off me, and even in the dimly lit club, I could read them clearly. He wanted me. The sweat was running down my back as I piled my hair on top of my head for the final song, which also happened to be a long time favorite of mine by Carlos Santana. There were couples surrounding me on the dance floor, but I didn't care. I had no problem dancing alone and with my eyes closed I began to move. Holding my hair in place with one hand, I gracefully moved the other hand at my side. My knees were bent as I stepped forward then back, twirled and bent, side to side, rolling my hips at a pace I never thought imaginable. I was thinking of Hayden and the way he held me that night an eternity ago. There on the dance floor I imagined I was in his arms. I was Baby from Dirty Dancing and he was my Patrick Swayze. Then I felt someone take me in their arms for real, and spreading their large palm against the damp skin of my lower back, pressed me into their hardness. I did not want to open my eyes because it felt good to be held by a man, even if it was a stranger. I was deep in a moment that I didn't want to end. If one of the desperate schmucks I'd refused throughout the night was trying to cop a feel, then this was his lucky night because I wouldn't stop dancing until the song was finished.

He was a good dancer that much I would give him, but after a while he stopped concentrating on his two legs and began to focus on his third. I continued to dance; our pelvises grinded against each others as my hips and bottom rubbed against his swollen crotch and he turned me and twirled me like a true expert. And there, above the loud music, I heard the almost deafening sound of my parents again turning over in their graves – again.

This poor fellow was burying himself in a painful hole that would ultimately end up with me going home *alone* to a soft oversized bed with heated comforters, and him soaking his groin with ice packs. It would serve him right! We were in the middle of the ramp up at the end of the song when I was pulled deeper into the moment; I let my hair fall and I circled both arms around my mystery partner's neck. I wanted to open my eyes, but wouldn't dare. We were moving then as he took control spinning me around the dance floor. His hands were moving up and down my thighs and back as we moved to the compelling rhythm, our bodies becoming instruments of movement. Then the music stopped in one final thump of the drums and the room erupted in applause.

For a moment I was still, not wanting to open my eyes, but I finally did to find Michael looking at me, his forehead glistening with sweat. I couldn't help smiling with relief as I turned to join the crowd in applauding the band. He was standing behind me with his arms wrapped around my waist, taking deep breaths. I was honestly thankful it was him and not a complete stranger. He didn't say anything as we walked off the dance floor and he helped me into my coat, which had miraculously appeared at our table. He stopped to talk to a few people and then we walked outside. We were silent most of the way home, which made me regret dancing with him the way I did.

"Did you have fun?" he finally asked, turning to face me as he ran his hands through his slightly damp hair.

"I had a wonderful time. Thank you for another nice evening. I haven't danced like that in a long time." I laughed then, "Actually, now that I think about it I don't think I've *ever* danced like that before."

"You could've fooled me. No one could keep their eyes off of you. *I* couldn't keep my eyes off you. You were amazing."

"I think that had a lot to do with this dress though, don't you?" He agreed and wrapping his arm around my shoulders pulled me closer. "Can I ask you something?"

"Of course, anything."

"I wanted to ask you last night and I forgot. That night at the resort when Hayden and I went off to find Max and the twins, you were coming to the car and Edward stopped you and said something. What did he say?"

"He told me he thought that trip was something you and Hayden needed to do together, more specifically *alone* and that I should stay there with them. I wasn't thrilled, but I understood. Why do you ask?" Interesting....I thought. Did Edward have his own agenda?

"No reason really, I just saw him say something and wondered what it was." We drove in silence the remainder of the way, as he continued to trail the tips of his fingers up and down my shoulders.

We pulled up to my house and he reached for the door. I was hoping and praying that he just wanted to let me out, but he got out as well and walked me up the stairs. I unlocked the door and stepped up on the landing as I opened the door slightly, not wide enough for an invitation. He was standing close to me. I took my keys out of the door and turned to face him, this is where I had to burst his bubble.

"This is where I say good night Michael." I could see the disappointment in his eyes as he leaned in and covered my mouth with his, snaking his arm around my waist to pull me closer. I kissed him back, opening my mouth slightly as his warm tongue slipped between my lips. I groaned as he grabbed a handful of my mane and tilted my head backwards so that he could kiss my neck. I wasn't groaning in pleasure, but out of the frustration that like Eric, there was something missing. His kiss was pleasant, in all honesty better than pleasant, but there was no spark. There were no contractions *down below* either. I pulled away.

"Come home with me. The night doesn't have to end Glory," he said with a raspy voice as I inched backwards into the house.

"I'm sorry, but that won't happen. It's too soon. I barely know you and like I told you before, I have a lot going on in my life right now."

"That won't happen tonight or that won't happen ever," he asked with a little smirk.

"Tonight," I responded with a laugh. "That won't happen tonight." He sighed at the thought there was still a hope he would sleep with me. He kissed me again more passionately this time, maybe in hopes of changing my mind, but it didn't. I waited a few seconds before pulling away.

"Good night Michael."

"I've never met anyone like you," he whispered. "Can I see you tomorrow?"

"Tomorrow as in Monday or tomorrow…"

"Tomorrow as in today!" he said with a laugh, bringing my hands to his lips. "Why do you persist in torturing me?" We both began to laugh.

"I'm sorry, but I can't. Max will be home this afternoon and I want to spend the day with him."

"What about…"

"And Monday I'll be swamped at work and I really don't like to go out during the week," I replied with an apologetic smile.

"So are you saying I have to wait until next weekend to see you?"

"Probably, but why don't you call me during the week and maybe we can do lunch or something?"

"Arrrhhh, all right," he groaned. "I've really enjoyed these past two nights."

"So have I. We'll talk soon," I said as I slipped my hand out of his and he stepped back giving me a complete once over. "I promise."

"If I didn't tell you before, you looked absolutely gorgeous tonight." He *had* told me for a total of seventeen times and like before I smiled and shyly thanked him. "Have fun with your son tomorrow."

"I will. Good night Michael."

"Good night Glory." I waited for him to get back in the car and drive off, before I stepped inside and closed the door. I slipped my coat off and hung it on the hook beside the door.

Leaning my forehead against the door I whispered to myself, "That was a little too close for comfort Dr. Strair."

"Far too close if you ask me!" came the angry reply from behind me. I couldn't help the scream that escaped my lips as I turned to find Max and Hayden standing in my dark foyer.

"*Oh meu deus, você assustaram-me!*" I screamed in Portuguese. I needed a moment to catch my breath as I dramatically placed my hand against my chest, feeling my heart pound against it. How long were they standing there? What are they doing back already?

"We frightened you?" Max yelled in disbelief flipping on the light switch.

"Yes, you frightened me!" I snapped. "What the hell is going on here? Do any of you care to explain what you're doing standing in my foyer at four in the morning when you're supposed to be in Colorado?"

"I wanted to come back early to surprise you!" He was becoming much too comfortable shouting and screaming at me. "We were worried sick mom. Where were you? Who was that? Do you know what time it is?"

"Max there's no need to yell," Hayden said calmly, even though I could tell behind those eyes he was also screaming.

"Sweetie, I'm sorry, had I known you were coming home tonight I wouldn't have gone out. I'm sorry I made you worry." I could tell he was genuinely worried and that was the only reason I would excuse his tone.

"Who was that?" he barked again.

"That was Michael Beckford." They both looked dumbfounded as Hayden turned and walked back into the living room.

"The guy from Colorado?" Max's jaw literally dropped to his chest.

"Yes. We went out for sushi last night and then tonight we decided to go dancing at a new Latin place downtown. There is no reason for you to be upset with me. It isn't as though I knew you were coming home and went out anyway. Now come and give me a hug," I said with open arms. He was reluctant, but finally came, although with the half-hearted hug he gave he might as well have not given me one at all. "So you came back early to surprise me huh?" I asked in a poor attempt to ease the uncomfortable silence now filling the house.

"Yeah so much for that...I'm going to bed. I'm tired," he grumbled and walking into the living room he gave Hayden a huge bear hug. The hug I wanted. "Thanks for waiting with me Dad. Will I see you tomorrow?"

"Of course. I've had an awesome two weeks." Hayden was fondly smoothing Max's hair.

"Me too. I love you!"

"I love you too son. See you tomorrow," and with that Max headed upstairs.

"What about me?" I openly begged, "Don't I get a hug and a kiss good night as well?" He just stopped on the stairs and looked at me.

"That would be gross mom. You were just kissing that guy!" and with that he ran upstairs with not so much as a glance over his shoulder. I was embarrassed and hurt, trying not to let the tears that were threatening to fall.

"Umm, I guess I'll take off too."

"Wait...don't leave yet," I croaked, quickly heading for the stairs.

"Glory are you cry..."

"Please...don't leave. I'll be...back in a minute. We need to talk." I ran up the stairs to my room wiping at my face. When I was safe behind my bathroom door I let my tears fall as I brushed my teeth. They couldn't have picked a worse time to come back. I'd done nothing wrong but still managed to feel awful. My son and the man of my dreams had just seen me kissing another man. I was mortified. This must be a sign that this distraction thing obviously wasn't for me. Of course if Hayden sees me making out with another man he's going to walk away. I was completely confused and in the same instance having a moment of complete clarity where I knew for sure I wanted to be with Hayden. Once I'd pulled myself together and washed my face, ten minutes later I headed back downstairs. I walked in to find Hayden gently running his thumb over my face in the only picture of Max and I on the fire place mantle. He snatched his hand away when he heard me walk in.

"Are you alright?"

"Embarrassed, but I'll live."

"Don't be. I…I should've said something when I realized the direction things were going, but I … I couldn't."

"Lately, I can't seem to do anything right with that boy," I said sitting down on the sofa as I massaged my temples.

"He'll be fine."

"I know, but it still hurts. Hayden, I know how things looked just now, but Michael and I aren't…"

"Glory you don't have to explain anything to me. You're an adult…"

"That's the thing…I *do* feel as though I should explain."

"*Don't*…I really don't want to…I prefer *not* to know," he was slipping his arms into his jacket.

"Hayden wait, please don't go!" he didn't hide the surprise at the urgency in my tone or at the fact that I didn't want him to leave.

"I *can't* stay. Being here with you, like this… in that dress isn't good for me, and I'm man enough to admit that."

"Please…I need to talk to you about something and find out how your time with Max was." He closed his eyes and let out a long sigh as though it pained him to be in the same room with me. What had I done? Did seeing me in another man's arms ruin any chance I had with Hayden?

"I'm sorry, I can't, not tonight. It's late and I have to leave, maybe we can talk tomorrow," and without a moment's hesitation he turned and walked out. With my hands akimbo I stared at the closed door for the longest while hoping he would walk back through it, but he didn't.

I went up to my room and had a shower, washing away the sweat from my body. Slipping on my pajamas I decided losing Hayden wasn't a risk I was willing to take. I needed to make sure there was no chance of *us* before I pursued things with Michael. There could be no more 'what if's' and 'why didn't I's'. Not to mention there was no way I was going to walk away again. If Lisa didn't want him I had every intention of fighting for him. Michael would have to wait, *or not*. At this point I really didn't care. Now all that I had left to do was figure out how to handle Brian Rafferty. Something about him scared me; no I was wrong – *everything* about him scared me.

CHAPTER SEVENTEEN

I don't know how long I sat in front of Glory's house before driving away, fighting every urge I had to run back in there, peel that sinfully tight dress from her body, and make love to her right on the spot before someone else did - Michael Beckford for instance. I might as well have changed my name to Yoda or Kermit because I was green with envy. He was kissing her. I could see through the paned glass that his hands were sliding up and down her hips, touching her the way I yearned to touch her. Hearing her groan was like pouring salt into my open wound. And then she wanted me to stay and talk? I was barely able to contain myself as it is and she wanted me to talk? Max knew that I had called things off with Lisa and that I had every intention of trying to become a family with him and Glory, if she would have me. He would not take kindly to her dating but, as hard as it may be for me, I had to support her decision, no matter how much I didn't like it either. It's not like I had been celibate these past twelve years. I wasn't successful at forgetting her, but I had *certainly* tried. I think my only option at this point would be to have a heart to heart with her about how I felt and have her decide from there. I knew she still thought Lisa and I were engaged and that was one of the main reasons why she couldn't tell me how she *really* felt, so I was interested in her response once she found out the engagement was called off and things between us were over.

As soon as I walked through the front door of the new apartment Hayley jumped up from the couch. "Hayden is that you?"

"What's up? I wasn't expecting you to still be awake. Isn't your bedroom comfortable?"

"Where were you? I've been calling your cell!" she seemed frantic.

"Uh, I left it in the car. I'm sorry, what's going on? Are you alright?" my hand immediately traveled to her round belly concern creeping into my eyes.

"Yes...I mean no!" I couldn't help laughing. Hayley had always been a scaredy-cat.

"Just like old times eh...."

"Stop it," she said playfully slapping me. "It's serious Hayden. I had a dream. A bad one." I wasn't laughing any more. I had learned a long time ago that when my sister had a dream you paid attention. "Alright...was it about Brian?"

"Yes. I'm worried...:

I cut her off, "Hail this is all going to be over soon. I won't let anything happen to you. There's nothing to be worried about."

"Hayden I'm not worried about me." There was genuine fear behind her eyes. "I'm worried about Glory. Something Brian said yesterday after our *talk* is bothering me. Have you seen Glory yet?"

She was making me nervous now. "Aaaah, as a matter of fact I just did. She wasn't home so I waited with Max, that's why I'm late. I left their house not too long ago. What's wrong? What does Glory have to do with anything?"

"I don't know…but I'm worried. I dreamt Brian tried…I dreamt he tried to hurt her," her voice trailed off. "And it made me think of something he said yesterday before we left the resort…"

On three separate occasions, while we were growing up, Hayley had dreams that came to fruition. My family had learned their lesson after doubting her the first time. She was eight at the time and scheduled to start ice skating lessons, fulfilling yet another one of my mother's dreams for her 'girl' child. The night before Hail's first day she had a dream that she got hurt really badly, something about having her fingers cut off. My mother tried to reassure her everything would be fine, telling her the only way that could happen is if she stuck her hands into a zamboni while it was still moving. It took almost two hours to drag her into the rink kicking and screaming, much to my amusement and my father's dismay, but my mother refused to give in. Needless to say the class went without incident as my parents watched with a see-I-told-you-nothing-would-happen type of look plastered across their faces. The following week it only took an hour to get her to the rink and once again the class went without incident. The next week she put up even less of a fight, until almost three months had passed.

It was the thirteenth class that made us never doubt her again, I remember it like it was yesterday. While she was sitting on the ice waiting for her friends one of the older girls skating by didn't see Hail and skated right over both her hands. The blades cut through the skin right to the bone breaking eight fingers except her thumbs. Seventy-six stitches and a hysterical mother later, my parents never doubted her again and neither did I. She only had two harmless dreams after that, but that one was enough to make us believers. You could call it whatever you wanted, a gift or a curse, either way it didn't settle well with me.

"Hayden are you listening to me?"

"Of course I'm listening. What…What did he say? Did he actually say he was going to hurt her?" my mind was going a million miles a minute as I tried to process what she was telling me. "I don't understand this. What does she have to do with anything?"

"I don't know, but his exact words to me yesterday were that I shouldn't believe everything I hear, especially from some Las Vegas whore! I didn't put it together at the time. He kept asking me what Glory had told me. I told him nothing and that we'd barely spoken. I thought he'd dropped it, but after everything happened and I told him I was filing for divorce, he started asking me about her again…"

"When? Where was I? I made certain that you weren't alone with him after we left Mom and Dad's room." My head was throbbing as I tried to find out what link Brian could possibly have with Glory.

"He called when you were talking to mom and Dad in the next room."

"And you answered? What did he say then?" This must have something to do with her reaction to him that night at dinner, but what could it be?

"He said I was making a big mistake and that none of this would've happened if Glory had minded her own business. He kept calling her a two-bit whore and slut. It was as though he knew her." The connection came then. "He said he loved me and that he would make her fix this even if they both died trying…"

"Damn it Hail why didn't you tell me this before?" I was pacing back and forth trying to figure out what to do with this information.

"I don't know! I thought he was just venting, then I had the dream. Hayden what is it? Does Brian know Glory? How did he know about Las Vegas?"

I took a deep breath, "He knows about Vegas because he was there Hail. He was also at the party that night I met Glory. If anything he was part of the reason why she wanted to leave." I grabbed a handful of my hair in frustration, as I wondered how far Brian would really go with this.

"For heaven's sake don't just stop there! I thought she wasn't feeling well? Did he do something to her?"

"Brian thought Glory was a prostitute…"

"Why the hell would he think something like that?"

"Because…because we all thought she was a prostitute."

"What? But I thought…"

I stopped her then and delved into the *full* story of how Glory and I came to be together that night. "Over the next year most of the guys found it pretty entertaining that I was making almost monthly trips to Vegas to find a prostitute named Glo!"

"Jesus Hayden," she announced once I was finished. "That could easily be the most romantic thing I've heard. She was a virgin? No wonder she left without a good-bye, she probably didn't know how to explain any of this to you. Her Aunt must have been a real bitch to make her do something like that."

"I'm not sure romantic is the word I would use. So you're fine with this?" I didn't try to hide my surprise at her reaction.

"Fine with what? What's there to be 'fine' about? You knew she wasn't a prostitute and even if by some stretch of the imagination she was, which I don't think is possible. It was all in the past. The woman is a brilliant surgeon now, who cares!" I was still pacing. I was worried about her. "Did she say anything tonight when you saw her?"

"No, but now I'm kicking myself because she seemed upset before I left and said she wanted to talk to me about something…"

"And? What was it?"

"I didn't stay to find out. I couldn't. I told her we would talk about it tomorrow!"

"God damn it Hayden! What the hell is wrong with you? Why didn't you stay and talk to her, especially when you know damn well she was all you could think about these past few weeks in Colorado? You aren't fooling anyone with this macho persona Hayden. Why?" My head was pounding and her ranting and raving at the top of her lungs wasn't helping. I'd forgotten how feisty the real Hayley was, before Brian.

"*Because* I'd just seen her lip-locked in Michael Beckford's arms for fuck's sake! He was kissing her; telling her how much he wanted her, begging her to spend the night with him. She was wearing this dress that…Damn it Hail! I couldn't handle it alright. I couldn't be so damn close to her. I want her so badly and it seems as though everyone else does as well. If I stayed, I would've done something she may not have wanted me to do." I couldn't help the passion that coated my every word, and I could no longer deny it. "Hail I love her and the thought that there's a possibility she may not feel the same way is driving me fucking insane! I can't eat or sleep. I see her when I'm awake and when I'm sleeping. I think about her every second of every day. I don't think straight when I'm around her. Do you really think I *wanted* to leave her side tonight? I sat in front of her house for twenty minutes trying to convince myself not to go back in there!" I didn't care that I was yelling. I wanted someone else to know how I was feeling and not just assume I was fine with this.

She walked over to me then and hugged me. "Alright, alright, shush. It's going to be all right. I'm sorry. This must all be very difficult for you. I didn't mean to yell, but you need to find out what it is that she wanted to talk to you about Hayden."

"I know. Something must have happened between her and Brian at the resort and he recognized her. That's the only explanation I can come up with for her leaving the way she did after they were introduced. Hail I swear to God if he harms one hair on her head I'll kill him myself."

"You don't think he would really hurt her do you? It was just a dream, right?" She was trying to be optimistic, but she knew better than anyone that it was more than just a dream. "I don't know how he expects her to fix this," Hail added.

I didn't know either and we spent the next hour figuring out what we should do next. In the end we decided to talk to Glory first thing in the morning, calling this early would only alarm her. And then we would get a feel for where Brian stood at the meeting with the lawyer on Monday.

Needless to say, I didn't sleep well. I didn't trust Brian Rafferty as far as I could throw him and as I tossed and turned I was angry with myself for not putting my foot down sooner with him and Hayley. This all seemed so preventable, now my sister was pregnant, sick and alone, with Glory caught in the middle.

CHAPTER EIGHTEEN

The sun was shining directly in my face as I squinted and turned away from the window. I could smell bacon…hmmm, Max was cooking breakfast. I quickly got out of bed, freshened up and ran downstairs.

"Max?" I called, but there was no answer. "Something smells good!" I sang as I ambled towards the kitchen looking forward to making the past two weeks and last night up to him. "I'm the one that should be making *you* breakfast." I walked into the kitchen and stopped dead in my tracks. There standing at my stove smoking a cigarette was Brian Rafferty. Max was no where in sight.

"What the hell are you doing in my house? Where's my son?"

"Calm down beautiful, I think he's still sleeping. At least he was still in bed when I checked on you both," he said calmly. *Checked on us? He was walking around my house while we were sleeping? Son-of-a-bitch! I was petrified.* I had to get Max and get the hell out of here.

"You were so rude to me last night on the phone I figured I would come see you in person so you could apologize. Now come here and give me a good morning kiss," his voice was cold and deliberate. He was beckoning me to come as though he read my mind and knew I had every intention of running, but I couldn't move. This wasn't happening. This man had broken into my home and except for my comatose son, we were alone. My mind was saying shout for help, but to whom? We lived in this house by ourselves and I wasn't sure if waking Max was the wisest thing to do. I would prefer if anything happened, that it happened to me - alone. The thought of him hurting Max made me feel faint. *Run!* I screamed inwardly. If I could run back upstairs and lock myself in Max's room then maybe I could call for help. But could I make it before he caught me? My brain was shouting orders, but my legs wouldn't obey.

"Come here." he repeated in the same tone. I still couldn't move. My bare feet felt like dead weights against the cool slate of my kitchen floor.

"Get out of my house before I call the police!" I barked in a sad unconvincing voice. My senses were trying to come back to me, slowly but surely. Again, as though he didn't have a care in the world he pressed his cigarette out in the frying pan with the bacon and tossed the dish towel on the stove. My eyes traveled to the butcher's block where the knives were neatly lined up and then back to him. He read my mind or knew exactly what I was thinking, because before I knew what happened next he was moving around the island quickly and standing in front of me. He kept walking forward until he had my back against the wall. He hadn't touched me, but was close enough that I could feel his smoky breath on my face.

"You'll do no such thing! Do you know why?" *Oh God, please don't hurt me*. Please don't hurt me, I kept saying to myself. I didn't answer and slamming his fists against the wall on either side of my head, I flinched; he asked again "Do you know why you aren't going to say anything to anyone about this?"

"*No,*" I whispered.

"Because I know where you live. I know where your son goes to school and hangs out!" My tears came then as I felt the walls of my bladder quivering. I was doing everything I could to control the urge I had to urinate right there. "Now, here's what you're going to do for me Dr. Strair. You're going to tell Hayley you were wrong about what you saw and…" I didn't wait for him to finish.

"What I saw? I keep telling you that I didn't say anything to Hayley about you and Lisa! I left the resort. I've never had a conversation with that woman outside of our introductions."

"Shut up you lying bitch! You may have everyone else fooled, but I know what and who you are. Remember? I was there when you had a line of men waiting to fuck you and politely told me I would have to take a number!" *I did tell him that didn't I?* "Up until I saw you in Colorado, Hayley didn't have a clue what was going on between Lisa and I; and now you want me to believe that you up and leaving the resort had nothing to do with Hayley suddenly wanting a divorce? Her parents won't even look at me! Her father and brother are going to destroy everything I've worked for, and you want me to believe that you had nothing to do with it? You're lying and I have no patience for this!" he screamed again as he pounded his fists repeatedly into the wall. "You should've kept your fucking mouth shut!"

All the blood had now drained from my head and was doing a Niagara Falls type rush towards the pit of my stomach. "Please… I swear to you… I said nothing!" I was beginning to second guess myself. Jeff wouldn't have said anything would he? No, it couldn't be Jeff because I told him what I saw *after* everything had happened and Hayley had already talked to Brian about getting a divorce.

"You know what you're going to do?" he leaned away from me and slowly ran his tongue over his bottom lip, back and forth. He was looking at my breasts, which made me feel dirty. He brought my hand from my side and placed it on top of something hard in the front of his trousers. He began to move my hand and I realized that I was stroking the cold steel barrel of a gun. I felt sick, turning my face away from his gross smoky breath. I willed myself to think, scream, or do something other than stand there like a frightened statuette, but I could do nothing, having some type of mental and physical paralysis. "You're going to *prove* to me that you didn't have anything to do with this."

"How can I prove it to you?" I asked incredulously and placing his hands firmly on my shoulders he started to push me down in front of him. When the realization hit of what he was asking me to do I began to fight, punching and flailing my arms wildly, clawing at his face as I tried to duck and get away from him, but he slammed his body against mine and quickly had my wrists crossed and held together over my head. I opened my mouth to scream and he immediately had his other hand over my mouth painfully pressing my lips into my teeth.

"Shut. Your. Fucking. Mouth." he growled as I closed my eyes in pain and fear. Letting out a long exaggerated sigh he blew tendrils of my hair away from my face. "I can see how this could all be very frightening for you, so I'll give you some time to think about it. When I take my hand away are you going to scream?" He was pressing even harder and what little will I had to fight him was quickly disappearing. I shook my head from side to side. He moved his hand away and then covered my mouth with his, sucking and biting on my lips, forcing his nicotine coated tongue between my teeth. Without a moment's hesitation he slipped his free hand down the back of my pajama pants cupping my bare bottom and spreading my legs as he dragged me towards him.

"Please don't... do this," I whispered when he moved his mouth down to my neck and earlobe, he was becoming aroused. "I have nothing to do with what's..." I had a sharp intake of breath as he forced his fingers into my vagina, jabbing angrily at my sensitive opening. "No, no, nooo," I cried as I closed my eyes and shook my head back and forth willing myself to wake up from this nightmare. *"This isn't happening to me. This isn't happening to me..."* I just kept repeating it, but he wouldn't stop his painful intrusion. He was hurting me and didn't give a damn. I could feel my tears pricking the back of my eyes.

"You're so wet Beautiful. You see? I knew you wanted me. All this playing hard to get isn't necessary." What the hell was my body doing? Encouraging him? My eyes were shut so tightly that my temples began to hurt, but Glory was no longer there, this wasn't me. I was floating high above looking down at the woman and the man, until he released me and withdrew his hand from between my legs. I cowered away from him further into the corner like the scared animal I was, bringing my knees into my chest to control my shaking.

"Look at me," he said, but I couldn't. I was going to be sick. Between my legs burned. "Look at me!" he yelled again and as I brought my eyes up to meet his he was sucking on his fingers. The vomit was burning my throat. "That's just a little taste of what's to come. This *is* happening and it will continue to happen until I get what I want. You should think about it Beautiful. I'm not asking for much. Talk to Hayley or pay me the way you're accustomed to, for all the trouble you've caused, that way I don't have to talk to Max personally." He was tapping the gun tucked in the front of his pants. "It's that simple! Please keep in mind the next time I won't be this gentle. And remember this is *our* secret, tell anyone and it will only make it worse for you."

By then I was in an all out wail, refusing to open my eyes even after I heard the back door close. I don't know how long I sat there quivering and sobbing, but the smoke detector started to go off. I could hear someone on the stairs calling for me, but I still couldn't move. Max ran right pass me into the kitchen and snatched the smoking frying pan and towel off the stove and dropped them in the sink turning on the water. All I could see was the smoke billowing in the air. It was only after I started to cough that he saw me over in the corner.

"Mom? What happened? What's wrong?" I couldn't answer. All I could think about was Brian Rafferty. His hands were on me. They were in me. Max was shaking my shoulders as he tried to pull me to my feet and out of the kitchen, but I refused to move. "Mom you're scaring me! What's wrong?" The phone was ringing and Max ran to get it. Everything seemed to be moving in slow motion. He said he would hurt Max. *My Max.* I should never have gone to Colorado, this is all my fault.

"Hello? Yes. This is her son. I don't know what happened! There was a frying pan and towel burning on the stove and…No I'm not hurt, but something's wrong with my mom…Are you sending someone now? I've tried to get her out, but she won't move! She's just staring off into spa...Alright, I'll try..." And with that he pressed off the phone and dialed another number.

~

Since I didn't sleep a wink I decided to go for an early run. The phone was ringing as I got back into the apartment, Hail and I picked it up at the same time. I could barely understand what Max was saying, but I heard 911 and that something was wrong with Glory. That's all I needed to hear before I was heading through the door like a mad man with Hayley at my heels in her pajamas. As I screeched to a halt behind the ambulance and fire truck, I was thankful that I lived so much closer. My heart was in my throat as I ran up the stairs and through the door.

"Dad!" Max exclaimed as soon as he saw me. I could smell the smoke and the chemical remains of burnt tephlon in the air. A policeman was talking to him and there was a flurry of activity through out the house.

"Are you alright? Where's your mother? Where's Glory?" I could tell he was close to tears.

"In the kitchen. She's in the kitchen. The police are trying..." I was already pulling him towards the kitchen. From the end of the hallway I could see Glory's bare feet across the floor and my heart dropped into the pit of my stomach.

"Glory! Glo..." I called. A large police officer stepped in front of me and stopped me from going any further. "What's going on? Is she alright? Glory? Get the fuck out of my way damn it!" I screamed, calling for her again as I tried to look around him.

"Sir, I need you to calm down. Are you a family member?"

"No...I mean yes. She's my son's mother. Please, is she alright?"

"We think so, but we haven't gotten much out of her."

"Please let me talk to her," I begged. He asked me to wait where I was as he went into the kitchen to talk to the other officers. Another one came out to me and asked my name. "Weiss. Hayden Weiss. Please I just need to know she's okay."

"She's fine, but quite shaken up? I'm Detective Smith. Is this your son?" he asked looking at Max.

"Yes."

"You want to tell me what happened son?"

"I already told the other officer," Max responded his tone dripping with impatience. "What's wrong with my mom?"

"That's what we're trying to find out," the detective responded. "Tell me again what happened."

Max let out a long sigh. "I was sleeping and I thought I heard yelling, but figured it was the TV since I'd left it on or that I was dreaming so fell back to sleep. The next thing I knew the smoke alarm was going off and I could smell smoke. I called for my mom and she didn't answer, so I ran into the kitchen and I saw the frying pan and towel on the stove on fire. I picked them up, threw them in the sink and turned on the water. There was a lot of smoke. That's when I heard mom coughing in the corner. She was just sitting there staring off into space crying. Our home security people were calling because the fire alarm was going off and then you guys came."

"Does your mom smoke?"

"No! Never! She's a doctor, plus I told you there was stuff burning on the stove, that's why the alarm went off!"

"It's okay, calm down," I said patting him on the shoulder.

"We found a couple cigarette filters outside the back door and the remains of another one in the frying pan."

"Well I'm telling you my mom doesn't smoke!" Max continued to yell.

"I believe you son," Smith reassured him.

"So what…are you thinking there was someone else in house?" I could feel Hayley squeezing my arm through my sweatshirt.

"That's the only explanation we have since she doesn't smoke and then there's one other thing." There was commotion behind him as I saw Glory getting to her feet. She was saying she was fine and wanted to know what they were all doing in her house. I followed the detective in the kitchen.

"Boss, I don't know what happened, but she just snapped out of it!" another officer was saying to the detective we were talking to.

"Max? Max?" She seemed frantic as she looked around for Maximus.

"Mom, mom, I'm right here!" She immediately flung her arms around his neck and asked if he was alright, touching his face and chest. "I'm fine! What happened?"

"Nothing. I…I got distracted and must have burnt the breakfast," she was walking away. We were all looking at each other as it dawned on us she intended to pretend like nothing happened. Then the female officer nudged the detective pointing towards Glory's pajama bottoms with her chin. There wasn't a lot, but through the light fabric it was obvious she was bleeding. I started to ask if she was alright, but was interrupted.

"Ma'am do you realize we've been in the house for the past half hour?" one female officer asked.

"Umm…of …of course I realize and that's why you all need to leave. Right now." Glory mumbled looking around as though she expected someone to come bursting through the door at any minute.

"You need to have a seat," the detective said gently taking her by the elbow and leading her to one of the stools around the island.

"I'm fine. Please just leave. You have to go." She seemed agitated as though she would burst into tears at any moment.

"I'm sorry but we can't do that. Dr. Strair what really happened here? Did someone hurt you?" She looked up at him, her eyes filled with tears.

"Hurt me? No...don't be ridiculous. I burned bacon…since when is that a crime?" she asked with a small laugh trying to play it off. "This is all an accident, a simple misunderstanding."

"So there was no one else in the house with you?" the detective pressed.

"*No*…there was no one else…"

Turning my attention to the Smith I asked, "What else is there detective? You seem to be convinced there was someone else here. Is there a reason you keep asking that?" And moving his eyes upward on the wall behind where Glory was on the floor, I turned to find multiple impressions where it looked like someone had punched the wall. "*Jesus…*"

"Mom I heard yelling," Max interjected and another officer quickly silenced him and asked him to come show him around the house. Max didn't need to see or hear any of this.

"If no one else was with you in the house then who put the cigarette in the frying pan Dr. Strair? Who was smoking on the back patio? Who punched your wall?" Smith pressed. Her tears started to fall and my heart ached for her. It was obvious she was afraid. I pushed everyone aside and took her in my arms, while she quietly sobbed.

"Was it Brian?" Hayley asked after a moment and Glory snatched her head away from my chest as I turned to glare at my sister for her poor timing.

"Who's Brian?" chimed in the detective and female officer.

"My soon-to-be-ex-husband," Hayley replied as she explained to the officers who she was and how she fit into this equation.

Glory began to pace. "I…shouldn't…shouldn't be talking to you. He said…he said I shouldn't say anything to anyone because he knew…where I lived. He…knows where Max goes to school and hangs out," she sobbed and right then I hated myself for leaving the way I did earlier that morning. I don't know what I would do if anything ever happened to her or Max. "He said he's coming back for me and that next time…next time he wouldn't be gentle."

"Dr. Strair we're here now. No one is going to hurt you or your son," said Smith, "but you need to tell us what happened."

"Did he…did he hurt you?" I asked. I was thinking about the Hepatitis and what a filthy pig Brian was, hoping he hadn't done the unthinkable. "Glory this is important. You have to tell us what he did." I couldn't drop this on her now. If anything ever happened to her because of me, I wouldn't be able to forgive myself.

Taking a deep breath she wiped away her tears and looked down at her hands, twirling her thumbs around each other as though she was playing an imaginary thumb wrestling game. "I thought it was Max in the kitchen cooking breakfast, but it was him. He said Max was sleeping when he checked on us. *Checked on us, Hayden!* He was walking around my house while we were sleeping. I told him to get out or I would call the police. He…he moved so fast I didn't know what happened next. He had me against the wall. He told me I would do no such thing. He wanted…he wanted me to..." she was shaking. "He had a gun and I tried to fight him, I tried to run, but my legs wouldn't move." Hayley was crying then as another officer escorted her from the room.

"Sssssshhh, it's ok now. *Did he rape you?"* I repeated again as my blood continued to boil and I hated myself for letting it get this far. Brian Rafferty had no idea who he was messing with and if he thought I only planned on destroying his career now I had every intention of burying him for good. I asked her again if he's touched her, to which she nodded turning her face further into the crook of my arm. The room was silent as I held her. After a few minutes she began.

"He put…he put his hand between my legs and kissed…" she started to gag and I knew then that he'd hurt her. Almost as though that's what they were all waiting to hear, the room burst into activity. The officer that was with Hayley insisted that she tell them anything that would help them track down Brian, while another officer got on the radio to request a finger print specialist. "Where's Max? I need him to stay with me!" Glory was becoming frantic again.

"Max is fine. Baby, I'm so sorry," I said as I took her in my arms, kissing her head, her forehead, and her eyelids. I didn't care who was watching, I wouldn't let her be alone ever again. An intense feeling of guilt took over me, as I fought the emotions running through me like lava.

"Dr. Strair, did he rape you?" the female officer asked the fateful question and again I ground my teeth fighting the urge I had to punch the same wall and hunt the bastard down myself. I don't think my mind had totally encompassed what had happened here. It couldn't.

"No…no. It didn't get that far."

"Ma'am, there's blood on the back of your pants," the officer said, at which point Glory twisted her body to get a better look. I could see the color crawling up her neck and cheeks. She was embarrassed as she quickly turned her back to everyone. "Where did that come from?"

"He grabbed me and put…and put his hand in my pajama pants… he must have scratched me when…he used his hand…he was forcing…," she stopped and turned to look up at me, those eyes, those sad eyes. "The night before I left Colorado I walked in on Brian and Lisa having sex in the linen closet. I didn't know who they were until Hayley introduced us. That's why I couldn't shake their hands at dinner and I left the way I did. He thinks I told Hayley and that's why she wants the divorce. I tried to tell him I did no such thing, but he doesn't believe me. He said I could fix things with Hayley or pay him back the way I'm accustomed to."

"What does that mean? *'Pay him back the way you're accustomed to?'*" asked Smith.

Glory took a deep breath, "Brian thinks I was a prostitute in Las Vegas and if I don't do what he says he's going to tell my son and my colleagues at the hospital. He called yesterday before I went out with Michael and told me he knew who I was and that unless I talked to Hayley he would tell everyone."

"Why would he think that?" pressed Smith.

"Because my Aunt owned an escort service in Vegas and one night when she was short staffed she asked me to fill in and promised I wouldn't have to do anything. Brian and Hayden were at that party. So Brian assumed I was a prostitute. But I'm not. I never was. This is just one big mess. I don't know how he got in or…"

"Sssshhh, we'll find him. This isn't your fault. Do you hear me? The police are going to find him and he's going to jail for the rest of his life if I have anything to say about it." I growled.

~

I felt better knowing that Hayden was there. He came in and took charge, not leaving my side while comforting Max and Hayley. She was devastated and couldn't help but think that she, in some way, was responsible for it all. I tried to reassure her otherwise because deep down I believed the fault ultimately lay with me. Everything that happened, from Las Vegas to Colorado and back to New York was because of something I did or didn't do. Hayley wanted to take Max back to their apartment until Hayden and I finished up with all the questions, but neither Max nor his father liked that idea. Hayden didn't want either of them out of his sight, but detective Smith agreed with Hayley and persuaded him to think of Max, adding that he would have one of the officers escort them home. Reluctantly Hayden gave in and they left shortly after promising to call as soon as they got home.

Initially when the police asked for specific details about what Brian had done to me that morning I was embarrassed, but that was quickly replaced by intense anger. Surprisingly I was angry with myself and no one else, to be frank, I was disgusted. How many times had I watched movies or read of instances where women had been attacked and could remember myself thinking or yelling at the television for them to run, fight, gouge his eyes out, hit him with something, kick him in the family jewels. *Do something!* I would yell, and there I was standing in a kitchen, of all places, with a plethora of utensils and weapons at my disposal and I did absolutely *nothing*. I couldn't even move, allowing a stranger to come into my home and assault me. I don't think I'd ever felt as weak and vulnerable as I did this morning.

The detectives had found some usable prints on the back door, kitchen counter and refrigerator door, but there was no progress in finding Brian since he wasn't home or at work; per Hayden a warrant had been issued for his arrest along with an APB on his car. I was asked to change out of my pajamas and give them to officer Suarez, then another officer swabbed under my nails where I'd scratched Brian.

Once the fire department and EMTs left, things started to quiet down a little more. That's when it really hit me how bad this situation really was. I mean yes he'd threatened me and yes he'd kissed and touched me, all of which I could probably live with, *but* the kicker was that he'd broken into my home and threatened the life and well being of my son. That was unforgivable. It was frightening. Brian had crossed the point of no return in my book and had solidified his own demise at the hands of Hayden Weiss. It was the phone ringing that scared the living daylight out of me, bringing me back to reality. For a while I just stared at it holding my breath and not moving until the answering machine picked up. Thankfully it wasn't Brian and I heard the unintentional exhales around the room when the message began.

"Glory, its Michael, you must be out with your son, so I'll try you back later. I…I hope you know how much I thoroughly enjoyed myself last night. You're an amazing dancer…we'll have to go there again some time. I really want to see you. I didn't sleep one wink thinking about…," there was a long pause, "umm I should probably hang up now before I say something I can't erase from your machine," he laughed nervously. "Don't make me wait too long. Please call me on my cell when you can. I want to see you again. Bye."

Needless to say, I was purple by the time he hung up; the awkward silence that remained in the kitchen wasn't helping. Hayden excused himself and went to the living room, as it was obvious that the thought of Michael and I together bothered him. Hurting Hayden was the last thing I wanted to do, but there was a twinge of pleasure in knowing he did have feelings and it wasn't sitting well with him that Michael was so actively pursuing me. I wanted Hayden Weiss more than I'd ever wanted anything in my entire life, and his reaction just now gave me hope that he may feel the same way about me.

Four very different men had now had their hands on my body, although the fourth was unwanted and there was no comparison between any of my experiences with them and what I shared with Hayden. I *wanted* to feel that again. I *longed* to know it was real and that I hadn't dreamt that night. I *needed* to feel the fullness that came only from having him buried deep within me, a fullness that Eric could never hope to provide. Groans that come not from frustration, but from the exquisite pleasure of having his hands moving against my flesh.

In that instant the contractions in my lower abdomen returned with a vengeance and my knees felt weak. Holding onto the edge of the counter I steadied myself and closed my eyes, having an intimate moment in the middle of a still occupied kitchen. Against my eyelids I could see Hayden's magnificent body on top of mine on the pillowy bed at the Bellagio. He had expertly lifted my legs from his sides, and while keeping them straight, crossed them at my ankles, and swung them over his left shoulder without withdrawing from me or losing his rhythm. His eyes hadn't left mine as he stared at me intently, still moving his hips at the same relentless pace. He was brilliant. This subtle change in position gave him unlimited access to that 'spot', I couldn't yet describe, deep within me that I never knew existed until moments before. And with each thrust another tidal wave of sensations traveled across my skin. His thick member continued its deep rhythmic strokes causing lone tears to run from the corners of my eyes and form puddles in my ears. Tears brought on by immense pleasure, and not from pain or discomfort.

One pump, two pumps, threee-e-e-e. Damn contractions! I was feeling weak again, my knees were buckling. A tingling heat wave was traveling up my body and I felt my nipples taunt growing against the soft fabric of my t-shirt. Then out of the blue there were strong hands lifting me, wait a minute that's not part of this daydream.

"Bring some water," someone was yelling. Shit! Did I faint? Someone was helping me into one of the chairs around the island. I cautiously opened my eyes to find three more pairs staring at me, Hayden, Detective Smith, and Officer Suarez. "All I saw was her sliding to the floor," Detective Smith was saying to Hayden. I quickly blinked away my confusion and focused on the concerned faces in front of me.

"I'm fine, please…I…I just lost track of where I was….I was just… daydreaming," I said in a small voice. How embarrassing is this? My knees were weak from an imaginary orgasm I had twelve years ago! The thought alone of the orgasm had caused me to *almost* climax again. Jesus I'm a mess! My skin was flushed as I gladly took the glass of water slipped into my hands and drank.

"I think she's had enough for one day," Hayden said with some authority walking beside me and snaking his arms protectively around my shoulders. If only he knew. "When can I take her home?" He was gently massaging my shoulders with the firm pressure of his thumbs being rotated in circular fashion over my scapulas. *Ooohh don't do that. Please don't…dooo thaaatttt. Aaaahhh.* This man had no idea what he was doing to me. In one more minute, they would all need ores and canoes to get out of my house because a tidal wave was coming and I couldn't control it if his hands remained on my body any longer. Detective Smith yelled over to the officers outside for a status and they replied that they were pretty much finished.

"It looks like we can be out of here in fifteen minutes or so," he said with a sympathetic smile.

"Will you call me…as soon as… you hear anything?" Worry crept back into my voice. Actually I wasn't sure if it was worry or having Hayden's hands on my body.

"Don't you worry about a thing; I will contact both of you as soon as we have him in custody."

"You've got my contact numbers, right?" Hayden finally stopped his massage.

"Yes I've got them all."

"Smith, I want to know the moment you've got him," Hayden said firmly.

"You'll know Mr. Weiss. You'll know."

Half hour later Hayden and I were alone in the house and I was trying my best not to show how nervous I was. He double checked all the locks on the doors and windows before following me upstairs to my bedroom. He hesitated before entering.

"I'm going to have a shower. I won't be long." I turned away quickly. I didn't trust my eyes not to reveal what I really wanted to do to him right at this moment.

"Take your time. I can pack Max's things while you're in the shower. Where do you keep your luggage?"

"Luggage? What do we need luggage for?"

"You're staying with me until this is all over," he replied matter-of-factly.

"Staying with you? No, no, no. I thought we were only spending the day…"

"Glory I don't want you or Max alone in this house until Brian Rafferty is behind bars!"

"I don't think that's a good id…" I tried to interrupt.

"Frankly I don't care what you think! This isn't up for debate. I will feel a whole lot better knowing you and my son are *with* me." I opened my mouth to protest again, but stopped myself, knowing full well I didn't want to stay here alone either.

"Is there enough room for all of us?" I asked, walking out to the hallway closet for the overnight bags.

"More than enough. It's a four bedroom apartment with an amazing view. I've already had a room decorated for Max and you can stay in my room." The small suitcase I was trying to reach in the hallway closet toppled to the floor beside me when my hand missed the handle, thanks to his last comment. I was looking at him and he was smiling. "This is where you say, '*I thought there were four bedrooms!*'" He was laughing at the face I was making, but was obviously reading my expression all wrong, since I thought sharing a bedroom with him sounded like a perfect idea.

"Umm, I thought there were four bedrooms," I in a small voice picking up the suitcase, doing a piss poor job of trying to pretend as though I didn't just make a complete ass out of myself.

"There is, but I was in the process of turning it into the baby's room, so I'll sleep on the sofa, unless…," he paused and held my wrist as I walked by, "unless you don't mind sharing my room with me."

"There's a lot that I don't mind," I replied fighting the urge to jump his bones right then and there. "Maybe it's time we cleared it all up." But right now wasn't that time. Even though I'd taken off my pajamas I could still smell Brian Rafferty on me.

"We'll talk later," he responded. "This isn't the time or the place. You've had a rough day and right now I just want to get you home."

"I couldn't agree with you more." Hayden packed Max's bag and after I got out of the shower I quickly packed mine.

"All set?" he asked as I came downstairs.

"Yes, I just need to do one more thing. I'll finish locking up and meet you outside." I walked pass him into the kitchen, waited until I heard the door open then picked up the phone, and taking Michael's card out of my coat pocket I purposely dialed his home number since he'd specifically asked me to try his cell. *Please don't pick up. Please don't pick up.* I did internal cart wheels when the answering machine came on. I cleared my throat. **BEEP**.

"Michael this is Glory. I'm sorry I missed your call this morning, but there've been quite a few…how shall we say this…uh… developments since we went out last night and…well… I don't think I'll be able to take *this* any further, *this* meaning you and me. Like I told you before I have a lot going on in my life right now and there are some things that I need to clear up and work out. It's only fair that I'm straight forward with you, so that you know where I'm coming from and you don't think I've mislead you in any way. Thank you for a wonderful evening and I hope there are no hard feelings. Goodbye." I quietly pressed off the phone and let out a sigh of relief.

"Why did you do that?" came Hayden's slow roasted voice behind me. I turned to face him and our eyes met. He immediately looked like he regretted saying anything. "I'm sorry I need to mind my own business. You don't have to answer that. I shouldn't have eavesdropped," and before I could respond he was already walking away and heading towards the front door.

"I did it for me," I whispered. "I did it for us." But he was already gone and out of ear shot.

CHAPTER NINETEEN

Once in the car I opened my mouth to say something, but Hayden reached over and squeezed my clasped hands gently rubbing them with his thumb. Nothing was said, but I understood that there would be time enough for us to say all that we wanted to each other. We drove in silence the remainder of the way with our only form of communication coming through us holding hands.

I loved this man.

Saying his apartment/penthouse/condo/mansion-thirty-stories-high, whatever you wanted to call it, was beautiful would have been a major understatement. The floor to ceiling windows that surrounded three-quarters of the space left me speechless. Max seemed completely at home, with it becoming obvious that he must have had some input into the design of his room since every facet of it incorporated many of his favorite things, like sports, math, and his favorite colors. It was a beautiful space. Both Hayley and Max looked comfortable, almost as though she'd been living there for months and he had known her all his life. Hayden gave me a quick tour and then he asked me to relax while he took a shower and made an early dinner. Even with Hail there, this all felt so right. Hayden was in the kitchen getting dinner ready, Max was lying in front of one of the windows finishing up his required reading for school, while Hail and I were in the middle of a scrabble game. I'm not quite sure how it happened, but what had started off as a horrific day had suddenly taken a 180 degree turn. Hayden made me feel safe. Brian hadn't been caught but I still felt as though I didn't have a care in the world. Once the lasagna was finished we had a lovely dinner in the dining room, listening to the several stories Max and Hayden had from their time together in Colorado.

"Max, you know what I forgot to tell you?" Hayden asked as he leaned over and started to clear my plate away. I wanted him so badly. It was awful, but I was sitting there wishing that Max and Hayley would go away and we could be alone. Did that make me a bad person? He smelled so good and the simple ribbed Nike t-shirt he wore had the perfect logo in bold across the front, '**JUST DO IT**', and boy did I want to take it literally.

"Nah Dad, what?"

"The twins live in this building!"

"No way!" Max yelled almost jumping out of his seat. "Really?" Hail and I couldn't help laughing.

"Yeah, they were one of the first tenants. If you want, we can give them a call and see if they're home since they flew back this morning." Turning to me he asked if that was fine and I told him it was. The Nealands were home and within minutes Max was on his way down to visit, it was still early but Hayden told him to come back up by eight since he had school tomorrow. Hayley, shortly after, commented that she was tired and was going to hit the sack early. Within fifteen minutes I got my wish and Hayden and I were alone. Now what was I going to do?

~

I could tell Glory was nervous as we packed the dishes away in the dishwasher and I immediately felt awful for getting rid of the others. With Max, I had genuinely forgotten about the twins, but then once I realized that the only thing standing between Glory and I being alone was my eight month pregnant sister, I threw a couple glances in her direction and she quickly got the drift and went scurrying off to bed.

"Do you want to go downstairs to the den? We can finish the rest of this wine and talk?" I did want to be alone with her, but knew full well that if she looked at me a certain way, the last thing I would be able to do is talk.

"That sounds nice," so I took the bottle and she carried the two glasses downstairs. I turned on the fireplace and poured the wine while she walked over and admired the view of the city from the window. "This is a beautiful building Hayden."

"Thanks. I've always liked it and promised myself if I didn't buy a house next, I would move here. I think Max and Hail really like it don't you?"

"Like it? He's like a pig in mud right now. I don't know if he'll ever want us to leave, especially with the boys being in the same building." She was laughing as she turned to face me. God she was beautiful. The city lights behind her cast a warm glow on her skin and even in simple jeans and a sweater the outline of her perfect shape was crystal clear. Those hips, those thighs, her breasts...

"That wouldn't be such a bad thing?" I added, opening a door that I hoped she would enter.

"What wouldn't be such a bad thing?" she whispered. Her eyes were dancing.

"If you never left." I held a glass of wine out to her. She came forward and in that instant I saw the same soft spoken girl that had turned me inside out that night so long ago. "Come sit beside me," I choked becoming surprisingly overwhelmed with the emotions I felt for this woman.

"Hayden I…"

"Please, come sit. I have some things that I want to say and then you can say whatever you want," I said softly. "Now, please sit." And obediently she took the wine and placed it on the coffee table, and slipped her hand in mine she sat beside me. Clearing my throat I began.

"If you haven't already heard, I've called off my engagement to Lisa." She didn't seem surprised which was a good thing, so I continued. "I would love to say that seeing you and finding out about Max, had nothing to do with it, but that would be a lie. Eighty percent of the reason was seeing you, another ten percent came with the realization that I never felt about her the way I felt about you, and the other ten came once I found out about her and Brian."

"Hayden…"

"Ssshhh, please let me finish," I rubbed the back of her hands. "Seeing you *was* the push I needed to call it off. I have never felt for Lisa, or about anyone for that matter, the way I felt when I was with you. Finding out that you were very real, and I hadn't dreamt what happened in Vegas put everything into perspective. I can't begin to explain to you how being with you that night changed my life forever; *forever* Glory. What we had was so much more than a one night stand. I knew I loved you then, that moment you quoted Shakespeare and Emily Dickinson, and I know I love you now." Her tears came as she looked down at our hands. "I knew there was something special about you and even if you did turn out to be…to be what we thought you were, I wouldn't have cared. I meant every word in Colorado when I told you I was prepared to wake up that morning and tell you everything there was to know about me. It wasn't just about the sex." Her warm tears were falling on my hands as she wiped them away.

"I know you've been alone all this time, but honestly I'm not sorry about that," she looked up at me with questioning eyes. "*I'm* the only man for you and I'm sorry it took twelve years to get to this point, but I promise to make you and Max happy and give you everything I possibly can. Eric and Michael could never love you the way I do. The way I *will*." She began to sob then, with the soft intakes of breath and shallow breathing, her shoulders shaking with little heaves. "I'll never forgive myself for leaving the way I did this morning. Maybe if I'd stayed things…Brian would never…"

"Don't…say…that," she cried placing her fingers over my lips, but I took them away.

"I don't know what I would do if anything ever happened to you. If I could turn back…"

"Hayden…it's alright!" she was gently rubbing the side of my face.

"No it isn't! I want you Glory. I want to love you, marry you, protect you, and be a part of yours and Max's lives. I want us to be a family and if you aren't ready for that, then I'll wait. I'll wait for you to find out that Michael Beckford and whoever else isn't the one for you and…I'll wait forever if that's what it takes…I love y…"

I didn't finish since her lips were on mine, tantalizingly warm and salty from her tears. She tenderly took my bottom lip in her mouth and rolled her tongue over it slipping it into my mouth. Aaaahh yes, I remembered that. I couldn't help the groan that escaped my lips as I circled my arms around her waist and dragged her onto my lap. This was it, the moment I'd been waiting for; waiting for what seemed like an eternity. I kissed her like I never had before, like with every twist and twirl of our lips and tongues, she was given the proof that everything I'd said was true. Curling my tongue upwards I ran it across the roof of her mouth, feeling her shudder and press her round bottom into my groin. Her body never lied to me and responded with naked honesty when she liked something I was doing. A simple shudder, moan, or shiver was worth a thousand acclamations in my book. And in response she dragged her teeth across my flesh and nibbled on my mouth, which was steadily driving me insane. She was still crying, soft silent tears were falling as I brought my lips to her eyes and kissed her tears away. She hugged me tightly burying her face into the crook of my neck and I just held her as the pain of this day and the loneliness of the past twelve years flowed out of her.

"I love you so much," I whispered, but she still hadn't responded. "This is where you say something," I said, bringing her face up so that I could look in her eyes. Her silence was making me nervous. What if I was wrong and she didn't' feel the same way? No, I couldn't be wrong; the way she just kissed me said it all.

She wiped away her tears and took a deep breath. "There's so… so much that I want to say to you. I guess as much as I hoped for it, I still can't believe you felt the same way about that night as I did. I never imagined that little inexperienced me could have that type of effect on someone like you. What we shared was perfect and indescribable and from the moment I saw you in the elevator in

Colorado I wanted it back. I wanted to lie in your arms again and have you tell me how being with me was unlike anything you'd done before. Hearing Edward announce that you were engaged and Hayley was expecting their *first* grandchild didn't help ease my anxiety. The fact that you were able to move on with your life made me feel even more stupid. I...I didn't want to be the reason things didn't work out between you and Lisa, but in the same breath I envied her." She took another deep breath, letting her head fall backward. "You were right when you said I've been alone for too long and some days were harder than others, but in the end Max was all that really mattered to me. I couldn't imagine my life without him. Having an abortion wasn't even an option..."

"I'm so glad you didn't. I can't begin to tell you how much it means to me, but if it takes the rest of my life, I plan on showing you," I said taking her mouth again. She willingly let me kiss her, moaning as I curled my tongue around hers, gently massaging her shoulders. Placing her hands flat against my chest, she eased back ever so slightly until our eyes met.

"Hayden, things between Eric and I..."

"Glo please... I don't want details...it doesn't matter. I just need to know that you feel the same way I do," I said slipping my arms from around her as I stood up and began to pace back and forth, again thinking back on the nightmare I had back in Colorado of her and Eric. The *last* thing I needed were details.

"You've said your piece, now let me say mine," she said firmly as she stopped me from pacing and sat me back down beside her. "Twelve years is a long time to go without feeling the way you'd made me feel that night in Vegas, and honestly, I was yearning for it. I needed to feel like that woman again. I needed to know she was real. What happened between Eric and I was a mistake on my part. I felt as if it was hopeless to keep looking for what I had with you and stupid for even expecting to find it. Life was slipping by me and Max needed a father figure. I felt as though I needed to hurry and play catch up; be a real mom to Max, get a husband, and maybe have another child. Financially I was finally in a position to relax and enjoy everything I worked so hard to build. So against every fiber in my being I took my relationship with Eric to the next level." I closed my eyes and looked away as she continued, hating the realization of what she was telling me. I didn't want to know. My imagination was already enough to drive me crazy. The last thing I needed was her verbal commentary on her sexual experience with another man.

"Hayden, look at me," she insisted and reluctantly I did. "I can't begin to explain to you how wrong being with him felt. It felt awkward...it felt...aahh what's the word I'm looking for," she said glancing up at the ceiling as she did a mental search. "Umm...yes...it felt unnatural," she finished with a smile. "Four minutes later I was miserable, unsatisfied, and wanting you more than I ever had before. I knew then I would never get over what we'd shared and I was content to be alone for the rest of my life if need be, because the emptiness of being with someone I had no feelings for was worse than pretending you never existed at all. After that night I began to back away from Eric and within a couple of weeks I broke things off completely." She smiled when she saw my lips curl at the corners ever so slightly. *Four minutes? Schmuck!*

"I love you so very much Hayden Weiss and I'm hoping that it's much more than the physical. I want you to take care of Max and I, and love us like you've never done before and in return, we'll love you the only way we've ever known how, completely." I leaned in to kiss her, but she stopped me. "There's one more thing you need to know before we move forward and I'm hoping that you won't hate me because of it..."

"Hate you? How could I ever hate you?"

"Because I...I knew Hayden was your real name?" she blurted out as I stood to my feet trying to comprehend what she was saying. "I told you I was out by the pool when I saw you leaving, but I didn't tell you that I was hiding there all night and I'd seen you turn away my Aunt and a few other girls." I grabbed a handful of my hair as I walked over to the window. "When the blonde man came out to you, he called you by your name. Hayden. Later at the hotel when you gave me your real name it caught me off guard and that's why I told you my nickname. It never crossed my mind to try and find you once I found out I was pregnant. I didn't want to. I was embarrassed at the situation, plus I didn't think you would believe me..."

"You should've given me the option damn it! You took all my options away when you decided *not* to find me. I had a right to know Glory. Max was my son just as much as he was yours!" I was angry, but not totally with her.

"I know, I know. I'm so sorry. I made a mistake," she was standing behind me circling her hands through my arms and across my chest. "Please forgive me! I lied before in Colorado when you asked me if I had it to do over if I would do the same thing and I said yes. I would do everything differently. I would've been there when you woke up! I would never have left the way I did," she cried onto my back and I could feel the wetness from her tears through my t-shirt. I turned and took her into my arms.

"I'm sorry I yelled. I just feel as though I've wasted the past twelve years of my life and things would have been so much different for me…for both of us if you had stayed," I took another deep breath and pulled her closer. "Everything happens for a reason. You never know, I may not have been ready then and now things are happening right when they're supposed to. I'm older, wiser, and know first hand what my life would be like without you in it. I don't want to lose you again Glo."

"Do you forgive me?"

"Of course I do, but there's really nothing to forgive. I can't blame you completely because of the situation, since…since I contacted your Aunt Miranda as well. I left countless messages at the club asking how I could get in contact with the girl that she brought to the party named Glo and she never returned my calls. Not once! So in part there were several factors working against us."

"Wa…wait a minute, you…you contacted Miranda?" I could tell she was trying to stop herself from crying, anger was building behind her eyes.

"At least five times that first month and then a few more times over the next year when I was there on business – even stopped by the club. The guy there wasn't helpful either, Carlos I think his name was. Both he and your aunt ignored my calls. Of course I didn't know she was your Aunt at the time, but still. All I knew was that they were the ones Tom had arranged the girls through."

"You were still looking for me a year after? I don't believe this. Why didn't she tell me? And when I told her I was pregnant she pretended like she didn't know who the father was, like she didn't even care. When all along it was because she already knew! She knew you'd been looking for me? God, if I'd known you were looking for me, I swear I would've come to you. You do believe me don't you?"

"Sssshh, sssshh calm down. It's alright," I said smoothing her hair, trying to comfort her. "Of course I believe you. Maybe she was trying to protect you?"

"Bullshit! Protect me from what? She kicked me out the minute...let me rephrase that...the *second* she found out I was pregnant. You would think that she would've gladly pawned me off on the first interested man. Why wouldn't she tell me you were looking for me even after she knew how hard it was for me with Max alone, in school, during that brutal residency, never really being apart of his life all these years? If I knew you wanted to find me it would've made all the difference in the world...Max would have been happier." Now she was the one pacing, becoming almost hysterical as she wondered why Miranda would've kept something like that from her.

"Glory, Glory, please, none of it matters now!" I tried to reassure her. "Max *is* happy. All that matters is that we're together and we love each other! A lot has happened in the last couple days..."

"You don't understand...things could have been so much different. We would be a family. I wouldn't have been with Eric and Brian wouldn't have..." her tears came anew and I just held her. I think the reality of what happened to her was finally sinking in. "He hurt me Hayden...*he hurt me*...and it could've all been avoided!" she wailed as I continued to hold her, vowing never to leave her again. She was shaking like a leaf against me.

"It's going to be alright, I promise you. Forget about the past and let me love you now," I said bringing her mouth to mine. I wanted to make everything go away except what was between us - our love. We were kissing again as I could feel myself growing against her abdomen. She slipped her cool hands up the back of my t-shirt pulling me closer. I picked her up and she wrapped her legs around my waist as I turned and sat down on the sofa. "I love you so much," I breathed as I nibbled and kissed her neck and shoulders. She responded that she loved me as well, but it was muffled by her sweater when she pulled it over her head, revealing a damn near dangerously sexy lace brassiere. God she was the picture of perfection.

We were kissing, this time more urgently as though we were racing to some imaginary finish line of intimacy. I was sucking on her tongue as she opened her mouth willingly. I could feel the heat from her body through the cotton fabric of my t-shirt. She felt just the way I remembered, like velvet against my skin. I reached between us and cupped her breasts, gently running my thumbs over her already taut nipples, drawing low moans from deep within her. They were fuller than I remembered, but I probably had Max to thank for that. I wanted to touch her intimately. I'd been dreaming about it for what seemed like an eternity.

Glory slipped her hand down between my legs as she stroked me with an irritatingly slow rhythm, which only added to my craving for her. She was calling my name softly over and over again, heightening my arousal.

"*I want you,*" she breathed moving her mouth away from mine and taking my earlobe between her teeth while flicking her tongue ever so slightly around my sensitive flesh. The stroke of her tongue was like being hit by an electrical shock over and over again. "I've wanted you for so long."

I groaned loudly, holding her by the hips as I pressed her further onto my growing hardness. Control yourself Hayden. You can't do this now. Not yet...

"I want... you too, but we...can't do... this right now," I managed to get out between her kisses as I took my hands away from her warm flesh. She pulled away and looked at me.

"Why not? Max won't be..."

"It's not about Max or Hayley. I...I want...I have an appointment to see my internist tomorrow to have a complete check up 'post' Lisa, if you know what I mean. And I think you should do the same after what happened with Brian today. Just to be safe," I said with a nervous smile, slightly embarrassed at what I was saying. There wasn't anything I wanted more than to make love to her at this exact moment. Being buried deep within her would've been a dream come true. But I was faced with the stark reality that both Lisa and Brian were sexually promiscuous people. I could tell she was disappointed, but her wellbeing meant more to me than the exquisite pleasure I knew would come if we made love right this minute. The fact remained that I made a poor choice in having Lisa for a partner and the thought of remotely hurting Glory as a result of that choice wasn't worth it.

"Brian gave my sister Hepatitis. He's been sleeping with Lisa for at least eleven months..."

"What?" I could see the surge of panic flow through her.

"I've always used protection with her, but I want to make sure. And after what happened today it wouldn't hurt for you to get a complete once over. I'm sure since things didn't...go very far, that you have nothing to worry about, but let's be on the safe side." Her tears fell anew.

"You're right. I guess we should hold off. This nightmare just seems to be getting worse," she responded in a low voice.

"You know I want you more than anything, don't you?"

"Of course I do its fine really. We have to take care of this first," she added with a smile as she reached for her sweater, but I held her hand to stop her.

"I just don't want to take any chances. I want things between us to be perfect from the beginning."

"I know…"

"I promise as soon as I'm given a clean bill of health I'm all yours!"

"Hayden, I've waited for years, I don't think a couple more days will kill me," she said with a smile and I kissed her again.

~

I'm not sure how long Hayden and I stayed like that, hugging and kissing, touching and fondling, but it was Max coming home that finally brought us back upstairs from our warm cozy love nest. We talked about the twins and the plans they'd made for later in the week and then went to bed. Unfortunately, Hayden had some work to finish so I went to bed soaking wet and alone. I knew we couldn't *do* anything, but I would've settled just to have his arms around me as I fell asleep.

I tossed and turned all night, having visions of Brian's neck in a guillotine, visions of me beating my Aunt to a pulp, and visions of Hayden and I getting married. My mind kept running through these 'what if' scenarios over and over again. It was a mess. *I* was a mess. In addition to everything that had happened today, I couldn't get my mind off the fact that Hayden had contacted Miranda. It was no surprise that I hadn't heard from her in months since I told her I wouldn't just give her ten thousand dollars and that she should forward her realtor's contact information to me, but for her to keep this from me all these years? And to think I was prepared to buy whatever house it was she wanted. Either way, I had every intention of personally going to see her once things went back to some degree of normalcy around here. She was deceitful and I'd be damned if I let her get away with it. I had held my tongue long enough with her and it was time for me to tell her exactly what I thought of her. She had gone through life walking over people and thinking only of herself. My mother would've been disappointed in how she 'turned out' and maybe she needed to hear that.

The apartment for the most part was quiet, but around midnight I could hear Hayden talking to Hayley in her room. It seemed like she cried all night. I felt so helpless. She had been a victim in this situation with Brian as much as I was. There was movement in the hallway, just outside Hayden's bedroom door causing me to sit up once the door was opened. Even in the darkness I could see Hayden's tall masculine frame enter the room quietly.

"Is everything alright?" I whispered through the silence.

"What are you still doing up? I thought you would have been asleep by now," he was making his way over to the lamp on the end table and turning it on.

"I can't really sleep. How's Hail doing?"

"She's having a rough night. Her obstetrician finally gave me permission to give her half a sleeping pill. Surprisingly it worked so she just fell asleep. I was trying to sneak in and grab some pajamas without making too much noise," he said sitting on the opposite side of the bed. "How are *you* doing? I didn't mean to wake you."

"You didn't wake me and I've been better. Every time I close my eyes I see…," I took a deep breath as parts of the day flashed across my mind. "I guess I can't believe this is all happening or happened."

"It's okay," he said reassuringly as he held my hand between his. "Everything is going to be fine. I'm here now, try to get some sleep." And as he swung his feet up onto the bed he pulled me into him. "I'm here."

I'm not sure when I fell asleep since all I could think about was the fact that I was spooning for the first time in my life and it felt damn good.

CHAPTER TWENTY

My internal alarm clock caused my eyes to pop open at six on the dot. Much to my disappointment Hayden was already gone. So I slipped out of bed, made it, and went down the hall to Max's room to wake him for school. I was showered and dressed half an hour later. Walking through the living room to the kitchen I noticed that Hayden wasn't in there either so I went downstairs to the den to find him sleeping on the large chocolate brown leather sofa. God he was a sight for sore eyes, disheveled hair and all. I took the blanket that was three-quarters of the way on the floor and tucked it back around his body lingering momentarily at his hips. There was the slightest frown played across his forehead, which made me wonder what he was dreaming about. I didn't want to wake him, but I *did* want to kiss him. Not caring that the man had probably only fallen asleep hours before I knelt beside him, closed my eyes, and gently pressed my lips against his.

"*I love you Hayden Weiss*," I whispered as I withdrew my mouth.

"I love you too Glory Strair," came his groggy reply as he slipped his arms around my waist and kissed me again.

"I didn't mean to wake you…"

"Ohhhh yes you did," he said with a small laugh, arching his back to stretch.

"Alright, maybe I did," I laughed. "Max and I are about to leave."

"Already? What time is it?" he tried to sit up.

"Probably a little before seven. Max has a 7:35 first bell and I have two cases this morning."

"Do you know what time you'll be home?" he was rubbing his thumb lovingly along my cheek.

"I'm free most of the afternoon. Why? What time do you leave work?" silently I wondered why this felt so good, us together so early in the morning, these questions.

"I probably won't go in today. I'll bring Hayley over to my parents this morning so she won't be alone then I'll go to my doctor's appointment. My Dad and I were going to take her to meet with the lawyers around lunch to go over a few things since today was supposed to be the day that she officially files for divorce. After that I'm free. What time does Max get out of school?"

"Two-thirty, but today is Monday so he has the math club and debate team which means Nancy won't drop him off until about 6:00 at my office."

"Who's Nancy?"

"My lifesaver," I said with a giggle, "no, she's a teacher's aid at the school; she earns extra cash by watching Max after school and bringing him to my office or home depending on the day."

"Can she bring Max here instead?" he asked.

"Umm, I don't see why not. Your apartment is much closer to the school or I could probably even pick him up today…"

"No!" the way he said it caught me a little off guard. "I'm sorry. I mean let her drop him off and maybe you could still leave work early and we could spend some quality time together." I couldn't help the smile plastered across my face.

"Ooohhh I see. A little QT sounds like just what the doctor ordered," I laughed.

"Good because I've always been told what a good patient I am," he was kissing me again.

"Here you are!" Max called from the stairs and I jumped back so fast that I hit Hayden in the chin. We both groaned. Max was laughing, "I'm sorry; I didn't mean to scare you. Mom didn't you hear me calling? We've got to go or we'll be late. Mornin' Dad! Love you," and without even a backwards glance he sauntered back up the steps waving goodbye to his father.

"I love you too!" Hayden yelled back still rubbing his chin and smiling.

"I'm sorry, is it me or did the fact that he just caught us kissing not seem to phase him?"

"Why should it?" Hayden asked pulling me into his arms again. "It's natural for moms and dads to kiss," and kiss we did until I finally managed to pull away. "Do you really have to go? Can't you call in?" he whined. I couldn't help but laugh.

"Call in? I can't just call in…"

"I know, I know, I was just teasing. But it was worth a shot," he said between kisses across my neck.

"I really have to go or we'll be late," I sighed, slipping out of his arms as I stood up.

"Alright, but what about our plan? Do you think you can get off early?"

"I'll be home by three," I replied over my shoulder as I ran up the stairs.

"Promise?" he bellowed.

"Promise!" I yelled back. *I'll be home by three*. That sounded like music to my ears. It was possible that even after all that had happened, I could still get everything that I wanted; a family and the man of my dreams.

I met with Jeff first thing when I got to the hospital that morning and told him what had happened over the weekend. Once his initial shock had passed, he was joining the lynch mob to destroy Brian. He was a good friend vowing to help anyway he could, starting with the mandatory three week vacation he was forcing me to take at the end of the week. Then he went with me to the lab and ordered a battery of labs for every STD known to man. I would have the results back as soon as possible.

After that my day progressed with me in some state of internal glee; humming, singing, and at one point I think I was actually skipping in the OR. It was almost as though nothing had happened with Brian and the possibility of living happily ever after with Hayden and Max made all traces of worry and regret disappear. I headed back to the office when my morning cases were finished; as I was walking through the door, my beeper went off with an emergency page from Rebecca.

"Hey Becca! What's…"

"I just paged you!"

"Yeah I noticed," I said with a laugh, but she wasn't laughing back.

"What's wrong?"

"Nancy just called because she was waiting for Max, but he wasn't there," my heart rate began to increase. "She went to the office and they told her they hadn't seen Max since lunch. Ms. Schwartz called the office when he didn't show up for Physics…"

"What are you saying?"

"I don't know…Max isn't at school and Nancy can't find him."

"It's now 2:30 they have lunch at 12:00, why didn't someone call me before?!" I shouted, shear panic taking over me. As I thought of all the things that could possibly have happened, but only one possibility made me physically sick. I was running down the hall towards my office trying desperately not to panic. Maybe Hayden picked him up early to surprise me or he's sick in some bathroom and no one even thought to look. My mind was going a millions miles a minute. "Get Nancy and the school secretary on the phone. Now!" I yelled over my shoulder.

"Right away," she responded, but I was already on the phone dialing Hayden.

"Hayden Wei…"

"Hayden its Glory…"

"Hi, I'm leaving the lawyer's office now and should be home by thr…"

"Hayden, Max isn't at school. He wasn't there when Nancy went to pick him up and no one seems to be able to find him since after lunch. Did you pick him up?"

"No, no of course not. I'm just leaving the office now. Wait a minute. What do you mean he isn't at school? Where is …"

"I mean I dropped my child off this morning and now he isn't there. They can't find him anywhere! He's not with you?" My line was beeping. "Hold on! I think that's Nancy!" I didn't wait for him to answer as I switched lines. "Yes Becca?"

"I have Nan…"

"Put her through." Once I heard the line connect I started. "Nancy? Where are you?"

"Dr. Strair, I'm still at the school."

"What happened? Are you telling me that none of his friends know where he is? Why didn't you call me before?"

"I'm sorry! I'm not even supposed to be here this early, but I got an email notice that the math club and debate team meetings had been canceled until next week and I had to drop some forms off to the office so I came in early before school got out." I could tell that the poor woman was becoming more distraught with each passing second. "Where could he be? This isn't like him at all! He would never leave in the middle of the school day…Pat? Patrick? Uh… Hold on I see one of his friends now… Patrick!"

"Nance you hold on as well I've got someone on the other line," I clicked over to Hayden. "Hayden?"

"Yeah I'm here! What did she say?"

"She doesn't know anything and she's getting more upset by the minute. Hayden tell me Brian wouldn't do this. Tell me I have nothing to worry about? Tell me!" My tears exploded out of me at the thought that the filthy bastard could have taken my son! "I've got to find him."

"Glory, don't leave your office. I'm calling Detective Smith and then I'm heading over there. Wait for me. I'll be there in fifteen minutes, alright? Don't leave…" But I had already hung up.

"Nance?"

"I'm…I'm still here."

"What did Patrick say?"

"He…he said his fa…father picked him up early!"

"Wa…what?"

"He said on their way back to class from lunch Max got a text on his phone and said he was leaving early because his father had a surprise for him." I think all the blood had officially drained from my head as I felt myself falling, missing my chair all together as I slumped to the floor, pulling the phone down beside me. "Dr. Strair? Dr. Strair? What's going on? Max's father? I didn't even know…"

"I…I have to go Nancy," I mumbled haphazardly putting the phone on the hook as I willed myself not to freak out! Becca came rushing in, just in time to see me burst into tears on the floor.

"Oh my God! Glory what's wrong? What's happened? Where's Max?" Rebecca was shouting.

I tried to gain my composure as, once again, I was disappointed in myself for how quickly I fell apart and became a useless crying idiot in these types of personal situations. I am a surgeon for Christ's sake. I make critical decisions on a daily basis. What was wrong with me? I tried to talk but I couldn't even form the words, as the only noises coming out of me were guttural sobs.

"Jesus Glory, say something, anything, but tell me what to do, please," Rebecca begged as her own tears also started to fall. "Should I call the police or Dr. Bruckheimer?" I still couldn't answer as behind my lids I saw Brian Rafferty's unforgiving face looking at me. *Pull yourself together!* Screamed the voice in my head. *Not again. You will not let the mere thought of this man render you in a complete state of fucking paralysis. Get up! Get up now and find your son god damn it! You've fought in the past for everything else. Fight now! Get up Glory, Max needs you.*

I didn't know who this woman was in my mind's eye viciously scolding me, nor did I care. All that mattered was that it worked. And as quickly as it came over me, the fear and sense of defeat was replaced by a seething rage at the thought Max may be in danger. Wiping at my face I quickly stood up and pulled myself in front of my computer.

"I think my son has been kidnapped…" I began to say.

"Oh God Glo…"

"*Listen to me Becca!* I need you to call Nancy back and have her meet me here. Also call Jeff and have him come down immediately, then I want you to contact I-Tel and see if they can give you the last number Max received a text from this morning." She still hadn't moved. "Go!"

"But…but who would…"

"BECCA! I don't have time for questions, time is of the essence! So go do what I asked. Hayden has contacted the police." I had already turned my attention back to my computer, when Rebecca bolted from my office. I pulled up my Vonage account online and realized I'd never loved these people more, as I clicked on the call log and pulled up all the incoming and outgoing calls to my home phone number in the last few days. *"Where are you?"* I asked to no one in particular as I skimmed through numbers. "There you are," I said, feeling calmer at that moment than I had in the past three weeks. Grabbing a pen I wrote down the number of the call that came in at 7:28 pm on Saturday evening, then dialed it. There was no answer, so I hung up and dialed again. This time waiting for the voicemail to kick in and feeling the slightest twinge of pride when I heard the correct voice on the other end. I left a message.

"Brian, I know you have my son, and as God is my witness, if you harm a single hair on his head I will make you sorry you were ever born! It's doesn't have to be like this. I will do anything, and I mean *anything,* if you return Max safely to me. I'm a woman of my word. I'm sure you have my mobile number so call me. Hayden has contacted the police so you've got about twenty minutes before they're crawling all over my office. You have until they come to reach me, so that we can make our *own* arrangements. If you've done anything to hurt him, I can't help you," and with that I marked the message as urgent and hung up.

Becca called to say that both Nancy and Jeff were on their way. I was standing in front of the window staring at my cell phone when Jeff burst through the door a short while later. He looked even more pale than I felt and saying nothing, he simply walked over and took me into his arms. My body was shaking with the tears I knew were threatening to break out of me, but I held it together, jerking free only when I heard my cell phone ringing. Placing my finger over my lips I motioned for Jeff to be quiet.

"Hello?"

"I don't think you're in any position to be making deman…"

"Where is my son? If you hurt him, I swe…"

"Calm down Beautiful, he's right here safe and sound."

"What were you thinking? He has noth…"

"Taking him was a means to an end…and that end is you. You know he's been really quiet since I told him how we all met in Las Vegas. I don't think he liked it very…"

"You didn't!" I hissed into the phone.

"Oh believe me Beautiful I did."

"Stop calling me that! How could…"

"I don't have time for this. On the message you said that you would do anything I asked correct?"

"Yes, as long as Max was returned safely."

"Well as I'm sure you're aware, I'm ruined and it's all because of you. My life, my family, my career have all been shot to shit because of you. You just can't seem to keep your fucking mouth shut and because of *it* things have escalated to this. Assault, kidnapping, rape, murder."

My knees threatened to buckle since I knew the last two actions on his laundry list of crime, were what he had in store for me. Rebecca had just walked in.

"Tell me what you want me to do." Jeff was asking who was on the phone as I turned away from him to concentrate.

"Meet me at the entrance of the Central Park Zoo in fifteen minutes. I know I don't have to tell you to come alone!"

"And you will let Max go…" I didn't even finish, as he had already hung up.

"Was that Brian?!" Jeff was asking as I hung up the cell phone and walked towards my coat hanging behind the door. "Glory where are you going? What did he say?"

"I have that number for you Glory," Becca was saying with a dazed look on her face as she tried to wrap her mind around what was happening.

"That's alright Becca, thank you, I already found it," and turning my attention to Jeff said, "He'll meet me at the Central Park Zoo to give me Max."

"You don't believe that do you? He's not going to just hand him over! We'll call the police and have…"

"Glory, Dr. Bruckheimer's right…"

"Listen to me, both of you! It's because of me that Max is even in this situation. *I* have to fix it," I said with some degree of finality as I buttoned up my coat.

"Please don't do this. Wait for Hay…" Jeff was pleading

"I've already made up my mind, nothing you can say will stop me from going, but promise me one thing," I said as I took both his hands in mine.

"What?" He was already shaking his head as though he didn't want to hear what I had to say.

"Promise that if anything happens to me you'll…"

"No. No. Do you hear me? No!" he continued to shout. "This isn't happening and you aren't meeting him anywhere until the police get here…," I silenced him by gently pressing four fingers over his mouth.

"I *have* to go. Please don't say anything to Hayden until I call and tell you Max is safe. Promise me Jeff."

"Glory I can't let you do this…it's obvious he'll stop at nothing until he has you." I knew then he wouldn't help me and I was wasting valuable time. Rebecca was now crying uncontrollably as she made a feeble attempt to block my passage through the door, but with the look I gave her she had no choice but to step aside or I would've plowed through her.

"Do what you want," I said over my shoulder as I ran out of my office, with Jeff and Rebecca calling after me. I took the stairs and was running through the park towards the Zoo's entrance ten minutes later oblivious to the frigid temperature.

CHAPTER TWENTY-ONE

Brian and Max were no where in sight as I approached the gate, stopping finally to catch my breath since my lungs were burning. I was looking around, but all I could see were the usual plethora of camera-clad tourists, children, joggers, and maternity mothers pushing carriages. It had been almost twenty minutes since Brian called as I looked back and forth between my watch and cell phone. I paced up and down within a few feet of the entrance, but tried not to go too far out of sight, incase he was looking for me. My phone was ringing, but looking at the caller ID number I recognized Hayden's number and didn't pick up. He kept calling and I kept letting it go to voicemail. The seventh call was Brian.

"Yes?"

"Did you come alone?"

"Yes of course I did. Where are you? Where is Max?" I was looking around frantically.

"Calm down Beautiful." This man had total disregard for the fact that I'd asked him not to call me that. In fact he had little regard for anything relating to me. "Do you see the black SUV across the street?"

I was moving through the annoying crowd trying to get to the railing.

"Yes, I see you."

"Come to me." His voice was low and lethal. I was hesitant looking around as I prayed I was doing the right thing.

"I need to know that Max is alright first." In the distance I saw the heavily tinted driver's window lowering and Brian smiling with the phone to his ear as he reached over and pulled Max to the window, by what I realized was a handful of his long hair. Max was wincing in pain. I could see his eyes tightly closed.

"Stop it!" I screamed at the top of my lungs, ignoring the stares and glances that were shot my way as people started to shun me, marking me off as another crazy New Yorker.

"Walk towards the car and I will let him go! Oh... and Beautiful? Don't forget I have my little friend."

"Alright! Alright, but don't lay another finger on him!"

"Again you fail to realize that you are in no position to be making demands." And raising his hand he showed me what I assumed was the same gun he had at my house. I snapped my phone shut as I placed both palms against the low wall and jumped over. I was waiting for the street light to change when my phone rang again. Hayden was calling. The light was yellow, now red. Brian was watching me intently. I stopped in the middle of the crosswalk.

"Let him go!" I shouted.

"Come a little further!"

He was taunting me, so I took a few more steps forward and Brian looked over to Max and said something at which point the passenger door opened. Oh thank God.

"Glory!" someone was yelling for me.

"Dr. Strair!" I could hear the commotion behind me and turned to see Hayden and handful of police officers running up the incline towards the street. Some had their weapons drawn.

"You lying whore!" screamed Brian at the top of his lungs through the window as he reached over and hauled Max, who was half way out of the car, back inside. "You had your chance. What happens next is on your conscience."

"*Nooo*," I screamed, running towards the driver's side, but he had already started to pull off narrowly missing a couple crossing in front of the car. "Please take me. Take me." I continued to scream as I heard Max shouting for me. I was hitting the windows of the jeep as he drove directly by me, but he didn't even touch his brakes. This can't be happening. I was so close. People were screaming for me to stop, drivers were honking their obnoxious horns, oblivious to what was going on around them, but I didn't care. I was running behind the car as he cut in and out between the traffic, jumping the curb when the cars in front of him slowed down too much. What little energy I had left was gone when he sped through the second red light and I finally stopped. I could hear the sirens behind me and then someone was holding me tightly, their arms wrapped around me as they planted quick tender kisses across my forehead. It was Hayden.

"Are you alright baby?" he was asking. "Why didn't..."

"*What have you done?!?*" I screamed, frantically pushing him away. "*You've killed him. You've just killed our son!*"

"Glo he would never have let Max..."

"Bullshit! He was practically out of the car when you all showed up shouting, waving guns and badges in the air!" I snapped. "We were a lot closer two minutes ago to having our son back than we are right now."

"What were you doing thinking you could handle this on your own? And then you didn't want Jeff to tell me?" It was only after the loud symphony of car horns that I realized we were still standing in the middle of the street. Detective Smith screeched to a halt beside us and Hayden practically dragged me into the car. They were talking to me, trying to ask if I knew where he was taking Max, but I only shook my head. I had nothing more to say to either of them until I had my child back. I was so close to getting him back on my own and they'd ruined everything.

Smith was on the radio shouting instructions and I could hear the helicopter over us as they were obviously trying to follow Brian, but everything after I got in the car was a blur. Between making his own calls Hayden was rubbing my hands and saying all these reassuring things, but my mind wasn't there. *"Well as I'm sure you're aware, I'm ruined and it's all because of you. My life, my family, my career have all been shot to shit because of you. You just can't seem to keep your fucking mouth shut and because of it things have escalated to this. Assault, kidnapping, rape, murder. Assault, kidnapping, rape, murder. Assault, kidnapping, rape, murder."* I kept playing what Brian had said over and over in my head until I was completely nauseated and detective Smith's driving wasn't helping much.

We'd come to an abrupt stop in front of the precinct and someone was opening my door just in time for me to spill what little breakfast I had in stomach onto the accommodating New York city side walk, narrowly missing the officer's shoes. I mumbled my faint apologies as Hayden picked me up and whisked me into the building.

Once we left the 'waiting area', I was surprised at how much the police station actually looked like the ones on television, with old wooden furniture, relatively out-of-date computers and stacks of paper everywhere. Anyone who didn't have a potential felon handcuffed to a chair by their desk was crowded around a desk in the corner watching television. Hayden got me a glass of water and put me to sit down as he joined Detective Smith.

This is what my tax dollars support, I thought in disgust; police officers watching sports when they could be solving crime and making the streets safe against people like Brian Rafferty. I had no concept of how much time had passed until Hayden's voice cut through the relatively loud station.

"For the love of God, Smith have someone stop him!" Hayden growled as I stood up and moved towards the group only to realize they weren't watching a game, but the car chase involving my son. I pushed through the dark uniforms until I was standing in front the television. The news flashed a picture of Brian in the upper corner and at the bottom of the screen it read 'LIVE POLICE CHASE OF SUSPECT IN KIDNAPPING OF PROMINENT INVESTMENT BANKER HAYDEN WEISS' SON,' while continuing to show the high speed chase taking place down the FDR Drive northbound toward the Harlem River Lift Bridge. There were numerous police cars and a helicopter in hot pursuit.

"He's got to slow down or he's going to get them all killed!" one officer announced as I simply glared at him. He was right. At the speed Brian was going, he would likely crash into the approaching Manhattan toll plaza; he was running out of options.

"What is he trying to do?" another genius asked.

"I think he's trying to get on to the bridge," Smith said. The next minute seemed like an eternity as we watched him narrowly graze other cars and cause multiple accidents as cars tried to get out of his way ultimately crashing into other cars and police vehicles as they did so. The news caster was saying that he was a couple miles from the toll plaza and the police were trying to clear the lanes up ahead before the Harrison Tunnel. It was like a scene out of an action movie as Brian's SUV dipped and swerved through the lanes. Hayden had made his way over to me and was now holding me as we watched the nightmare unfold before our eyes. The news station helicopter was not letting him get out of sight for more than a split second. I still couldn't believe this was happening, realizing I had totally underestimated how crazy Brian was from the beginning. I never thought he would go to these lengths to save a marriage he had long since left.

As they approached the tolls two cruisers now had the SUV flanked. Brian swerved to try and hit the car on his left but the officer pulled away. You almost knew what was going to happen before it did. The driver didn't take into consideration how close he was to the toll booth and in trying to avoid a collision with Brian's car put himself directly in line with one of the booths. If he saw it coming it was too late, the car crashed into the booth head-on causing a large explosion that made the television crew pull back.

"Jesus!" came the outbursts through out the room as other superlatives were thrown in the air simultaneously. I turned my face into Hayden's arm not wanted to see what happened next. The reporter was screaming into the headphones stating what anyone watching had just seen for themselves. Brian didn't let up for one minute and if anything, seemed to be going even faster.

"What the hell is he trying to do?" another officer shouted in frustration to no one in particular, since it was likely that he'd just lost a colleague and friend.

Another police cruiser was coming up beside his car and yelling for him to pull over. Brian swerved again to hit the cruiser but the officer anticipating his action slowed down, which resulted in Brian missing him altogether and slamming into the guard rail. I couldn't help the scream that escaped my lips. The inevitable happened and he was losing control of the car with it swerving across all the lanes from guard rail to guard rail. I was digging my nails into Hayden's arm as we both watched in horror. Then there was nothing. Brian had now entered the tunnel and all we could see on camera were the orange sparks from him grazing the railing and tunnel wall. The helicopter pilot flew over the tunnel so we had a perfect view of where Brian would exit. No one saw what happened in the tunnel, but the car was still swerving out of control as he came out of the darkness. My heart was now in the pit of my stomach and my screams deafening as I watched the car flipped over and over and then finally slid to a halt on its crumpled roof against the guard rail almost half a mile from the tunnel. I wasn't sure what was worse, watching it all unfold before my eyes or having the detailed commentary of the shrieking reporter as it all happened.

I couldn't hear anything over my emotional screams as I beat against Hayden's chest. As I closed my eyes I saw Max, naked and beautiful as they laid him in my arms after I'd given birth. I tried to recall the first time he said mumma, his first birthday, his first step, his first tooth, his first fall, but I couldn't and that was because I'd missed most of those important steps in my son's life. I was too busy building my career and for what? At what price? The most important thing in my life was now gone. The pain in my chest was excruciating as the blood curdling cries continued to pour out of me. Looking at the television, we saw the police cars and emergency vehicles come to a stop about a hundred feet away from the smoking remains of the car, as the firefighters hurried to assess whether or not the car could explode any minute. The relentless camera man had now zoomed into what was obviously Brian's limp and mangled body curled up in the crushed cockpit of the car. The reporter once again stating the obvious that he was lifeless and didn't appear to be moving, which only brought another gut wrenching wail from deep within me. Smith was shouting orders to turn the television off; there was nothing more he could do at this point. It was over. My beautiful son was dead.

CHAPTER TWENTY-TWO

The extent of my despair had been reduced to whimpers and uncontrollable shaking in the corner of a vacant conference room. Everyone was now there; the Weiss's, Hayley, Jeff, Nancy, and Rebecca as I tried to physically work through the sorrow and guilt on the verge of crippling my body. Hayden hadn't left my side, but didn't broach my personal space, saying he was sorry countless times since I'd made him feel as though he were the one driving the car. He was met with frigid silence. Half hour before I'd gone on a rampage blaming my son's death on Hayden and fact that he somehow thought he was in charge, ruining any chances I had of getting Max back. I threw anything within arm's reach staplers, filing bins, chairs and two keyboard trays directly across the crowded room aiming straight for his head. Screaming at the top of my lungs I told him I would never forgive him and that I would never speak to him again. Nothing he could say would make me feel otherwise. It took 45 seconds too long for them to get me under control; by the time they had it looked like a miniature tornado had passed through the NY-3 precinct. After being restrained by the surrounding officers, they had tucked us away in a back room, free of sharp or potentially lethal objects. Neither Harriett, Hayley, Nancy, nor Becca had stopped crying, but I couldn't see past my own grief to think about consoling them as I mentally checked off how I was going to make Miranda pay. Next to myself, Hayden and Smith, Miranda was the only other person I had faulted for my son's death.

All these years she knew and said nothing. After I'd helped her so many times, this is how she repaid me. Well I would show all of them. I didn't know how or when, but I knew she would pay dearly.

Detective Smith had just walked in and called Hayden and Edward over. I wasn't sure what they were talking about, but Hayden had a look of confusion spread across his face.

"Wa..what's going on?" I asked trying to swallow the scratchy pain in my throat. Detective Smith opened his mouth to say something, but Hayden stopped him. "He is *my* son god damn it and I want to know what the hell is going on! You talk to *me* Smith, no one else. *I'm* his mother! Your family's name may have been plastered across that television screen, but he is my son. I raised him not you. Three weeks of playing daddy does not give you to right to control this situation." I snapped, glaring at them.

"Umm…yes…Ms. Strair, I was just telling your husband -"

"He is *not* my husband," I hissed. I almost didn't correct him, but decided that his assumption was part of the original problem. He took orders from Hayden like *he* was the one in charge. If they had just let me handle it Max would be safe right now. My anger was rising again.

"I'm...I'm sorry. I was telling Mr. Weiss that I got a call from the fire chief on site at the accident. I'm not sure how to say this..."

"For Christ's sake spit it out Smith." What little tolerance I had was long gone.

"They can't seem to find... Max's body wasn't in the car." *A spark of hope flickered.*

"Maybe he was thrown from the car," Jeff interjected. *The spark was squelched.*

"That was my sentiment exactly," countered Smith, "but they've looked and can't find him anywhere around the crash. It's almost as though he wasn't in the car..."

"*He was in the car! I saw him with my own eyes,*" I cried, willing myself not to fall apart again. Becca tried to put her arms around me but I shoved them away.

"Could Brian have hidden him somewhere?" Edward asked.

"No, I don't' think so. He wouldn't have had a chance. My men were on him the second he drove off from in front of the zoo."

"Obviously not," Hayden yelled, "because my son was in the car and now he isn't. We were all watching Smith!" My mind was going in circles, questioning if my eyes had been playing tricks on me at the zoo, but I knew what I saw and Max was in that jeep.

"Did they check the tunnel?" I asked. *The spark had returned.* "In the tunnel was the only time we really lost sight of the car..." I wasn't finished before Smith was on the radio instructing the men to check the tunnel. The first minute passed and then the second. You could hear a pin drop in the room as we waited. The third minute had almost passed when Smith's radio crackled to life.

"Lieutenant?"

"Go ahead Walters."

"We've found him. He's alive! Pretty beat up, but alive. It looks as though he jumped from the car when they went through the tunnel and rolled into a drain off gutter. The EMTs are getting ready to take him to St. Ann's now."

Anything that was said after that was drowned out by the screams and cries that erupted in the room. *He was alive.* I was in the air as Hayden picked me up and twirled me around high above him.

They were all hugging and kissing, but I could only cry. Max was alive. Brian was dead. It was over.

Again.

CHAPTER TWENTY-THREE

It had now been one long month since that tragic weekend. The week that followed was even more of an emotional rollercoaster if that was at all possible. My brilliant son had indeed jumped from the car, which caused Brian to lose more control as he tried to pull him back inside, and as a result Max dislocated the still weak "Slit Throat Gulge' shoulder, broke his collar bone and a couple of ribs, but we knew firsthand it could've been a lot worse. Then while we were all piled into St. Ann's emergency room waiting to see him, Hayley's water broke, followed by sixteen hours of labor and the birth of beautiful healthy, six pound two ounces Hanna Elizabeth Weiss.

The night of the accident it was decided that there was no need to break the Rafferty's hearts anymore with the sordid details of Brian's deeds. Hayley wouldn't file for divorce, but she would change her name. Brian had been buried without incident a week later in a quiet media free service with the Weiss' and his family present. They had so many questions, but the police gave few answers, only saying that he was wanted in questioning for a separate case and that the chase ensued when he took off. The Rafferty's were at a loss, but that was better for them. The less they knew the better.

As for the Weiss', in the quiet of Hayley's hospital room, while we waited for Max to have another CT scan, they were told the full, 'unedited' version of what happened from Las Vegas to the accident. They were upset, Harriett more so than Edward, but there wasn't much they could say until Hayley dropped the bomb about the Hep B which left them even more upset and sympathetic towards her. But in the end she appeared to be doing better than we could imagine. It was as though she was thankful it had ended this way; no messy divorce, no awkward meetings with his parents, or nasty custody battle. It was all over and in most of our minds Brian had gotten what he had coming to him, which was pretty sad.

Things between Max and I were strained the first week, although much to my dismay nothing had changed between him and his father. He'd been through so much and was in a lot of pain, but besides the obvious reasons, I could tell he was upset with me. Unfortunately, we were never alone long enough for me to bring it up. He wasn't rude, but he wasn't particularly chatty either. If anything he was simply dismissive and I hated it. We didn't get a chance to talk until his first night home at Hayden's.

There wasn't much of a choice as to where we would stay since I signed a contract and paid a deposit to have my kitchen completely demolished and remodeled on the Wednesday after the accident. My decision was made when I stopped home quickly from the hospital to grab a change of clothes, and as I walked through the door my nostrils were assaulted by the strong smell of smoke and burnt tephalon, causing the memories to come flooding back to my mind. I used every ounce of my strength and blinked them away but was unsuccessful. I went to double check that the doors in the kitchen were locked and saw the holes Brian punched in the wall and the scorched frying pan in the sink. The memories came back with a vengeance since I could've sworn I also saw Brian Rafferty's cold hard face looking at me through the back door. I was hysterical by the time I got back to the hospital, falling to pieces in Edward's arms outside Max's room as Hayden helplessly looked on. I knew it was hurting him that he wasn't the one consoling me, but I couldn't bring myself to go to him.

By Thursday morning I'd contacted the contractor that had previously done work on my house and told him to do whatever he wanted, but that I wanted a new kitchen. *Everything* had to be replaced. There was to be nothing that would remind me of the old kitchen and he gladly accepted. I later called Jeff and requested a six month leave of absence which he approved before I could even recite my explanation. I needed a mental break, and for the first time in my life, I had to make Max my top priority. I had saved enough over the past few months so that we would be comfortable.

Hayden and I moved our clothes over with Edward's help so when Max came home from the hospital a week later everything was there for him. We came home on the same day as Brian's funeral and at Hayley's request, Hayden had to attend to provide additional support. Hence Max and I were finally alone.

He'd fallen asleep soon after we got home and like I had done countless times over that week I crawled in bed beside him to watch him while he slept and ended up dosing off myself to wake and find him watching me. He just smiled as I made a funny face and reached up to kiss his chin.

"How long are you going to stay mad at me?" I asked when it was clear he wasn't going to volunteer to start the conversation. He remained quiet for a long time and then for the first time since it had all happened he burst into these gut wrenching sobs that tore at my heart strings.

Brian had indeed told him *his* version of what had happened in Las Vegas and Max admitted that he'd felt betrayed. He'd never thought in a million years that I would ever lie to him, but I did. He wasn't mad at his father because he knew I'd probably instructed him not to say anything. I listened and apologized, admitting that if I had to do it all over again I would've handled things between his father and I much differently, but that I still wouldn't have told him exactly how I came to be at the party, because those details weren't important. I told him what I thought he should know, how special that night was to me and what a gentleman his father was. I promised him that things would be different and that I intended to prove to him that he *was* the most important thing in my life, not work. He seemed to understand and almost immediately, things between us were almost back to normal.

Michael Beckford had called several times over the past month the instant it hit the news that the child involved in the crash was my son, but somehow the conversation always turned to *'us'*. I had to reiterate what I'd said in my voicemail, that much to his disappointment, *'we'* wouldn't go any further. It wasn't something he wanted to hear, but he didn't have much choice in the matter. The good news was we ended, what had never really begun, on a friendly note.

I hadn't had a chance to visit Miranda yet, but I called to tell her everything that had happened. She was sorry to hear about Max, but outright denied ever receiving the calls from Hayden, so there wasn't much I could do about it. I told her what I had to say and left it at that, promising to come see her in person once Max was better. She was a liar and a deceitful person. The way I see it, what goes around comes around and she would get hers soon enough, if she hadn't already.

Today at Max's and Hayley's urging to get out of the house we went over to the Weiss's to spend the day since Hayden was out of town on business. I was hesitant because even though she hadn't said anything, I could certainly feel that once Harriett knew the truth her feelings towards me changed. We were cordial, but something was different, my assumption was that she probably thought less of me and there was nothing I could do about that. I certainly couldn't blame her.

I didn't say much about Hayden being gone, but Max was pretty verbal about how much he missed him. I did too - immensely. Since the accident, to say I behaved differently towards him would be an understatement. We hadn't kissed or touched since that morning before Max and I left his apartment and that was mainly because I refused to be alone, much less carry on an independent conversation with him. When ever there was a remote possibility it could happen, I would find myself going to sleep early, hanging with Max in his room, or helping Hayley with the baby. I knew he picked up on it, but I didn't know what else to do. I couldn't find the words to apologize for the hurtful things I'd said to him that night in the police station. I knew I still had feelings for him, but was appalled at how quickly my heart became hard towards him that night. I couldn't understand if I loved him so much, why those feelings came so easily for me. I was second guessing my heart and doubting the authenticity of my feelings. The worse part was…he was letting me. When he tried to approach me the third time in the hospital I shunned him, so he'd stopped trying.

It was his house, but he worked around me and my schedule. I woke up at six so he was gone by 5:30 for his run and then off to the office. He'd shortened his days significantly at work and was home usually by six on the dot. I would have dinner ready and try to give Hanna her bath while he and the others ate. It was childish I know, but there wasn't anything else I could do. Both Hayley and Max had tried to bring it up on separate occasions, but I refused to talk about it. In a couple of months my kitchen would be finished and I would be back in the safe confines of my own home.

It was becoming harder and harder to be so close to him and not touch him or stay in a dry state for that matter. My heart would literally leap in my chest at the sight of him. When he came through the door in the evenings, I had to physically leave the room so I wouldn't run and jump into his arms, kissing and telling him how much I loved and missed him. He probably saw it as me being obnoxious and leaving the room because I couldn't stand to be in his presence, but that was hardly the case. And then there were the two near fatal instances when I was using a knife and he walked by in just his pajama pants and I almost lost my fingers. Needless to say I tried to stay out of the kitchen when he was home.

Harriet was calling me, but as usual I was in another place, my mind lingering on Hayden as I rushed to clear my thoughts and become cheerful.

"What do you think?" she asked joining me in the bay window that over looked the back of their brownstone house. Once again I realized I'd missed out on some joke or comment because everyone was now looking at me with questioning eyes as though they expected a response from me. "Glory, what's wrong?" her brow furrowing with concern.

"Oh nothing, I'm sorry I was thinking about the house and…"

"Nonsense! Unless the house is 6'3" and named Hayden Alexander Weiss you aren't fooling anyone!" she said abruptly. Edward and Max started to laugh which didn't help the hot flush traveling up my cheeks. Hayley was the only one that seemed to sense how close I was to a mental break down.

"Mom, that's enough. Let's get that game of Scrabble going while Hanna is still sleeping," Hayley said with a nervous laugh trying to change the subject.

"It's not enough," Harriet argued as she turned her attention directly to me, "someone has to stop this madness. I've certainly had enough. You and Hayden aren't fooling anyone Glory. Why are you doing this to yourself? Fighting something as natural as love," her icy blue eyes piercing straight through me. "What's in the past is in the past. The situation wasn't optimal, but it's over and done with. There's a saying I've heard that says: '*Build a bridge and get over it.*' No one in this room thinks you meant anything you said that night in the police station. You were hurt. We all were," my eyes were filling up with tears at the thought of my transparency. "Please for Max's sake try to get pass this. Initially I was upset, but that was stupid of me. Forgive me. We love you. I just want things to be like they were before. Hayden was doing what he thought was best on that dreadful day. I know you can see that. Can't you?"

"I…I…," trying to respond my voice cracked with emotion and I bolted from the room outside onto the patio gasping for air as though with each question she asked someone was squeezing the air out of my lungs. It was Max who came out to comfort me a short while later.

"Mom…"

"I'm sorry…I'm just…" I couldn't say anything else as he slipped his good arm around my waist and rested his head against my shoulder.

"It's alright," he said reassuringly as I smoothed his hair, "but grandma is right." I loved how affectionately he called her that. "I know how much you love Dad and he loves you, but it's over now. We need to start over. If Dad thinks he's hurting you, as much as it hurts him, he won't say anything to you. He'll stay away, if that's what he thinks you want."

"Did he tell you that?" I wiped at my eyes.

"No he didn't tell me anything, but I know. Please talk to him. He thinks you hate him!"

"Did he say *that*?" I questioned again.

"Not in so many words, but he thinks you blame him for what happened."

"I don't..."

"If it's any consolation I'm glad you weren't in that car. I couldn't bear anything happening to you."

"Well now you know how I feel..."

"And how Dad feels," he finished. "You were asking him to choose between his child and the woman he loves. He did what he thought was right at that time mom. You can't fault him for that." I was looking at him, wondering which of us was the parent and when had he blossomed into such a wonderful young man? "Promise me you'll talk to him when he comes back home tomorrow. I know you've been miserable. You aren't fooling anyone." His eyes were pleading with me. He was right, they all were. "I just want you to be happy. We all do."

"I promise I'll talk to him when he comes back. I love him so much Maximus, but this is all new to me. I don't want to mess up again."

"You won't, but you quit before really getting started. Talk to him," he coaxed.

"Alright, I'll talk to him."

"Great. Now let's go kick some butt in Scrabble."

~

Things hadn't been the same between Glory and I since the accident and I knew there was a good chance that they would never be. I just couldn't see her getting over this. My parents had tried and Hayley had certainly tried, but no one knew better than I did how much Max meant to her; and the fact that it was my fault that she'd almost lost him was a tough pill to swallow – especially for me.

Living in the same house and being so close to her, without having the ability to touch her was torture. I couldn't kiss or hold her and she was never in any room long enough to say two words to me, so that wasn't helping. Her sweet scent constantly lingered on my sheets and in my bathroom after her baths. I would conveniently brush my teeth or have a shower as soon as she was finished, just to be enveloped in the smell of her scented oils and bath gel. The fragrant steam would coat the air as I stood in its mist desperately

220

trying to feel closer to her. I wanted so much for our warm naked bodies to be intertwined in passionate love making, and wanted so much for the pain of the past month to go away.

She was the first thing I thought of each day and the last thing I thought of at night. Nothing could take my mind off her and the endless possibilities of us being together. Max was so much like her that it seemed everything he did, how he laughed or smiled reminded me of her in one way or another which only made the pain of losing her harder to bear.

Looking out at the gorgeous San Francisco view I thought my current business trip would be a welcomed distraction, but I was wrong, since I missed them more than I could've imagined. My life was fuller than it had ever been with Max, my restored relationship with Hayley, and my beautiful niece, yet there was something missing - Glory. A knock at the door startled me since I hadn't called for room service; peering through the peep hole I was shocked to see Lisa standing there.

She'd called countless times since Colorado, but I refused to take her calls. She had even shown up at my job unannounced and if it weren't for the client I was with, I probably would've thrown her out on her ass, but thought against it, simply giving her a look that read *If you say one word to me or embarrass me you'll regret it.* She stopped in her tracks and I walked right by her like she never existed and now this.

"What are you doing here?" I asked through the closed door.

"I came to talk. You won't see me or take any of my calls, so what am I supposed to do?"

"You're supposed to take a fucking hint!"

"Hayden please…you moved all your things without a single word to me. We have over ten years of history. Let's just talk about this. Do you realize we haven't talked about *this* once?"

"What's there to talk about? What can you possibly tell me that I don't already know for myself?"

"Please…just open the door?" And against my better judgment I opened the door and she walked in.

"Talk fast. I've had a long morning."

"I'm sorry about what happened to your son. I saw you at… at the funer…"

"Lisa let's cut through all the bullshit and the pleasantries. You didn't follow me all the way to California to tell me you're sorry about your lover kidnapping and trying to kill my son. What the hell do you want?" The tears started then, but she was playing these games with the wrong person. I'd had enough. If only she knew how hard I was trying to avoid breaking her neck at that exact moment she probably would never have risked coming.

"How long did you know about Brian and I?" she choked. I really didn't want to do this now.

"I found out the day before you came to Colorado, but my sister knew the entire time." She tried to hide the shock that ran behind her eyes, but I'd already seen it.

"And she didn't say…"

"No she didn't say anything – just like how she never said anything about the abortion you had when we were in college. Care to tell me what that was about?" *That* topic I was genuinely interested in. Again she did a piss-poor job of hiding her shock or increasing discomfort.

"Um, um, there's nothing to tell. I didn't think we were read…"

"*We*?!?" I laughed loudly at her audacity to imply that the child was mine. "Don't even go there Lisa. Who was the *real* father?" She became quiet, realizing I could see straight through her lies. "Well?" I pressed, when she continued to remain silent.

"*I don't know*," she whispered and again I couldn't hold in the laugh that burst out of me.

"You don't know? You don't know?" I was dumbfounded. "How hard could it be? Let's see," I said rubbing my temples. "Your last year of college…umm, well that could be one of several people: your communications professor, my ex-buddy Tom, my polo coach, Mike from the rowing team, Blake the quarterback, or for all I know Brian," her eyes kept getting wider and her skin kept getting paler with each name. She looked like she was going to be sick at any moment and I was loving every minute of it. "Oh I'm sorry, did you really think that I didn't know anything about your sleazy late night escapades with any Joe-Schmo you would let crawl between your legs? I was stupid before and let a lot of things go unsaid, but not any more, life's too short," I finished and she, for the moment, still remained mute and deathly pale.

"Soooo all of that being said, what could you possibly want to talk to me about? What could you possibly tell me that I don't already know?" Still no answer. "All right Lisa I'll make this crystal clear for you. That rotten bastard died before I got a chance to destroy him, but *all* that rage and hate is still here," I said pounding angrily on my chest taking a step towards her. "Give me one reason to let it all out. Give me one reason to pour my wrath out on you for all the pain you've caused my sister. Give me a reason to tell the world what type of person you are. Don't ever contact me again. Let this be the last time you take it upon yourself to show up anywhere I am. If you know I'll be there, then it would be wise for you to un-invite yourself. Don't ever let my name or any member of my family's name cross your lips, or else I will take it as a personal insult and we both know I've already been insulted far too many times." Her tears continued to fall and I only became angrier at the thought that I'd let it get his far. I was mad at myself. "Get out of here," I yelled, but she still didn't move. "GET OUT!" I shouted again at the top of my lungs causing her to jump and run out the door sobbing.

Once she was gone my head continued to throb, I had come up to the room after my morning meeting because I wanted to use the afternoon to get some rest but now, sleeping was the last thing on my mind. Leaning across the bed, I picked up the phone to call home with the silent hope that Glory would answer. I only needed to hear her voice.

CHAPTER TWENTY-FOUR

The remainder of my day with the Weiss' was less eventful. I had a long nap after I blasted them to high heavens in Scrabble with the word CRAZY, using the triple word as well as the Z falling on the double letter score, sealed my victory, much to Edward's dismay. When I woke up they were all still in the living room goo-goo'ing at Hanna.

"Good mom, you're awake. Can I spend the night? Aunty Hayley is staying over with the baby. I have clothes and grandma said it isn't a problem. Pah-leeeaase…" Max begged before I had fully entered the room.

"Is it that late already? Why didn't you guys wake me?"

"You don't nap often so we figured we would just leave you be," Hayley said. "Let him stay. We'll have a blast."

"Umm, are you sure that's alright Harriet?" I asked with a smile. Max already couldn't contain his excitement at the possibility of spending the night with his grandparents.

"Of course it's fine, that way you can head home and have the evening to yourself." Hayley was nodding at what a great idea it was as Edward and Max had already started talking about what they would do tonight. They loved him so much.

"Well I guess it would be a treat," I said, actually looking forward to an evening alone. "I'll pick you guys up in the morning."

"Oh that isn't necessary," Edward interjected. "We can bring them home tomorrow afternoon."

"OK then, I guess I'll take off and milk this for all that its worth," I said with a little laugh as I hugged them good-bye. "Call me if you need me."

I was driving down the beltway fifteen minutes later, and was being serenaded by Luciano Pavarotti as I soaked in a warm bubble bath of rose scented oil, forty-five minutes after that.

The music was probably a little too loud, but I didn't care. There was no baby to wake and little chance of upsetting neighbors since we were the only occupants on this entire floor. I was alone and needed to be enveloped by the words of my favorite opera, La Bohème's Act IV *"O Mimì, tu più non torni"* -- *O Mimì, will you return?* Relishing in the moment as the rich voices poured out of the speakers.

I finished blow drying my hair, slipped on my nightgown and sashayed to the kitchen to refill my glass of wine.

I could see this libretto so clearly. The ending was near. *Mimì was back, but she was extremely weak from her illness, and all her loved ones had come to assist the dying girl. Musetta and Marcello left to sell Musetta's earrings to get money for medicine; while Colline and Schaunard left to pawn Colline's coat. Mimì and Rodolfo were left alone, to recall their past happiness.* Like all the times before when I'd heard it I was now in an all out wail as I tearfully sang along with Mimì and Rodolfo's duet *"Sono andati? -- Are we alone?"* I drank my wine and twirled my bare feet across the cool hardwood floors of the spacious apartment as I imagined how they were feeling.

The others had returned and while Musetta prayed aloud, Mimi died. Schaunard checks on Mimì and sadly announces that she's dead. Rodolfo is horrified, cries out Mimì's name and starts sobbing. My chest was tight with the thought of how I would go on if anything ever happened to Hayden. The higher the crescendo went the harder I cried at how completely miserable I was without him in my life. I mean he was in my life, but not *in* my life. I wanted him to hold me again and tell me how much he loved me. The unbearable, but familiar cramping in my lower abdomen had returned, reminding me of its emptiness. Rodolfo's voice was piercing me; my arms were open as I let my head fall back, willingly becoming him as I wept openly for my love. The tears flowed freely, his voice was riveting. We were one, but not the same. Unlike him, my love was not yet gone forever. I still had a chance. And as his voice trailed off into the distant heavens I cried, as I knew Hayden was the only man I would ever love.

It was the sound of the door closing, in the now silent apartment, that snapped me back to reality. And as if out of some beautiful dream, I turned to see Hayden standing there. I didn't know how long he'd been watching me, nor did I care. He was a sight for sore eyes with his gold and navy striped silk tie loosened around his neck in a perfectly tailored dark blue suit, and his hair messy from his travels. We just looked at each other, my chest still heaving from my sobs and awful singing. We were reading each others eyes, as I hoped mine were screaming how much I missed, loved, and wanted him. His eyes left mine and darkened as they trailed the full length of my body, barely being covered by the translucent cotton nightie.

"Glory…" he breathed as he let his garment bag drop to the floor with a loud thud, but didn't move and that was the only invitation I needed before I was running across the floor and leaping into his arms. My legs were around his waist as I took his mouth in mine. I

was ravenous, frantic even, moaning loudly as I grabbed handfuls of his hair. His arms snaked around my waist tightly as he drew me closer into him. His lips and tongue were ready and willing to meet my urgent need to taste him. My nostrils were filled with the scent of him and God did he smell good. The faint smell of expensive aftershave mixed with his natural scent, made me want to be under his skin. His face was now buried in my neck as he grabbed a handful of my freshly blow dried hair and gently pulled my head backwards so that he could have easy access to that sensitive spot just below my jaw line.

"Is it fair to say you've missed me?" he asked with the debonair smile, putting an abrupt halt to our kissing frenzy.

"More…than…I can…even…begin…to tell you," I mumbled between slipping my tongue in and out of his mouth. Picking up my feet from dangling at his hips, I wrapped them at the ankles and using my thighs, pulled the hot flesh between my legs further on to his abdomen, in an effort to lessen some of the contracting there. I'd missed him so much over this past month and now I had every intention of proving it.

"If you can't tell me, then you'll have to show me," he responded, his voice deep and coarse with his arousal. His large hands had now traveled down my back to cup the underside of my naked butt cheeks as he walked down the hall towards his room. The movement of his thighs and hips were bringing his fingertips dangerously close to that spot I was longing for him to touch, caress and finally enter. "I love you so, so much," he was saying as he reached out to close the bedroom door behind him.

"I love you too baby."

"This month has been miserable for me. Can you forgive…"

"*Sssshh, no more talking now,*" I whispered. "*Show me.*" I wasn't sure how he did it so quickly, but he laid me on the bed and removed my nightgown in what seemed like one flowing motion. I was now completely naked as he longingly gazed at me. My body was covered with tiny goose bumps as he slowly started to undress. His liquid dark eyes not leaving mine. *I* should've been the one undressing him, but I couldn't move an inch even if he paid me. I was paralyzed with anticipation. Stepping out of his slacks I could clearly see his massive erection straining against his catalog-worthy jockey shorts. Oh my God…all of that was for me? I could feel a warm flush spread across my body as the center of my body began to ache.

"Don't blush love, it's all yours and no one else's," he said with a small chuckle easing the sides of his boxers down as I wondered if I'd said my thoughts out loud. And as if it's sole intention was to surprise me, out bobbed the delicious head of his penis. In my mind I heard myself say 'peek-a-boo'. All I could do was bite my bottom lip and moan in expectation of the goodies to come. "You're the most beautiful thing I've ever laid my eyes on," he said, his eyes lingering on my torso, "always were."

"Believe me I feel the same way about you."

He crawled on to the bed and laid beside me gently rubbing his fingers across my abdomen; the warmth of our bodies radiating from each other. Turning into him, he kissed me so deeply it took my breath away. It was like paradise. I continued the exploration of his hard body with my hands and he did the same with mine. Our hands were getting to know each other again. He was squeezing my hips, thighs and bottom. His chest was smooth and holding my palm flat against his skin, I dragged it down his chest and muscular abdomen to finally take his fullness in my hand. My fingers didn't meet as they circled *him* and immediately the contracting in my loins increased at the shear width of it. A deep groan escaped his lips when I began to stroke him slowly and he continued kissing me. This time less frantic, as he kissed me with the same rhythm, in which I was stroking him. He finally dragged my hand away as he took one of my already puckered nipples into his mouth, rolling it against his tongue. I couldn't help the little squeal of pleasure that escaped my lips as I writhed beneath him. Hayden was using his teeth and fingers to squeeze, pinch, twist, and nibble as I was convinced, that alone would've brought me over that glorious edge, but it didn't.

The tightening between my legs worsened and thankfully he was using his knee to spread my thighs as he slipped between them. Grabbing the sides of his face I brought his mouth down to mine as I devoured the natural sweetness of his saliva. "I want you so badly. I can't wait anymore." I nuzzled against his ear as I felt him positioning his large head at my opening. I was ready, lifting my hips eagerly to meet his. It was clear now that neither of us could wait another second. He pressed into me, but nothing happened. The soft flesh of my vagina bent inward slightly, but wouldn't give way to completely accept him. I guess Max wasn't that big after all. Easing back he moved the smoothly bulbous tip up and down my opening in an attempt to spread some of the moisture, as I moved my hips slightly, and then tried to enter me again. This time there was a lot of pressure that was soon replaced with a burning sensation. I must've made some type of painful sound because he pulled away.

"I'm sorry baby," he said immediately easing away to look into my eyes. "Are you okay? Did I hurt you?"

The embarrassment at my own dryness and my body's lack of cooperation showed as plain as day on my face. Damn it! I wanted him so much. On any other day I was like the Colorado River... *white water rafting anyone?* and today, the day I needed it most, my body's response had been reduced to a dripping faucet.

"Don't be sorry...it's me...I don't know what... It's been a long time since...I'm sorry," I nervously mumbled as I tried to move from beneath him reaching for my night gown strewn across the end table, but he silenced me with a kiss, holding me in place as he interlaced our fingers on both hands.

"Stop apologizing," he said softly easing off of me. "You have nothing to be sorry about. If anything I should be the one apologizing for rushing this..."

"You aren't rushing me Hayden. I want *this*. I want *you*, now."

"No, no, you don't understand what I'm saying. I meant rushing *this*," he drawled trailing his eyes down my body as his hands followed. "I should've known better," he continued apologetically. "You see, I've wanted nothing more than to be buried inside of you since the second I saw you in Colorado and just now I was being selfish, trying to hop-skip straight to the finale. Forgive me."

"It's not you..." I tried to insist.

"Please," he said silencing me with his fingers across my lips, "let me apologize to you. There's more to this thing they call love making than meets the eye," he said sincerely. "*I* should've been taking it slow. It's been a long time. Your body needs to warm up - literally."

And with that we were kissing again as he brought my arms around his neck. He was kneading my thighs and buttocks in some type of sensual massage and it wasn't long before the cramping returned with a vengeance. He gave my breasts the same royal treatment like before, as he moved from one to the other, then up and down my body. Hovering over my abdomen, he traced a line of wet kisses from the top of my pubic area back up between my breasts and down again.

"Are these from Max?" he asked in a soft voice on his final descent. I peered through lowered lids to see what he was talking about. He was using his lips to trail the little stretch marks on either side of my stomach below my navel. My body tensed up.

"Yes," I replied, subconsciously bringing my hand to cover them.

"Please don't do that. That's not what I meant Glory. I think they're beautiful," he said again moving my hand away as he kissed each one deliberately. "They're mine. They're there because of me. You don't ever have to hide from me," he finished lovingly, moving farther between my legs as he placed a mixture of bites and kisses along my inner thigh. I thought I would die. His hands were stretched along my sides as he cupped both my breasts and continued his religious pinching of my already painfully hard nipples, pausing only to lift my legs on to his shoulders.

I thought this was it. I held my breath in anticipation of the moment that I'd dreamed about for over a decade, but it wasn't that moment. He moved on, lingering at my knees, making large circles around my kneecaps with his tongue. Then it was on to my ankles, as he lovingly suckled every joint, finally slipping each of my pedicured toes into his mouth twirling his tongue around them. I was panting as he explored my body at length. Everything felt so good I was shivering with delight, but I was also on the verge of holding him by his ears and dragging him to the spot still starved for his attention. Just when I thought couldn't bear it anymore; he slithered back up between my legs and hovered over my quivering mound.

"The last time it was chess and now? What is this?"

"A spiral," I whispered breathlessly, to which he just smiled.

"It's beautiful." I too smiled at the compliment since it could've quite easily been the hardest design I'd attempted a few days ago, during a desperate attempt to stay in the bathroom as long as possible so I wouldn't have to say goodbye to him before he left on his trip.

For a long time he did nothing but hovered, like he was taking in the scent and sight of me and loving it. I could feel the tip of his nose and tiniest edge of his lips as he moved his head in slow tiny circles still barely touching me, but what was most maddening of all was the steady stream of air that came out through his nose as he breathed. I had to dig my hands into his shoulders as I felt the tightening intensify in my lower abdomen. His cool breath tickled and seemed to heighten every nerve ending in the general area. My inner lips were swelling towards him as if begging for his tongue. Christ almighty he was good, spectacular even. All of this and he hadn't even touched me *there* yet.

"*Hayden*," I whispered, but whatever I was going to say next went flying out of my mind when he covered my drenched lips with his mouth. I dug my heels into the mattress and instinctively raised my hips. He moaned as though he'd just tasted something so delicious it had rendered him speechless. His tongue was calling me as he curled it up and inward repeatedly in a silent 'come here' gesture. When he wasn't using the tip of his tongue like a calligrapher to seemingly write love letters against the soft walls of my womanhood, he was sucking and grazing his teeth ever so slightly over her sensitive hood. The shaking returned. Then he gently slipped one long beautiful finger between my dripping folds, then two, and I was certain that would be the end of me, but once again it wasn't. He did just enough to bring me to the brink of insanity and then he pulled me back; brought be to the brink and then pulled me back again. His explorations were leaving me weak and wet.

Mission accomplished! You couldn't find a fish, anywhere in the world, wetter than I was at that moment as he slurped and lapped at my creamy offering like a man dying of thirst. "*Pu...pu...lease*," I openly begged, feeling the tingling increase all over my body. "*I don't know how much more I can take*," I said softly, placing my hands at the sides of his head as I grabbed handfuls of his hair, caressing his scalp with my fingertips. If he heard me, he didn't acknowledge it right away as he continued his diligent work of getting reacquainted with his long lost friend. He seemed content to stay there all night. "*Hay...Hay...den*," I whispered again and this time he acknowledged me, turning his face into my palm to kiss it.

I didn't know if it was at all possible, but as he positioned himself over me and between my legs I could swear his penis was even larger than before. Was I fighting a losing battle? Again he laced our fingers together.

"*Look at me*," he said softly in a deep slow roasted voice that in itself would've caused me to climax. I stared at him intently as I chewed on my lower lip. Wasting no time he was there and with one steady push entering me as I felt my moist flesh give way to willingly accept him.

"Aaa...ahh...aaaahhhh," he breathed as I tried to get used to wonderful fullness and heaviness he was producing between my legs. He was moving with slow deep strokes as he brought my thighs up to rest on his hips. His eyes were closed as his frown lines deepened in concentration. Each deep stroke drew a low moan out of me.

My day dreams had served me well over the past twelve years, but they couldn't have been farther off. Nothing I could ever imagine held a candle to what I was experiencing at that exact moment. It was even better than I remembered. Placing my hands on either side of his waist I pulled him further down onto me as I raised up to meet him, since I wanted to make sure I'd taken all of him.

"Ohhhhhh ssshhhhit bab…" the ending of 'baby' was swallowed by the primitive growl that came out of his mouth when I tightened my muscles around his throbbing shaft. "Do…do… that again," he managed to get out and I gladly obliged as this time he held still within me and let me move around *him*. I dragged myself up and down his thick pulsating penis as I simultaneously clenched the fist of my loins around it repeatedly.

Uuuuuuuppppppppp then, *ddddddddddooooowwwwnnnn.*

When he could bear it no longer he held my hips firmly as he brought me down hard and fast onto him repeatedly. I thought I would explode or be split into a million pieces, but then he slowed down. We were looking at each other as I tried to remember when I'd ever experienced anything in my life that felt so damn amazing.

"Now if my memory serves me correctly," he was saying, "I think its here." And as he said it he made a sudden thrust a little to the left of my womb, the head of his penis hit that forbidden spot only he'd been able to reach and which I'd forgotten about.

"Oooohhh," I groaned. "You…remembered," I breathed, gently rubbing the sides of his face where his skin was glistening with a layer of sweat covering his body; and in the cool purple evening glow of the New York City lights outside his window I knew I was in heaven.

"How could I forget," he smiled taking a couple of my fingers into his mouth to suck them lovingly while making slow sweet love to me.

We went on like that for what seemed like an eternity as he shifted me effortlessly from one position to another, only heightening my pinnacle of pleasure. My legs were up and then they were down. I was on either side, then on my back. My feet were spread-eagled going in every which direction and then they were tightly squeezed together creating an even thicker wall of flesh around his pulsing member. All of that and he never withdrew from me. I had never felt as alive as I did at that moment. Each cell that laid dormant over the past twelve years was coming back to life under his expert tutelage and affection.

Hayden's muscles were starting to quiver as he began a repeat session of his fast deep strokes. My breath, like the hundreds of times before, was once again caught in my throat and any words of praise or encouragement I could hope to offer him were held captive there. Hearing the erotic sound of his testicles slapping against my bottom seemed to urge him to the finish line, but my orgasm was still painfully aloof as I groaned in frustration. He suddenly withdrew himself from me and I immediately felt empty.

"Please don't stop," I moaned. "You can finish without me, its okay."

"Don't worry, I'm not stopping and I'll try my damndest *never* to finish without you," he said with a smile. "Now turn around," he said firmly and I did as I was told, turning on my knees with my back to him. With firm but gentle pressure, he held under my abdomen and pushed me forward slightly as he entered me from behind. I don't know why, but that felt different. Incredibly good, but different as if new nerves were being used in this position. He appeared to have even easier access to that infamous spot deep within me as I began to shake against him; maybe my orgasm wasn't as distant as I had thought.

Instinctively I moved my hands forward so that I could be on all fours, but he stopped me; holding me by my shoulders as he brought me up so that I was leaning against his broad chest.

"No," he breathed, "I want you just like this," he finished as he wrapped his arms around my damp body. One hand came around my waist and up between my breasts to gently caress my neck as I turned my face to the side to take his mouth. And the other went down between my legs to take my bud between his thumb and index finger.

"Mmmmm," I moaned, while he maintained his steady upward thrusts. There wasn't much I could do in this position as he controlled everything. I continued to clench my muscles around him rotating my hips to match his rhythm. I loved how his pubic hair felt against my smooth bottom. He was squeezing the tiny bud between my legs with his fingers and I could feel the tightness growing in my lower abdomen. I knew I wouldn't last much longer and the excitement of experiencing the way I felt twelve years ago was enough to leave me weak. We were still kissing as I sucked on his tongue and nibbled at his lips, tasting the mixture of saltiness from our sweat and natural sweetness of our saliva.

He increased the speed with which he was turning my dial. My body began to tremble, small shudders at first. *"Oh Deus...Oh Deus,"* I cried throwing my head back against his shoulder in wild abandon as I brought my arms over my head to hold the back of his neck for support, convinced if I didn't I would fall forward. As though that was what he was waiting for all along, he took my hands away and bent me over, starting deep raw thrusts into me, burying his penis in my meaty folds to the hilt just as my shuddering became increasingly violent. "*Hay…Hayden. Meu amor…meu amor…I love you!*" I cried out sporadically. Grabbing handfuls of the sheets I buried my mouth in the mattress in a feeble attempt to lessen my yowls. I was now bucking against him like a wild mare as he stopped the vigorous massage of my rosebud and turned his attention to that spot deep within me, holding both my cheeks with his large hands as he spread them apart widely. And for the first time it crossed my mind that those two spots could be connected in some way. Since the intense journey to my orgasmic explosion continued without altering its course and he soon joined me on the same beautiful road heading for that long awaited finish line.

"I love you Glory," he rushed between his grunting and moaning, but I couldn't respond my vocal cords again were being held under arrest.

He was trembling behind me, but skillfully maintained his relentless pummeling of my core as we neared the finale together. Officially he got there first but I was a nose length behind him as I arched my back, pressing further on to him and feeling every muscle in his body stiffen as he exploded in my vagina, the hot liquid coating my insides. We were making the same guttural sounds that had filled the air in the Bellagio suite that night so long ago, our bodies shaking against each others. Leaning forward against my back, he wrapped his arms around me as I gladly welcomed the heaviness of his wet muscular body against mine. Then we were still, only moving when intermittent aftershocks rippled over us. I rose up off my hands to lean back against his heaving chest and could feel his heart beat pounding against my back as our lungs expanded like accordions to get as much air as possible.

"Baby," he said in a barely audible voice, "I have to get off my knees. I feel like I'm treading water."

"Me too." I slid forward, feeling the sudden emptiness as he pulled out of me.

I realized at that second that Eric was so far off base it was unclear to me where he was, as I solidified that we were *definitely not* at the same address that night at my house. *This* is what making love was supposed to be like.

Hayden and I laid in each others arms quietly until our breathing returned to normal. He just held me close rubbing his finger tips across my damp skin, interrupting the trickles of sweat running down between my breasts. I was the one to say something first, turning to face him.

"I'm sorry about what I said that night in the police station and how I've been behaving towards you these past few weeks. I was hurt and distraught. I didn't mean to hurt you," I whispered rubbing my thumbs over his sexy lips, wondering if it was too soon, to do it all over again.

"It's alright. I'm sorry too. I understood what you were trying to do Glo, because I would've done the same thing, trade my life for Max's, but I couldn't let *you* do it. I just couldn't. Maybe it was the wrong choice, but at the time I thought I did what was right."

"I don't think there could ever be a right or wrong way to deal with that situation, but I shouldn't have said the things I did. Can you forgive me?"

"Like I said, there's nothing to forgive. I love you more than life itself," he said kissing my mouth tenderly. "I don't want to lose you again. I refuse to."

"You won't," I replied. "I love you too." Again we said nothing for a while, hugging and kissing.

"What are you doing home anyway? I thought you were at my parents," he asked sleepily between two huge yawns.

"I was, but how did you know that?"

"I was miserable in California and I just couldn't keep my mind off you, so I called here primarily hoping to hear your voice and to let you guys know I flew home early, but when I didn't get an answer I called my parent's house. They said you were sleeping at the time, but that I should head straight home and get some rest instead of coming over."

"You mean your parents knew you were coming home early?" I couldn't help bursting out with laughter at the thought that they'd suckered me - all of them.

"What's so funny?" he drawled, his eyes heavy from well-deserved exhaustion.

"They didn't say anything to me about you coming home early. I woke up from my nap and Max asked if he could spend the night because Hayley and the baby were, when all along they just wanted to get rid of me and make sure we were alone!" He was now laughing along with me.

"Glory?"

"Yes my love."

"*I'm glad they did*," he whispered softly.

"So am I. There isn't a doubt in my mind that your mother spearheaded that plot," I said kissing his nose then lips, but he was

already sleeping and for the second time in my life I fell asleep
naked in this man's arms.

235

CHAPTER TWENTY-FIVE

It was around three thirty in the morning when I woke up to the beautiful sound of him breathing next to me. My head was on his shoulder with his face turned into my hair.

Rubbing my legs together I could feel the sticky remnants of our union. I smiled rising up quietly to prop my head on my shoulder as I watched him sleep. The moonlight was casting a similar glow across his body as I had flashbacks of the way the city lights made his skin look as he'd made love to me earlier. Soon the sticky friction between my legs was replaced by the smooth gliding of my thighs against each other as the new moisture formed.

I slowly peeled the sheets from over his body until his flaccid appendage was in plain sight. Even in its 'unexcited' state it still lay across his thigh effortlessly. I was becoming hungry for him yet again. My womb contracted as though she too also remembered and yearned to be filled to capacity with his thick member. I rose up so that I was kneeling beside him and he still hadn't moved. Perfect. I ignored the tenderness between my legs from our earlier session as I greedily focused on having an encore. I wanted to get as far as possible in my endeavor without waking him and positioning myself beside him I took his soft penis in my hands and brought him to my lips, quickly taking it into my mouth.

Closing my eyes I relished in the texture, taste and smell of him trying desperately to ignore the rampant contractions ravishing my womb as it seemed to have a mind of its own, begging me to fill her, wanting him all to herself. It was a beautiful thing to witness him growing in my hands and mouth almost instantly; from soft and rubbery, to smooth, firm and rigid. He was beginning to squirm as I continued stroking, sucking, and licking him.

"Ummmm, Glory?" he drawled in a groggy voice, obviously not sure if he was awake or dreaming. Peering up at him I realized his eyes were still closed as he bit his bottom lip. I took all of him in my mouth again until he gently nudged the back of my throat, running my tongue over the cool crinkled flesh of his testicles. As I brought my head up I dragged my teeth along the full length of his shaft. It was time to wake up! At this point between my legs continued to ache, so all I could think about was having him hard and deep inside me.

"Glo….ry?" he called again, this time his eyes were open as he tried to focus in the dimly lit room.

"Yes baby," I replied, taking him out of my mouth as I rose up and swung my knee over to straddle him positioning myself perfectly over his throbbing penis. He was about to say something else but couldn't, as I slid my swollen lips down his length until I'd taking all of him, impaling myself in the most delicious sense of the word. The sensation of my sore flesh being stretched so wide was overwhelming, plus the feel of his bulbous head pressing against that infamous spot only made me shudder. I controlled everything now.

He groaned on the exhale as I slowly glided my warm moist folds down his still growing member. Drawing my thighs into his sides tightly as I increased the speed with which I brought myself up and down on him. Five, ten, fifteen times, I lost count, until he seemed to be close to the edge, grabbing my cheeks as he arched his back moving his hips beneath me.

"God you feel so good," as he attempted to match my intensity by thrusting upward.

"Oh no Mr. Weiss," I breathed sitting down fully on him, "I'm running this show now." He stopped moving and with that I came straight up onto my knees so that only the thick head and a few inches of his shaft remained in me and then I squeezed. Clenching the soft fist of my womb around his sensitive tip as I simultaneously rotated my hips in deep tight circles. I moved my hips in a circular motion while he bucked beneath me. His breath caught in his throat as I came forward to interlace our fingers above his head. His mouth was still open as I took his bottom lip in mine suckling and biting on it, running my tongue along the inside. I repeated that series of fast slams and slow top-side rotations until it didn't matter which one we were doing as our moans and groans of pleasure began to overtake us. I was blind with ecstasy. We were wrapped in a vortex of passion ending in sensual pleasure.

As I reached closer to my explosive finale, a thousand sensations and emotions tore through my body, robbing me of all reason and thought. This time it wouldn't take too long for me to reach the point of no return, since my body seemed to remember and was eagerly getting back into the grove of things.

Hayden had let out several superlatives and growls, but didn't do anything to stop me from getting mine, almost urging me on. My palms were flat against his chest as I listened to the erotic sound of my cheeks slapping against his thighs and the slurpy, gurgling sounds coming from the over flowing well of my vagina. My stomach muscles were tightening as I felt the spasms spread to my lower back and I sat down fully on him too exhausted and sore to run across the finishing line I intended to walk. *Slowly*. Moving my hips in a rocking motion forward, then back, and forward again; back and forth, back and forth; figure eight, the letter S. My hips rolled against his. I could feel the little nerve endings firing sporadic blasts, coming from the tips of my toes crawling up my body until even my ears and the top of my head tingled.

"Hayden I'm co...come...coming," I whispered softly. I was trembling as I closed my eyes and let my head fall back. Hayden began moving now as he held me in place and rocked his hips in a similar back and forth motion, picking up where I'd left off. I couldn't move.

This orgasm was taking over my body as I began to shake more violently. My eyes were tightly closed and my brows furled as I let his name roll off my lips. Even though I knew the end was coming, it still took me by surprise as I felt the explosion erupt across my body and my shudders turned to uncontrollable shaking. All I could do was feel him and that moment of pure uninterrupted bliss, as he spasmed inside me. Arching my back I stiffened and pressed myself further onto him and when the last wave rolled over my body he stopped moving as I collapsed on his chest gasping for air.

"I love you," we both said simultaneously making us laugh at the corniness of it.

Taking my head between his hands he brought my face up to meet his and took my mouth. I could feel him still hard and thick within me and the thought of it made me shiver again. Wrapping his arms round me, he expertly rolled so that I was now beneath him without withdrawing from me. He was looking at me with so much love in his eyes planting soft quick kisses across my moist skin.

"Have you had your fill Mrs. Weiss?" he asked with a wicked smile stretching his body out on top of mine as he brought one of my legs up to rest by his hips.

"Um hmm," I groaned with a small nod loving the sound of him calling me Mrs. Weiss.

"Good, because it's my turn," he finished with a smile and with deep smooth insertions he slowly began to walk across the finish line as well. He was in no hurry and neither was I. I knew right at that moment it was all about him, but it felt so bloody good, like he was giving me a deep tissue massage *down there*. Nice n' easy. It seemed like forever that we went on and I admired his control, but when I started clenching my infamous fist that was all she wrote as he buckled on top of me like a row of dominos and fell into my arms.

"That wasn't fair," he said with a laugh once he was finished and able to talk.

"I know, but I couldn't help it," I laughed snuggling further into the crook of his neck. "I didn't mean to wake you," I chuckled.

At which point he kissed me, "Yes you did!"

"You're right I did."

"If it's any consolation you can wake me like that anytime you want," he smiled. Then becoming more serious he said, "You are everything I thought you would be and more," his voice choked with emotion. "Almost makes everything that we've been through worth while because now we appreciate each other so much more." I rubbed his face tenderly. "I promise that what we have right now and all I plan to give you in the future will make the past twelve years all worth while…"

I kissed him then, deeply and pulling my lips away said "… Priceless even." We moved closer to each other as he circled his arms around me. I whispered sleepily, *"I gave myself to him;"*

Hayden joined me then. *"And took himself for pay. The solemn contract of life; Was ratified this way; The value might disappoint, Myself a poorer prove, Than this my purchaser suspect, The daily own of Love."*

And for the fourth time, in what would likely be an eternity, we fell asleep in each others arms, the sky ablaze with the colors of dawn - the ironic symbolization of a new day and a new beginning - our new beginning, mine, Hayden and Max's. I'd never been more content.

EPILOGUE

*B*y my next birthday I'd received my previous wish ten times over. Hayden and I were married a few weeks after that night in a small private ceremony and our appetite for each other has remained insatiable. Hayden had said it before, but now more than ever I could appreciate what he meant when he said that he wasn't sorry I was alone these past twelve years. I can't imagine being in another man's arms and letting him touch me the way my husband did. Every opportunity he gets he blows me away with his attention to detail, but more specifically, his attention to my wants and needs - wants and needs I never knew existed. I only have to think about something and somehow he knows. I only have to look at him a certain way before he's willingly stripped and at my disposal and vice versa. The love I have for him is overwhelming and knowing that he feels the same way makes it even more special.

We enjoyed a family summer of traveling and Max was happier than I'd ever seen him. And as much as I loved my job, I didn't miss it one bit, not looking forward to my October return.

Having another baby had come up in conversation a couple times with Hayden and I, but we decided that we would wait and although we wouldn't try for it, we wouldn't stop it from happening either. The longer I had him to myself the happier I was.

Late in the summer when I tried to get in contact with Miranda to schedule a visit, and finally have the opportunity to give her a piece of my mind for keeping Hayden from me all these years, I was informed that a month before, she had overdosed on heroin. Carlos, her "boyfriend" was in jail when she died, and no one knew how to get in touch with me at Hayden's, so she was buried without ceremony by the state. The interesting thing was that I was neither sad nor happy about her death; I felt nothing.

Hayley seemed to be given a fresh start and was now enjoying life as a single parent and working at a reputable PR firm. Her surgery had gone well and she stayed in the apartment while Hayden moved into the house with Max and I. We had become closer; with her being my closest friend next to Rosie and Becca, who was the maid of honor in my wedding and finally about to graduate from nursing school. I was proud of both of them.

Edward and Harriett gladly relinquished their socialite crowns to adorn ones of loving and dedicated grandparents, spoiling Max and Hanna to the fullest.

I knew my parents were happy for me. Jeff had gladly donned the father-figure role and gave me away at my wedding, but over all I was happier than I'd ever been – in a state of constant euphoria. Happily ever after doesn't come for most, but luckily for some. Thankfully I was one of the lucky ones.

Coming Soon

Noelani

By: Deborah S. Jones

The Beginning of the End

Ethan

I couldn't feel my finger tips as I used my elbows and forearms to clean the heavy snow away from the windows and doors of our SUV. From the soles of my feet up to my thighs were numb, and moving around through the deep snow was becoming increasingly painful. Jesus, it was freezing. I couldn't remember ever in my life being as cold as I was at that exact moment.

My brother Paul and I left Clayman's Ridge six hours before with our girlfriends Tara and Grace; now cuddled (much to Tara's horror) in the back seat trying to keep warm. One hour into the trip our, practically new, rental died - CAPLUNK - in the middle of the street. No warning lights on the console or smoke coming from under the hood, nothing; it just died. Paul and I managed to push it off to the side of the road and had looked under the hood a total of twelve times and still couldn't figure out the problem. We hadn't made a dent in the gas, so there was a little less than a full tank in there, the oil level was fine, no wires or cables seemed to be out of place, but the expensive hunk of metal still wouldn't budge.

We were on our annual winter retreat. The plan was to make it back to our lodge a couple hours away before the blizzard hit, but with a stalled truck and no cell phone service out in the middle of nowhere, we were screwed; too far to walk in either direction, plus the weather was getting worse by the minute. Originally, once the snow started we decided to stay put and keep warm, but between the rapidly dropping temperature, several inches of snow falling an hour and the wind drifts the car was almost covered when we heard the first car approaching and by the time we managed to get one door open, it had already passed. I thought it was in our best interest to keep the windows and doors clean with an on-the-hour ritual clearing away of the snow. Now, on our fourth hourly ritual, Paul was tackling the passenger side and I was on the driver's side. I just kept saying to myself that *I can't die like this. Ethan get control of this situation!* Sheer determination was keeping me going right now as I kept on willing my arms and feet to move and cooperate with my brain, but Paul was having a hard time. I could see it. He was moving slower and on several occasions not moving at all. Damn I was cold. Grace was banging on the glass trying to get our attention.

"A car's coming! A car's coming!" she continued to yell pointing out the back window. And sure enough even with poor visibility, we could see the faint headlights of a vehicle approaching. Thank God.

"Paul someone's coming!" I tried to shout over the howling wind and immediately started flailing my arms wildly over my head trying to get the driver's attention as Paul made his way around to the back of the car to join me, but it didn't look like they were slowing down, so I went further into the street, pushing my way through the deep snow to a point where I knew they could see me.

"Damn it, slow down you stupid bastard!" I yelled, when it became obvious they weren't trying to stop. I was determined not to move as the truck came skidding to a halt, the front of the plow kicking up waves of snow. I could hear Grace and Paul yelling for me to get out of the way, but I would be damned if I waited another four hours for a single car to pass by. We could be dead by then.

The truck was swerving now as the snow covered road made getting any traction close to impossible, but it finally came to a sliding stop a few yards from where I stood sending a large snow wave at me with its abrupt halt. Without hesitation the driver's door flew open and the tall hooded driver jumped out and marched towards me.

"What the hell are you trying to do, get us killed?" barked the distinctively female voice over the howling wind. Her face was completely wrapped and under the enormous hood of her winter parka, you couldn't even see her eyes.

"I'm...I'm sorry about that, b b b - but ...we need your help and it didn't look like you were trying to stop," I breathed.

"Of course I wasn't trying to stop. We happen to be in the middle of a blizzard, you fool!"

"I said I was sorry, but we've been stuck here for the past five hours and we're completely frozen. Please...I didn't have a choice. We can't stay out here!" My face felt like a giant icicle as I willed my lips to move. It hurt to talk. She was looking around me to Paul, who was coming over.

"Well jumping in front of my truck isn't the way to get help. I'm of no use to you if I'm dead." she exclaimed with her hands akimbo. "How many of you are there?"

"Four. Our girlfriends are in the car," answered Paul. I could tell she was hesitant. "Please... you can drop us at the nearest hotel and we'll wait the blizzard out there..." he pleaded.

"Hotel?" I think she almost laughed. "There's no hotel around here. The closest thing to where we are is my house a few miles away and... and you staying there isn't a good idea," she added becoming more serious. "I would really like to help but I have to get home. I can't be late. I will make a couple calls when I get there and send the sheriff to get you..." she was already turning away from us.

Was I hearing her right? Did she really want to leave us out in the worse blizzard in history? "You can't leave us out here." I pleaded,

"Please we'll be no trouble at all." I saw her shoulders rise as she obviously took a deep breath.

"Pleeease," Paul begged openly.

"Alright, alright," came a barely audible tone, "but you have to hurry I've got twenty minutes to get home and I can't be late, so get your friends," she snapped, abruptly turning away to head back to the truck.

Late? Late for what? We were in the middle of a god-damned blizzard. What the hell could be so important that she couldn't help us? In no time Paul and I were shouting orders for the others to come on as we tried to get our overnight bags out of the car.

"Don't make me leave you. For heaven's sake leave that stuff, we have to go now!" yelled the woman impatiently over her shoulder as she put her hands up in front of her face to protect it from the biting snow and wind.

"Like hell I am," muttered Tara under her breath. "There no way I'm leaving my Louis Vutton luggage out here in the middle of no where for some hillbilly to take!" I couldn't help rolling my eyes at her ignorance. There was a chance that the only person *semi-willing* to help us, was about to leave us all to die outside in the tundra and she was worried about someone taking her hideous oversized luggage. Sometimes I couldn't believe her. Grace, Paul and I were all high-tailing it towards the truck. My legs felt like frozen blocks of ice as we piled into her warm pick up truck.

"Where's the other one? You said there were four of you," the woman shouted.

"She's coming," Grace replied.

"I swear to God, if she isn't in this car in the next five seconds I'm going to leave your asses to die in the …" she stopped just as Tara opened the back and threw her three pieces of luggage in. Once she got in, the door wasn't fully closed before the woman was speeding away, skidding all over the road from her quick acceleration. No one said anything as she drove the beast of a truck like it was a Miata on a LA highway, going way too fast for the current weather conditions. We all had a look of terror as we approach a steep incline, wondering if we'd made a terrible mistake coming with her. Freezing to death versus a horrific car accident that could leave us mangled and bleeding in the snow, started to seem the better of the two.

Despite the painful stinging that started in my finger tips and had now spread all over my body, the warmth in the truck felt good as I placed my hands a few inches from the vents. I could hear the others rubbing their hand and shoulders to get warm.

"Thank you for helping us," Grace said, but it was only met with cool silence. The woman seemed to be concentrating on the tasks at hand; getting us to our destination alive and not being late for whatever the hell she was in such a hurry to get home for.

The truck was having a hard time with the incline as the back tires struggled to get traction and reaching forward the woman gently rubbed her gloved hand across the dashboard and said, "C'mon baby, you've gotten me this far, just a little further, please…baby…c'mon…," she urged. "Thatta girl," she finished proudly as the truck lurched forward as if it were physically being pushed up the hill. We drove a little further then turned off the main road. Straight ahead we could see what looked like a three-story farm house and a barn in the middle of a wide open space. Steam was billowing from the chimney and you could almost imagine the warmth that waited for you inside. Everything was white from the snow, so it was hard to tell where things ended and where they began, but it was obvious the house sat on a large piece of land. It was beautiful, almost like it came straight off one of those winter wonderland postcards at Christmas time.

As we approached it was noticeable how much she'd slowed down, as though she was sneaking up to the house. She put the truck in park and then asked to no one in particular, what time it was as she unzipped the top of her coat and pulled out an old fashion gold time piece hanging around her neck.

"It's 6:06," I replied.

"*Chikusho! Dammit!*" she whispered once she'd confirmed it for herself, then looking around at us she said, "Please try to be as quiet as possible when you go in the house," and before we could respond she was out and trudging through the thigh-high snow as we hurried to grab our things and keep up with her. Silently I wondered what the other language she spoke was. The high winds were blowing the snow off the roof of the house and creating even more of an Artic whirlwind affect as we tried to make it inside.

When we finally reached the porch she quietly pushed as much snow aside as she could to open the storm door and then the large front door. We managed to crowd into the foyer, thankful for how warm it was inside. "*Take your coats off and wait here,*" she said in a voice barely above a whisper, then turned to walk away, but quickly looked back, "*and please be quie…*" she didn't finish before Tara began to loudly stomp the excess snow off her boots, verbalizing how thankful she was to be out of the wretched cold. The look of terror that entered the woman's eyes as her eyebrows raised in disbelief at the blatant disregard for her instructions, was clear, as we all turned to glare at Tara who was oblivious to what she'd done, but it was too late.

That was when we heard it. It wasn't a shriek, nor was it a scream, but it was just as painful to the ears. The woman closed her eyes and her shoulders curled inward in an act of defeat that comes from being helpless.

"NO-EH-LAN-EEEE IS THAT YOU? COME IN HERE RIGHT THE MINUTE!" a woman screeched, and with slumped shoulders and a dejected demeanor the woman silently turned and walked slowly towards the room at the end of the hallway where the voice was coming from. As soon as she opened the door the voice of the older woman yelled, "Where have you been? You're supposed to be home at six on the dot! Where were you?"

I turned to verbally lambaste Lisa, but stopped to listen to what was happening in the next room.

"You were with a man weren't you? I knew letting you work at that diner was…"

"Obaasan I wasn't with a man. There's a horrible blizzard out…"

"Don't you dear talk back to me, you insolent girl. You're just like your mother."

"Please let me explain. There were these people who needed…"

"BE QUIET!"

"They jumped in front of the truck. I almost crashed…"

"SHUT YOUR MOUTH!"

"Please listen…I've never been late since I started working and there was no way I could make it home on time in all that sn…," the woman continued to beg. I knew that was a lie because if she hadn't stopped to help us she probably would have made it home on time.

"URUSAI! *SILENCE*! You are late and that's all that matters. Now…you know what to do!" the older woman continued to shout and in the dead silence we could hear the sound of a jacket being removed.

"Do something," whispered Grace, tugging on my shoulder. She was right. This woman was *six minutes* late because she helped us. I began to slowly walk toward the door when a sound I'd never heard before, but recognized instantly, stopped me in tracks. **WHAP, WHAP, WHAP.**

"I've told you – **WHAP** – not to – **WHAP** – disobey me - **WHAP** – I don't care if Buddha – **WHAP** - himself – **WHAP** – stops you – **WHAP**…" My body flinched with each biting lash.

"Oh my God! Ethan do something," Grace continued, fighting back the tears I could hear caught in her throat. Paul was holding her back as she attempted to step forward. I'd forgotten how emotional my best friend could be.

"…I want you – **WHAP** – in this house – **WHAP** – at six – **WHAP**…"

"Hell…hello?" I yelled, the hesitation in my voice bothered me. "Ma'am?" I called as I continued to make my way towards the door. The beating had stopped.

"Who is there?" came the agitated response.

"We're the people who your grand-daughter helped. It's our fault she's late. We…uh…we tried to hurry, but the roads were treacher…" I became silent as a beautiful silver haired Asian woman wearing a red silk kimono covered with cherry blossoms entered the hallway. She gracefully moved a long silver lock hanging at the side of her face and tucked it back in the tight bun at the back of her head. The lock of hair had probably been set free during her onslaught against that poor woman or girl, now I couldn't tell how old she was. All I knew was that she didn't deserve what had just happened to her.

"How rude of me," she said softly, "My granddaughter should have told me we had guests," she finished as I tried to hide the disgust across my face. I couldn't believe this elegant being standing in front of me was the woman we'd just heard. If she cared that we had just witnessed her beat that woman for no apparent reason at all, she didn't show it, flashing a beautiful smile at all of us.

TO BE CONTINUED…

Concrete Rose Publishing Order Form

1. Keyshawn, the lies he told, Renarda Huggins $15.00
2. Caught Up In Drama, Latifa Sanchez $15.00
3. Dilemma, Latifa Sanchez $15.00
4. The Prodigal Daughter, Patricia Enyi $15.00
5. City Is Mine, Karma $15.00

Please send the novels that I have circled above.

Shipping and Handling $1.99
Total Number of Books _______________
Total Amount Due _________________________

Send check or money order to:
Concrete Rose Publishing
1 Corman Road
Mattapan, MA 02126

Name

____

Address____

City_________________________________ State________
Zip Code__________

Please Allow 2-3 weeks for delivery.

www.ingramcontent.com/pod-product-compliance
Lightning Source LLC
Chambersburg PA
CBHW061611100726

47898CB00002B/609